HOLDING THE MAN

Timothy Conigrave was born in Melbourne in 1959 and educated at Xavier College and Monash University. He trained as an actor at the National Institute of Dramatic Art, graduating in 1984. He appeared in such plays as *Brighton Beach Memoirs* and *As Is* with The Fabulous Globos. He initiated the project *Soft Targets*, seen at Griffin Theatre in 1986. His other plays included *The Blitz Kids* and *The Thieving Boy*. Timothy Conigrave died in October 1994, shortly after completing his book *Holding the Man*.

HOLDING THE MAN

Timothy Conigrave

Foreword by David Marr

PENGUIN BOOKS

PENGUIN BOOKS

UK | USA | Canada | Ireland | Australia
India | New Zealand | South Africa | China

Penguin Books is part of the Penguin Random House group of companies
whose addresses can be found at global.penguinrandomhouse.com.

Penguin
Random House
Australia

First published by McPhee Gribble, 1995
This edition published by Penguin Group (Australia), 2015

Cover design by Samantha Jayaweera © Penguin Group (Australia)
Cover photograph by Ben King
Typeset in Galliard by Post Pre-press Group, Brisbane
Colour separation by Splitting Image Colour Studio, Clayton, Victoria
Printed and bound in Australia by Griffin Press, an accredited ISO AS/NZS
14001 Environmental Management Systems printer.

National Library of Australia
Cataloguing-in-Publication data:

Conigrave, Timothy, 1959–1994, author.
Holding the man / Timothy Conigrave.
9780143009498 (paperback)
Conigrave, Timothy, 1959–1994.
Gay men – Australia – Biography.
Gay male couples – Australia.
AIDS (Disease) – Patients – Australia – Biography.

306.766092

This project was assisted by the Commonwealth Government
through the Australia Council, its arts funding and advisory body.

penguin.com.au

Life is nothing if not change.
  my friend Laura

Foreword

I read Tim's manuscript in a hotel room in Melbourne in
1994. Penguin wanted a line for the cover. I was hope-
lessly busy but said I'd take a look. And that weekend I
found myself hiding in the room, all work abandoned,
reading and reading. I haven't heard of anyone since
who has consumed *Holding the Man* any other way: in
great chunks, as much as possible at a sitting.

The minute I finished I rang Nick Enright who had
helped Tim beat the manuscript into shape. I wanted my
old friend to know straightaway how excited I was; how
funny and horny and sad and truthful I found the book;
and how much it had told me about myself. Nick seemed
a bit distracted. I asked him when I drew breath what the
din was in the background. He said: 'It's Tim's wake.'

I didn't know he had died. That he managed against
all the odds to write the book and then work with Nick
up to the last moment is all of a piece with the Tim that
emerges from *Holding the Man*: a master of the close
shave, brave and stubborn and determined to have his
say. Did anyone ever shut him up? Death certainly didn't.

Holding the Man is a story almost perfectly told.
You don't have to be gay to wonder where you will find

love – or where love will find you – but for Tim and John Caleo to discover each other in the same classroom at Xavier is the sort of blazing good luck we'd hardly believe in a magazine.

Xavier was clearly a hotbed of romance, which is fine, and the priests are often on the side of love, which is a good thing. But there's anarchy in the classrooms. Sometimes John is sitting across from Tim; sometimes he's sitting in the row behind and gently massaging Tim's back. Finally they are side by side: 'Father Bradford was talking about the disturbance of the natural order in *Macbeth*. John and I were rubbing our knees together, caressing each other in long gentle strokes.' At which point, discipline had entirely broken down. Terrific.

Tim writes beautifully about the small milestones of life. That it's gay life is crucial and at the same time hardly matters. It's life.

Blue jocks and the first inkling of desire.
The first wank – immediately announced to his
    mother.
The first kiss – Tim writes particularly wonderfully
    about kissing.
The first fuck – hats off to Fr Wallbridge and his
    retreat at Barwon Heads.
The awful disappointment of the first Gaysoc
    meeting at Monash.
The first mirror ball.

The first adultery.

The first reconciliation.

The first symptoms.

This is also a book about dying. The same candour that makes *Holding the Man* an irresistible account of love and partnership also makes it an irresistibly moving account of dying, death and loss.

Tim seems never to have been anything but candid. He couldn't help himself. He opened his mouth and out rushed the truth. He was an outrageously tactless human being. He nearly ruined his sister's wedding by choosing that of all nights to tell his parents he was HIV positive. By some miracle he was dissuaded. He reports this near-catastrophe with all the scorn he deserves.

Tim's candour falls like a bright, soft light over his life and this book. It's that light and his voice that makes us read *Holding the Man* with such greedy impatience. He can admit lust, disloyalty and foolishness; admit the most fugitive and inappropriate longings; admit he's a master of mistiming; and confess his shocking curiosity.

As John was brought back one night from the operating theatre, Tim saw the huge scar that ran from his solar plexus to the back of his ribs. 'I wish I could have seen the operation,' he writes. 'I would love to know what my boyfriend looked like inside . . .'

And there is the moment only he could write, the scene readers of *Holding the Man* talk about afterwards with a kind of awe: that last homecoming fuck. In ways we find hard to face, Tim was able to admit he was a human being. We love him for that.

When the book appeared with my line on the cover, I was embarrassed to find people assumed I'd known Tim well. His friends would 'remind' me of hilarious episodes in his life and shocking lines he had delivered. After a while I stopped explaining that we had never met because it struck me that I knew Tim and John as they are going to be known by everyone, through these pages and now from Neil Armfield's haunting film.

The publishers cut my line in half because they wanted something short and snappy. Now is my chance to say what I want in full. This is a fine, tender and sexy book. Life, it says, is precious and we must not waste a day of it.

David Marr

PART ONE

A Head Full of Boys

Chapter ONE

Me

At the end of the sixties the world seemed very exciting for a nine-year-old. Things were changing at an incredible rate. And most of the changes seemed to be for the better, like the afternoon we all sat in the library watching a man take his first step on the moon of planet Earth. Even schooling was changing. My Grade Four teacher at the state school treated us like adults who were able to think for ourselves. He was open to all forms of learning. My last year at this school was spent drawing, writing poems; building Aboriginal humpies, dams and watercourses. We discussed space travel, pot and why boys should be allowed to have long hair.

In contrast was Miss O'Leary who gave us Catholic kids our injection of religion, all five of us in a cupboard at the end of the hall. At Christmas she gave each of us a crucifix made of foiled glass. As she handed me mine she said, 'You don't deserve this because you're wicked.'

She got into my head at the age when I was loading the operating system that forms self-image. Sure, the software was a mix

A HEAD FULL OF BOYS

of creativity, sunshine and games with the girls, but I was also becoming a Catholic. And looming large was the awareness that I was about to take a leap into Catholic manhood: an all-boys school, Kostka. Footy, cricket, smelly socks, and Jesuits in cassocks.

Even though Kostka was at the end of my street, all I knew of it was the high pale-orange brick walls and large copper gates, beyond which I occasionally glimpsed a concrete playground lined with oleanders and yew trees, and a whirlpool of boys in grey uniforms.

After I'd sat an entrance exam my mother and I were interviewed by the headmaster, who wanted to know whether, since she had married a non-Catholic, her children went to Mass. My mother's face was scrunched up as we walked back to the gates. 'That stuck-up bully sitting in judgement of me! Surely it's obvious that I want my children to be brought up in the Church, or we wouldn't be wasting our money putting you through a Jesuit school.' I found it odd that she was so vulnerable.

This was to be my first experience of dressing exactly the same as everyone else. The first time I heard 'fuck', 'shit' and 'arsehole'. The first time I had textbooks: the Jacaranda atlas; a catechism full of groovy drawings of doves, wheat and a Jesus who looked like a hippie; my first dictionary, and a book called *Roget's Thesaurus* with the words 'Find, Seek, Search, Discover' on its cover. Learning at Kostka was going to be a different experience. I spent hours writing my name on the title page of my books, covering them in sweet-smelling soft plastic, filling my drink bottle with orange cordial and putting it in the freezer.

The first day all the new boys met in the library. The headmaster's secretary drilled us on punctuality and compulsory sport. We were taken to our classrooms where boys were lined up waiting for the door to open. I tried to be inconspicuous, aware that everyone was looking at me and the other two new guys.

At the front of the line was a good-looking boy wearing

sunglasses. From the other boys' gibes I learnt that he had almost poked his eye out in a sailing accident. They didn't bother him. He looked really cool.

My first year at this school was a big shock. I was keenly aware that these boys had a different life from mine. They were fulfilling expectations that they would be doctors and lawyers. 'Play' for them meant football. What I knew about footy you could have written on a piece of toilet paper. In order to survive I learnt to know which team was on top of the ladder and to say things like 'carna Saints'. But as for what 'holding the man' meant or which team Jezza played for . . .

Grade Five Red was in the neglect of Mr Geddes. His idea of teaching was to write on the board 'Page 13, Exercises 4–9' and make us do them in silence. He'd sit on a desk and order one of us to scratch his back. He liked to terrorise us, picking his nose and wiping it on us, knocking our books off the desk, opening someone's bag and eating his lunch.

One day a boy called Kevin asked to be allowed to go to the toilet. Mr Geddes made him stand on the platform and sing 'Twinkle Twinkle Little Star'. Kevin did so, his legs jiggling in an attempt to stop pissing himself. 'Now with actions.' None of us laughed. We were just glad it wasn't us. Kevin did the nursery rhyme with actions and then ran for the door.

Another time Mr Geddes told us to read a chapter about Cromwell and the Roundheads and left the room. We were doing as we were told when his head suddenly appeared through an open window. He ordered Kevin up on the platform to get the strap.

'But I wasn't doing anything, sir.'

'Exactly. You should have been reading about Cromwell and the Roundheads. Get up there before I make it the full six.' Heavy with persecution, Kevin sloped up to the platform and took his punishment.

The other regular victim was Andy, a milky fat kid with a skin rash and a permanently running nose. Geddes would tease him until he was in tears and then would get us all to sing a version of a folk song: 'Oh Andy, don't you weep, don't you mourn.'

When the bell went we would tumble out into the playground and rough-house each other, asserting our strength so that we would never become the milky fat kid who was so loathsome.

Damien

Out of this landscape appeared a boy called Damien. He was from a working-class family; his father and brothers were in the army, but he was a rebel. His hair was long, his attitude defiant. He thought football was stupid. With a shock of glossy black hair tumbling into his eyes, he looked like Mowgli from *The Jungle Book*. Our point of contact was born of this rebelliousness: smoking.

I had already been experimenting. One Friday night I sat on my parents' bed watching a St Trinian's movie. Two girls were smoking in the toilets. I lit a match, blew it out and drew back the fumes. I felt sophisticated despite the sulphurous burning in my throat. Another time I filled a paper straw with lawn clippings and nearly set my lungs on fire as I drew back the burning grass.

Damien and I were going up to the park when I spied a cigarette butt on the ground and put it in my mouth. He pulled out a whole pack of Craven As and some matches.

'You smoke?'

'Der.'

'Wow. What's it like?' He offered me one.

'Not here!'

'Where?' He was testing me. I showed him a couple of hollow pine trees that were hiding places for local kids, their branches smooth from years of polishing by children's bums.

This sanctuary was to become ours. We were partners in

crime, a secret society in our secret headquarters. Our ritual always started with a cigarette. The smoke provided safety as we talked about school, what a dickhead so-and-so was, or the time Gilligan built that car out of coconuts.

I liked Damien, and I was happy that he liked me. Although we weren't in the same class we always found each other at breaks and played handball in the concrete squares of the playground, practised tricks with Coca-Cola yoyos or climbed over the back of the green shed to have a cigarette.

The bench I was sitting on was slowly being torn from its place by the roots of the liquidambars that surrounded the lunch quadrangle. All around me the broken asphalt said that these trees were winning a war. I was trying to finish my lunch before English. I hadn't done my homework and had spent the break composing a poem about 'scraping away to the inner essence'.

Sitting nearby was the sunglasses boy. I was thinking about his looks. *What makes me think he's handsome? I like the way he is. Calm, and cool. Would the other guys think he was handsome?* As I lobbed the soggy remainder of my lettuce-and-Vegemite sandwich into the bin, I spied Damien walking across the playground. *He's really good-looking. Even the way he walks is really good.* He walked towards me, smiling.

He sat on the bench, opened his hand and revealed a superball. 'It's Andy's.'

'God, he'll be spewing!'

He put his arm around me. There was a kind of stirring, a buzz coursing through me. I wanted to break away from him but I also wanted to put my head on his shoulder. The electronic bell pealed.

I headed off to the toilets. Damien said he'd save me a place in the assembly hall.

Friday afternoons were a bludge. Mr Steed the science teacher would show us documentaries – about Campbell's attempt at the land-speed record in his futuristic Bluebird, or the development of the Merino by CSIRO. It was a strategy to stop us sleeping our way through the last period of the week, but it gave us a chance to play up as the excitement of the weekend loomed.

The assembly hall was a fibro hut, painted pale green like a public toilet. The carpet was a splotchy synthetic red. It resembled pizza and smelt like pizza. Black curtains were drawn across windows that were wide open. The roof was corrugated iron and even in winter the heat could be smothering. On this summer day the room was an oven filled with boys basting in their own juices.

I could make out the short figure of Mr Steed fumbling at the projector. We sat totally still until he squatted down beside the machine, and then the room became a snowstorm of paper balls and planes. Mr Steed stood up and the storm abruptly stopped.

The projector threw a white square of light onto the screen, which immediately came alive with rabbits, dogs, thumbs-up, and peace signs. Someone did the VO-5 symbol from the television ad. The rabbit became a two-finger salute.

Where is Damien? I heard a whispered call and turned to see him on his own, up the back behind the projector. He patted the seat next to him.

Mr Steed was agitated. As he lifted an arm to brush his oily fringe off his thick glasses I could see the sweat stains in the pit of his mustard-coloured shirt. The projector jumped into life and the screen read, *The Prickly Menace*.

Damien took my arm and put it around his waist, smiled and turned to the screen. The film was about a cactus getting out of hand somewhere and the moth that was helping to keep it under control. It could have been about Auschwitz. All I could think of was my arm around Damien's waist. It felt like it had found its home. It felt right. It felt safe.

We sneaked looks at each other and smiled. Then he put his lips to my cheek and let them sit there until I whispered, 'Don't!'

He smiled and whispered, 'I wish you were a girl.' I wasn't sure what he meant but said I wished he was a girl too.

We stayed entwined until the film whipped out of the gate and slapped the projector, stirring Mr Steed awake. He fumbled to turn the machine off. Damien stretched and released me. The darkness was broken by boys pouring out of the assembly hall.

'Come back here until the bell goes,' barked Mr Steed. As if to make a fool of him, the bell went.

A couple of Grade Fives stood on the footpath waiting for someone to pick them up. One grabbed the other's bag and lobbed it over the wall back into the playground. The victim kicked his friend's bag into the traffic and ran back into the grounds.

'Got any durries?' I turned to see Damien coming out of the school ground with his cap pulled to one side. He put his arm around my shoulder. I showed him the pack of Escorts inside my bag.

'Are you two boyfriends?' An older boy with carrot-red hair was leaning against a wall, hands in pockets, feet crossed at the ankles.

Damien turned to confront him. He picked Damien's cap off his head and threw it onto the road. Damien went to snatch the redhead's cap but was gripped by the wrist and shoved. 'Poofters!' jeered the redhead and sauntered across the road in triumph.

Neither of us said anything as we walked to the park and climbed our trees. We sat on the bum-smoothed branches and started our ritual. The smell of pine oil hung in the air. Damien said he was going off to get an Icy-pole. When my cigarette was down to the butt I took out another and did a donkey root. I could see his bag at the base of the tree. *He's going to come back.*

I felt I had done something wrong, and Damien was angry with me. I wondered what it would be like if Damien were a girl. Or if I were. Then we could be boyfriend and girlfriend.

Damien reappeared and held out two Icy-poles. He tossed them up to me. I reached in my pocket but he shook his head. It was a present. We sat cocooned in our trees with dripping Icy-poles, dripping sweat, and burning cigarettes.

I started to feel dizzy. I wanted badly to fart or burp but nothing happened. My throat felt scratchy. I had to lie down. I tried to do it on the branch but I slid down to the grass at the bottom of the tree.

'How many cigarettes have you had?' said the Cheshire cat from his branch. I'd had four or five. 'You tonk, you've got nicotine poisoning.' He slipped down the trunk and lay next to me. I didn't have to look at him. I could feel him there beside me. We lay together with our hands behind our heads, watching the sky through the branches. Damien put his arm across me. I drifted on a cloud of contentment.

The man in the kiosk was chatting up a girl while the rest of us stood shivering in the wind at Brighton Beach. The sun was hot but the breeze coming off the bay stung with cold.

Casanova was taking so long that I dried off and was left with salty skin. I picked at the peeling sunburn on my shoulders. My turn finally. I asked for a pack of Marlboros. 'For me mum,' I lied, pointing to some fat lady asleep in a deck-chair.

He didn't believe me but he gave them to me anyway. Someone grabbed them from my hands. It was Damien. He jumped up on the rail and held the cigarettes high in the air.

'I was grounded for calling my sister a slut,' he said. 'But Mum's working at the TAB. Long as I'm back by four-thirty.' He raised an eyebrow, smiling. 'Have you seen who's on the beach?' He tilted his head over the rail at a Beaumaris surfie chick called Puck. 'I think I'm in love.'

My stomach gripped. 'She's nearly fifteen. Why would she be interested in a twelve-year-old?'

He slipped over the rail down to the sand. I followed, feeling like the milky fat kid, all thumbs and not an ounce of cool. He opened the smokes, took out the foil and a couple of cigarettes and threw them on the sand. 'Don't want to look like we just opened them.'

He walked over to Puck and a freckly girl I didn't know. 'Got a match?' said Damien in his best Paul Newman voice.

'My bum and your face.' She was everything everyone said about her. *Why does Damien like such a rough girl?* My stomach gripped even harder.

Damien took out a cigarette and lay down in the sand. 'You gonna light it for me?'

'If you give us one.' He offered her the pack and she took one. She pulled out a box of matches, took his cigarette, lit both at once and handed his back.

I asked Damien for the smokes. He threw them at me, not taking his eyes off Puck. When I asked for a light, Damien handed me his lit cigarette and I donkey-rooted it.

Damien punched a hole in the sand to make room for his private parts. Every time I looked at Puck I caught her looking at me. This was all too much. I said I was going for a leak.

I ran through the sunbaking bodies, up the burning hot concrete steps and into the change-rooms. As my eyes adjusted to the light I caught sight of a guy, about eighteen, taking off his purple boardies to reveal pale blue jocks. I walked past him into the other room. There was the rank smell of stale piss. I was standing at the urinal when he walked in. I could see him out of one eye as he dropped his jocks and put them on one of the hooks. He disappeared from view. I heard the hard stream of the shower.

My body was on fire. I couldn't relax enough to piss. *Can he tell I'm not pissing? He must think I'm a pervert.* My full bladder and I left the change-rooms. I went to the railing and yelled to Damien.

'I've gotta go.' I ran through the rusty turnstile. I was pissed off, but I couldn't figure out why. I walked home as fast as I could.

The chapel was an octagonal building in beige brick with a vaulted roof and a ring of stained-glass windows representing the Stations of the Cross. So far only three of the stations had been completed. Today was the Assumption of the Blessed Virgin Mary and we had to be absolved of our sins, as it was a sin to receive the Eucharist without this having been done.

Damien was chuckling quietly with Grant, a tall good-looking blond boy. I slid in next to Damien and knelt, pretending to say a prayer. 'What's so funny?' I whispered.

Damien knelt beside me. 'Grant reckons we should see who gets the biggest penance.'

Grant chipped in. 'Make up something really good. What do you reckon? You in?' *Lying in confession! That's a big one!*

The door of the confessional opened. It was Grant's turn. Damien and I stayed kneeling, our shoulders pressed against each other. I felt happy, strong, calm.

The confessional door clicked open and Grant burst out. He winked. 'Six Hail Marys and two Our Fathers.' He slunk over to a pew and knelt. Damien went in. I dug into the deepest pit of my bowels to drag up a story but couldn't think of anything. The door clicked open.

Damien was smug. 'Ten Our Fathers. Told him I titted off my girlfriend.' The judges gave him the thumbs-up.

It was my turn. The mahogany cave was draped in red velvet. I pulled the door shut and knelt. A small curtain was drawn on the other side of the rattan grille.

'In the name of the Father, the Son and the Holy Ghost. Bless me, Father, for I have sinned. It has been two weeks since my last confession and these are my sins.' I froze.

'Yes, my son?' I could smell garlic and figured it was Stinky.

'Me and another boy were in the shower together and he dared me to see who had the bigger erection. We abused ourselves.'

'And that was all?' *Damn, he doesn't seem to be fazed by it.* A top idea flashed into my head. 'That was a lie. It never happened.'

There was a long silence. *Got him!*

'Son, many young men get confused. God can be very forgiving if you are repentant.'

'Nothing happened. I was lying to you. It was a dare.'

I heard him take a big breath and sigh, clear his throat and then mumble the absolution rapidly. 'For your penance you must recite the rosary.' *I win!*

As I left the confessional I heard the other door open. Stinky was trying to see who I was. He shook his head in disgust and shut the door. I went over to Damien. 'The rosary.' I knelt in the glow of a champion. Damien punched me in the arm. *He's proud of me.* The bell went and Damien stood up. 'I've got to do my rosary,' I said, not moving.

He smiled. 'You're such a Catholic.' I got halfway through the first Hail Mary and leapt after him, putting my arm around his shoulder.

Mass that day was quite a spectacle. Father Larkin in full gold regalia and the altar boys in red soutanes and lace surplices genuflected in front of the altar, swinging the incense and ringing the bell.

I stifled a yawn as we all sat down. Father Larkin opened his hands and began the reading. I drifted off to the land of questions. *I wonder if Jesus really did have a loincloth? But imagine if he didn't. The guy who carved the statue would have had to carve his dick and balls. I guess he would have been circumcised.*

We all stood again and mumbled a prayer. *I wonder what Father Larkin would look like with his clothes off?* A wave of panic crashed over me. *God, I hope no one can read my mind.* As the bread was broken it dawned on me that such thoughts were sins, and that I shouldn't take Holy Communion without confessing them. As boys started filing up to the altar I hoped no one would notice that I didn't join them.

'Race ya!' said the disembodied head of Damien, bobbing around in the waves in the middle of the baths. 'Last one to the board is a scab.'

I cut my way through the water to the deck. Being a stronger swimmer than Damien I arrived at the ladder first, but as I was climbing up he snatched my ankle and used me as a lever out of the water, grabbing my shoulders and clambering up me. There we were, like dogs, one on top of the other, his body surrounding mine. I tried to break his grip, prising his fingers from the rails and shoving him with my bum. I was alive with glee and effort as we jostled for the trophy.

'Shit. You're hurting me,' he gasped.

'Give in, suck, and the pain stops,' I said, prising him off the ladder. I heard a loud splash as he fell back into the water. I climbed onto the deck and bolted for the wooden steps to the board, slipped in the slimy water but recovered beautifully, and won! Standing with arms triumphantly crossed I asked, 'So, scab, what now? Biggest bomb?'

We stood in line at the diving board, shivering in the breeze, watching girls swan-diving and boys bombing. I stepped over the coir matting and walked to the end of the board. As I bent my knees to spring, Damien rushed out to bounce me. I knew he was going to do it and reduced my spring, making Damien bounce himself. 'Sucked in!' I laughed evilly as I took flight, pulling one knee up to my chest. I surfaced to hear the fallout, ultimate proof of an excellent bomb.

Damien was standing still on the end of the diving board. *What's he afraid of?*

'I don't want to be a poofter anymore,' he announced, then took off and dropped another bomb. My brain was a mess of crossed wires. It suddenly cleared. Only one thought was possible. *Fuck, I'm a poofter.*

I had just one delivery for the day. I took the package from the pharmacy servery, walked out into the summer afternoon sun and hopped on my trusty three-speeder. *Halifax Street. Doesn't this lady have a chemist closer?* I liked this work because I was on my own and it was outdoors, which was great in weather like this.

But I felt as if I'd forgotten something, not something from the shop – something else was chewing away at me. *Something not good has happened.* Then the memory came back. Damien. The diving board. And that thing he said. My mind went suddenly blank. Ambling past me was a teenage girl in netball gear, a short red skirt and a busty green top. *Please God, make me like girls.* I made myself stare at her breasts and imagine how it would be to fondle them. *It'd be sort of nice. Wonder what it'd be like to kiss them?*

'What are you staring at? Piss off, you pervert.'

I blushed and rode off as fast as I could, my mind on fire, thoughts crashing in, my muscles working at their peak. Before I knew it I was at the address in Halifax Street. A dear old lady came to the wire door. I gave her the package. *I wonder if she can see that I have a heart heavy with sin?* She handed me a small chocolate wrapped in cellophane.

I didn't eat it in case it was poisoned.

Boy in the Blue Jocks

He takes off his purple boardies, revealing pale blue jocks. He is muscular and deeply tanned, his hair sun-bleached. He captivates me with a smile.

'Can I help you?' I don't know. He picks up his towel. 'Do you want a shower?'

He swaggers towards the shower room. I watch the muscles

working in his back and his hard round bum. As I follow he leans against the wall, hands behind his back, standing on one leg, the other foot halfway up the wall. Still smiling, he points to where the wall should be. Now there's another change-room. He wants me to keep following. I walk to the archway. This room is much larger and there are five or six men at different benches and lockers, all wearing bathers or jocks. I walk through the room towards a corridor and see the men watching me. I stop at the entrance to the corridor and my friend with the towel places an arm around my shoulder. The corridor is dark but at the end there is a brighter room, open to the sky. There are two men, naked, kissing. In the centre of the room is a large bonfire. It melts into the floor and becomes a swimming pool, lit from within. 'It is time to become a man, to find your fire, your strength.' He places the towel around my waist and pulls me toward him. 'Your strength is in this.' He places his mouth on mine and I am charged. I am strong, I am a man. We sink into the water. I am cocooned. I am whole.

Kevin

Kevin's parents were going to Sydney for the weekend. They bred trotters and had a two-year-old pacer running in the Regal Handicap.

Kevin was a year older than me. His parents didn't think he needed a babysitter – someone to sleep over was enough. He asked me if I would stay with him. *Shit, I hope he doesn't want me to be his friend. It will be playground death if the other guys think I'm his friend.*

I hardly knew Kevin. He was the best long-distance runner in the school but he was a real loser. Teachers picked on him. He wasn't a wimp, in fact he was quite beefy from all the running and could defend himself well, but he was so easy to get a rise out of. I felt sorry for him. He was quiet and very nervous about asking me. The poor bastard probably felt I was the only person who wouldn't say no.

The street was short. Kevin's parents had pulled down all the other houses and built their own, with tennis-court and pool. I stood at the white door with my schoolbag over my shoulder and pushed the brass bell.

Kevin opened the door wearing track pants and a windcheater. He was like an excited puppy, eager and nervous. He took my bag and offered me a glass of milk, some Twisties, a seat in the living-room. I sat but Kevin stayed standing, looking lost.

The interior was all white brick and stained beams, with parquet floors, bright pink shag rugs and a purple vinyl settee. The pride of the room was the Fantasia lamp, a hairdo of optical fibres that changed colour. I found it mesmerising.

He offered to show me the trophies. I followed him into the billiard room where he took a photo off a shelf. 'This is Red Falcon. She won the Finster Derby three years in a row. She broke her fetlock a couple of weeks ago and had to be destroyed.'

On another shelf were many bottles of different shapes, one like a monkey, one like a bunch of grapes, filled with coloured liquids. 'Prizes. Liqueurs, I think.' He took down one that looked like a windmill and pulled the cork. He sniffed it and then took a swig. He offered me the bottle. I said no.

'It's nice, it's like chocolate. Have some.' I let the sticky chocolate run down my throat. It had a hot aftertaste. I handed it back but he was up on a stool trying to get another one down, a big yellow cone with a soldier painted on it.

'Won't your parents have a spak if they find out we've been drinking the trophies?'

'They won't know if we only have a mouthful of each. Like bottle-o.'

I had only been drunk once before. Damien, Grant and I had hired a squash court a few weeks before and drunk some red wine I had stolen from Dad's cellar. We felt weighty and stupid as we left the courts. On the way back to Grant's house I pashed with a dog, then took a chuck on his parents' driveway, fascinated by the vomit splashing on my shoes. Grant's old lady drove me home to a very embarrassed Mum. As I lolled around on the bathroom floor I spotted my sister. 'Anna, you gotta do my chemist round, I'm pissed.' Dad was very understanding but asked me to pay for the wine.

'Wow, nice. Mint.' Kevin took a couple more swigs. 'This was my favourite pacer.' He read the inscription on the plate around the bottle-neck. 'Shakespeare's Daughter.'

'Slow down. Not so much. Your folks are going to know we've drunk it.'

'Not if we put water in it.'

As I took a swig, that weighty feeling started to come back, and with it a sick feeling. I stumbled to get my Craven As out of my schoolbag. *Shit, I'm more pissed than I thought*.

Kevin grabbed another bottle, took one mouthful and handed it to me. *I'll pretend to take a swig*.

'I'll fill this up.' He headed out of the room but the bottle of green stuff slipped from his hand and smashed on the parquet floor.

'Oh shit!' Kevin tried to pick up the pieces. 'Better get the brush and pan.' He stumbled into the kitchen. I sat there smoking, the air filled with sticky mint, then went to look for an ashtray. Kevin was standing at the open fridge. 'I'm starving,' he said, opening the freezer. He took out a bag of frozen chips and I took a bite out of the side of the pack. Pulling pieces of plastic out of my teeth I let the chip defrost in my mouth. It tasted quite good. Kevin took a bite out of one. 'It's revolting, you spak!' He took my cigarettes from me and lit one. 'Let's go for a walk.'

We stumbled into the street, then Kevin pulled me back into the house, seized by an idea. He rooted around in the broom cupboard and found a can of paint and a brush. I followed him back out to the street and down the path to the railway line. A long corrugated-iron fence ran along the path. 'Needs a big sign, don't ya reckon?' said Kevin. 'You keep a lookout. Got any ideas?'

'Led Zeppelin?'

'Lead what?' *He is such a dag.*

'Stop the H-bomb.'

Kevin struggled to get the can open. I watched him paint the words and then throw the can and brush into the grass. The paint flew through the air like cream in slow motion. We tore off back to the house. Out of breath and exhilarated we crashed through the front door and fell about laughing on the parquet.

'I'm rooted. Gotta lie down.' He climbed the stairs. I grabbed my schoolbag and followed. As I arrived at his bedroom door, I saw a small mattress on the floor with a sleeping-bag. 'That's you there, unless you want to share the bed.' He struggled to get his windcheater over his head. He sat on the edge of his bed, drunk, his body lean and muscular. His room had the tangy smell of sweat and running shoes. He fell back onto the bed, kicked off his runners and drifted off to sleep. Fascinated, I stood watching his stomach muscles heaving. *Got to lie down.* I struggled to change into my PJs, trying not to lose my balance. I unrolled the sleeping-bag.

'You don't have to sleep down there,' Kevin slurred into the universe. I said I'd be right. I crawled into the bag and listened to him breathing heavily.

I was bothered some time later by the hardness of the floor and the bright light on the ceiling burning into my brain. I turned over to shade my face and rolled onto one of Kevin's running spikes. 'Oh, fuck!'

He'd seen what happened. 'Come up here.' I said I was fine. 'Suit yourself, I've gotta take a piss.' I watched Kevin's red track pants walk out of the room. *Fuck this, let him sleep on the floor.* I crawled into the warmth of his bed and rolled over to the wall.

I heard him come back in. He crawled in beside me. I pretended to be asleep but every cell of my body was suddenly alert. Kevin turned toward me. I felt his hand reach around to my crutch and check out my dick, which swelled in his hand. We lay like that for some time. Hormones, adrenaline, testosterone.

The boy in the pale blue jocks is standing beside the bed, nodding gently.

Kevin rolled me onto my back and climbed on top of me. I could feel he had a fat, he rubbed it against me through his pants. He undid my pyjamas, slid his trackies down and lay back on top of me, our cocks flesh on flesh.

His warm breath smelled of cigarettes, banana, stale chocolate. His warm hand wrapped around my tool, tugging it gently. He undid my pyjama top. Hard chest and sweet burning skin.

The boy is in the corridor to the change-room. He puts his hands on top of his head, revealing tufts of hair in his armpits. We are hurtling down the corridor. The boy and I are in freefall.

'Kevin, get off me, gotta go to the toilet! I'm gonna piss myself.' *I can't stop it. Hold it in!* The weight of his body was crushing me. 'Get off me,' I barked.

I slid off the bed and stumbled out to the toilet. I stood at the bowl, holding the wall with one hand, trying to piss. But nothing happened. On the window-sill was a ceramic clown with a cactus growing out of his stomach. My pyjamas were wet, my stomach sticky. *How embarrassing, I've pissed on him.* I put the toilet seat down. I sat drifting between now and the boy in blue, a long way away.

I hauled myself back to bed and slept badly, until I saw the sky coming to life through the window. Small birds cut across the blueness. My head was a fog of hangover and hunger, my mouth dry, my guts tired and achy. Kevin was asleep beside me but tossing a lot. *Does this mean I'm not a virgin anymore?* Suddenly he sat upright on the edge of the bed and put his head in his hands. He tried to shake himself awake, like a horse whinnying.

He pulled on his track pants and skulked out of the room. I could hear him crashing around downstairs. Broken glass was thrown into a bin, taps ran, cupboard doors closed. He crept back into the room. I smiled and he tried to smile back but he wasn't really looking at me. He was changing into his running gear, red satin shorts and a red singlet. He waved and left.

The sun was beginning to bleed into the room. I got up, dressed and started to put my stuff into my schoolbag, dragging myself into the day. I felt sick. *Better go while Kevin is out running*. I stole downstairs to find the front door open and Kevin sitting on the doorstep, dripping with sweat. 'Going?'

'Lots of homework.'

'Me too.' Now he looked like the guy we all picked on at school. 'I need a smoke.'

'You've just been for a run.'

'Feel like shit, may as well really do myself in.'

We sat smoking in silence. Kevin started to undo his running shoes. 'You remember much about last night?' He wasn't looking at me. 'What'd we do? I can't remember anything.'

Should I risk it? 'I think we compared dick sizes.'

'Yeah. I remember that. Not poofters or anything?'

'No.'

He threw his butt into the far gutter, stood up and stretched. 'Better get going. Got heaps of geography.' I wandered off along the street, the street with only one house.

I was very busy that day, reading the newspapers cover to cover, watching television, doing an exceptional amount of homework. Things I had put off for weeks toppled: my book report, counting my money jar, filling out my record-club membership. I was proud of how much I achieved but somewhere in my head was a nagging feeling. I didn't seem tired at all, perhaps a little foggy but not tired. But the feeling stayed with me, even as I watched the Sunday night movie.

'Tim, turn off the television.' Mum, in her dressing-gown, was in the kitchen pouring Riesling from a cask. 'What about your homework?'

'Finished it hours ago.'

She settled at the dining-table with her wine and her book, but didn't read. She was going to sit watching me until I went to bed.

I tried to change quietly in the dark so that I wouldn't wake my younger brother Nicholas. I fell into bed thinking I would be dead to the world any minute, but all kinds of demons began to creep onto the ceiling above me. *I didn't know Kevin was gay. I hope no one can tell what we did. Wonder what it would be like to suck him off? To lick his balls. What we did was probably wrong but I liked what he did. It was like . . .*

I grabbed my cock. It didn't feel the same as when Kevin had done it, so I reversed my hand as though he were holding me. I played with my knob and put the pillow on top of me so I could pretend it was him. He was the boy in the blue jocks. I was rubbing my cock against the pillow, trying not to make too much noise in case my brother heard me. It felt nice, weird, like hurtling down the corridor again. *Does Kevin really forget what he did? Oh God, I'm gonna piss myself again. I can't believe this.*

I bolted into the toilet. *Jesus. What's that?* Claggy stuff was coming out of the head of my cock. I stood watching it spurt, mesmerised by its pulsing, dribbling. I stood in wonder at what had happened. In silence, reverent. *Spoof! Sprog!*

I slipped back into bed and fell asleep before my head hit the pillow. I slept very deeply, the deepest in a long time.

'Tim, Nicholas, quarter to eight,' called my mum, the alarm clock. I leapt out of bed and into the shower, secure in the thought that I was a man, that I had sprogged. I bounced into the kitchen. Mum was sleepily squeezing oranges. 'You're very buoyant this morning.'

'You can tell?' I poured my Special K into the bowl. 'I can be a father.'

Mum was visibly shocked, motionless in mid-squeeze. 'Who have you got pregnant?'

I laughed. 'No, I was . . . I had a wet dream last night.'

She sighed and shook her head. 'What makes you think I'd want to know that?'

Because I wanted everyone to know I'd sprogged. I even announced it later to Joe McMahon, the brainiac of my year.

'How do you know it was sperm? It was probably just pus,' he sneered.

'It was spoof.'

'What a liar. Prove it.' The gruff voice of Quin chipped in.

'Oh sure, deadshit. Here? Now?'

'Bring it in a jar. I'll be able to tell you if it is or not.'

Sanctuary

Sanctuary.

A head full of boys. Nipples. Armpits. Lips.

Vaseline. Stroking. Tugging. Baby oil. Pulling. Dencorub.

Surfers changing on the beach near the baths. The surfer with the amazing eyes asking me to help him out of his wetsuit.

Rubbing the bed with my cock. On top of my pillow. Fucking a T-shirt.

The boy in the blue jocks, his bush of pubes slowly revealed. His hardening cock trying to escape. Franco in the change-room shower.

Sitting on the floor of the shower, the warm wet stream pulsing against my cock and balls. Trying to hold it back.

Three billion people in the world. Someone else must be having sex right now. Or whacking off. Spoofing as I spoof.

Stacker's bush of black pubic hair. The Watermouth twins. A clothesline full of jocks.

Coming again.

A head full of boys.

Nipples. Armpits. Lips.

Sanctuary.

The Wood Princess

Brother Reynolds was late. Guys were up the front, pushing his desk to the front of the platform so that if he put any weight on it, it would fall. Mission achieved, we all sat down and tried to look cool as he marched in, followed by a boy called Billy, red in the face. Billy went straight to his desk without meeting anyone's eye.

'Apologies, tadpoles. Bill's been in an incident this morning that involved the police.' *He's been shoplifting again.* 'I asked his permission to tell you about it and he's very generously agreed. Bill went to the toilet at the railway station this morning and while he was standing at the urinal, a businessman offered him five dollars –'

'Two dollars, sir,' Billy chipped in.

'Two dollars, to put the man's penis in his mouth.' The room came alive with whispers. Fucken poofters. Devos. Should be shot. How sus.

'Billy did exactly the right thing. He remained calm and said, "No thank you," then went out to the main entrance and told the police, who arrested the man. I think what he did was very brave. Remember that you can't always pick a homosexual, but should one approach you, remain calm and go and get the police. The policeman is your friend.'

Wonder which railway station? I would have done it for him.

'All right, this morning we're going to look at a play called *The Wood Princess,* which is based on an old Hindu myth. Rankin, you read the part of the hunter. Conigrave, you can read the part of the princess.' *Instant death.* He handed us copies of the play. A paper ball smacked into the back of my head. 'Hi Princess,' Quin whispered behind me.

'Scene 13, at the riverbank,' said Brother Reynolds.

HUNTER: Why did you run away?

PRINCESS: It is not right for – ['We can't hear you, Conigrave.'] It is not right for you to approach me like this. We cannot be in love.

HUNTER: I only want to provide for you, catch squirrels and build
           a home where we can play with our children.
PRINCESS: You must go. I cannot tell you why.

As I choked out each word, I could feel all chance of survival in the playground receding.

Brother Reynolds thanked me and Rankin and asked us to read the whole thing for the class next week. *Gee, can't wait.* The teacher's desk fell with an almighty crash. Brother Reynolds was unfazed. 'Andy, pick that up.'

Within days, I was christened Princess, then Princess Tina and eventually Sue, which became my nickname for some time.

A week later Rankin and I were coming to the end of the reading. My legs were wobbly, my hands so wet that the pages of the play were stained with sweat, and my face was on fire. I ploughed on.

PRINCESS: Do not kneel before me. It is not punishment I desire. It
           is your love.

We took our bows like real actors. The guys went spakko applauding. Brother Reynolds sat in silence, shocked, maybe even touched. He looked up and dismissed us with a wave. We were let out of class three minutes early.

'Bit heavy on the makeup, don't you reckon?' It was Quin.

'Wasn't wearing any.'

'Bullshit. You look like a girl.' He walked away angrily across the quadrangle.

I stood stunned. When I was a small boy, shopkeepers would sometimes call me little girl, but this was an outright attack. *What have I done? He was so angry.* I went into the toilets. I looked in the mirror. I saw my fringe falling into my eyes, the brown lines around them, my ruddy cheeks, my blood-red lips. I was flushed from acting in front of a hostile class. I did look like I was wearing makeup.

As I walked out of the library after school I saw the gang hanging around the verandah: Grant, Damien and Quin with Sandilands, a bear of a guy whose greatest trick was being able to slag into the air and catch it again in his mouth. I heard them boasting about the orgy they had been to on the weekend.

'Three fingers, mate, I swear,' Quin was boasting. 'She was begging for it.' *What bull, no chick would let such a grot near her. They're all bullshitting.*

Sandilands saw me. 'Hey, Sue!' Damien looked uncomfortable, almost embarrassed, as though he felt he should intervene but couldn't. Sandilands put his arm around my neck. 'Damien reckons you know a way into the tuckshop.'

I led the way. The gang looked suspicious at any time. Today they looked like bank robbers. Telling them to try to act normal, I sidled over to the counter. Underneath was a half-door with a hinged section over it, like the one on *Mr Ed*. It was unlocked. Grant was salivating. I could see their minds ticking over. My nickname might be Sue but I was approved.

That weekend, there we were: me, Damien, Grant, Sandilands. Four bandits in windcheaters scaling the walls of the school, crashing through the oleanders. I crept round to the front of the tuckshop. The concrete desert echoed. I had never seen it like this. Across the yard I could see a Jesuit whipped by the wind slowly opening his mouth to reveal fangs. *It's only an oleander, you dickhead.*

I prised the door open with my fingers, got inside as fast as I could and crawled across the floor to the back door. I undid the bolt. The others were pressing so hard on the door that it smashed into my hand, spraining a finger. Damien and Grant tumbled in on top of me.

'Where's Sandilands?' I asked.

'He's keeping guard.'

We were in Aladdin's cave. Jupiter Bars. A box of Colvan Chips. Twisties. Chocolate frogs. I pushed my stuff out after the others, bolted the door behind them and crawled out the front and over the fence. We headed back to my place, trying to walk casually, as though we always carried entire boxes of lollies.

We made it to the cubby-house in my backyard. An old beach kiosk, it had been many things to us as kids: a horror house; a comic club, and now a discotheque with foil walls, beanbags, a poster of Suzi Quatro, fluoro artwork, and red cellophane over the windows. Spinning torches hung from the roof. Most important of all was Mum and Dad's old mono record-player that I'd painted yellow and covered in little foil stars.

We crashed in to find my twelve-year-old sister Anna and her friend Therese sitting among clouds of strawberry incense, listening to Carly Simon's 'You're So Vain'.

Caught, I stopped in the doorway but the others pushed past me. Anna was shocked by our booty. 'Where'd you get all that stuff?'

I ignored her and stashed the goods in the denim-covered chest.

'School tuckshop,' mumbled Sandilands with a mouth full of Jupiter Bar.

'You guys are such dicks. If Mum catches on she'll chuck a birko.'

'Only if you dob.'

'As if.'

I saw Therese looking shyly at Damien. He was staring at her. He introduced himself and asked her name. Before she could answer I plonked myself down next to her and offered her some Cheezels. 'This is my girlfriend Therese,' I said.

'Am not!' She hit me.

Damien lit a cigarette and bent down to the record-player and changed the record to *Aqualung*. We sat around talking about

Janis Joplin's *Pearl*, David Bowie's *Space Oddity* and what a dick John Denver was. Living in the seventies.

Damien put his cigarette out and walked outside without saying anything. Grant and Sandilands followed. I had an empty, hollow feeling. I became aware of the throbbing of my sprained finger.

A few days later I was walking out through the gates when I saw Quin sitting on the low wall that formed the flowerbed. He asked how my maths exam had gone. I said I'd be lucky if I got a C.

'Fair dinkum, Conigrave. You always play this game and then you top the class. It's funny, school ending, don't ya reckon? Here we are the older boys, but next year in senior school we're the little fish again. Weird, that. And with two junior schools, suddenly we're eight hundred boys in one school.'

I asked if he was nervous about it. He shrugged but I could tell he was. His place in junior school had been clear. He was the stirrer, the ratbag. Who knew what things were going to be like next year? We asked each other about our holiday plans. He was trying for a job at the bowling alley.

I said I was cleaning windows for the neighbours. 'And then the folks have got a house down at Somers for January.'

'Damien going with you?'

'Don't know what he's doing. Do you want to come down for a coupla days, Quin?'

'You can call me Bernard. Nuh. Folks wouldn't let me.' He was staring at his shoes as if to make sure they were clean. 'Big school. Pretty scary.' He wanted to say something. 'I reckon you should stop this girl stuff. They'll rip you to shreds up there. Nothing personal.' He smiled and jumped to his feet. 'Better kick off.'

I watched him walk away. *That was so weird.*

Chapter TWO

John at a Distance

Xavier College, the senior school, merged boys from two junior schools. It was in Kew, on the other side of Melbourne, a garden suburb all silver birches and manicured lawns. The days of leaving home ten minutes before school were over.

Getting to school would now mean a walk to Brighton Beach station, a twenty-minute ride in a carriage full of smoking kids, changing trains at Richmond for another ten-minute ride crammed in with migrant shift-workers from the textile factories, and then running down a ramp to fight for a place on the Glenferrie tram. The tram was a microcosm of human survival. As one pulled up, we would climb over each other to claim a bit of runner-board and a grip on a handle. The conductors were so jammed in amongst the acne and athlete's foot they couldn't collect fares. We ended up making a profit; our fares became money for Redskins or Choo-choo bars.

On my first day at Xavier I followed a stream of older boys in through the hurricane-wire gate. The other Kostka boys spotted some mates and I continued up the driveway by myself. A large grass quadrangle opened before me, shaded by lofty elms and flanked by two-storey red brick classrooms. At the far end was a large Victorian hall with huge windows and a slate roof.

I walked up a set of stairs, pulling out my information sheet to find the Third Form master's office. As I tried to make sense of the map, Damien came up behind me. 'Hey, buddy,' he whispered. I tried to smile but we were both uncomfortable. Neither of us had made contact over the holidays. 'Well, here we are,' Damien said awkwardly. 'Good holidays?'

'Not bad. You?'

'Tops. Went surfing with Makka down at Lorne, hot-doggin' chicks.'

I found it hard to look at him and began to spot Kostka boys. The faces I didn't know, Burke Hall boys, were different from ours. There seemed to be many more Italians and Greeks.

'You're in the A-stream, Latin and shit?' Damien asked. I nodded. 'Poor bastard. I'm in D-stream. Should be a real bludge. Don't know if I'll stick it out, but.'

Makka arrived. He was always tanned because he spent his summers at Lorne, his winters at Falls Creek and his September holidays at Surfers Paradise. His long hair was forever blond. His voice was husky, though maybe that was a put-on. Perhaps he wanted us to believe he was Rod Stewart.

'Was wondering where you got to, Dame.' *He calls you Dame? Doesn't sound right.* He whispered something to Damien, who squeezed my arm as they wandered off together.

Grant and Sandilands came up. Then suddenly Quin was on my back yelling, 'Jezza,' pretending to take a spectacular mark. We shuffled our way through the throng to the noticeboards. Joe-the-brainiac saw us and called out across the heads of the others. 'Welcome, comrades.'

On the far side of the crush I noticed a boy. I saw the body of a man with an open, gentle face: such softness within that masculinity. He was beautiful, calm. I was transfixed.

He wasn't talking, just listening to his friends with his hands in his pockets, smiling. *What is it about his face?* He became aware that I was looking at him and greeted me with a lift of his eyebrows. I returned the gesture and then looked away, pretending something had caught my attention. But I kept sneaking looks. *It's his eyelashes. They're unbelievable.*

A stocky boy with long fuzzy hair and ruddy cheeks recognised Grant from a football game the previous winter and introduced his group. 'Patrick Barrett, Vince Alliotti, Neil Garren, John Caleo.' *His name's John, John Caleo. Italian, that explains the eyelashes.*

Grant introduced us. 'Lex Sandilands, Bernard Quin, Tim Conigrave.' We shook hands. I couldn't bring myself to shake John Caleo's hand.

'You were ruck rover weren't you?' Grant asked John. He smiled and nodded.

'Captain actually,' someone chipped in, 'but don't tell him that. His head's big enough.' *Captain of the prep-school footy team. How?* 'You guys play footy?' We were unsure how to answer.

'Firsts basketball,' I said with as much dignity as I could muster.

The bell for assembly went. I tried to keep up with our new friends, I wanted to watch him. Even from behind he was calm and beautiful.

Suddenly we were in the hall, eight hundred boys in grey uniform with red and black stripes around the collars and cuffs and tops of socks. On the platform were six boys in sports blazers who turned out to be prefects, a number of Jesuits and lay staff, a track-suited sportsmaster and a middle-aged woman – the librarian.

The headmaster, Father Brennan, talked about the importance of leading a life in Christ, of loyalty to the school, of hard work and respect for those who wished to impart their knowledge to us. 'And when you are in uniform,' he reminded us, 'you represent the school.' We prayed, thanking our parents, our teachers, our religious leaders and the Father for this opportunity to improve ourselves.

We were sent to our classrooms. *Will he be in my class?* He stopped at his locker and took out a folder, a tartan pencil-case and some textbooks. I walked past him, as though by accident. I grabbed my bag, still lumpy with books, from the top of the lockers and made my way to maths class. I took a desk and watched the door.

An Italian boy with well-cut glossy black hair and lots of style strolled through the door. He was very sophisticated and elegant, but not the boy I was waiting for. Then he walked in, the boy with the amazing eyelashes, and sat a couple of desks in front of me. John Caleo was in A-stream.

'If you have a population problem that causes difficulties, like the diseases that come with overcrowding, what can you do?' Father Kelly was giving one of his famous talks on aid to India in Thursday morning religious instruction.

'Couldn't you make an exception about contraception?' suggested Biscuit, so named because he was one short of a packet.

'There are other methods, methods recognised by the Church.'

'The rhythm method,' offered Neil, one of thirteen children.

'That can have its problems too.' Distracted by two boys talking, Father Kelly watched them until they became aware of his gaze. One of them was John Caleo. 'Perhaps you've got some insight into this dilemma?'

The class erupted into gibes and applause. Father Kelly was stunned by the reaction. 'It's John Caleo, Father,' Patrick Barrett, one of the stirrers, was stirring. 'He never gets into trouble.'

'But deserves to?'

'No. He never does anything wrong.'

'A Goody Two-shoes?' I could see that John was blushing.

'No, he's a good bloke.'

Father Kelly sighed. 'John, sounds to me like you have a lot of respect among your mates and that's why they're taking a rise out of you.' He raised his eyebrows. 'I'll never understand you lot. Back to our dilemma.'

Patrick leant over and gave John a friendly punch in the arm. John looked quite shaken. I wanted to put my arms around him. Just to hold him.

Terry

Outdoor rock concerts had a culture of their own. Two types of kids went to them. There were the sharpies, a kind of skinhead peculiar to Melbourne. Boys and girls alike had their hair shorn with clippers, except for a set of rats' tails at the back. They wore high-waisted baggies, platform shoes, and short striped cardigans.

We were the surfies: baggies and striped oversized T-shirts under silky Hawaiian shirts. Our shoes, known as treads, had soles made of car tyres, and uppers of woven suede in contrasting colours. We wore a silver marijuana leaf or a shark's tooth around our necks on a piece of leather thong. We kept a hand up to our mouths as though we were biting a fingernail.

This particular concert at the Myer Music Bowl, a fundraiser for the famine in Bangladesh, was a mixture of glam bands like Hush, heavy rock like Lobby Lloyd, and folk-singers like Jeannie Lewis. After interval my friends said they were going home. I wanted to stay for Little River Band.

'Admit it. You want to stay for Sherbet. See you at school tomorrow. Give our love to Darryl.'

The sun setting over the Melbourne skyline, the cold night air descending and Little River Band playing gave me some thinking space. I became aware of the bass player. He looked like Biscuit at school. *I never thought Biscuit was good-looking. Maybe he's his brother.* The bass player had a beautiful smile and his bum looked nice in his satin baggies. *I wonder if he's gay? He looks like he could be. I can't imagine him with a girlfriend.* I sat there fantasising about him and what it would be like to be his boyfriend. I would feel safe, protected. I floated on these ideas for the whole set.

They finished and I figured I should go. I couldn't handle the thought of anyone catching me watching Sherbet. On the way to the station, on the platform, and then sitting in the carriage, all I could think of was the bass player. *What do the other band members think of him being gay? What would it be like to have sex with him?* I was in love.

The carriage was empty. The breeze coming off the Yarra made the windows rattle, and every so often there would be a whirring clink-clank-clunk as the engines turned over. Suddenly, the door slid open with a crash and in stepped a young guy of about eighteen with short hair, Clark Kent glasses and a purple quilted parka. *Must've missed the sixties.*

He checked out the whole carriage and then came and sat opposite me. I kept catching him looking at me. He gestured at the poster I was carrying. 'Good concert? Who played?'

As I named the bands and rated them he looked nervously around him, one foot tapping furiously. *Perhaps he's a spy using me as his cover.* I reached into my bag and pulled out Asimov's *I, Robot*. The minute I opened it he started chatting.

'What school do you go to?' I told him. 'Where's that?' In Kew. 'Yet you live down this way? What sort of school is it? Catholic? No girls? Just lots of frustrated boys, I bet.'

He introduced himself as Terry and asked my name. 'I should give you some of my magazines, Tim. Show them to your frustrated friends. You'd probably be shocked, being a Catholic.' I realised he was testing my reactions. 'You think you'd be shocked?' I shrugged. 'These are pretty different. They're not just boys and girls.'

His eyes were fixed on my forehead. 'Some of them are boys and boys.' I tried to look unfazed. 'So you wouldn't be shocked?'

'No.' I was nearly choking. 'I'm bi.'

His leg gently worked its way towards mine and our knees touched. We were pulling into Elsternwick, his stop. 'What station do you get off at?' he asked.

'Brighton Beach.'

'I think I'll stay on. Is that okay?'

I nodded nervously. His knee was pressing against mine. We didn't say much until we pulled into Brighton Beach, then he asked, 'Do you know where we can go?'

'There's a footy oval across the road.'

'You lead the way.'

And I did. On this cold autumn Sunday night there was not a soul around. He grabbed my hand, indicating the door to the change-rooms, which had a brick screen in front of it. He leant against the door, reached down and grabbed my crutch. I took his lead and did the same to him. He started to unzip me and I did likewise. We stood in the cold with our pants around our knees, tugging at each other's cocks. I wanted more, wanted to feel him against me. My hands went up under his shirt and jumper and into the warm protection of his back and I pressed my cock and balls against his. He was probably only a couple of years older than me but his cock was so much bigger than mine. I rubbed up against him, like I was fucking the T-shirt in my bed, and before I knew it I'd come on his leg. He grabbed my hand and put it on his balls, spat into his own hand and pulled himself off holding my still-hard dick. As he came his whole body nearly collapsed. He groaned, his eyes shut, and spoofed over the ground. We let go of each other. He reached into his parka pocket, pulled out a handkerchief and wiped off his leg. He offered to walk me part of the way home.

'How do you think your school mates would react if they knew you were bi?' He had opened a floodgate. At last, here was someone to whom I could blurt out all the feelings that had been trapped in my head for three years. I asked if his family knew he was gay. He didn't live at home anymore.

'What about the people you live with?'

'I think my boyfriend is okay about it.'

I was shocked. 'You've just cheated on him.'

'We have a deal. As long as we don't bring people home.'

'I would never do that if I had a boyfriend.'

'Is there anyone you like at school?'

I smiled and nodded.

'What's he like?'

'He's shy but really good-looking. I don't think he's gay. He's captain of the Under Sixteens.'

'Doesn't mean a thing.'

'You'd better stop here. This is my block.'

'I'll give you my phone number in case you want to catch up again.' He wrote on the back of his train ticket, handed it to me and shook my hand.

When I got home I headed straight for the shower and thought about what had happened. It was nothing like what I'd imagined. *He didn't even kiss me. The boy in the blue jocks kisses me.* I drifted off thinking about what it would be like to kiss John.

The next afternoon I snuck into Mum and Dad's bedroom and pulled out the well-fingered train ticket from the coin pocket of my school pants. I'd taken it to school in case Mum found it in my room. I dialled and the number rang and rang. *Maybe no one's home. Maybe he gave me a false number.* Then a man answered.

'Terry?' I faltered.

'I'll just get him for you.' He put the receiver down. 'Terry? I think it's the kid from last night.'

'Hi, Tim.' Terry's cheerful voice. 'I didn't think you'd call.'

'Um . . . sort of ringing to say that we'd better leave it here. I just think it's too risky.'

'We don't have to do anything. Just talk if you want.'

'I don't think I should.'

'Are you worried you might blab to your folks?'

'No. I just don't think we should see each other. But thanks. Bye.'

I hung up. My heart was pounding and blood had rushed to my face. I felt bad.

Berry

Carolyn lived across the road. We had been friends since we were seven. We'd been through puberty together and she was the first person I showed my first pair of jumbo-cord flares to. She burst into tears once when I gave her a birthday card that said, 'Rah rah, sis-boom-bah, nobody else could fill your bra.' Her room was wallpapered in pages from fashion magazines.

The Easter of my first year at high school I spent in a small country town called Maldon, near Castlemaine, with Carolyn and a friend of hers called Kelly. The highlight of the weekend was to be the annual bush dance at the nearby town of Burringup. Kelly had someone she wanted me to meet.

The dance was in a weatherboard hall decked in crêpe bunting which came together at an oil painting of the Queen. The Burringup Bushrangers, three old men and an even older woman, were setting up the drum kit, piano and music stands. Kelly led over a young girl wearing a cloth driving-cap and a blue V-neck jumper tucked into the top of her baggies. She had extraordinary dark brown eyes and glossy chestnut hair. Her breasts were really big for a girl of her age – fourteen or so.

'This is Berry,' said Kelly.

Barry? She could see the confusion on my face. 'Berry, short for Berenice.' I blushed.

'I get it all the time. Do you dance?'

'Not to this sort of stuff.'

Berry dragged me into the throng on the dancefloor. It was weird to be in the hands of someone I had just met. But I was picking up the steps and began to feel I knew what I was doing. The music began to slow down and the band leader told us to 'bring the little lady back to earth.' Berry twirled herself under my arm. 'See! You can dance.'

The bandleader announced a jazz waltz and off we went. I was a little more confident about this one, having been shown how to waltz by other kids and Dad. I was feeling quite good until one of my left feet caught the hem of an older woman's skirt. She stumbled and landed on all fours. Berry and I tried to help her up but she gave me a look that could have fried eggs. Angrily she left the dancefloor.

'She deserves it. She's so pretentious. Let's sit this one out.' Berry took my hand and led me off the floor, but not to where Kelly and Carolyn were. Without looking at me Berry said, 'You have amazing eyes.' As we got to the edge of the dancefloor she turned and looked at me. 'An unusual green. Very clear. Nice.' I started to feel that this was some TV show I was watching.

'You have nice eyes too.' She was very beautiful.

'Did you notice if there were clouds tonight?' She took my hand and dragged me towards the door. We walked out into the autumn air. 'Just look at the stars!' She spun with her arms out. 'You don't see these in the city, do you?'

'No. They're amazing.' We stood looking up at the night sky, then stretched out on the ground with our arms behind our heads. We spent ages talking about the universe. Was there life on other planets? Did we believe in God? Then we talked about ourselves. She was the daughter of a headmaster, she sang on television every now and then, and she was going to be a lawyer.

Towards the end of the dance all four of us joined in the Pride of Erin, then the hokey-pokey, almost falling over with laughter and exhaustion. I felt I had made a new friend in Berry, but I wondered what it would be like to have a boy treat me like this. That thought felt right. Nice.

As I was getting dressed on Sunday morning I saw Berry arrive with a basket full of Easter eggs. She gave the girls an egg and a kiss then turned to me. She handed me a card and kissed me. Snoopy lay on his kennel with Woodstock sitting on his chest under the words 'Happiness is a new friend'. Inside Berry had written, 'It was really nice to meet you last night and I hope we can stay in touch. Here is my address if you'd like to be my penfriend.' She handed me an Easter egg.

We spent the morning making and eating an enormous country breakfast, playing Monopoly and creating ways to smash our Easter eggs – headbutting them, throwing them against the wall or jumping on them. We then made ourselves truly sick by making and eating honeycomb and drowning it in mint chocolate milkshakes.

Fading into a sugary haze we succumbed in front of the television to a cartoon about a bunch of furry animals witnessing the crucifixion. Kelly had fallen asleep over the arm of the couch. Carolyn dozed off with her head in Kelly's lap.

The midday movie was *The Greatest Story Ever Told*. Berry said that should be fun for a good Catholic boy like me. We smiled at each other and sat in silence for a while. *She's really pretty. I almost think I could go with her. I wonder what that'd be like? It feels sort of different. I don't know.*

We started chatting. Did I believe contraception was a sin? Did she like Pink Floyd's *Dark Side of the Moon*? What did I think *2001: A Space Odyssey* was about?

The three family dogs were asleep in a pile in front of the television. 'God,' I moaned, 'a household full of sleeping animals. Last night Buster pissed on my bag.' Buster the beagle lifted his head to see who had called his name and Max the mongrel stood up. The two of them started playing in front of the television. As Moses parted the Red

Sea, Max tried to mount Buster. Berry and I pretended not to notice, until I couldn't stop myself smirking and both of us burst into laughter. By now Max had succeeded in his plan and was bumming off Buster. We were hysterical. Carolyn woke up. 'What's so funny?' She saw what we were laughing at. 'How disgusting,' she said and went back to sleep.

I couldn't stop laughing. 'How embarrassing.'

'Don't be silly.' said Berry. 'They do it all the time. They're boyfriends. I think it's really sweet.' I could feel the blood rushing to my face. 'You're blushing.'

'Always happens when I laugh. I've got to go to the toilet.' Trying to look relaxed, I walked slowly out into the hall. I went into the bathroom and sat on the edge of the bath, angry. *Why do I blush? Can she tell? I don't think she'd mind. I know she likes me. Perhaps I should ask her out. I really like her. I don't know. What if she wants more from me?*

I went back to the living-room. Before I could stop myself I asked Berry if she wanted to go round with me. She looked curiously amused, leant over and kissed me gently on the cheek. 'How sweet.' For the rest of the day we held hands. It was nice, but I was very conscious of what the others must be thinking.

Dear Tim,

        I've got some good news. I was singing at the Maldon Fête yesterday and a woman said how much she liked my singing. She works for . . . drum roll . . . *The Ernie Sigley Show* and she wants me to call her to talk about singing on the show. Wouldn't that be a gas? I'm going to ring this woman now. I was writing to you hoping to get some courage.

Berry
PS: Snoopy says hello.

Dear Berry,

That's good news about Ernie Sigley. It means you'll be coming to Melbourne and we can see each other. Life is going pretty well, although I'm finding school a bit boring. Better go now. Maths homework!!!!

Your friend,
Tim

'Hello, Berry . . . That's good, Tim will be pleased . . . Yes, of course. We've got a spare bed in the front sunroom . . . Dick will pick you up from the station . . . I'll get Tim.' As she handed me the phone Mum said with a satisfied smile, 'She has lovely manners.'

We had won the Saturday morning basketball match against the Protestants. I was in my gear, waiting for Berry with Dad. I pointed to a young woman in a large denim coat with a wing collar, her hair under a red crocheted beanie. She looked much older than fourteen.

'Son, she's beautiful,' he said under his breath. *Of course she is. You think I'd go round with an uggo?*

At lunch, Dad was almost embarrassing. 'Berry, sit here. What would you like to drink with your lunch, perhaps some wine?' When Dad and I were in the kitchen making the coffee he confided, 'Son, she is very beautiful. And intelligent.' He put his arm around my shoulder and gave it a squeeze.

Berry and I headed for the beach after lunch, walking hand in hand. We sat on the sea wall with our arms around each other, watching boys riding waves beside the Brighton baths. 'I didn't think you could get waves in a bay,' Berry said.

'Whenever there's a westerly there's a bit of a swell.' This was well known to the surfies in surrounding suburbs. I often went down to watch them getting in and out of their wetsuits. Once a boy with straight sandy hair asked me to unzip him from the back because his zipper had jammed. I recalled the slow revelation of tanned smooth skin speckled with moles. There had been another boy spearing a stingray off the sea wall whose shorts had ripped at the crutch, revealing his red jocks.

That night was the Third Form social, the first chance to wear my new baggies with the side pockets. I tucked my blue and white striped T-shirt into the top of my baggies and climbed onto the toilet to check myself out in the mirror. I donned my ox-blood platform shoes and I was ready.

I walked into the dining-room where Mum sat with Berry, who wore a floral chemise and huge red bubble-toed platforms, her hair pulled back by a red Alice band. She handed me a present wrapped in red crêpe paper. Inside was a little enamelled bluebird on a silver chain. 'It's grouse, thanks.'

'Let me put it on you.' Mum smiled as Berry undid the clasp and put it around my neck. 'Very cute.'

Dad dropped us off at the main entrance and we walked through the gardens to the lower quadrangle and the Montague Theatre. Outside was a group of guys from my class, none of whom seemed to have girls with them. *There's no way I could have come to the dance without a girlfriend.* I walked past holding hands with Berry. Then I noticed that John was among the group. *He doesn't have a date. He should be able to get one. I guess he's too shy. I wonder what he thinks of Berry?*

In the theatre the chairs had been stacked against one wall to clear the parquet floor for dancing. On stage was an earnest schoolboy band called Crimson Lake. We tried to dance to their attempt at 'Horror Movie'. I noticed Derge Camilleri, a small Maltese guy from my class, looking at me and Berry, giving me the thumbs-up. I started to wonder what people thought of us. The more I thought they were looking, the better I danced. Rhys, a very good-looking boy dressed much more formally than the rest of us, was holding hands with a beautiful girl with a blond dolly haircut wearing a handkerchief dress. He led her over to us. *He looks really good dressed like that. And I've never noticed his skin before, so brown against those green eyes.* 'Frances, this is Tim and . . .'

'Berry. This is Rhys.'

'Nice to meet you, Berry.' I could smell Brut mixed with sweat. *I never realised he was so . . . I dunno, attractive. Girls must think he's a real spunk.* 'What do you think of the dance?'

'What's the bet the next song is "Stairway To Heaven"?'

He laughed. Frances was playing with an earring. 'I think it's very pleasant.'

'If only the boys weren't such pigs,' Berry said.

Rhys laughed again. 'Not all of us!' *He has such a cute smile.* Frances grabbed Rhys's hand, saying, 'I want some fresh air.' She dragged him up the stairs and into the quadrangle.

Berry grinned. 'She thinks I'm trying to crack onto him.'

'He *is* very good-looking.'

'Do you think so? We have the same taste in men.'

I thought I was going to blush. I grabbed her hand. 'Let's go outside, I can't stand this music any longer.'

We climbed the stairs out into the night air and walked along the verandah with our arms around each other's waist. Suddenly Berry dragged me into a dark corner. She leant against the wall and stood like a siren tempting me. She took my head in her hands and put her lips on mine. I put a hand gently on her breast and she opened her mouth. *She tastes sweet: strawberry lipstick.* Our tongues played with each other. *C'mon hard-on, where are you? Enjoy. Doesn't this feel good? Nothing's happening. Wonder if she can tell. Pretend she's Rhys. She doesn't smell like Rhys. A small stirring. Yes, c'mon.* I rubbed my crutch against her. *Yes c'mon. Rhys. It's not happening. Gotta stop.* 'I need to go to the toilet.'

We hardly spoke in the car on the way home. Dad must have

thought we'd had a fight. We didn't talk much before going to bed. 'Thanks for tonight,' she said as we parted.

'That's okay.'

She looked stunned. 'Is that all?' She went to bed, obviously disappointed.

We talked little over breakfast. Her eyes were bleary. *Fuck, has she been crying? It's because of me. She's getting too involved. Too intense.*

In the car on the way to the station we held hands. I felt a lump in my throat.

A few days later Berry rang. 'Is everything okay?'

I hesitated. 'Perhaps we should call it off.'

'Have I done something wrong?' No, I told her. Silence. 'You don't like me?' I said I liked her a lot. 'Please think about it and write to me. Okay?' She sounded like she was going to cry. 'Promise?' I hung up feeling really bad.

That night I dreamt I told her I was gay and we had a punch-up. She stood on the verandah at school yelling that I was a poofter. I made love to her and she laughed at me.

I woke up feeling it had all really happened. At school next day I was distracted, ashamed of leading her on, feeling that I did really like her but knowing we could never be boyfriend and girlfriend.

Finally I wrote to her to explain. After a pile of failed attempts came one that said what I needed to say.

Dear Berry,

> I've wanted to tell you for ages but didn't
> know how you would take it. I hope you can
> understand and not be too angry with me. I think I am
> gay. I've known it for some time, since I was about
> eleven. I've had a couple of crushes on guys at school.
> That is why I went into such a spakko mood at the
> dance after we got so close, because I think that you

want something from me that I can't give you. I want to
say I'm really sorry about leading you on, but some of it
was because I really do like you, only not like that. I
hope we can still be friends.

The letter sat on my desk all night. I woke up thinking, Tear it up!
Tear it up! I dreamt that I had torn it up but next morning it was still
there. It burnt a hole in my chest as I ate my bowl of Special K.

On my way to the station I hesitated at the letter-box,
imagining my letter sitting on top of the others. Then I let it drop.
Can't do anything about it now. It's done.

When things got boring during French or science I would
try to imagine where my letter was. *It's at the post office. It's on the
train to Maldon. Can't do anything about it.*

Mum and her friend from across the road were sitting in the living-
room, chatting over a glass of wine. I was still in my school uniform,
watching an episode of *The Partridge Family* when the phone rang.
My heart jumped into my throat. *Berry must have my letter by now.
She's probably so disgusted that she won't ring.*

'Mary-Gert speaking . . . Hello Berry . . . Very well, thank
you. I'll get Tim for you.'

I suddenly felt I was going to throw up. 'I'll take it in your
room.' *In ten seconds my life will be over.*

'I got your letter. It's okay.'

'It's *okay?*' My mind was flooded with questions. *Did she suspect?
Was it a total shock? What was it like opening the letter?* But I didn't think
this was the time to ask them and we sat in silence for a moment.

'I still want to be friends,' she said at last. *Does she know any
gay people? Do I look gay?* 'I really want to see you.'

We agreed that I would visit her that weekend. I hung up the
phone and sat there, numb. All at once I was hit by a wave of

excruciating relief. Tears trickled down my face. I wasn't crying or even whimpering, just shaking my head, my face wet with tears.

I climbed under the shower. Supertramp were on the radio singing 'Dreamer'. I joyfully sang along as though it had always been my favourite song, my tears mingling with the running water. 'You silly little dreamer, can you put your hands in your head? Oh no.' *Whenever I hear this song I'm going to remember this moment.*

There had been little rain around Castlemaine for some time. All the grass was the colour of straw. I was getting restless as my stop approached, unable to concentrate on *The Midwych Cuckoos.*

I went to the dining-car, where a young man in a red waistcoat was cleaning up. 'We're closed.' His eyes flashed green. 'We get to Castlemaine in about ten minutes.' His full red lips parted again. 'I'm sorry.'

I fell instantly in love. I asked if I could sit there for a moment. He was beautiful, his curly brown hair moving about his broad shoulders. Every now and then he'd give me a little smile and lift his eyebrows.

The train slowed down as we approached the outskirts of Castlemaine. I slid off the stool at the counter. 'It was nice to meet you.'

He looked surprised, then smiled. 'It was nice to meet you too.' *Why did I say that? How embarrassing.* I tried to walk away as though that's what you always said to a waiter you'd met two minutes ago.

I spotted Berry on the platform in her denim coat and crocheted beanie. I alighted and we hugged. She asked how the train trip had been. I couldn't say I had just seen the sexiest waiter in the dining-car.

We walked hand in hand along the main street of the town, looking in windows. We didn't say much until I spotted a camp oven in the window of a tent shop. 'Just my lucky day,' I quipped.

It wasn't much but it was enough for her to open the topic. 'How long have you known?'

'Two or three years. But I can remember having a crush on my cousin's boyfriend when I was about eight years old.'

Walking through the town, and then in Berry's bedroom with her Peanuts posters and her stuffed Snoopy, we talked about many things: Carole King's *Tapestry*, Woody Allen's movie *Sleeper*, and The Topic. 'Do you think I look gay? Did you pick it?'

'Don't you think it's a bit early to make up your mind? You're only fourteen.'

'I don't have feelings about girls, but the guys at school . . . All the time. That guy Rhys you met at the dance . . .'

'He had his girlfriend with him.'

'So did I.' This hurt her. She was hugging her Snoopy doll and turned him to look at her. 'There's also this guy, John. I don't know, it sounds so dumb, but he's different. He's really quiet and gentle and has beautiful eyes, dark brown with these eyelashes. He's captain of the Under Sixteen football team.'

'You never know. Maybe it's because you're at an all-boys school? Have you ever had sex?' I nodded, too embarrassed to go into detail. 'With a girl?'

'No.'

'Then how do you know?'

'I know.'

She was annoyed. She put Snoopy down, sorted out the things on her desk, and finally sat back on the bed and took my hand. It was okay. I had passed the test.

The rest of the day we were two friends who shared a secret. I felt a special kind of bond with her, the kind that I hoped one day I would share with a boy. When it came time to catch the train back to Melbourne we parted good friends.

We kept in touch by letter until Berry got a job playing

Dorothy in *The Wizard of Oz* at a Melbourne shopping centre during the Christmas holidays.

We were sitting on a jungle gym in the park near her sister's house. I told her I was sad that I couldn't be her boyfriend and she snapped. 'I'm sick of this. Why do you have to make such an issue of it? There's more to you than being gay, but it's all you ever talk about.'

'You're the only person I can talk to.'

'What's there to talk about? You say you're gay, I've said that's okay. What's the big deal?'

'I've been hiding all this stuff for years. I'm sorry that you're copping it all but I don't know who else to talk to.'

Obviously her frustration was deeper than this. One afternoon when I was hanging around the show the Scarecrow took me aside. 'Berry says you think you might be gay. Don't you think it's a little early to make that decision? You've got your whole life ahead of you. No need to close off your options.'

The more he said, the more I was convinced that he was wrong. He'd sown some doubts, but all I had to do was think about Damien, Rhys, John and my head full of boys to know what was true.

Geoff

The local cinema, where *Soylent Green* was showing, had a hand-written advertisement seeking a junior usher for the Christmas holidays. The owner, Mr Ward, had only one question: could I start on Monday morning?

Next day I stood letting in the small audience for the eleven o'clock session, mainly kids without parents. Jaffas started flying, then milkshake containers. A fat kid jumped over two rows of seats and started to chase his victim. 'Hey you lot, settle down or you won't be seeing the movie,' yelled Geoff the projectionist. There was a big 'whooa' from the stirrers.

'Isn't that sweet? Normally they'd just stab you.' Geoff was standing next to me, his hands behind his back, bouncing from foot to foot. He was a young, heavily built guy with surfie-blond hair, wearing a striped T-shirt and white flares. 'How are you, cutie – settling in?' *Did he just call me cutie?* I was taken aback. *Is he gay or is he just being silly?*

'Why don't you pop up to the projection-room when the film starts? Unless you want to see *Benji* again.' He smiled, then turned and headed up the stairs. I thought what a nice body he had – broad shoulders, nice hard bum. He turned, caught me looking at him and winked. *Why did I do that? Oh no, he'll think I'm interested.* I felt a thrilling cocktail of fear and excitement.

The upstairs foyer was dark but I could find my way by the ultraviolet light of the large fish tank. I opened the projection-room door to find a small ladder. Geoff called down to me over the clatter of the projector and I clambered up into a warmly lit room.

As he was showing me how the projector worked he noticed the bluebird round my neck. I said a friend had given it to me.

'And what's your friend's name?'

'Berry.'

'Barry? So you are camp?'

'Yes, I am, but her name is Berry. She was my girlfriend. Why did you think I was camp? Do I look it?'

'Probably not to the rest of the world but I can pick it. Takes one to know one. Was Berry a cover to keep the guys at school off the scent?'

'No, I really liked her. But I told her I was gay.'

Suddenly the door at the bottom of the ladder flung open and Shirley the ticket seller shrieked my name. 'Mr. Ward's looking for you. You'd better get your bum down here.'

He was waiting for me in the foyer, his voice bouncing off the pebble-crete floor like a whisper in a cathedral. 'Your job is to sit inside when the public is in there. If there's a disturbance or, God help us, a fire, you have to be there. That's what you're paid for.' *Great.* Benji *over and over, twice a day for four weeks.*

The following day I stood guard at my post. Suddenly Geoff was there again. 'What have you done to your top lip?' I had cut myself shaving. He chuckled. 'How old are you?'

'Fifteen.'

'You don't need to shave. You're only a baby. I've got a doughnut for you up in the projection-room.' I told him about Mr Ward's lecture. 'He's probably just jealous. Wants to keep you all for himself.' He saw I was shocked. 'Joke. See you upstairs.'

Eating my doughnut in the little room, I asked Geoff how old he was. 'How old do you think?' I thought he'd be twenty-three at most. He was thirty.

'You don't look it.'

'Thanks, pet. Being gay keeps you young and attractive.'

The room became a kind of secret school where I could ask all the embarrassing questions I'd been squashing for years, where I learnt what being gay could mean.

'Does anal sex hurt?'

'If you don't know how to do it properly. Being in love can help. But anyway, not all gay guys do it.'

He told me about saunas where men went to have sex with strangers. He shocked me with the story of his last boyfriend, Graeme, who was out skateboarding late at night and got pulled over by two policemen. One was a 'real honey', more interested in frisking Graeme than anything else. They got off together in the back of the paddy wagon while the other cop kept watch.

He told me that some camp guys had one-night stands and some had long relationships. He knew of one that had been going for eleven years.

I felt totally safe with Geoff. He never made fun of my questions and he never tried to feel me up or make a pass at me. But somehow I did get his address.

I had told Mum and Dad I was going out to photograph railway stations for an art project, but I had other things in mind.

I was outside a large Victorian house surrounded by an overgrown garden. I opened the front door onto a dark corridor smelling of cabbage and garlic. I stood there in my duffle coat, holding my camera. I patted my hair to make sure it wasn't sticking up, braced myself and knocked on the door to Geoff's flat. I thought I heard a noise inside, but no one came to the door. *I've come all this way and now he's not home. He should be, it's Sunday morning.* I knocked again.

'Who is it?' The voice was groggy.

'It's me, Tim.' I could hear more noises. *Perhaps he's with someone.* Bleary-eyed he ushered me in, wearing only a pair of board shorts. He pulled on a T-shirt and ran his fingers through his hair. The flat was one room with a double bed. A bay window held a kitchenette. He put the kettle on as I explained that I was out taking photos for a project. 'I was in the area and you said to drop in some time.'

He offered me a cigarette. 'I'll give you a tour of my mansion while we wait for old mother to boil.' Some unfinished cabinets ran around the walls. 'My pride and joy. I'm making them myself. That's my bed, don't look too close or you might get a fright. This is my altar to Marilyn.' A large poster was surrounded by pictures cut from magazines. Below this stood a brass vase with a single plastic rose and a small ceramic candle-holder that was Marilyn as the Statue of Liberty.

'Can I hug you?' Geoff asked apprehensively.

I croaked out a timid yes. He put our cigarettes in an ashtray near the bed, then wrapped his large arms around me. We hugged a long gentle hug. He smelt of cigarettes, aftershave and sweat. *Is this what it's like? Is this what I want? Why am I doing this? Does he think I'm trying to crack onto him?* He kissed me on the forehead.

The kettle boiled and Geoff let go of me, suggesting that I

take off my duffle coat. I hung it over a kitchen chair as he made tea. He brought two cups to the bed. 'Sit here.' He patted the spot beside him.

'It's okay, I'll stand.' *What do I look like? I must look like such a dickhead. But if I sit down he'll think I'm easy.* I sat down. Geoff rubbed my knee. *My God, it's just like in the movies.* He took my cup of tea from me, placed both mugs on the floor and lay back. His hand was rubbing my back. 'It's all right. I don't bite.'

I lay back. He started undoing the buttons of my shirt. 'Is this okay?' I nodded. He undid my shirt all the way. 'Hello, little bluebird.' He popped the top button of my jeans, sat up and grasped a shoelace. 'Can I take these off?' I nodded and he took off my shoes, socks and, after making sure I was okay, my jeans.

He took off his T-shirt and shorts. We lay there in our underwear. He caressed me. *Wonder what he thinks of my body? What happens now?* Geoff started to lick me all over. Before I knew it my hard-on was in his mouth and he was sucking me. *Feels okay. Not as good as I thought. Those orange café-curtains are terrible. Wonder if anyone can see in?*

He sucked me for some time and eventually kissed my dick and lay back. *Guess I'd better do him.* I moved down the bed and pulled out his erect cock. *My God, how am I going to get that in my mouth? I'm gonna choke. My jaw is aching.* I gagged and dry-retched.

'It's okay.' Geoff took a bottle of oil from the bedside table, squirted some in his hand and rubbed it into my hard-on. He kissed me with an open mouth. He rolled me onto my back and continued to stroke my cock. After not very many strokes, my semen splashed onto my belly. 'There's some tissues beside you,' he said.

'Don't you want to come?' I asked him.

He said he didn't need to come every time.

'Is it because I can't do it right?'

Geoff drew on his cigarette. 'It was nice just making you come.'

I fumbled to get my jocks on and took a Marlboro from the kitchen table. A strange feeling came over me, a mixture of relief and hollowness. *That wasn't quite like I imagined. Something missing.* 'I hope I meet someone my own age,' I mused. 'It's not that I don't like you. But I'll have more in common with a guy my age.'

We sat in silence and drank our tea. I don't think he was hurt, just unable to find anything to say.

John in the Change-room

In the white wonderland of the shower-room the warm water was welcome on my tired muscles. My calf smarted from the grazing it had copped as an opponent went for the ball at soccer.

I turned off the water and limped through naked bodies into the change-room, its cold concrete heavy with the smell of crushed grass and mud. I grabbed my towel from the rack.

Out of the corner of my eye I saw a football boot thrown against the wall. 'Fucken one-eyed dickhead,' said John, dragging his other boot off. I got dressed, trying not to stare. John's voice cracked. 'How can he call himself an umpire? I'd let go of the ball, but the jerk threw me to the ground. And do I get a free kick?'

Father Wallbridge stood over him. 'That's no excuse for shoving him.'

'Their ruck had been picking on me all through the match. Something just snapped.'

'Let out your frustration in here, not on the field. John, you're up for the Best and Fairest medal. You're lucky you didn't get a suspension.'

Wally Wallbridge walked away. John leant forward on his knees and took a deep breath.

Putting on my shoes and socks I watched him undress. He pulled his footy jumper over his head, revealing a muscular chest. He caught my eye and I tried to be supportive. 'Sounds like it was pretty tough out there?' He gave a half-hearted smile and slipped off his red jocks. His genitals peeked out from their black nest of pubic hair. He ambled towards the shower room, hooking his towel on the rack as his muscular bottom disappeared into the fog.

John picks up his towel. I am watching the muscles working in his back and his hard round bum as he disappears into the land of fog. I can hear the taps squealing and the hard stream of water hitting the white tiles. I see him standing under the fall of the shower, his eyes closed, drinking in its warmth, his wet hair curling around his sweet face. He sees me and opens a hand to call me over to him. I step into the stream realising that I still have my pyjamas on . . .

I woke to the reality of my bedroom. Darkness. Rain outside. *What was I dreaming? John.* I realised that I had a hard-on. *Let me go back to sleep.* I began rubbing my cock against the bed. *In the shower with him, our bodies pressed against each other. No. I shouldn't, not John.*

But my hard-on beckoned. It was not going to let me sleep until it had been satisfied. I snuck out of my bedroom holding my cock in case anyone was awake, crept into the dining-room where mum's towers of magazines were kept, and searched out a *Cleo*.

I lobbed the magazine onto the bed and went to my desk to get out my trusty come-rag, an old green T-shirt now covered in brown stains. It was not there. My erection started to wane. I would have to baptise a new T-shirt. I opened the drawer to find my come-rag neatly washed and folded on the top. *Poor Mum must have found it and washed it.* The realisation took some of the edge off my orgasm.

It was a crisp winter morning. I had slept most of the way to school on the train and knew that to sit in the sun streaming through the window would be instant death, so I sat on the other side of the classroom. I was still tempted to catch some zeds before Mr Cameron arrived, but my attention was caught by John.

He was mucking round with Derge Camilleri a few seats in front of me. He nudged Derge's folder and books to the edge of the table. Derge grabbed them and tried to push John off his seat. John resisted, gripping the railing. *He is so cute. Warm. Genuine. Untouched. I'd love a boyfriend like him.*

Mr Cameron dropped his books loudly on the desk. 'Differential calculus. What is it? Joe?'

'A formula that describes a rate of change.'

Holding hands with John. Meeting him after school. Meeting at lunchtime. Studying together, I watch him and he lifts his eyes and catches me looking at him. We both laugh.

'Conigrave? Acceleration or deceleration?' I was lost. 'Perhaps you could honour me with your concentration.' I wasn't even at the right chapter. I could see John's neck as he made notes. *He leans back and I wrap my arms around him. He turns and kisses me. I wake up beside him and lie there watching him sleep. He opens his eyes and smiles as he stretches.*

Pow! I was struck by a duster. My head spun in a cloud of chalk dust. 'There you are, Conigrave, an example of deceleration.' Mr Cameron smirked. I felt the blood rushing to my face as I brushed the chalk off my jumper.

Chapter *THREE*

Rhys's Baby

By Fifth Form the school recognised that we were adults and had the right to feed our addictions. First they set up a smokers' room – a sandstone dungeon in the basement of the old hall, a better place than the unsanitary environment of the toilets where we might pick up the habit of loitering. But after a few weeks of their sons returning home in uniforms reeking of tobacco, parents put the boot into that idea. So the school created a coffee room. We met in one of the classrooms during breaks for biscuits, and coffee or tea at twenty cents a cup.

This morning I was starving, even though I'd had breakfast. My stomach had been grumbling all through maths, and in biology even the slime moulds looked edible. I was tucking into my sixth Milk Coffee when Patrick Barrett piped up, 'Hope you're buying tomorrow's biscuits.'

'I'm starving.'

'Perhaps you're pregnant,' Derge Camilleri chuckled. 'Have you been having any morning sickness?' He took my pulse.

'No, Doc. I think I'd know if I was pregnant.'

'Still, we'd better do the test. Give me your coffee.' He picked up a sugar cube. 'If this floats you're not pregnant. But if it sinks . . .' The cube sank into the coffee. Patrick, Derge and the onlookers cheered.

'What's going on?' Rhys asked as he entered the room.

'Conigrave's pregnant.'

'Tim, you told me you were on the pill.'

'I hope you're not angry. I'll get rid of it if you want.'

'Get rid of our baby? How could you suggest such a thing? We'll go through this together and it'll be a beautiful child.' Rhys winked.

'You guys are sick.' Neil was disgusted.

Next morning Derge handed me a pastizzi. 'A present from my mum. Remember you're eating for two now.'

In the middle-school library stood Mr O'Connell, our English teacher, a massive bulk of culture who wore an academic gown and swept his blond fringe continually.

'Your book reports are due in three weeks, cretins. If you haven't chosen a book, you see before you the largest collection of second-hand paperbacks in the Southern Hemisphere.'

I was sharing a table with Patrick the stirrer, Marcello the spunk, Maltese Derge, Rhys and John. I sat opposite John. It was hard not to stare. He looked up from *The Swiss Family Robinson*. 'Any good?' I asked.

'I've just started it but I think it's pretty good,' he answered shyly.

Derge leant against me and chuckled. 'What about when they find that cave with the society of little robots?' John looked bemused. He had never watched *Lost in Space*!

Patrick was incredulous. 'Danger, alien approaches,' he said. Mr O'Connell was on his way over to our table.

'I thought you boys were reading aloud but you're just gossiping. Put your jaws to some use and tell me what edifying works you're reading.'

'*Catcher in the Rye*,' said Marcello to Mr O'Connell's approval.

'Patrick Barrett?' Nothing. 'Get over to those shelves and find something.' Derge held up *The Exorcist*. 'Dear oh dear, if you must.' Rhys proudly showed *Hotel*. 'It's like an airport bookshop. Find something else. Conigrave?' I had *Chariots of the Gods*. 'No, no, no! I will not have you reading that garbage.'

'But I found it on the shelves here,' I protested.

'Find something else.'

Amongst the paperbacks my eye caught a red cover with a cartoon of a curvaceous Mae West-type being fondled by a muscular sailor: *Myra Breckinridge*. I took it back to the table. *This could be fun. Might curl a few of O'Connell's hairs.*

As I went to sit down, Derge pulled my seat out from under me and I crashed to the floor. 'My God, the baby!' A chorus of three boys jumped to their feet. As Mr O'Connell looked up, a deathly hush fell on the group.

'Do I understand that you are pregnant? That some miracle has occurred?'

'It's a joke, sir, a running joke.'

'And you participate freely in this running joke?' I nodded. He took a deep breath. 'You're an idiot, Conigrave. Not only do you make a mockery of one of the Lord's greatest gifts but you degrade yourself with this pretence of otherness.'

He shook his head in despair. 'You make me sick. Sit down.'

Myra Breckinridge turned out to be quite a horny story. But I couldn't bear Mr O'Connell knowing I had enjoyed it, so I gave it a damning report: a mindless pornographic romp, I called it.

I got fourteen out of twenty, but a large note was scrawled

in red across the report: 'Pornography is in the eye of the beholder. *MB* is much more than it appears; that is why it is a masterpiece.'

Romeo and Juliet

I was at the noticeboard outside the form-master's office when Chook Hennessy the Ancient Greek teacher sidled up to me. 'Auditions. Lunchtime today, 3C. *Romeo and Juliet.*' He headed down the stairs, but stopped at the landing. 'Real girls this year.' He winked and scuttled away.

I had often contemplated being an actor and would watch things on TV, repeating lines. Now I thought I'd give it a go.

The doorway to 3C was crammed. I could barely see through the throng of grey jumpers. A wiry boy was on the platform giving his all.

Chook was pacing, listening intently, murmuring lines and conducting the boy through his speech. Ash fell from his cigarette as his hands cut the air. His bottle-end glasses slid to the tip of his nose every time he squinted.

'I think you'll make a good Mercutio. Who wants to try out for Romeo?' Two boys put their hands up: Pietro, a 'boy-next-door' from the year below me; and a very pimply boy, Jack. *No harm in trying.* But as I put up my hand a rush of panic descended on me.

Pietro went first. Then a very nervous Jack, who stumbled along in a feeble monotone. Chook was frozen in horror. He dismissed Jack and butted his cigarette on the sole of his shoe. 'Tim?'

I managed as well as I could with Chook's interruptions, his squinting and fidgeting with his glasses. *There's that feeling again. All the blood is in my hands and feet.* I ploughed on. 'That'll do,' called Chook. 'I'm not sure. Let's have a go at this scene. I'll read Juliet. Go.'

I took a deep breath.

If I profane with my unworthiest hand
This holy shrine, the gentle sin is this,
My lips, two blushing pilgrims, ready stand
To smooth that rough touch with a tender kiss.

Chook lightened his voice, making it almost falsetto.

Good pilgrim, you do wrong your hand too much . . .

There were sniggers in the room. Chook pushed his glasses
back up his nose and eyeballed us angrily. 'Hilarious. I'd like to see
you lot do better. Pietro, I'd like you to play Romeo. Tim, you can be
Paris. Jack, I don't know, we'll find you something. There are scripts
here. Read it by the first rehearsal. The whole thing, please, not just
your bits.'

'Thou art thyself though, not a Montague.' Pepe, a feisty young
woman with short auburn hair, stood in the old pulpit that was to be
her balcony. Chook acted the part along with her, muttering between
sucks on his Benson and Hedges. 'What's Montague? It is nor hand,
nor foot . . .' She stopped, distressed.

Chook came to the rescue. 'Nor foot, nor arm, nor face nor
any other part . . .'

'I'm sorry, sir. I think you would play the role very well, but
I'm afraid you're putting me off.'

At the back of the theatre we boys tried not to laugh out
loud. A boy at the other end of the row, one of Romeo's gang, stood
up cagily, checking out the Sacre Coeur girls on the stairs beside the
stage. I'd been finding something about him remarkable. Now it hit
me. *He looks like John.* I tried to observe him without anyone else
noticing. *Maybe he's John's brother. It's the eyelashes. Gentle. Maybe I'm
obsessed.*

Joe was reading. 'Hey, Brainiac, what's so interesting?' Patrick leant over from the row behind him.

'Something you wouldn't understand. *The Selfish Gene*. It explains why specimens like you insist on reproducing yourselves.'

'Have you laid eyes on that girl with the long straight hair?' Joe didn't look up from his book.

'She's a nice specimen. How do you reckon she'd go in the reproduction stakes?'

'Only one way to find out. Now go away.'

By the end of rehearsal, the guys had decided which girls they were going to work on. They even had a few nervous encounters as they pressed sweaty palms with their partners in the ball scene. As Paris, I had to dance with Juliet. Each time we turned upstage my eyes searched out John's brother, for he was indeed a Caleo. *I am obsessed.*

The only person who made any real progress was Joe. A girl called Gina was Lady Capulet to his Capulet. As we tried to remember the steps of our galliard he said to her, loud enough for us to hear, 'Gina, there's more to get out of this scene. Would you like to work on it at my place this weekend?' She thought that would be nice.

Patrick muttered enviously, 'How does he do it, men?'

I waited for the train with the guys from the play. Someone called from down the platform. I turned to see Joe near the subway stairs, beckoning. I joined him. 'I thought you might want an excuse to get away from that bunch of mental defectives,' he said. 'How do you think rehearsals are going? I don't think they're very challenging.' I could see the train snaking its way along the track. I edged back towards the gang, but he asked me to ride with him.

In the last carriage, Joe and I sat opposite each other on cracked and slashed mock-leather seats.

'I read something in *Science and Nature*, a study of dolphins that showed they're primarily homosexual.' He looked at me as if gauging my reaction. 'They swim in single-gender packs and a lot of their play is sexual. They only come together with the opposite sex to procreate.'

He hesitated, then went on as if he had decided it was safe to continue. 'To say that homosexuality is unnatural is ridiculous when clearly it occurs in nature.' *He's testing me to see if I am. God, I hope he doesn't like me.* 'But what evolutionary purpose does it serve?' *Maybe he's trying to let me know that he's gay?*

'I don't know. Population control?'

'It's not as though the oceans are overcrowded with dolphins. Freud said that we are all born capable of sex with either gender. Do you think that's true?' I didn't answer, distracted by the thoughts traversing my brain. He was watching me intently. 'I'm sorry, I'm boring you.'

'No. I'm just tired.'

'You should try Royal Jelly. It's full of vitamins and amino acids. I use it every day. It's expensive but I can let you have a capsule.'

We sat in silence until we arrived at his station. 'See you at school tomorrow, man of wax.' I didn't understand. 'Isn't that what the nurse calls you?'

I am sunbaking at the beach. There is another towel laid out parallel to mine but I don't know whose it is. Someone stands at the water's edge looking out to sea, a silhouette against the glare of the bay. Maybe it is John.

The figure turns and waves. He comes to sit on the towel next to me. It is John. 'Have you learnt your lines? I'll hear them for you, if you like.'

I turn over and realise I have an erection. I am nervous that he'll notice. I cannot remember a single line. I panic. He'll think I'm a liar. 'Maybe we should do it later. I need a little more time.'

He lies beside me and puts his hand gently on my erection. 'Does this help?' I am awash with intense feeling. I come.

As I walked into geography class, I noticed that the desk beside John was free. He looked up at me with those big brown eyes and the dream suddenly felt real. *I wonder if he had the same dream, if he dreamt that he was on a beach with me. Like astral travelling.* I could still remember what it felt like to have his hand on my cock.

I sat next to him. I said I was in the play with his brother Paul. He looked up from his doodling. 'You playing Romeo?'

'No. The competition.' John looked confused. 'Paris, the one Juliet leaves for Romeo.'

'Poor Paris.' He smiled and went on doodling. I tried to sneak fleeting glances at him. Suddenly we were both looking at each other, aware that we had run out of things to say. *Say something . . . anything!*

'You're up for the APS Best and Fairest.'

'Think I've ruined my chances. Which team do you play for?'

'I play soccer.'

'A soccer choc!'

The teacher arrived and our conversation was cut short. I found it difficult to think of anything other than last night's dream. I was so aware of him I could almost feel the heat coming off his body. The cover of his clipboard was right next to me, calling me like a siren to the rocks. I wrote, 'You shall win.' He smiled.

For the next few geography classes, writing on his clipboard became my way of expressing affection for him.

A poem: 'There's hope for the living and hope for the dead/But there's no hope for John 'cos he's gone in the head.'

A slogan: 'If it feels good and hurts no one, do it!'

Finally: 'John has asked me to stop writing on his folder, so

I won't do it anymore. See, I've already stopped.'

Now I always looked forward to geography.

Paris was at the Capulet mausoleum. 'Sweet flower, with flowers thy bridal bed I strew.'

'You've lost your fiancée, not your wallet. Can't you do it sadder?' I tried again, my face contorted with sadness, my hand on my heart. 'Stop, stop. You don't sound very real. Do you know anyone who's died?' I didn't. 'Could you imagine what it would be like to lose, say, your girlfriend?' *John?*

'I guess so, sir.'

'See her lying in her tomb, cold, the colour gone from her face, lifeless.' *John dead, lying in a coffin, cold, lifeless.*

The obsequies that I for thee will keep
Nightly shall be to strew thy grave and weep.

Chook clasped his hands together as a sign of approval. I heard laughter. Chook turned to see who it was. Joe and Gina were giggling to each other. They held hands, his leg on top of hers. Chook frowned. They extricated themselves from each other but took every opportunity to remind us that they were together.

When rehearsals finished I grabbed my bag and ran. I didn't want to get stuck talking to Joe.

'Hey, Conigrave. Your boyfriend wants you!' Patrick pointed down the platform where Joe was waving. 'Give him a kiss for me.'

I dragged my feet down to where Joe was waiting. Nothing was said until we had taken our seats. 'Do you think Gina is good-looking?' he asked. I agreed that she was. 'She's the best-looking girl in the cast. I really put it up those others by getting there first. What makes her good-looking?'

'She's pretty.'

Joe dug into his schoolbag and pulled out a Spirex notebook. 'Can you be more specific than *pretty*?'

'Shiny hair, clear skin, nice smile.' Joe scrawled in his notebook.

'What are you doing?'

'I'm collecting data about how we decide that someone is good-looking. Name a guy at school you think is attractive.'

John. 'Rhys.'

'And what makes him attractive?'

'His suntan.'

'Anybody else? What about that Italian boy I've seen you talking to? John. What do you find attractive? His build?' I nodded. 'His eyes?'

'And his eyelashes.' Joe scrawled away.

'Is this a science project?'

'If you know what others find attractive you can manipulate things so you're attractive.' *I think the wires in his head are too tight*. He chewed the end of his pen. 'The real challenge is to stop the ageing process. I'd like to be the one who discovers the fountain of youth. I never want to grow old. And because I believe it strongly enough I know I never will.'

Father Brennan stood at the microphone on the stage of the Great Hall. Behind him sat a couple of staff and two boys in sports blazers. One of the blazers was John.

'Xavier has once again shown that a good footballer has many of the qualities of a good Christian: taking the talents that God gave you and using them to your best ability, working in a team to achieve a common goal. So it gives me great pleasure to award the following trophies on behalf of the Association of Public Schools. Justin Healy for Top Goal Score, 1976.'

Justin accepted the trophy. 'And John Caleo, Best and

Fairest, 1976.' John shyly stepped forward to equally loud applause, trying hard not to smile too much.

Later that day in geography I thrust my hand forward and said congratulations. His hand was soft and warm. He opened the front cover of his pink clipboard. I could see my comment, 'You shall win,' and gave in to temptation. I crossed out the middle word. It now read, 'You win.' John looked pleased and gave that little smile that lately had been causing my heart to twitch.

The following Monday morning I was struggling to balance my physics folder on my knees and do the homework I'd avoided all weekend: a heap of circuit diagrams for which we had to work out voltage, amplitude and resistance. As the train pulled into Joe's station, he saw me and appeared at the door of my carriage.

'Cramming? I should be doing some too. I didn't do any work over the weekend.' He was bursting for me to ask him why.

'Busy weekend?'

'Very. Pietro came back to my place after rehearsal on Saturday and he only left last night.' He raised his eyebrows lewdly. 'I've begun my experiment to prove my theory that we are all bisexual.'

'But he's got a girlfriend.'

'So have I!'

I was dumbstruck. *He's had sex with Romeo.* 'How did it happen?'

'During rehearsal we got talking about music. I told him about my synthesiser and he seemed interested. We mucked around with music, then we went for a swim. Pietro in a pair of boardshorts is worth seeing. I told him I thought he had a good body and that his girlfriend must like it, and he complained that she won't do anything and that he was getting frustrated. Then we talked about wanking and one thing lead to another.' He smiled a satisfied smile.

'Does this mean you're going out together?'

'No. It was just some fun. He's got Michelle and I've got Gina.'

'Are you going to tell her?'

'If Pietro was a girl it'd be different, but this way there's no competition. Can I copy your answers when you've finished? I'd better start on my Latin.'

I was shocked. *Wonder what Pietro is thinking now? Joe makes it sound so easy. Wonder if I could try the same thing on John?* I was barely able to concentrate on the circuit diagrams.

Later, in the study hall, John sat in the desk behind me. *I won't be able to concentrate with you sitting there.* He pulled books out of his bag. I was going over my lines for *Romeo and Juliet*.

'When's it on?'

'Thursday and Friday.' My voice was calm.

'You must be nervous?'

'Shitting myself.'

'Poor Paris.'

I was taken aback by his use of that name. 'Are you coming?'

'I don't know much about theatre. Or that Wobbledagger fella.'

I didn't get it.

'Shakespeare. Sorry, bad joke.'

'I thought you'd be coming 'cos your brother's in it.'

'I guess I should try. Thursday maybe. I'd better come along and keep an eye on you.' *Beauty.*

There was an air of controlled excitement in the room beneath the stage. A large curtain divided it, and on one side the girls were dressing in crushed-velvet frocks with laced bodices, hair ribbons and ballet slippers. We wore tights and velvet jackets with padded shoulders. And ballet slippers. I also scored a small cloak for the tomb scene.

The chemistry teacher had made large tubs of face cream in the school laboratory and was distributing them. As I applied the panstick I was suddenly twelve again and at my first night of Scouts, terrified that the boys in my troop would give me a hard time about my ruddy cheeks, red lips and the dark lines around my eyes. *Mum's got that cream that makes her look like she's got a suntan. Perhaps in this drawer? Yes, Mother of Pearl Beauty Fluid.* 'Tim, you're going to be late,' called Mum, then stopped in her tracks. 'What the hell do you think you're doing?' She handed me some Pond's Cold Cream and tissues. 'Your first night of Scouts and you're putting on makeup! Your father and I worry about you.' She sighed and left the room. A hollow feeling, the realisation that I had nearly done something dangerous, ate away at my stomach.

Chook Hennessy swanned through the dressing-room delivering copies of the program. Its front cover showed a boy and a girl holding hands inside a large heart. 'Remember, if anyone laughs at you, they don't have the guts to do it themselves. Good luck.'

'You can't say that, sir. It's bad luck,' Bartels prodded.

'You're right. Break a leg, boys.'

'Break a leg,' pondered one of the other boys. 'Why don't they just say split a bowel?'

The play began with a *tableau vivant* as the prince gave a run-down of the story. As we left the stage I waited in the wings. I was scared that if I went downstairs I would miss my entrance, the scene where Paris asks Capulet for Juliet's hand. Terrified of forgetting my lines, I went over and over them till I no longer knew what they meant.

My next memory was of leaving the stage after my first scene, my hands and feet tingling. *Maybe it went all right.* By interval I was feeling more confident. *Not much to this acting game.*

For the final scene the lights went down and the dry ice started to bubble. The stage became a mausoleum. I marched on, asked for my torch and dismissed my page. The audience was quiet. I suddenly realised the crutch of my tights was getting lower. *Shit, I must look like a baby with a full nappy.* My mind went blank. I stood there afloat in nothingness, the words refusing to come. *The line, what's the line? Graveside. John dead.* From the wings I heard Chook whisper, 'With flowers thy bridal bed . . .'

The flowers in my hand started to shake. I struggled my way to the end of the speech and then walked off as calmly as I could, though tempted to run. I was devastated. *What must John think of me?*

After the show Chook triumphantly thanked us all. He spotted me taking off my makeup. 'Bit of brain death?' he laughed. 'Believe me, no one noticed.'

Dad stood in the foyer with Mum. 'Here's our own Larry Olivier. We're proud of you, son.'

'I forgot my lines.' I was scanning the foyer to locate John. *Perhaps he's gone to the toilet.*

'We wouldn't have noticed except for the prompt you got.'

Pepe came over with her mother. 'Tim, this is Marie.'

'These are my parents, Gert and Dick.'

'You must be very proud of your daughter, Marie,' said Dad.

'And you of your son.'

'Few shaky flowers at the cemetery,' Dad chuckled, 'but we're very proud.' The numbers in the foyer were dwindling. John was nowhere to be seen. Dad rubbed his hands. 'We should get going, you've got school tomorrow, son.'

Pepe and I walked back to the change-room to get our bags. 'Are you all right?' she asked. 'We all forget our lines sometimes.'

'I thought a friend of mine was going to be here tonight.'

Lying in bed that night I tossed around all kinds of scenarios. Perhaps he was sick. Perhaps he forgot. Perhaps he was only being polite when he'd said he'd come.

As I showered next morning, as I ate my tomatoes on toast, and as I sat on the train to school watching the aniseed plants beside the railway line whizzing by, I wondered how to find out if he'd seen the show. And if he did see it, why he didn't stay. And if he hadn't come at all, why not. I didn't want to interrogate him or make him feel uncomfortable. I didn't want to hassle him. Well, I did but I didn't want him to feel hassled.

As I entered the study hall I could see John from the door, hunched over some work. The desk behind him was free, so I sat down casually. Brother Cahlill was walking slowly down the aisle, his eyes fixed on me. *Shit, what have I done?* 'Fine performance last night, Tim. The girl who played Juliet is very good.' I thanked him and he walked on.

John turned round. 'Sounds pretty good.'

'I take it you weren't there?' *Shit, I sound like I'm ticking him off.* He wasn't. He apologised. *More. I need more.* 'Are you coming tonight? I'd really like you to.' *Shit. Too far.* He said he'd have to see.

I wanted to jump on his desk and throttle him. *What do you mean, you'll have to see? There is no reasonable excuse. It's a Friday night. What could be better than seeing me in the play? Would you rather do homework?* I nonchalantly mentioned that there was a party after tonight's show. That sounded good to him. *He's going to come! Perhaps – don't jump to conclusions. But imagine if he did.*

That night I walked out into the foyer, my face still greasy and my fringe wet. I was on a high, having given what I thought was a good performance. John would be waiting for me. I spotted his brother Paul with people who could only have been his parents. His mother was a very tall, neat woman, her hair immaculately set. Her husband was a fumbly wombat of a man, his hands formally crossed in front of him. Both wore their Sunday best. John was not with them. I was crestfallen.

'Your friend's not here again?' Pepe put her arm through mine. I shook my head. 'He doesn't know what he missed.' She rubbed my hand reassuringly. 'You like this boy?'

'What do you mean?' Perhaps I was a little too defensive.

'Whatever you like.' She was smiling gently.

Pepe and I rode to her party with Jackie and Juliet, two of

the Sacre Coeur girls, babbling away: it was so much fun; they'd miss everybody; we must keep in touch.

Pepe's place was a rustic open-plan house. Her attempts at sculpture graced bookshelves flanked by the biggest stereo speakers I had ever seen. It was perfect for a party. Pepe handed me a glass of green liquid with mint leaves floating in it. 'I hope we're going to be friends. I have this feeling about you. So who is this boy?'

She smiled. I had no choice but to answer. 'His name is John. He's a boy at school, Paul's brother actually.'

'And you like him? Perhaps more than like?'

I felt a rush of warmth mixed with sadness. 'I'm bisexual.'

'I've grown up with gay people all my life. Mum's best friend is a lesbian. How are we going to get you two together? Dinner at your place Wednesday night, I'm cooking. And we should ask some of the others. It's settled.'

I sat smiling, content. I raised my glass to Pepe. 'Here's to our friendship.'

'And here's to your relationship.'

'You're so pushy.'

Through the sea of boys in the corridor preparing for the first class of the week, I caught the eye of John walking towards me. He opened the locker a few along from mine. 'I'm sorry I wasn't there on Friday. How did it go?'

'It went okay. Good actually.' I was trying to smile, but my face was in a wrestling match with the disappointment I felt.

'Paul said the party was good.' *Would have been much better if you'd been there.* 'I was out on a run and when I got back there was this note from Mum saying that she and Dad had gone to see Paul's play. That's when I remembered. Sorry. I'd better get off to Latin. I'll see you at the break.' He started to walk away. *Does he want to see me at the break or was that just a throwaway?*

'John?' He turned. 'I'm having an end-of-term dinner on Wednesday night with some of the girls from the play. Would you like to come?'

'Getting home might be a bit difficult.' *You can stay over.*

'Pepe lives over your way. I'm sure you could get a lift with her.'

'Sounds good.'

At the break John was with his footy mates in the coffee-room discussing the grand final, so I had to stand by, listening. Still, over the next couple of days I felt there was a secret between John and me. Okay, I couldn't go toe-to-toe about football, but it didn't matter – John was coming to dinner at my place. And then an ugly thought descended. *Perhaps he's only coming to meet some girls.*

On Wednesday night I was cutting up tomatoes for a salad when Pepe arrived with a large ceramic pot and a bottle of champagne. She gave me a kiss. Jackie and Juliet followed. 'We wanted to get here before lover-boy,' said Juliet, handing me another bottle of champagne. I was taken aback. 'It's all right darling, I knew from the moment I met you.'

We lounged around on the couches in the living-room. I munched on pretzels, unable to relax or join the conversation. I looked at my watch. It was quarter to eight. Pepe caught my concerned look and told me to relax.

At that moment the doorbell went, ripping through me like a bolt of lightning. I stood and cleared the pretzel out of the corners of my mouth with my finger. I took a swig of champagne, braced myself and headed to the front door, where his silhouette showed through the glass, schoolbag over his shoulder. I opened the door. He was dressed quite formally and looked nervous.

'I got lost on the way from the station.' He pulled from his bag a bottle of soda water and a bottle of lime juice.

I took him in, introduced him, organised drinks and sat down on the arm of the couch next to him. Pepe, Jackie and Juliet were all staring at John in silence. An agonising silence.

'You and Tim are at school together?' burst out Jackie. Pepe and Juliet looked at her in disbelief. Again we fell silent. John fumbled with his glass.

It was Juliet's turn. 'What did you think of the play?'

'I didn't see it,' John said apologetically.

'So I can tell you that we were fabulous?'

'I'd better serve up the ravioli,' Pepe said. 'Tim, can I have a hand?'

The pot came out of the oven. 'Tim, he is so sweet. So shy.' She left me to bring in the food and went out to seat everyone. 'Jackie and Juliet there, John next to Tim here, and I'll sit on the other side. Dig in.' We helped ourselves and complimented the cook.

The kitchen door opened. 'It's only us,' Mum called. 'We won't disturb you. Oh! That's an interesting seating arrangement.' I introduced the gang to Mum and Dad and they disappeared into the front of the house.

The ravioli and salad were demolished. I found making coffee a challenge after all the champagne I had drunk. When I sat back at the table Pepe announced, 'We're a new group of friends, so we should pass a kiss around the table as a kind of bond. Jackie, you have to kiss Juliet.'

As they kissed it dawned on me that I was going to have to kiss John. The thought filled me with terror. *What if he refuses?*

Juliet kissed Pepe. Their kiss lingered. Pepe came up for air. 'Tim.' As I kissed her she opened her mouth. Her tongue was exploring mine. I felt trapped. I was afraid to stop kissing her because I knew what was coming. *I don't want John to think that I'm enjoying this.* Before I knew it my hand was on his knee, as if to let him know it was him I wanted. His hand settled on mine as Pepe continued kissing me. I couldn't shake the feeling that I was a virgin being led to the volcano to be sacrificed.

I turned to face him. He shut his eyes and pursed his lips.

Everything went slow motion as I pressed my mouth against his. His gentle warm lips filled my head. My body dissolved and I was only lips, pressed against the flesh of his. I could have stayed there for the rest of my life, but I was suddenly worried about freaking him out and I pulled away.

I caught sight of his face – fresh, with chocolate-brown eyes and a small, almost undetectable smile.

'Last but not least.' Jackie threw her arms around John and gave him a smacker on the cheek.

Not long after that the front doorbell went, and Pepe's mother Marie was there to be the taxi home. We said our goodbyes. The secret between John and me was solid now. I could barely stop myself from begging him to stay. Instead I said, 'I'm going away with some of the guys from school next week. Is it okay if I call you when I get back?'

'Sure.'

I gave him a quick peck on the cheek. And as Pepe kissed me on the cheek she whispered in my ear, 'He's divine.'

'Do you think he's gay?' I whispered back.

'It doesn't matter. He obviously likes you and that's all that's important.'

I kissed the others goodbye and stood on the footpath watching the car disappear, feeling an excited sort of contentment. *There goes the boy I've kissed. Marie, his life is in your hands. I better not hear you've had a head-on with a tram.*

The Week Away

'That's them on the corner.' I pointed to six small weatherboard huts as the bus turned into the main street of Warburton, a sleepy village by a rocky river overhung by trees. It was late afternoon. The sun had already gone down behind the hills, bringing a cold twilight to the blanket of mist and smoke from the woodfires.

Our hut was pretty spartan. A spongy double bed, a spongy double bunk, an old fridge, a cold-water tap over the sink, one stark light-bulb and, the feature of the room, an open fireplace over which hung a sign: 'Breakages are to be paid for'.

I had arrived with Matthew, a chunky sandy-haired boy. The following day Neil, Patrick the stirrer and Rhys would join us for a week of fishing, drinking and freedom. Matthew and I spent the rest of the day playing house: unloading food, putting beer in the fridge, chopping and stacking wood, making a fire. Matthew, a little drunk, was raving on his favourite topic, The Rolling Stones. 'The Beatles never wrote a song as good as "Sympathy For The Devil" or "Jumping Jack Flash".'

I was starting to feel tired. After a couple of beers and a large plate of sausages and mash I was almost asleep. We both stripped down to our jocks and climbed into our sleeping-bags. Matthew offered me the double bed.

'No thanks, I'm happy here. Least I know I won't have to share my bed tomorrow night.'

'I don't mind sharing. Why don't you come over?' There was a stirring in my cock. I tried to brush him off. 'I'm serious. Come over here.' By now I had an erection. 'C'mon,' Matthew coaxed in a childlike voice, 'come over here with me.'

I was very turned on. I bounced across the floor in my sleeping-bag and plonked down next to him. He looked into my eyes and slowly started to unzip my sleeping-bag. When he got halfway he stopped. 'You're going to let me. I can't believe it.'

He jumped up, went to the fireplace and took out a cigarette, lighting it off the coals. 'Would you have let me?' Before I could respond he said, 'I don't want to know.'

Too embarrassed to move I stayed where I was. He came back to the bed and we tried to go to sleep as though nothing had happened. But an hour later, too tense to sleep there, I snuck back across the room and quietly wanked.

The door burst open and Patrick, Rhys and Neil marched in. 'Woah, a double bed, better check for fresh stains,' Patrick joked.

The troops unpacked: beer in the fridge, tins of biscuits from mothers, fishing gear in the corner. Packs of cards went onto the table and Rhys pulled out a jar of two-cent pieces, his betting money. 'Here kitty, kitty.' He lovingly placed it on the table. 'Prepare to die, the lot of you.'

It wasn't long before Matthew, Patrick, Rhys and I had settled around the laminated table to play pontoon. Neil, who didn't believe in playing cards for money, had gone out fishing. He returned with two small trout.

'That's not going to feed us all,' Matthew said.

'I've got some loaves in my bag,' quipped Patrick.

By now beer and the open fire had given us ruddy cheeks. Neil cooked and ate the fish while the rest of us had bowls of Weetbix and continued our card game. Rhys was sent for more beer because he looked eighteen. We loaded him up with money and sent him on his way.

He was soon back. 'Nice town, nice pub, but Jesus it's cold out there.'

'Good streaking weather, huh?' Patrick said. We all looked at him and then at each other. As we excitedly removed our clothes, the rules of the race were sorted out: first one back wins, last one back pays for tomorrow's beer. Neil was appalled. He headed off to the pub to watch television.

Four boys, naked except for running shoes, tumbled outside into the freezing air. I suddenly felt how quiet the night was, as we broke the silence with laughter and the pounding of rubber on asphalt. 'Neily boy!' we all cheered as we passed him on the highway and turned into the main street. No one raised an eyebrow as we streaked past the pub.

I came in behind the others, my throat burning. *Got to give up smoking.* I'd be buying the beer tomorrow.

Patrick had crashed on his li-lo, Matthew on his bed. For some reason Rhys was lying on my bunk. He waved me over to him and patted the mattress. 'Sit here.' I did so. 'I think you're a really good bloke. Genuine. Lie down.' *What would the others think?* 'I want to give you a hug.'

'I'm going outside.' I was testing him. I stood on the doorstep, lit a cigarette and looked at the stars. Rhys came outside and my heart jumped.

'Can I have a puff?' He was running his fingers through his hair. He leant against me, his face in my neck. He smelt warm and sweet. His hand worked its way into my jeans and took hold of my hardening dick.

We walked down the hill to the paddock that ran along the river, climbed the barbed wire and squelched through long wet grass.

We hugged. Our flies were undone. We rubbed our cocks on each other's bellies, holding each other's balls, pulling each other. We collapsed to the ground and lay there on the dewy grass. We rubbed and pulled and grabbed until we both came.

Rhys sat up, crowned by the moon peeping from behind the clouds. 'Better get back, eh?'

As we climbed over the barbed wire I noticed that he was covered in something dark, all down one side of his body. *Mud, perhaps.* 'Rhys, look!'

He looked at himself and then at me. 'You too.' He smelt it. 'It's cowshit.'

A chorus of kookaburras cut through the haze of my hangover. I lay in my sleeping-bag, aware that my bladder was bursting. Bang. I remembered. *Rhys. Me. The embankment. His sweet smell. John. Oh God. I wonder what Rhys is thinking?* I sat up just enough to see him on the other side of the bulk that was Matthew. I tried to go back to sleep but my bladder's alarm had gone off. I climbed out of my sleeping-bag, opened the door gently and stepped outside.

The kookaburras started their laughing again. *You having a go at me? Come down here and say that.* It was so cold my breath formed little clouds. I stood waiting for my morning glory to slacken enough to let me piss. My head felt like a genie was trying to crush it.

On the way back to the cabin I suddenly felt a sharp pain up my leg. *What the fuck have I done?* I found a paling from the woodpile hanging from my heel by a rusty nail.

I disimpaled myself, watching blood form a bubble on my foot. *Fuck. Rusty nail. Tetanus. Rhys. John. Fuck.* I squeezed the puncture, hoping the blood would flush out any tetanus. I was starting to shiver.

I hobbled back to bed and when I woke some time later, Neil and Patrick were trying to make bacon and eggs. Rhys was not in the cabin. I grabbed my towel and headed up to the toilet block, greeting the kookaburras and the paling on the way up. As I stepped into the shower I caught sight of Rhys's back in the laundry. I called out, asking how he was.

He turned with a look of apprehension, shrugged and didn't answer. I wanted to touch him. He kept scrubbing cowshit off the clothes in the basin. He was so distant.

'I stepped on a nail. If I died you would have been the last person I made love with.'

He looked shocked, but went on scrubbing away the mess of last night. I knew then that he wasn't a potential boyfriend.

It Begins

I'd been back from my jaunt in the country for three days, but for some reason I put off ringing John. At the cinema watching *Earthquake*, doing homework, or listening to Pink Floyd, I would get these stabbing feelings. I was scared that the image I had been holding of us kissing at my dinner would all be taken away if he was cold to me on the phone. *But I said I would ring.*

I braced myself and dialled. John's mother said he was at the shops and took my number. *If he rings back, what am I going to talk about?* The phone rang. My heart jumped into my mouth. I let it ring a few times so it wouldn't seem like I was sitting by the phone.

'Um . . . you said to call. Well no, actually I said I'd call.'

'How was the country? Hope you guys didn't get up to too much mischief.' *Rhys.*

'Five guys in a cabin, things are bound to happen.' *That doesn't sound right.* I told the adventures of the week. How many fish I'd caught, the rusty nail. And the big streak. 'You're not shocked, are you?'

'Like you said, five boys in a cabin.' His week had been a lot quieter, watching the Test against England, playing pool with his brothers and doing homework.

I asked if he'd like to see a movie. His family were going off to their beach-house next day, so we wouldn't see one another till the next week at school. But the image of him was just as warm as before the call. It was so nice to hear his voice.

John was telling me about Christmas Island. When he was nine, his father had been posted there to help set up the radar for the Navy. The family moved to this small Australian territory in the middle of the Indian ocean for six months, the best six months of his life.

He was describing the annual migration of red crabs. They would crawl out of the jungle and head off to the water, forming a prickly red carpet across the roads. You had to accept that if you used the road, crabs would die.

Biscuit leant in between us. 'You two seem to be getting along very well. I thought Tim was going out with me. Maybe we should have a triangle.' He was smiling, wide-eyed.

'Sorry,' I said. 'My heart belongs to someone else.' It felt so nice to say. John seemed unperturbed.

Towards the end of lunch, Biscuit and I sat looking over the basketball courts. 'Are you gay?' he asked, with such innocence that I wasn't shocked. But I wasn't sure how to respond. 'Nothing to be ashamed of,' he continued, tossing a piece of chalk and snatching it out of the air. 'I wouldn't mind being bi myself, like David Bowie.'

He squatted on the ground and wrote with the chalk, 'I love Paula. Tim loves –' He smiled teasingly then filled in the space. 'Tim loves B + F.'

He saw the incomprehension in my face. 'Best and Fairest.'

'Maybe.' I felt naked. 'You won't tell anyone?'

He scrawled over the writing, then said with that devilish smile, 'Trust me.'

Wow, someone at school knows that I like John. God, I hope nothing goes wrong.

A few days later our English teacher showed a video of *The Go-Between*, a book we were studying. I was sitting in front of John. Suddenly I felt a hand on the back of my chair. I turned to find John leaning his chair against the wall and holding on to the back of my seat. He apologised and snapped his hand away. *Put it back. Why did I turn? I've embarrassed him.*

A couple of minutes into the film, John put his hand on the back of my seat again. Then I felt it move. I thought I must be imagining it, but no, he was rubbing my back, softly. I used my back to caress his hand. My spine melted into his fingertips. When Alan Bates and Julie Christie spooned on the screen they were John and me.

Out of the semi-darkness Biscuit appeared, sliding in next to me. John's hand left the back of my seat. 'I'm getting jealous. You have to drop him,' Biscuit said. 'Tell him you're going out with me.' I said yes, just to shut him up.

That afternoon as the train rolled past the Rosella factory the smell of tomato soup wafted through the carriage. It would usually make my stomach grumble with hunger but today my thoughts were distracting me. *I'm breaking up with John. 'There's something I have to tell you.*' I imagined John choking back the tears. Sadness washed over me. *Half-brain, you're not even going out with him. None of this is real. Then why do I feel so sad?*

'Are you okay?' It was Joe-the-brainiac. I shrugged. 'It usually helps to talk about these things. Your secret's safe with me.' *Why is he being so helpful? Does he want gossip?*

'This dumb game has started up between Biscuit, John and me. A love-triangle. Today Biscuit asked me to drop John.'

Beneath his calm psychiatrist's exterior I thought I could see a wolf waiting to pounce. 'Do you like this John?'

'A lot.'

Joe raised his eyebrows. 'Does he know that?'

'I don't know. I haven't told him as much.'

'Tell him. Ring him. Tonight.'

'I couldn't.'

'He doesn't seem freaked out so far.' I dissolved in terror. 'When I see you on the train in the morning, I want to hear that you did it. Onward and upward.'

I felt contractually obliged to ring John. I did it that night.

'Mrs Caleo, can I speak to John please?" She asked who was calling. I choked out my name.

I could hear voices, then footsteps approaching, but they passed the telephone and disappeared. *It's like waiting at the steps to the gallows. Maybe they've forgotten I'm here.* A jagged piece of fingernail caught my attention and I was gnawing at it when someone picked up the receiver. I tried to look relaxed, then realised I couldn't be seen.

'Hi Tim.' We sat in silence for a moment. 'This is a nice surprise.'

'That's good. There's something I want to tell you.'

'I'm all ears.'

'You know this stupid game that Biscuit's been playing? Today he said I have to drop you, and I don't want to.' *Should I risk it?* 'I'm being serious.' *Maybe he doesn't understand.* 'What I'm trying to say is I like you.'

'That's good.'

I was fumbling. 'I really like you. I've liked you for some time.'

'I like you too.'

'Does this mean we're going out together?'

'You haven't asked me yet.'

'John Caleo, will you go round with me?'

'Yep.'

The undisclosed had ejaculated into daylight. I told him that I had known I was gay since I was eleven but had never had a boyfriend. When I asked how long he'd known he was gay he said he didn't know if he was. He'd only ever had one girlfriend. 'This is new for me,' he said. 'I've always wanted to be married with kids. I want kids.'

'I'll have to be their godfather.'

We talked about how others might respond. Our families. The guys at school. We both agreed that no matter how things turned out we would always be friends.

My mother appeared at the door. 'Tim, you've been on the phone for ages.' She gave me five more minutes. The conversation re-ignited. We had so much territory to cover.

Mum was at the door again. 'You've been on the phone for more than two hours.'

'Okay, okay.' I asked John, 'Did you hear that?'

'Has it really been two hours?'

'Feels like twenty minutes.'

We talked a little while longer then I tried to say goodbye. 'See you tomorrow. Sleep well.'

'You too.'

'I don't want to hang up.'

'Me neither.'

'This is it, I'm hanging up.' I didn't move. Then I said, 'Sweet dreams, my boyfriend.' It felt so good to say.

It was the public school sports day at Olympic Park, a glary white-sky day with the threat of rain in the air. I was among the crush of boys in uniform pressed against the fence, cheering their schoolmates and wolfing down hot dogs and packets of chips. For me it was a chance to perve on spunks.

John was in the final of the hundred-metre hurdles. In his red singlet and satin shorts he walked up to his starting block, shaking out his legs and hands. He looked so nervous. The gun went and six bodies flew down the track. It was over before it began. John came third. I called his name across the heads of the other boys but he didn't hear me. He was preoccupied, perhaps even angry with himself.

We had arranged to meet at the main entrance at the end of the day. He was already there, leaning against a wall and looking vulnerable, his hair still wet from the shower. I wanted to throw my arms around him and tell him how proud I was, but I knew there wouldn't be much chance here. 'Congratulations.'

'Third.' He shook his head. 'I can't believe it. Can we go for a walk?'

Olympic Park was set among rolling lawns and large ornamental trees. We wandered over into Kings Domain. We spoke hardly a word. There was some other language passing between us.

We came across a gully rich in ferns and sat on a bench overlooking a small waterfall. John put his hand on mine. Suddenly we were locked at the mouth, two schoolboys in uniform pashing on a park bench. Our fever was broken by a couple walking hand in hand. The man cleared his throat and gave us a warning look.

We went looking for somewhere more private, where we could be schoolboy lovers. Nowhere seemed secluded enough. We ended up in the doorway of the fire escape of Allen's Sweets. I had spent many hours at Flinders Street Station, looking across the river to Allen's and its large fireworks neon. Now it was providing refuge for John and me.

We stood against the door, kissing freely, holding each other, hugging, pressing against each other, breathing the intoxicating smell of warm wool. *Pepe was right, you can tell when a boy has an erection.*

John came up for air. 'It's getting late. Mum'll start worrying.'

We said our goodbyes. From the platform I could see the neon trail of fireworks curving up into the sky, exploding and twinkling as it descended back to earth. *My boyfriend and I were just there.*

Chapter FOUR

Desire

My boyfriend and I were on a date. We watched Woody Allen chew himself up with guilt, but our desire to touch each other overrode what was happening on the screen. I realised if I folded my arms and leant on the armrest between us I could touch his upper arm. I stroked him gently for some time. His hand reached out and took mine. There we were, in a theatre full of people, holding hands – sort of – pretending to watch the film.

As I walked him to the station John said, 'I wish we could hold hands properly.'

The weight of what he said sank in. 'Maybe one day, when things change.'

The boom-gates started to ring and the train tooted somewhere down the track. 'I'll catch the train after this one,' said John. 'I don't want to go just yet.' We crossed the road and walked along the cliff-top, looking at the grey sea. 'Is there somewhere we can hug?'

We found the shelter-shed in the park. 'This corner over here is pretty secluded,' John said. My boyfriend's big brown eyes were calling me over. I sat next to him. He took my hand and we sat there, drinking each other in. I desperately wanted to hug him and tell him I loved him but instead I said, 'I can't believe this.'

'What?'

'This. I've liked you for ages and here I am sitting with you holding hands. I would never have thought it could happen.' John leant over and kissed me lightly on the lips. He then lay back and pulled me down onto him. We kissed and held each other with no concern that we might be sprung.

My erection was getting caught up. I leant on one elbow and rearranged myself. 'I'm so turned on I'll have to go straight home and pull myself.'

'You don't do that, do you?' *Is he joking? I don't think he is.* 'I don't think it's good for you. Why do you need to do it?'

'It's fun.'

'Why don't you see if you can stop?'

I was so rapt in this guy I would have done anything for him, even stop wanking if that's what he wanted. But God alone knew how. I was ready to blow in my jocks then and there.

I could never be a Buddhist monk. The very act of denying myself something makes the desire for it unbearable. Now every night in bed was a challenge. I'd lie there with a raging hard-on, wondering if pulling myself might jinx things between us.

A new *Cleo* arrived. *I'll take this to bed but I won't look at the centrefold. Nine days since my last pull and I've lasted this long. I can be adult about this. I don't need to look at the centrefold, so it's okay if I do.* I was greeted by pictures of The Daly Wilson Big Band. Most of them were overweight but there were some very erotic younger men. *That guy holding the saxophone is gorgeous.*

I turned onto my stomach, kidding myself that it was just to make myself more comfortable, but my erection brushed against the bed and I ejaculated into the front of my pyjama pants. The afterglow of the orgasm lasted about three seconds and was replaced by a much bigger sense of failure. *I'm sorry, John.*

We were standing on the verandah of the chapel after First Friday Mass when we saw a flashy red MGB with its top down making its way round the playing fields towards the main steps. The driver hopped out of the car, put his cigarette out in the gravel and headed towards us. He was a handsome dark man wearing the black trousers and shirt of a Jesuit. He took off his Pierre Cardin sunglasses and asked directions to Father Brennan's office. We stood staring, our jaws hanging in amazement. 'He's a Jack.' He had a little crucifix on his collar.

'What about the car? And the sunglasses?'

'Maybe the Jacks have worked out this is the seventies.'

That day he was introduced as our new housemaster, Brenton Lewis. Offered the chance to speak he said he'd rather answer questions. We were a little hesitant at first but he took our enquiries well. Brenton was born in Rhodesia to Greek parents, had grown up in Perth and spent some time living in San Francisco, in Haight-Ashbury. He had been engaged to be married when he received his vocation. He chose the Jesuits because he believed it was important to feed the mind as well as the soul, and because they tended to be more radical. He was doing his PhD in behavioural science.

He was calm and collected, like a pop star at a press conference. *He seems really nice. I'd like to know him better.* I introduced myself at break, boldly asking him how the MG fitted in with his vow of poverty.

'It probably doesn't, but it was a gift. There are lots of things about me that don't fit.'

'Yeah. A bit groovier than most of the Jacks.' I nudged him.

'I'll take that as a compliment. Have you got a few minutes?' We went into his office. He wanted to know a lot. Which staff members did I like? Were there any that he should be wary of? Who was top dog in the playground? I grilled him about Haight-Ashbury, the hippies, the artists and the gays. Did he live in a commune? Then the bell went. I was due in chemistry class.

'Do you want to go? If you want to stay I can write you a note.'

I had more questions. 'Do you think being gay is a sin?'

'I can't imagine that God would have a problem with two people loving each other. Why? Do you think you might be gay?'

'I know I am.'

He seemed slightly taken aback by my certainty. 'Do you have a friend?' I smiled and nodded. 'Another Xavier boy?' I didn't want to give away too much. 'Well, if it is respectful I wish you all the best.'

Brenton lit a cigarette. I remembered the undertaking that John had got from me. 'Your vow of chastity, does that mean no masturbation?'

'For me it does.'

'So you don't masturbate?'

'Haven't for more than three years.'

'Wow. I can't imagine that.' It was comforting to know that there was a kindred spirit among the staff.

We were meeting the gang for dinner at Lebanese House. John rang and asked me to arrive half an hour before the others. *He wants to talk. About what? He wants to adopt children? What? My God, he wants to break it off!*

My heart was in my mouth. My guts were going through their own personal snuff movie. As I turned into Russell Street he was leaning against the front of the restaurant with his hands behind his back. He wore Bogart jeans (very trendy), a pressed short-sleeve shirt and a bow-tie. His hair was immaculate. He looked like a little boy whose mum had dressed him up for Sunday School. *Jesus, what do I look like? Why the hell am I wearing my surf shirt? I should have worn my green windcheater. Relax. Walk slowly. Cool. Masculine. Act like nothing's wrong.*

I copped a full flash of those chocolate eyes. He smiled, a warm welcoming smile. Or was it the smile of an executioner? He reached out and brushed my elbow. We started walking.

'Is everything okay?' I asked. He looked at me quizzically. 'Why did you want me to come early?'

He shrugged. 'How was your day?'

'Nice weather we're having,' I riposted with sarcasm. *Oops.* 'Sorry. Sorry. Sorry.'

'Tim, relax.' *Relax! Yes, relax. What do people see when John and I are together? Do we look like homosexuals? Can they see that we're together? That we're breaking up?*

His hand brushed against mine. It was a bolt of electricity tearing up my arm. *God, it would be nice to walk hand in hand.*

'You said you wanted to talk,' I ventured.

'I wanted some time to ourselves. You guys are going to be talking about film and art and stuff.'

Our hands brushed again and his little finger hooked mine, but I wanted people to know we were in love so I took his whole hand. He turned sharply down an alley and we found ourselves against a wall. He looked around. 'Not here, we can be seen.' Another sharp turn down another alley. He took both my hands and leant against a large green roller-door. We were standing holding hands, looking. I think this was the first time that we had ever really looked at each other. Boys do not look at each other like that.

I reached out and touched his hair. He turned and kissed my hand. I moved closer until we were standing against each other. He smelt like soap and clean clothes. Gentle. Just holding and kissing gently. Little angel kisses.

If this had been it, if I had died then, I would have said it was enough.

My hand was cupped around his balls. They were made for each other, my hand and his crutch. I undid the button of his jeans and unzipped his fly. My hand was on a mission. His jocks had little octopuses and men in diving-suits on them. Cute. But through the deep-sea scene I could see what I was looking for, hard and standing to attention.

He pulled away suddenly and did his jeans up. 'We should get back, the others will be waiting.' *I've freaked him out. Why the fuck did I do that?* As we walked out of the alley and into Russell Street I looked back to where we had been. It looked familiar. I had seen it before. Then it dawned on me. The building at the start of *Homicide*.

'John, look where we were.'

His jaw dropped. 'Russell Street Police Station!'

I pissed myself laughing but he didn't seem very impressed.

Dear John,

It's 4:30 in the morning and I can't sleep. I'm confused about what happened tonight. I think I went too far too soon when I undid your jeans. All I can say is I'm sorry. I don't want to put pressure on you to have sex or anything like that, especially if you don't feel ready. I love you and if all we ever do is hug, that is enough for me. When I give you this letter, I won't say anything. When you are ready, talk to me.

Yours sincerely,
Tim

I gave him the letter just before chemistry. Biscuit snatched it. 'What's this? A love letter?'

'Give it back,' I barked, snatching the letter. I calmly gave it to John, who looked stunned.

He sat at the lab bench in front of mine. I saw him read the letter and put it in his pocket. Sometime later – it felt like an eternity – he turned and smiled. He mouthed, 'Everything's all right.'

Birthdays are minefields. There is nothing scarier than expectant eyes watching as you unwrap the plastic lobster or the nylon denim-look jacket. But this year my family did pretty well. Mum and Dad gave me a large box wrapped in the paper from Dad's birthday a month before. It was a clock radio. 'It's got a snooze button, so your mother won't be calling you sixty times a morning.' Next was a present from Anna and Nick, the new John Lennon album *Walls and Bridges*.

'I played it last night. It's really good,' said Nicholas.

'Let's hope you didn't scratch it.'

I'd never received a present from John so I didn't know his taste. This would be a test of how well he knew me. My beautiful boyfriend with the big eyelashes was leaning against the wall. He held what looked like an album wrapped in black glossy paper and red ribbon. 'Essendon colours,' I laughed.

'Of course. Only the best for my Tim.'

The card said, 'No longer sweet sixteen, hope the next seventeen are as much fun. I love you, John.' The present was *Let's Stick Together* by Bryan Ferry. *Success, he does know my taste.* 'I like the song a lot.'

'He's really good-looking. I saw him on *Countdown* the other night and I felt all . . . I don't know, sweaty. Oh. One last present.'

He handed me a small enamelled Snoopy in psychedelic blue swirls. *I'll have to wear it or he'll be hurt. Maybe it could accidentally fall over a cliff.* 'It's cute, thanks.'

We stood gazing at each other. He looked around and,

seeing the coast was clear, kissed me gently on the lips.

The bell went and we headed off to geography. I suddenly thought of something. 'Father Wallbridge is organising a retreat at Barwon Heads. I reckon it'd be great if we both went.'

In the off-season Barwon Heads is a ghost town. But the house where we were holding our religious retreat was abuzz with boys in their civvies claiming beds and eating Twisties. By the time John and I arrived all the good beds had gone. We ended up in the dorm, a large rumpus-room lined with bunks. At least we were in the same room.

In the afternoon a barbecue was organised: rissoles and salad, with *Sergeant Pepper's* on the cassette player. This was followed by a class in Buddhist meditation, and then Father Wallbridge on helping a friend in need. 'Little Johnny has been depressed of late, he's feeling listless, failing his schoolwork; he's masturbating every day . . .' *How disgusting, call the police.*

We sat around in our pyjamas in the dorm. Biscuit and Joe-the-brainiac leaned against my bed playing Snap. The others were asleep. John and I were lying head to toe on my bed. It was nice to be close to him like this. I could feel the warmth radiating from him. John took hold of my feet, held them close to his cheeks and started to kiss them gently.

'What are you doing?' I whispered, alarmed.

'I don't know. I just want to.'

My feet were alive with his soft stroking and gentle kissing. 'You'd better stop, I'm cracking a fat.'

'Good, so am I,' John said seductively.

'What are you two up to? A bit of a foot fetish, John?' Joe was watching us. He suggested that we all sleep on the floor. John and I could lie together without looking sus, so we agreed. As we hauled the mattresses off the beds, Biscuit winked. 'Never know what might happen.'

Among the mattresses, pillows, and throw-cushions, we lay like a sheik's wives in a harem. In the darkness Biscuit and Joe whispered and giggled. John and I were nuzzling noses. He smelt sweet.

Lips caressing lips. Exploring. Our lips slightly parted, exchanging breath. Hands slipping into each other's sleeping-bags. His warm body in cotton PJs. Running my hand up his spine, feeling the muscles in his back. His hand going in under my pyjama shirt. Skin of his hand against the skin of my back. My hand slipped into his pants and stroked his downy bum, pulling his hips closer to mine. I wanted to reach around to the front and hold his sex but was scared that it might spin him out. I moved my hand to his stomach and slowly worked it down to play with his bush of pubes, occasionally brushing his erection.

His eyes were shut and his breathing was getting faster. I took hold of his cock in one hand and his cool balls in the other. He started to groan gently in my ear. He was coming in my hand.

He took my cock and held it against his body, undoing his pyjamas. I pumped it against his belly until I came on his stomach. John touched my semen. 'Wow.' He smeared it over his chest and stomach. 'Can you touch me again?'

I took hold of his cock, which was still hard. He started pumping my hand until his body arched and he came again. Still puffing, he hugged me and whispered, 'I love you.'

We drifted off to sleep, deep, blissful, complete. Through the night we would wake and start kissing, fondling, tugging and coming again. We were two suns, exchanging atmospheres, drawn into each other, spiralling into one another.

I woke in a patch of early morning sun. In front of me was the angelic face of John asleep, almost smiling, his eyelashes against his cheeks. *My boyfriend. And last night we made love for the first time.*

Everyone else had left the room. I was content to lie there looking at John, but he woke, his eyes opening suddenly as if he knew

I was watching him. He stretched. 'I feel exhausted, like I've played a grand final.' He gently kissed me. We lay there, caressing.

Suddenly Father Wallbridge walked in. He mumbled good morning, crossed the room and went out through the sliding glass doors. We looked at each other, wide-eyed. 'He was more embarrassed than us.' We burst into laughter.

Father Bradford was talking about the disturbance of the natural order in *Macbeth*. John and I were rubbing our knees together, caressing each other in long gentle strokes that became slower and more sensual. I wrote, 'I'm getting turned on.'

John whispered, 'Better check that.' His hand slid across the seat and up my thigh. He reached into my pocket. I nearly gasped. Part of me was shocked, but the other part of me wanted to see how far we could get. John was holding my hard-on in a class of twenty boys and I had no sense of time or place.

Father Bradford was speaking to me. John's hand shot out of my pocket. *What did he see?*

'Sorry, Father, I didn't hear the question.'

'What event sets the world on its ear?'

'Uh . . . the murder of the king?'

'Correct. Would someone like to read the scene between the Macbeths?'

As two boys read I took revenge and put my hand in John's pocket. He smiled impishly and shook his head. 'The other side, suck.'

I thought I'd make him sweat it out so I kept making false advances, until finally my hand found its warm home in John's pocket. There it sat in contentment, holding his hard-on.

The boy behind us knocked his pencil-case onto the floor. He ducked under the desk to retrieve it. John and I jumped. I banged my knee under the desk.

'What's up with you two?' *Shit, he must've seen something.*

'You'd think I was going to feel your bum, the way you jumped.'

Towards the end of the year, Neil asked me to go to New Zealand with him over Christmas. We would travel on the cheap, hitching and staying in youth hostels, or perhaps with my cousins.

Now the year was almost over and the New Zealand trip was looming. Exams had come and gone and nominations for the next year's prefects had been posted. John and I were on the list. We were staying at each other's houses at every opportunity. We'd fix the room so it looked like we were sleeping in separate beds, but we'd both be on the mattress on the floor doing the wild thing.

We were lying there one evening in each other's arms in a post-orgasmic haze when John asked what I was thinking about. I had been wondering about being a prefect. 'You think you'll get it?' he asked.

'I hope so. Then I can turn it down. To make a stand. I think it's revolting to set one group of boys apart, give them power and ask them to dob in their mates. It's just a form of policing. And they always choose the guys who excel at sport. I find the whole thing elitist.'

'Not everything has to be political.'

'Maybe that's where we differ.' I unlocked myself from him and moved away. We lay there in our separate bad moods.

Biscuit threw Neil and me a farewell party at his house, a large Victorian mansion with a pool and tennis court. Neil and I were showered with Australiana: badges of the flag, koala pins, and jars and jars of Vegemite. John wanted to talk in private, so we found an unoccupied bedroom upstairs.

John was shaking. 'I don't want you to go.' *He can't be serious.* 'What if something happens to you, some weirdo picks you up and I never see you again? I couldn't handle it.'

He was crying. I took him in my arms and hugged him. 'Neil will be with me and I promise we won't get into cars with any weirdos. I'll write a postcard every couple of days.'

'Better not. I reckon Mum's already suspicious.'

'I'll sign them Michelle.'

Dear John,
          Am on the Cook Strait ferry between North and South Islands on way to Nelson. So beautiful. Like what I imagine Europe to be like. Neil has worked out a way to attract lifts. We kneel and pray to the passing cars. Works like a bomb.

Missing you heaps,
Michelle

Dear John,
          Have just been through the west coast of the South Island. Like a fantasy. Misty mountains, cabbage palms and weird rock formations that look like pancakes. Full of communes. Met a nice gypsy girl on the bus. I'm writing this to you from the Franz Josef Glacier – a huge wall of ice with an enormous river pouring out from its face. It's hard to comprehend. Only ten days till I see you again.

Love,
Michelle

Dear John,

It is Christmas Day and I'm missing you really badly, so I thought I'd write you a letter this time. I'm sitting on the verandah of my uncle and aunt's house in Clyde, a small country town. The reason I'm missing you (besides the reasons you'd expect) is because yesterday I had an accident – don't panic, I'm all right – I came off my uncle's new racehorse. My back and elbows are fairly cut up from the gravel. I'll show you my war wounds in five days. Can't wait. No weirdos sighted yet. Miss you, miss you, miss you.

Sending love across the Tasman,
Tim

As soon as I returned to Australia, I went straight to the Caleos' holiday house. John was waiting for me by the bus-stop and my heart jumped as his face lit up. He rubbed my elbow, but real affection would have to wait until we were in private. I was like a puppy barking at his heels. There was so much to catch up on.

Later that night John and I walked to the beach to watch the sunset. I hummed songs from an album I'd bought in New Zealand, *Second Childhood* by Phoebe Snow, singing to John as a kind of serenade. There was privacy in the darkness so I put my arm around him. We started to kiss. John unbuttoned my boardies and started to take off my T-shirt.

This was not what we thought it would be. There were crashing waves and a gentle breeze, but the sand got into everything, our mouths, noses, the crack of our bums, and, worse, all over our hands. Pulling each other was like wearing gloves of sandpaper. We started to laugh. I spat sand out of my mouth. It was nice to be home.

Sursum Corda: Lift up Your Hearts

'The staff congratulate the following boys for their selection as prefects for 1977 and welcome them into the Xavier family.' I scoured the list but could not see my name. *They've spelt it with a K. No. My name's not there. John's is. But mine's not.*

I stood there, crushed that I had been deemed unfit to be a prefect. John walked up beside me. 'Congratulations,' I squeezed it out, trying to disguise my disappointment. My attempt at a smile was a flop. 'I can't believe I didn't get one.'

'You were only going to turn it down.'

I rolled my eyes in self-mockery. 'I failed in the popularity contest.' I was starting to feel a little better. 'So, my little prefect, the coffee scrolls are on me at lunch.'

A week later the school newspaper carried humorous profiles of the chosen twelve. The one about John walked a very thin line.

NAME:	John Caleo
BEST FRIEND:	Tim
HIGHEST ACCOLADE:	1976 Best and Fairest
FOOTY TEAM:	Essendon
HOBBIES:	Anything that involves Tim
FAVOURITE COLOUR:	Essendon black and red or whatever Tim is wearing

I had to reread it. In a funny way it felt good to have our relationship acknowledged. It seemed accepting, it wasn't malicious. But I couldn't tell how it would be taken by the other guys. Would it feed the ridiculous rumours that were sprouting, like the one that I had sucked John off in the aisle at *Rocky Horror*?

Brenton called me into his office. 'The piece about John in *Sursum Corda* . . .'

'I guess you know now, it's John I'm going with.'

'I'm sorry to say it's been the stuff of discussion in the

staff-room for a while. Their own lives are so boring they have to spice them up with gossip.'

'Why hasn't someone tried to stop us?'

'Some of the lay staff would love to.'

'I would have thought it'd be the Jesuits.'

'They argue for you two to be left alone. They see it all the time, it's part of growing up. I wonder if some wish it were them.'

'I can't understand why everyone is talking about me.'

'As my friend Pamela says, only magical people get talked about.' I wished I could believe him.

Coming Out

Anna, Nicholas and I were watching *Countdown*. Mark Holden threw carnations to the throng of weenyboppers while we wolfed down popcorn drenched in honey and butter.

'Your friend John is really sweet,' ventured Anna. I nearly choked on my popcorn. I had often wanted to tell Anna that I was gay. Since John, the desire was so much stronger. Now I had an incredible urge to blurt it out. 'Does he have a girlfriend?' she asked.

'Sort of.' There was fear in Nicholas's eyes. I steeled myself. 'Me.' It was on the table, like a big dog turd. There was silence. Anna adjusted the angle of her head, as though that would help her comprehend.

'You're gay?' Anna leant across and kissed me on the cheek. Nick hurried out of the room and Anna went after him. I sat in silence. Molly Meldrum was running through the latest albums.

Anna brought Nick back into the room. His eyes were red. 'I've been defending you at school ever since I started. They all talk about you as the school poofter. Then to find out it's true . . . I wonder why I bothered.'

I felt well and truly ticked off. I put my arm around him and all three of us hugged. 'I'm sorry if you've been hurt by this, but understand that it's nothing I've done. I'm really grateful that you stick up for me.'

'How am I going to do that now?' Nick left the room.

The rest of the night Anna grilled me about John. How did we meet? Did his family know? It was wonderful to share my feelings about him.

But I started to worry that John's brothers would hear the gossip and, disaster of disasters, mention it to his parents. I was terrified that I would be confronted by John's father, Bob.

One day, after I had stayed the night in John's room with its racing-car wallpaper, I was sitting at the table with the remains of lunch. His mother Lois was in the kitchen clearing up. Everyone else had left the table except for me, Bob, and John's little brother, who was pulling apart a Lego truck.

Bob fidgeted with a box of toothpicks. *This could be it, the moment I've been dreading.* Then he spoke. 'Lois and I are very grateful for what you've done for John.' I was taken aback. 'Since you boys have been hanging round, John has really come out of himself. We'd like to thank you.' He turned the box in his fingers, almost too embarrassed to look me in the eye.

'He's a great guy,' I said. We sat in silence unsure what to say next. *If he knew the half of it . . .*

On a grey winter afternoon some months later the school bussed us to Wesley to support the Xavier Firsts. This had special meaning for me because it was the first time I would see John play football. As ruck rover he was able to play the whole ground, so he would sometimes be only a couple of feet away, his sinewy muscular body in slow torsion.

A few minutes into the final quarter, it looked like the game had stopped dead at the other end of the ground. Both teams started moving to stay warm, hands on hips. Someone was hurt. Straining my eyes I could see a couple of people running onto the field, someone else running off. There was a body lying on the ground.

'It's a Xavier boy.' We surged towards the other end of the ground. An ambulance with its sirens going appeared at the gate. *Jesus, must be serious.* 'It's Caleo,' I heard someone say.

My heart skipped a beat and I could hear the rush of blood in my head. 'What happened?'

'He collided with one of the Wesley guys.'

I could see the ambulance men lifting John onto a stretcher. His hand was on his forehead as though he were in great pain. *He's hurt his head!* I felt so alone. I was scared but I couldn't share it with anyone. I didn't want to draw any more attention to our relationship. I stood watching the ambulance disappear, hoping to God that he was all right, feeling as bare as the large elm trees that surrounded the ground.

When Mum asked me how my day was, I wanted to break down and yell, 'My boyfriend's been injured and no one will tell me what's wrong. It could be brain damage.' But I said calmly, 'John was injured today in a football match. They even called an ambulance.' *Held that together pretty well.*

I was nervous about ringing John's house. I imagined Lois crying as she told me that he'd had a brain haemorrhage and was on a respirator. The phone rang and rang and rang. No answer. *They're at the hospital deciding whether or not to take him off the life support. Fuck.*

I tried again half an hour later. Still no answer. *Where could they be?* Then suddenly the phone rang. It was John. He was okay. 'Bit of a broken leg but I'm fine.' He'd broken his fibula and had plaster almost up to his hip.

'A broken leg?' I laughed. 'You gave me such a fright. I saw you holding your head as you were carried away . . .' I was choking back the tears.

'You're going to have to think of something funny to write on my plaster.' We sat cuddling over the phone.

When I was formally introduced to the plaster I wrote, 'When I said break a leg, I was only wishing you luck, Tim.' And, 'There's hope for the living and hope for the dead, but no hope for John 'cos he's broken his leg, Michelle.'

The lump had to be incorporated into our lives like a pet dog. We learned to sleep with it, make love despite it, and take it for regular walks with the aid of a walking-stick.

One afternoon, we were lying on the bed and I started to think how it would have been if John had had brain damage, or had his leg amputated. I knew I would still love him. And so I told him.

Nick and Anna were doing their homework. Dad and I were sitting on the lounges and Mum was stacking the dishwasher. She stuck her head through the servery and told me to go and pack for tomorrow's trip to Sydney.

I said I didn't think I would go with them. They asked why. There was a chill in the air, as though I'd said I wanted to be a woman. 'I've got things I want to do here.'

'This is meant to be the whole family going away together,' Dad said. 'You spend your weekends with friends and when you are at home you're on the phone most of the time. You never tell us anything . . .'

'You only open your mouth to fight,' threw in Mum.

'This is not a hotel, son. It's a family home and there are certain things expected of you.'

I knew what I was going to have to say. I'd been through it in my head many times. After this moment there would be no going back. 'There's something I think you should know.' My mouth was dry. 'I'm gay.'

In the scenarios I had created they put their arms around me and said, 'You poor bastard, that makes so much sense of your moods. Being gay is not easy but we'll help you through the difficult times.'

In reality Mum stared with hatred in her eyes, her arms folded. 'Why are you saying this?'

'Because it's true.'

'You're just saying that to hurt us.'

'Gert, let the boy speak,' Dad interjected. 'Son, what makes you think you're gay?'

'I don't know, I just know I am.'

'When I was your age, guys used to muck around in the shower at the yacht club while the parents were sitting in the bar. Everyone did it. You'll grow out of it.'

'I hope you do,' Mum said. 'Otherwise you're going to have a sad life, a very lonely life.'

'Right now, I couldn't be happier.'

Mum fixed me with her stare. 'It's John, isn't it?' I nodded.

'I kept telling myself that I was being stupid. I suppose Anna and Nicholas know?' I said they did.

Mum went into the kitchen and poured herself a glass of wine. 'I brought you up the only way I knew how and I'm sorry if I failed.'

Dad and I sat for a moment. 'You've really upset your mother. I think you'd better come to Sydney for her sake.' I said I would. 'Good,' he said, 'I'm off to bed. Sleep well.'

I was shell-shocked. I should have felt the lifting of a burden from my shoulders but instead I felt shame. And I could see storm clouds gathering on the horizon.

We stayed at the Rushcutters Bay Travelodge, where we could look down through Moreton Bay figs to moored yachts.

After dinner on the first night I was in Mum and Dad's part of the suite when a call came for Mum: her brother David in New Zealand had just died of a heart attack. Their mother had died when

Mum was only eleven and she had been brought up by her brothers and sisters. David had been her favourite, but neither she nor Dad would be able to go over for the funeral.

Dad gave me a signal to go into the other room. 'I'm sorry about David,' I said. I told Anna and Nick what had happened and stepped out onto the balcony to have a cigarette.

It was a warm evening. Halyards rattled against the masts of yachts. There seemed to be people walking around the canal, among the fig trees. I realised they were all men. *This must be one of those gay pick-up places I've heard about.* A man stopped near another man. They looked at each other, said a few words and walked off together. *I wonder where they do it?* I leaned on the rail watching, wondering what it must be like to pick someone up like that, excited by the knowledge that these were gay men.

The glass door to the balcony opened. Dad stepped out and asked for a cigarette. I asked if Mum was okay.

'Never can really tell.' At that moment we heard Mum laugh uproariously on the phone. Dad looked out over the trees. Then he glanced down on the action below. He shook his head. 'Sad. Thank God you'll never be like that.'

'How do you know?'

'You're not homosexual.'

I was stunned. Hadn't they understood me the other night?

Dad's eyes darted all over the place. His mouth was moving but no words came out. 'I don't think we should talk about this now. It's going to be hard enough looking after your mother.' He threw his cigarette down onto the homosexuals.

Those were Dad's last words to me that weekend. He barely looked at me. He clenched his jaw so hard that his temples pulsated. The best response I could get to anything was a grunt.

Back in Melbourne, I was at my desk in the sunroom doing some physics homework. There was a knock on the door. 'Can I come in, son?' *He's talking to me again!* Dad walked in looking like a four-year-old who'd lost his blanky. He put his arms around my neck and tried to hug me. His body was shaking. He was crying. 'Please don't do this to us.'

There was no point in challenging this. Whatever I said would be like picking a scab. I sat there rubbing Dad's arm as his tears fell onto my homework.

'I'm sorry.' He wiped the tears from his eyes and hurried from the room. That was the first time I'd seen my father cry.

Brenton offered to speak to my parents. 'But first you'd better find out if they want to speak to me.'

Mum and Dad were a little suspicious at first, but warmed to the idea, and so a Sunday lunch was organised. We sat outside in beautiful spring weather feasting on smoked trout, stuffed mushrooms and a green salad. Brenton was an absolute charmer, witty, engaging. Mum laughed so hard at times that I thought she'd wet her pants, and even Dad loosened up. Brenton then gave me my cue.

I made my way into the house with the plates, put them in the dishwasher and stood at the sink trying to look like I wasn't watching.

Mum's laughing face became solemn. She was tense, her shoulders up around her ears. She looked tired. All I could see of Dad was his back. It was rigid. Mum wiped away the odd tear. Dad's hand reached out and patted hers. I couldn't believe my sexuality could cause so much pain.

I wasn't sure when to go back out, but figured it was better to take too long than not long enough. I turned the percolator down. Just my luck, it started to vomit almost straight away and the kitchen was filled with the heady aroma of coffee. I loaded the tray. 'Is it okay to come out now?' I called. Brenton consulted Mum and Dad and waved me over.

They looked embarrassed until Dad toasted me with coffee. 'We love you, son.' Brenton's wink reassured me that everything was okay. We walked him out to his car and waved him goodbye. 'He's a very special man,' Dad mused.

A few days later I sat in Brenton's office. 'I believe your parents' reaction is based in love. Your mother believes that only bad things can come of this and she's genuinely concerned for you. I told her I believed that whatever you and John do, you will do it with dignity.' I was impressed. 'Your father thinks you shouldn't make a decision just yet. He's worried that you're closing off your options. I'm inclined to agree. But that doesn't invalidate your present feelings for John.'

He had something else to say. 'Your mother is concerned about John staying over. It might take them some time to get used to the idea. These are new things for them. And I think they're blaming themselves. Give them time and don't push too hard.'

I still felt anxious but knew I had Brenton and John to help me through this.

To say goodbye to us, the school threw a Valete dinner. Before it the headmaster said Mass in the school chapel. John and I sat together, our parents with us. It was a chance to introduce them. The dads shook hands, the mums waved to each other.

John had been selected to read the lesson and was quite nervous. His legs were bouncing in anticipation. He shuffled out of the pew and climbed up to the lectern. Someone behind us started whispering. I had a strong urge to turn and ask him to be quiet while my boyfriend was reading. When John returned I patted his thigh to congratulate him and then realised what that must have looked like.

In the Great Hall were long trestle tables covered in white damask. A large buffet was laid. I looked round the tables and sadness washed over me. I probably wouldn't see these guys again. I recalled the crushes I'd had, devastating and more often than not unrequited – Rhys and all the rest. The next news I'd hear would be that they'd married so-and-so, a good Catholic girl.

The meal was followed by a prize-giving. The winners had

already been sent to a bookshop to choose their prizes. I had won the politics prize and chose *The Complete Works of D.H. Lawrence*, hoping to find some more gay references.

The book had the school emblem embossed on its cover. I was nursing it on the way home when out of the blue Dad said that John's mother was very striking. *Perhaps my attraction to John is inherited from my father.*

The worst was yet to come: the Higher School Certificate, the exams that could determine the rest of our lives. We had two weeks to study. I made up a timetable, trying to convince myself that since school was a six-hour day, I could get by on the same timetable at home. However, I soon realised I'd need to work longer than that if I was to revise everything. And worst of all, there was going to be little or no time to see John. We spoke to each other every day and met on Saturday afternoon but it was hard to relax. *Gotta go. Gotta revise valency.*

But eventually it was all over and the holidays were here.

In the last few months of school John and I had hung round with a new group of guys, Da Boyz. Biscuit, Eric – from John's football team, lean like a marathon runner – and Rick, tall and strongly built with glasses and a wicked sense of humour. Da Boyz were going on holiday to Eric's family shack at Kallista in the Dandenongs. It would be a chance to drink, share war stories about our exams and bask in our new freedom.

The others decided to cycle the whole thirty-two kilometres from Melbourne, but John and I took the train part of the way, realising only when we got to Belgrave that the hardest ride was ahead. At every bend the road got steeper and cliffs dropped further. I hopped off my bike and walked up the next hill. John had stopped quite a way in front of me. With hands on hips and an evil smile he yelled that perhaps we should stop for a cigarette.

'I'm giving up, okay? I have to stop for a sec,' I wheezed.

The road eased off a bit but my legs and lungs were yelling at me to stop.

At last we arrived at a small village. The air was cool and moist with a heady smell of rotting vegetation, but the house was on a hill bathed in sunlight. It stood before us, a weatherboard castle. I let my bike crash to the ground, followed closely by my weary bod. John, smug about his superior fitness, went to find the fuse-box. *Jesus, I've got to find a couch.*

The interior was open and airy. A mock fireplace held fake logs that looked like grilled steak. On the mantelpiece, the window-sills, and in a small display cabinet were endless knick-knacks – glass animals, Snow White and three dwarfs, a vase decorated with a painting of Hanging Rock – probably relics Eric's mother couldn't bear to part with but was too embarrassed to have in her swanky Balwyn residence.

In the olds' bedroom I plunged onto the marshmallow mattress. *I wonder how many of Eric's brothers and sisters were conceived on this bed?* I was in heaven. On the dresser was a bottle of baby shampoo which wasn't clear yellow but an opaque blue-green. *Time for some scientific investigation.* I clicked the lid open and took a cautious sniff. *Avocado moisturiser. Does his mother buy it in vats and decant it? This could be handy if things get a bit sexy.*

'The fuse-box was hard to find.' I turned to see a sweaty John taking off his T-shirt. He wiped his face and armpits with it and threw it to the floor, then crawled onto the bed beside me. We lay there on our backs, hands behind our heads, smiling at each other. I could feel the heat from his body even though we weren't touching.

'Hi, spunk,' I mouthed. John leant on one elbow, put his hand on my chest and kissed me very gently. Things were getting a bit sexy. Nuzzling noses in sweaty jocks. Slow release of hardened cocks. The smell of workers on the docks. I leapt off the bed towards the avocado moisturiser, my hard-on bouncing joyfully against my stomach as I crossed the room with my shorts around my ankles.

The squirty sound of the stream of avocado. Hands full of

cock and moisturiser and soon to be spilling over with our offspring. 'Ye-e-es. Oh, yes.'

We lay in a blissful coma, me with my shoes and socks still on and John's head on my chest, his arm across my body and his warm breath caressing me, and the sticky chlorine smell of our spoof mixed with the avocado moisturiser.

'Wakey, wakey, hands off snakey!' Rick put his head around the door. 'Oops, sorry!' He pulled the door to, but we could hear whispering and laughing.

I was embarrassed. Putting shorts on over my shoes wasn't as easy as having John tear them off. 'Relax, Tim. They don't care.'

I cared. The top button of my shorts popped and rolled into the black hole under the bed. I laughed and bounced back beside my little lustbucket. 'I suddenly realise how Catholic I sound.'

'You are a Catholic.'

'So are you!'

'It's not an insult, Tim.'

I became aware of a burning sensation around my dick and balls. Then I found John was in agony too. 'What was in that bottle?' he wanted to know.

'Moisturiser. Wasn't it?'

'It's not yours?' John asked as calmly as he could.

'No, it was here. I'll ask Eric.'

I grabbed John's T-shirt from the floor, wiped the spoof and the green slime off my stomach, and ventured out.

Da Boyz sat on the lounge in total silence. Then they broke into a round of applause and stomped their feet. 'Bravo, bravo!' *How do you maintain dignity in the face of such humiliation?* I drew Eric into the kitchen. It was bare except for a tray of Ratsak on the bench. 'What was in the bottle on the dresser?' I said under my breath. 'It's a baby-shampoo bottle but it has some green stuff in it.'

'Anti-dandruff shampoo. Joy buys it in bulk at some discount chemist and then decants it.'

I called John. There was another standing ovation as he crossed the lounge. 'Thanks, guys.' I took him by the hand and led him to the bathroom where we flopped our bits into the basin and drowned them. They were getting a major workout this particular day.

'You're only supposed to leave it on your head for five minutes,' John said. 'We were probably asleep for half an hour. Maybe longer. Maybe we should ring the poisons information people.'

'And say what?'

'I don't know,' John snapped. 'You're the expert on everything.'

Time heals all things, even scrotums. Over the following days we saw the soft pink flesh of our bits turn dark brown and grow tough as leather. It was like when you leave a sausage uncovered in the fridge for a few days. And then we peeled! Huge tracts of penis dandruff, incredibly itchy. The desire to help the peeling process along was almost overwhelming. It was a gruelling test of restraint and a waste of three days of love-making.

Pepe brought her friends Prue and Kate up for a picnic. They and Da Boyz checked each other out like dogs meeting in the street. As we sat out in the backyard under the trees and the Hills Hoist, chewing on makeshift sandwiches, I described our collision with the shampoo to intense laughter. My head was in John's lap, my favourite place in the world. This was where I belonged, part of a gang, a gang that included my boyfriend.

The next day when Da Boyz took a walk through the bush, our shirts off so we could work on our suntans, Biscuit tapping the ground with a stick to scare off the snakes, that sense of belonging was there too.

John had been spotted by a talent scout and asked to train with the Essendon Under Nineteens. It meant that he might one day play for the Essendon seniors, which would be a dream come true. Training started in summer, so John had to leave Kallista early. Rick also had to be back in Melbourne, so Eric, Biscuit and I figured we'd share the same room. We dragged a mattress from the other bedroom and placed it between two beds for a kind of slumber party.

'What's the most bizarre sexual thing you've heard of?' someone asked.

'A guy who cored an orange and used it to wank with,' came the reply.

'Farm boys get the poddy calves to suck them off,' Eric said. 'Poor calf's waiting for milk but gets a mouth full of spoof.'

I felt safe in the dark, safe to open up. 'I've got something I want to ask. We all wank, right? Well, how do you do it? I sort of pump the bed, like I'm fucking it.'

'Making little baby beds,' Biscuit joked.

'That's kind of like what I do,' Eric said. 'Leave my jocks on and then put a flannel down the front and pump it.'

'Don't you share your bedroom with two brothers?'

'I can come without making any noise.'

Biscuit said, 'I rub the head of my cock with my thumb and finger really fast until I come.' He added quietly, 'I think I might do it now.' Silence. We all did it. Biscuit's way must have been efficient because he came really fast. I found it horny to be in a room full of boys wanking, so it didn't take me long either.

'C'mon Eric, you can do it,' Biscuit teased.

'Shut up, will you.' And then he came, but not as quietly as he'd said. It wasn't exactly a circle jerk but it was a ritual moment in our friendship.

PART TWO

Out in the World

Chapter *FIVE*

Young Gays

John went to college to train as a chiropractor. Most of the Xavier guys wanted to go to Melbourne University and be lawyers or doctors. I chose science at Monash, partly because of its history of student activism.

During the Vietnam War there had been large student demos and a sit-in in the chancellor's office that took days to break. There were still remnants of that radicalism: the Wholefood Restaurant run by the anarchist collective, a small café thick with dope smoke; and the Community Research Action Centre, a collective of the political left, including the Trotskyites, the Gaysoc, and the anti-uranium lobby.

If this wasn't enough to keep you from your studies there was an array of activities, film clubs, band nights and, the biggest hook for me, student theatre. Its office was a hotbed of ideas and gossip that was always far more interesting than physics, and so my studies began to suffer.

There were lots of good-looking men, some available, some gay. I started to feel I wanted to broaden my horizons, to explore my sexuality. Perhaps I was missing out on something because I had been with the same guy for two years. But I felt I lacked experience. If I did go to bed with someone, would I know what to do? Would he laugh at me, even run away in horror, if I did something I liked doing with John? This feeling kept me from straying too far, but it didn't stop the crushes or the flirting.

Grandma was no longer using her car, so, as I was about to get my licence, Dad approached her about giving it to me. The car was sent over from Adelaide by motorail, and Dad and I went into town to collect it – a pale blue Morris Major Elite with white trim. It was like a Noddy car, but with flash wings on the back like retro rockets. *Noddy, I think that'd be a good name.*

A week later I bounced in through the kitchen door and found Mum talking to Tom, a boy I had known since demanding an invitation to his seventh birthday. We had become intellectual sparring partners, arguing about who made the universe (Tom was an atheist). We were extremely competitive and sometimes our arguments became fights. But our families became quite close, even spending vacations together. I held up my driving licence with a conqueror's grin. Mum and Tom congratulated me. I offered to take him for a drive.

Tom was in a talkative mood, rambling on about the different styles of his lecturers. Approaching a stop sign, I put my foot on the accelerator instead of the brake and we catapulted through the intersection, narrowly missing a car that swerved to avoid us.

Tom went on as though nothing had happened. 'My English professor, who I'm sure is gay –' I interrupted to ask how he knew that. 'He shares a room at college with another man and he's obsessive about Oscar Wilde.'

'I'm gay.' I let the words sit in the air.

'How funny. I think I am too.'

We both laughed. But we didn't do the 'How long have you known, how's it been for you?' number. For some reason I felt embarrassed, naked, exposed. After a silence Tom spoke. 'Actually, I quite like your friend John.'

I burst out laughing. 'John is my boyfriend.' He looked despondent.

I rang John to tell him my great news and arranged to pick him up at Princes Bridge. 'See you there, Peter Brock,' he laughed.

I could see John waiting, neatly dressed. I tooted, and his face lit up at the sight of me driving. He got in and patted the dashboard. 'Hello, Noddy.'

I drove us to Point Ormond. I guessed from the number of parked cars that it was probably a lovers' lane. We sat holding hands, looking over the bay sparkling under the moon. Now we could be alone together whenever we wanted, without parents breathing down our necks. John leant over and kissed me. He tried to move closer but bumped his knee on the gearstick. I leant down to kiss it better but found the gearstick in my chest. We climbed into the back seat and sat there kissing, our tongues mingling. John suggested we lie down. That wasn't easy either. Our knees and feet were squashed up against the window. Then John kneed me in the balls. We'd have to open the door. But not there.

We drove around looking for a secluded place to open the door and finally, in Port Melbourne, found a huge street lined with big factories and not a single car or person in sight. We hopped into the back, opened the door on the gutter side and lay down with our legs hanging out the side. It was still difficult but at least we were lying together comfortably, face to face. Slowly jeans came undone, jocks slid down, and we pulled each other off.

'I wonder what Grandma would say if she knew what we were doing in her car?'

Mum and Dad had relaxed their stand on John staying over, as long as he slept in the front room. So we'd wait until everyone was asleep, then he'd sneak down to my room and we'd get naked and sexy.

On this night John was writhing on my bed as I sucked his

cock. I loved having him in my control, in my face. This had become a regular part of our lovemaking.

'Stop. I'm going to come.' I crawled up to be near him. 'That was great but I want you inside me.'

'You want to suck me?'

'I want you to screw me,' he said in my ear. I was very turned on by the prospect but it clashed with deep feelings that anal sex was unnatural, dirty.

'Please,' John implored. He turned onto his stomach and presented his arse to me. I nudged his sphincter with my cock but it wasn't going to open. 'Keep trying.' I kept nudging until my cock felt it was about to break in half. Suddenly I was in. John caught his breath. 'Gentle. Gentle.'

'Can I go in further?'

'Slowly.' He caught his breath again. I wasn't enjoying the pain. I started to caress him and kiss the back of his neck. I took one of his earlobes into my mouth and chewed on it. Suddenly I was a lot further in. I could feel his pulse through his warm moist rectum.

I looked down to see what it looked like. I could only see half my cock, the other half was inside him. I slid back and forth. It was a totally new sensation for me and seemed to be hurting John. He wanted me to stop. I withdrew, which also seemed to cause him some discomfort. We lay in each other's arms, rubbing our cocks against each other until we both came. We fell asleep like that. I woke some time later and looked at my clock. It was nearly four.

My sleepy-eyed boyfriend kissed me goodnight, tucked me in and waved from the door.

I hated winter. The sun went down at four-thirty, making everything gloomy. And Noddy's heating system never started to work until I was nearly home from uni. I was looking forward to a nice warm snooze on the couch in front of the teev. I called hello as I walked in through the kitchen door.

'Could you come in here please, son?' *Oops, that doesn't sound too good.* Dad was sitting at the dining-room table. Mum got to her feet and put her hands on his shoulders. *Shit, somebody has died.* 'Sit down please.' I sat obediently.

Dad was still in his suit. His eyes looked red. He took a deep breath, looked at Mum and then spoke in rapid-fire. 'You and John can't see each other anymore. His father was in my office this morning, waving a pack of letters at me and yelling at me that you had corrupted his son, a good Catholic boy, trying to make him homosexual.'

I could feel every corpuscle coursing through my veins.

'He made me read one letter. Something about putting pressure on John to have sex.'

'Where the hell did he get that?'

Mum spoke. 'While John was staying here last night Mr Caleo went through his room. He obviously expected to find something. He accused your father of being a party to the whole thing.'

'Do you understand?' asked Dad. 'You're not to see each other. The man's threatening court action.'

'Who knows what he'll do the next time,' Mum chipped in.

'Do you support him?'

Dad's head fell. 'You know we've never been happy about this lifestyle you've chosen. We've tried to stay out of it. But this morning was the most humiliating moment of my life.'

'You can't stop us.'

'Of course we can't,' said Mum, 'but John won't be staying here anymore and you won't be invited to the Caleos'.'

Dad added, 'And you can't use the phone to call him.'

I lost it. Sometimes you smash doors and furniture. But sometimes you grit your teeth and say with quiet disgust, 'Fucken poxy traitors, I hope you get cancer.' Then slam the door and yell, 'Fucken poxy cunts,' so all the neighbours can hear. And that's what I did.

There I was at age eighteen, running away just like I did when I was four. No promise of an icecream was going to work this time. My hands were buzzing. I was hyperventilating. I pulled into the carpark at the top of the cliff. I started crying, the kind that starts in your feet and moves all the way through you. Even my hair was crying.

It wasn't that John and I would never see each other, or anything so melodramatic. I felt betrayed. *Poor John. What's he going through? I wish I believed in telepathy. I've got to find out.*

I knocked on the door of Tom's room at college. He opened the door a crack, bleary-eyed, in a paisley dressing-gown. 'Sorry, mate, but it's an emergency. I need you to ring John for me.' I told him what had happened.

'You poor things. Let me get dressed.' We went down the corridor to the student phone. 'It's Tom here. Could I speak to John?' I could barely get my breath. *It's going okay. Everything will be all right.* 'John, it's Tom. Tim just told me what happened. Are you okay? He wants to talk to you.'

'Hi, bubby. I love you,' I said. John started to cry. 'Are you okay?' I asked. 'We'll get through this.' John couldn't speak. He was choking back the tears. 'We'll be okay. I love you.'

'Me too. I'd better go,' he got out finally.

I sat on the stairs with Tom next to me, his arm around me. 'You know what pisses me off? Us being together never hurt anyone but it's okay for that dickhead to destroy his own son.'

I spent the night on Tom's floor, hoping my parents might sweat it out a little. When I arrived home I walked in without a word and went to my room, where I drifted in and out of sleep. I heard the phone ring. Mum knocked on my door and came in. 'It's John. I'm not very happy about this. Just don't let your father find out.'

John was still upset but calmer than the night before. 'Dad wants me to see a psychologist, some guy at college recommended by our parish priest. I know there's nothing wrong with me. I'll go to shut Dad up. I hope he won't take Dad's side. Can you meet me at college for lunch tomorrow?'

Lunch was so nice. It confirmed that nothing had really changed. He still had all his limbs and his sense of humour. It was difficult not being able to show affection, especially when he looked so cute, but we managed some furtive holding of hands and rubbing of knees under the table. His appointment with the psychologist took place that afternoon.

'Unbelievable,' he reported. 'This guy asked me all sorts of questions. How long have I had these feelings? Am I comfortable with them? How do my friends react? And then he leans back in his chair and says, "You seem well adjusted. I think your father is the one with the problem. Would you like me to speak to him?"'

'When I told Dad this he looked like he was going to burst open. "How dare he? I don't need help. How can he call himself a Catholic?" I know it's wrong, but I really enjoyed giving him the shits.'

I pulled up outside Pepe's house in Templestowe to find the front door open. She was in the galley kitchen fighting with a huge pot of macaroni.

'My boy!' I heard the husky voice of Marie behind me. She held out her arms and ash dropped from the obligatory cigarette as we hugged. 'The whole thing is so offensive. I've made up the spare room. It's only a single bed, I'm sorry.'

I thanked her. 'I don't think John will be able to stay anyway.'

When John arrived he was comforted with lots of rubbing and patting, but that was not what he wanted. We went into the yard, and out among the leaf litter and spiderwebs he pushed pebbles around with the toe of his shoe. 'Dad and I had a really big fight.'

'Does he know where you are?'

'I wasn't allowed to leave the house until I told him. I guess the more I deflected the question, the more he was convinced I was about to commit a mortal sin.'

'And you are,' I joked. John didn't even smile. 'Sorry.'

'When I told him I was coming here he says, "But Pepe is a friend of Tim's. So will Tim be there?"'

'And what did you say?'

'He was staring at me like he couldn't believe . . . like he was really ashamed.' John took a deep breath. 'I just cracked. I've never spoken to him like this, never spoken to anyone like this. I called him an arsehole! I told him that if he can't accept you and me, I don't want him to be my father.'

I took my boyfriend in my arms and hugged him. I could feel John convulsing. For a split second a wave of guilt overwhelmed me. *This wouldn't be happening if it weren't for me.* He broke away from me.

'Dad said he was sorry I felt like that, that he loved me as his son, but that the Church tells him that what we are doing is wrong. It's a sin and he can't condone it.'

John bent down and grabbed a handful of pebbles and lobbed them over the canopy of gum trees. He looked at me with his chocolate eyes and somewhere out of my brain fell the words, 'Will you marry me?'

I couldn't tell whether he was taken aback or appalled. *What a stupid thing to say. You just said it because it sounded romantic.* And although we never talked about it again, in that moment I think it confirmed for him that the fight he'd just had was worth it.

We were halfway through our beetroot soup when the phone rang. Marie answered. Her mouth opened as if she couldn't believe what she was hearing. 'I don't think it's any of your business. I'd prefer that you didn't ring here again. Goodnight.' She hung up and growled. 'I'm sorry, John, but your father is a very rude and irritating man. He asked me if I realised there were homosexuals at my dinner table.'

We partied hard that night. John fell asleep in my arms as we sat on a canary-yellow beanbag. Marie stuck her head around the corner. 'See you boys for breakfast in the morning.'

John mumbled, 'I don't think I can stay, Marie.'

'You must stay. You've done the hardest part.'

'Dad'll be waiting up.'

'Serves him right, don't you think? Eggs, bacon, muffins and great coffee.'

'John doesn't drink coffee,' I said.

'An Italian who doesn't drink coffee!'

'I'm only half Italian.'

'Then half a coffee. See you at breakfast.'

John and I made our way to bed feeling that even though we were safe in our cocoon, the world outside was a dangerous place.

I knew there were bars for gays but John and I had never ventured into one. Lately I had started to wonder what we might be missing. One of the guys in student theatre told me about a nightclub called Bernhardt's and wrote the address on a piece of paper. John was trying to read this as we drove down a dark lane. He spotted a semicircular facade with the name on a backlit leadlight.

In the foyer a large effeminate man sat behind a counter. 'Hi, boys. Five dollars, please.' His aftershave was so strong that when his assistant lit a cigarette I imagined us being consumed by a fireball. We handed over our money and he gave us a raffle ticket. 'Hold on to those, there's a door prize.' As we headed off he said, loud enough for us to hear, 'Did you see those eyelashes? And they're real.'

The dancefloor took up the whole room. There were flashing

lights and a mirror ball. I stood mesmerised by the sight of men dancing together, embracing and kissing. *These are all gay men.* I stared at a very manicured Indian boy in a suit, dripping with gold jewellery. *I could have picked him.* The rest looked like ordinary young men. I had the desire to run up to all of them and ask, 'Do your parents know you're gay? How did they take it? Tell me about your life.' I saw a strongly built guy who looked like David Cassidy. *I'd especially like to ask him. He's beautiful. What would it be like to have sex with him?* We watched the boys dancing, some delicately, some funkily, and some as if they were in Disneyland on Ice. I suggested we start talking to people.

John turned up his nose. 'What do we say? "We're Tim and John and we'd like to be your friends."? Let's see what's upstairs.'

There was a café selling coffee and toasted sandwiches. We sat in a red vinyl booth. A tall blond man plonked himself down and breathed whiskey over us. 'You boys are new here?' He'd obviously been dancing as he was sweaty and hot. 'Didn't think I'd seen you. I'm sure I'd remember.'

The waiter slunk over to us. 'What can I get you girls?'

'A hot buttered man on toast,' said our sweaty friend.

'Fresh out, lovey.' *Why do they all talk like that? It's like the gay characters on Benny Hill.*

I wasn't comfortable. John and I had hot chocolate and toasted cheese sandwiches while our friend rabbited on about how Babs had sold out making *A Star is Born.* I stood and said politely, 'It's been nice chatting to you but I think we'd better go.'

John wanted to have a dance. 'Disco Inferno' was playing. It felt weird, even slightly daring, dancing with my boyfriend in a room full of strangers.

But driving home in the car I felt down. I had expected good-looking masculine men to run up to us and invite us to meet their friends. Instead there were lots of guys giving each other furtive looks. I remembered what my mother had said about it being a sad lifestyle.

As we reached John's house, to my amazement he asked me in.

'Mum and Dad don't get back from the beach-house until Monday. You could stay if you wanted.'

'What if they come home early?'

'They never do. Please.'

'I just hope your father hasn't installed Tim detectors.'

I felt as though I was about to step onto an electrified floor but when I smelt the sweet homely smell of the house, warm memories came flooding back and I relaxed a little. John and I climbed the stairs and went straight to bed, where we made love like we were reclaiming old territory.

I found it difficult to sleep. Every time there was a noise outside I'd snap awake. I lay there with John's arm around me, remembering the time he and I decorated his room after the renovations, choosing the colours (chocolate, beige and yellow), and painting his piggy bank gloss-yellow. Lois and I had gotten on really well. I think I was the first boy she'd met who was interested in her new kitchen curtains. I was sad that now things had broken down so badly.

I drifted off to sleep again, but was woken by a sound. It was morning. I heard a car door slam. Another door slammed and then we heard the sliding door open and John's mum asking Anthony to bring the blue bag inside.

'Shit!' John leapt out of bed and pulled on his tracksuit pants. He grabbed my clothes and pushed them and me into the louvred cupboard.

I stood in the shadows among John's coats and shirts thinking of all those cartoons with the lover hiding in the cupboard. But this was real. *It's happening. I can't believe it. How do we get out of this? Create a diversion?*

John came back into the room and opened the cupboard. 'I've told Mum you're here. She said Dad's on his way.' He bustled me outside.

Lois had parked me in. John asked her to move her car and she came out with Anthony in tow. He was obviously glad to see me. She said hello very formally. She moved her car and I made my escape, thinking how much worse it could have turned out.

Later that night John rang. 'Mum isn't going to tell Dad. She feels the whole thing is absurd.' It was nice to think that we might have an ally.

The campus gay society, Gaysoc, met on Tuesdays in the small meeting-room of the union building. I had already walked past a few times and nonchalantly taken a squiz, which had proved a little disappointing. There had only been six or so people in there. Now I sat outside trying to get up the courage to go in.

Before I knew it I was walking through the door, as if my body had a mind of its own. 'Is this the Gaysoc?'

A large guy with long curly brown hair introduced himself as Woody. I sat with my back to the door in case anyone I knew walked past. 'We're discussing Sexuality Week and what we want to do for it.'

As they talked about having a same-sex couple kissing in the lift in the Menzies building I looked around the group. *They couldn't be more different from the guys I saw at Bernhardt's.* Most of them looked like hippies, in alpaca jumpers and T-shirts with political slogans on them. And there were a couple of women. I didn't find anyone attractive except perhaps Woody. He asked for a report on Gay Blue-jeans Day.

Lee, a small bald guy wearing a May Day T-shirt, said he needed some volunteers to screen-print posters. When I asked about the event, he said, 'We ask everyone who's gay to wear blue jeans. Most people wear them anyway, so everyone has to make a choice that might force them to consider their prejudices.'

I started to feel relaxed. They seemed pretty laid-back and

even happy. And it was good to meet people who were trying to do something to change the situation for gays.

At the end of the meeting Woody came over and asked me to join them for coffee. *What if someone sees me with them? But how would anyone know these people are gay?* 'Okay.'

My eyes scoured the caf for faces I knew. No one ran from the room screaming. Four of us sat at one table, Woody next to me. He asked if I was in a relationship.

'With a guy called John. We've been together nearly three years.'

'Three years?' Lee chipped in. 'You must have been a baby.'

'We were at school together.'

'How did the other kids react?'

'The guys that knew were fine about it.'

'That is so sweet,' said Woody.

'It's encouraging. It's what we're fighting for,' added Lee.

We talked about our sexuality and our families. It was weird how comfortable I felt with these guys. They were older, hipper and more politically radical, but none of that mattered. We were connected by our fight to make things better for gay men and women.

Dear Editor,

I am surprised by the level of anti-gay thinking on this campus. I don't understand how people can hate gays when they are just like everyone else. My boyfriend was captain of the football team at school. He is strongly built and masculine, and if you were to meet him you wouldn't know he was gay. He isn't like the stereotype. We have been together for three years, which is longer than most of our straight friends' relationships. We love each other the way most couples do. Some of you would say it's unnatural, but so is having a haircut or driving a car. Some of you would argue it's wrong because our sex doesn't produce babies. Where does that leave infertile couples? I just hope that we can learn to accept each other for what we are.

Tim
First-year medicine

A few days later in the community research centre, Lee sidled up to me. 'Did you write that letter in *Lot's Wife*? I thought you were doing science?' I said I didn't feel brave enough to sign my real name and faculty. Lee burst into laughter. 'Fabulous, some poor first-year med student has been dragged out of the closet whether he's gay or not.'

'Was the letter okay?'

'Perhaps a bit politically naïve, but your heart's in the right place.'

I'd been given an elephant stamp. Then I started to worry. *Politically naïve?* My elephant stamp was a bit smudged.

As I sat with Woody in the caf drinking a swampwater milkshake (lime and chocolate flavouring) I was on edge, trying to formulate the question I wanted to ask. 'You know when you're making love – ?'

'Do you mean fucking?' I was taken aback. 'You're talking about anal sex?'

'Have you done it?' I asked him.

Woody broke into a big grin. 'Many times. I think it's important. Men being intimate or being penetrated challenges the patriarchy.' I pretended I knew what he meant.

I lowered my voice. 'John screwed me for the first time last night and I found it painful. It would hardly go in and it felt like I needed a shit.'

'It takes practice, my friend. You've just got to try to relax. I get my lover to chew on my earlobe. It distracts me and before I know it, he's in.'

'Thanks. Oh, one other thing.' I lowered my voice further. I was finding this one harder. 'My bum wouldn't close and the come kept dribbling out for about half an hour.'

'Your sphincter was probably in shock. It'll get used to it with practice. It's worth it, because when it works it's mind-blowing.'

It saddened me to have John's and my lovemaking reduced to dick-in-the-bum mechanics, to fucking. But the power of peer pressure meant that I wouldn't use the old term for some time.

The same six or eight people were turning up to Gaysoc meetings each week. I thought they were great, but they were older than me and I wanted to meet some people my own age. Where were they?

'Think about it,' I addressed the meeting. 'There are eighteen thousand kids on campus, and if we believe the statistic of one in ten that means nearly two thousand gay guys and girls.' I felt audacious and confident. 'So where are they?'

'Library toilets,' Lee joked.

Woody chipped in. 'It's too confronting for them to come to a group like this.'

'Why don't we set up a gayline where they can speak to one of us anonymously? I spoke to the woman in student counselling. She's happy for us to use her phone for one hour three days a week if we attend some training sessions.'

At that moment, two good-looking boys stuck their heads around the door, disappeared from view and then entered the room. They sat together across from me. It was hard not to stare. Imagining that these beautiful boys were gay gave me a pang like unrequited love. Before the meeting ended, they slipped out as quietly as they'd slipped in. *They're the kind of people I'm talking about.*

'Probably a couple of straight boys on a dare,' Woody said as we sat over milkshakes in the caf.

'We could at least have introduced ourselves. It was almost as if they weren't there.'

'Except for your jaw on the table and the dribble,' Lee joked.

'Would you care so much if they hadn't been so good-looking?' a woman called Rose challenged me, watching for my reaction. *She's probably right.* 'Or if they'd been lesbian?'

I put on my best Queen Victoria voice. 'Surely that's not possible.' There was a deathly hush over the group. Rose grabbed the table and tipped it and all the milkshakes over me. I was shocked. 'What's the matter!'

'Work it out.' Rose stormed off. The three of us sat dripping milk. I set the table back on its feet. 'I don't understand what I did wrong.'

Woody put his hand on my arm. 'Rose's big beef is lesbian invisibility. Your comment only confirms it.' *How am I going to face her again?*

Next day I saw her in the open area of the union building. She was writing, her legs drawn up to her chest. I was nervous but there was no table to throw at me. I quietly said her name. She looked up at me.

'I'm sorry I upset you yesterday.'

'I'm sorry about making such a scene.'

'Woody told me you're angry about lesbians being invisible.'

She rolled her eyes. 'It's much more than that. It's all the men in the group, the language they use, the way they talk over women.'

'Why don't you do a session on it?'

'Women are sick of being responsible for educating men. It's your turn to educate yourselves. Go and read a book. Now, if you'll excuse me I want to finish my letter.'

I walked away feeling helpless. I don't enjoy upsetting

people. Later that day I ran into Woody in the community research centre, where he was cutting out letters for an anti-uranium banner. He pulled a stool over and sat me down. 'Rose has had a very bad time of being gay. When she told her parents, her father asked if she was telling him she wanted to be a man. He had her committed. Her girlfriend helped her escape. When she went back home to collect her things her father had burnt everything.'

'That's outrageous. Poor Rose. It's amazing that she isn't fucked up more.' I wanted to put my arms around her but I suspected this was not the right moment.

The student counselling room was a small office with large cushions on the floor. Woody and I lay on them waiting for the telephone to ring. The lack of response was disappointing.

'It's a new thing. It might take some time before people get the courage up.' Woody stretched. He turned to me and smiled. 'Can I have a hug?' He rolled on top of me. He was a big guy, much bigger than John.

'Woody, you're crushing me!'

'Sorry.' He rolled off to one side and stayed there with his arm over me. It was nice to be cuddled by a big bear. I felt protected from the outside world. He nuzzled my neck. 'You smell nice.' Then he started kissing me and I flew into a panic. *He wants more than a cuddle. He's nice but I don't find him attractive.* I sat up. 'What's the matter?' he asked.

'You said a hug. I'm in a relationship. And so are you.'

'We're not monogamous.'

'But that's what a relationship is. Isn't that what everyone wants?'

'I don't believe all my needs are satisfied by one person. My lover Peter likes to play tennis and I don't, so he plays with other people. Why can't sex be like that?'

This started me thinking. *Sex with John is pretty good but it's becoming a bit routine. There're only so many ways to skin a cat. But John would be hurt if I told him my needs aren't being met.*

I stood in the stream of marchers trying to read the various banners: Victorian Teachers Union, Christian Students Alliance. But no Gaysoc. It was extraordinary to be among all that energy, the air charged with purpose.

We marched down Collins Street. It was eerie to walk down a major city street and hear no cars or trams. 'Keep uranium in the ground. What do we want? No uranium. When do we want it? Now!' The chants bounced off the glass towers along with the whistling and playing of guitars. I was marching alone but feeling strong, like part of a tidal wave about to crash down and change the landscape forever. I wondered if this was what the Vietnam demonstrations were like.

'Hey! You with the nice bum!' I turned to see Woody holding a banner that said, 'Uranium – not a good look. Monash Gaysoc.' I jumped all over him. Both Woody and the boy at the other end of the banner were wearing red bandannas. *He's very cute. Mediterranean-looking. Why haven't I seen him at Gaysoc?* Woody introduced his lover Peter Craig, who asked me to take his end of the banner. *The photo on the front page could be me holding a Gaysoc banner.* But I wanted the other marchers to see a proud gay person and so I took it.

Every elevated place had a photographer on it. Press, students documenting the march, and probably ASIO. I might have a file by now.

When the march reached the main intersection we were asked by a marshal to sit down. Cars were already banked up, honking their horns. An irate taxi driver jumped out and started abusing us. We were powerful but I don't think we were making many friends.

After the march Woody, Peter and I went to a greasy spoon

in Swanston Street. A volleyball nut as well as a tennis player, Peter was into all sports.

'Like my lover John.'

'He didn't come to the march?'

'It's not really his bag.'

I liked Peter. 'Hope I see you round,' I added as we said our goodbyes. I wanted to make a time and place then and there, but was afraid of appearing pushy.

John and I went to the fourth National Homosexual Conference at the Universal Workshop. As we climbed the stairs, he took my hand and we walked into the foyer holding hands. I felt proud and secure, as though I was wrapped up in a blanket.

The atmosphere was abuzz with anticipation. Smiling people greeted each other with kisses and hugs. *I love seeing men kissing men and women kissing women.* We were given name badges and the conference program, which included workshops on gay teachers and students, and growing old with dignity.

I spotted Woody. When I asked if Peter was with him, he told me they had just broken up. He didn't want to say any more. John and I went off to the first workshop: Get Your Filthy Laws Off My Body.

At lunch a young guy with curly hair came over to us. 'A group of young gays want to set up our own group, because there's nothing in the program dealing with our issues. We're meeting next Saturday at the graduate lounge at Melbourne Uni.'

At the final plenary session, a confident young woman named Alison took the microphone and addressed the conference. 'We the newly formed Young Gays are disappointed by the lack of workshops dealing with our issues. Being young and gay in 1979 is probably easier than when you were coming out, but things are still difficult. Kids still get hassled at school, some attempt to take their own lives. Your attitude that we should have to deal with it because you did is patronising, and not very community-spirited. Being young and gay is political. It forces people to confront adolescent sexuality. I hope our group can be strident enough to challenge the old theories about recruitment of the young.' Her motion of support for Young Gays was carried. Young Gays looked like being a formidable part of the gay community.

The group began to meet on Saturday afternoons at the Universal Workshop. At the inaugural meeting the people running the group were confident, political and vocal, and there was a sense that anything could be achieved.

The next few meetings were spent trying to work out the structure. Collective? Committee? We decided it should be democratic, with a rotating chair. There were house rules, like confidentiality and one person talking at a time. This group found both very hard.

A letterhead was designed, two smiling stick-figures holding hands, and 'Young Gays' in a child's handwriting. The group then decided to write to school counsellors to let them know how to get in touch with us.

As word got around, the group soon swelled to forty people. There were so many good-looking boys I fell in love at every meeting, at a picnic near the floral clock, a day of beach volleyball. Kids have ever-changing best friends; I had ever-changing boyfriends, whom I flirted with and who appeared in my masturbation fantasies. Often when John and I were having sex, my eyes would close and I would be having sex with the beautiful Eurasian boy, or the guy in the singlet.

I wanted to share all this with John but felt I couldn't. Occasionally he would ask if I thought so-and-so was cute. Guilt would wash over me and I would deny it.

John and I were on our way to a cottage at Warburton that belonged to a friend of my parents. I'd asked Mum and Dad if I could take a couple of friends up there. I didn't tell them it would be fifteen to twenty young gays.

There was an infectious feeling of expectation as we explored the surroundings, made cups of coffee, fought over sleeping arrangements and flirted madly. Some people had brought tents and set them up outside.

After dinner the group decided to go into town to the pub. We found a corner near the fire, dragged a circle of chairs together and plonked ourselves down. I was aware that people were watching us. *Perhaps it's the earrings and groovy haircuts. I guess they don't see boys with earrings much around these parts.*

After a few drinks the group became openly affectionate, sitting on knees, holding hands and kissing. It seemed that lots of the gang were pairing up for a night of doing the wild thing.

A guy at the bar whose yellow T-shirt stretched over a beer belly walked over to Alison. 'Do you know your friends are poofters? Don't you think it's disgusting?'

'I'm a dyke, you deadshit.'

He shoved her, she fell to the ground and he started kicking her. Alan and another guy from our group went to help her, but were swamped by men with moustaches and beerguts swinging punches. The wives stood on the sidelines trying to call them off.

Someone came over to John and asked him, 'Are you a poofter?'

'I don't want to fight you.'

'I asked you a question.'

'I heard you.'

'Fucken smartarse poofter.' He swung at John, connecting with his jaw. It made no noise, no whack like in the movies. I laughed out of shock, before it dawned on me what had happened. We got out as fast as we could.

'Should we go to the police?' someone asked.

'They're not going to be interested in a bunch of poofters and dykes.'

Alan's forehead was bleeding. He needed stitches. The nearest hospital was back towards the city, in Box Hill. Alison bundled him into her car. It was two o'clock in the morning before our war hero returned. He'd had to be observed for four hours. He held up a pamphlet, 'After a Head Injury'. 'If I start acting strangely you have to take me back.'

'Darling, you always act strangely,' one of the boys joked. Alan got lots of stroking. The incident at the pub had bonded us stronger than anything.

John and I lay awake for some time, our ankles crossed over each other, talking about what had happened, and what would have happened if one of us had been seriously injured. I was still very angry and running through scenes of what I wished I'd said. 'We should go back tomorrow night and trash the place.'

'It's not the owner's fault.' We were safe, snuggled up on a very soft double bed as we drifted off to sleep, John's arms around me.

John had gone to a meeting with other student organisations to work out how to set up a gay group at his own college, and had met Peter Craig. 'Amazing to meet a gay guy who's into sport. We're going to play tennis tomorrow at Clifton Hill.'

Peter and John played while I sat in the umpire's seat watching the two young Mediterraneans thrashing it out, their sinewy bodies working hard in the sun.

We went back to Peter's place in Fitzroy to have a cold drink. While John and Peter were making up lemon barleys, I picked up the *Advocate* from the coffee table. On the third page a headline asked, 'Is There a Gay Cancer?' *Gay cancer? What does that mean? Cancer that only sleeps with cancer?* 'Doctors with large gay practices in San

Francisco and New York are reporting the appearance of a cancer called Kaposi's sarcoma, previously seen in older Mediterranean and Jewish men but never in young men,' I read. *It doesn't make sense. Cancer is not contagious.* I showed John the gay cancer story. The three of us wondered where it came from and how it could be spreading. We hoped to God that none of us got it.

The night before Melbourne Cup Day there was a party thrown by the *Gay Community News* people. John was studying for an anatomy exam later that week, so Peter and I went together.

When I called for him he came to the door in a towel, his sinewy body still glistening from the shower. *A seriously sexy man.* Eventually he emerged in blue satin running shorts and a blue and white striped singlet. 'It's Cup Eve. I thought I'd dress in my racing silks.' I felt daggy next to him. He offered to dress me the same way. There was something very sexy about wearing the clothes of a man I found so attractive.

Dressed alike we attracted a lot of attention at the party. One man even referred to Peter as my boyfriend. Late in the night, Michael Jackson's *Off the Wall* was playing. We weren't dancing but sort of moving to the music, watching the other people in the room bathed in red light. The combination of dope and alcohol made me feel brave. Giggly. Sexy. 'Rock With You' came on. I put my arms around Peter's waist and started rocking with him. I could smell him, a musty man-smell mixed with shampoo. I started kissing his neck.

Peter tried to push me away. But I was aroused and pressed my hard-on against him. *Maybe he's embarrassed to be doing this in public?* 'Can we go back to your place?'

'Sure, but not for sex,' Peter warned. 'I couldn't do it to John.'

'He doesn't have to know.'

'I wouldn't feel right about it.' Peter walked away. It was the first time I'd tried to initiate something, and it was my first rejection. The worst part was trying to pretend that nothing had happened.

Chapter SIX

Adventure and Separation

A few months later, early in the summer of 1980, I had moved out of home, and was lying in my flat in St Kilda looking at the palm tree outside my window. I was feeling so jealous of my friends' exploits: picking up someone at the Screech Beach changing-sheds, starting a romance with someone in a sauna, or going home with the spunk of the party. These were things I would like to try. I was nearly twenty-two, and compared to my friends' my sexual experience was limited. It had been mainly John, and although it had been mostly good it hadn't been very adventurous. And John needed the experience as much as me, I rationalised. I was the only person he'd had sex with. He might learn some tricks and techniques that would reignite our sex life. But how would I feel if I heard that he'd had sex with someone? I really didn't know. And how would I bring this up with him? Maybe he was feeling the same things, but I suspected not. I didn't want to hurt him.

John and I went to see *Nine to Five* and had coffee in a city café. I was preparing to drop the bomb. *I wonder if dropping the whole thing would be easier?* 'How would you feel if we were to open our relationship?'

His forehead creased. 'You mean have sex outside the relationship? Who with?' I said no one in particular. He stared at the table and his breath was rapid. 'I don't understand why you would want to.'

Fuck, I didn't think he'd be this upset. 'You know I love you?' He didn't say anything. 'But I'm worried that we're missing out on what people our age are supposed to be experiencing. I feel sexually inexperienced. Don't you feel that? You've only ever had sex with me.'

'I don't want to have sex with other people.'

'Okay. But would you allow me to?'

'I don't know why you'd want to. Is it something about me?'

'No. I don't believe that it's fair to expect our lovers to fulfil all our needs. From you I get affection, companionship, love and sex. But what I'm not getting is the thrill of the hunt or experiencing different men's bodies.' He seemed to understand my argument but he wasn't buying it. 'Life is about experience.'

'I don't want to talk about this. Not here in public.' *I think that was a no.*

A group of us gay boys met at Churchill Park for a barbecue, to drink beer in the sun and play games. Peter brought his volleyball net. He also brought along his new boyfriend Ian, whom we liked even though he took his politics too seriously. Ian was the sort of guy who wouldn't buy Nescafé because of Nestlé's history in Africa, and expected everyone else to do the same. On this day he was wearing bib-and-brace overalls without a shirt, so you could see his lithe brown body, his nipples bobbing up and down behind the bib. It was a horny look.

After lunch John and Peter and a couple of others went up the hill to play volleyball. Someone suggested a game called Train

Tiggy. Whoever was It tried to tag someone, who then became the front of the train. They'd have to run together to tag someone else. Ian offered to be It.

It was hard to run on a full stomach so when Ian approached me I couldn't be bothered trying to escape. Besides, the prospect of running around with Ian was not unattractive. Ian put his hands on my hips and he and I tried to catch our next victim. Eventually we were all in a train formation one behind the other. Ian said softly, 'Bit like a daisy chain.'

He put his hand up inside my T-shirt and started to play with my nipple. 'Ooh, erect already.'

I put my hands behind me and slid them into the slots in the side of his overalls. *I wonder what sort of undies he's wearing?*

At that moment the volleyball came down the hill, John full pelt after it. He and the ball broke through our train. Ian and I had broken from the rest of the group but were still locked together. John looked angry. I pulled away from Ian, and John murmured, 'I'm really sorry,' then punched me hard in the stomach. He walked away and Peter put his arm around him. *Fuck! The drive home's gonna be fun.*

But John started to leave with Peter. It was like another punch in the stomach. Feeling like a heel, I pursued him. 'Please let me drive you home. We need to talk.' *I have no idea what I'm going to say.* John's jaw was clenched, but he agreed. We drove for ten minutes before John asked what I wanted to say.

'I'm sorry that I upset you. I wasn't doing it to hurt you. I guess I was a bit pissed.'

'I can't believe it. After our discussion the other day I did some thinking and I was coming round to what you suggested. But not if you're going to flaunt it like that. Now everyone thinks I don't satisfy you. You know how that makes me feel?'

We didn't talk for the rest of the journey. My head thumped. John stayed in his cloud of anger. When we arrived at his place we kissed goodbye. I asked him to call me: 'I might let you sweat it out for a while.' He closed the car door. *That's fucked that. I am so stupid sometimes.*

In my search for adventure, however, I did start trolling.

First there was Harry, a Turkish boy who was at his first gay party. Harry was drunk not just on alcohol but on excitement. 'Are you gay? This is my first gay party. God, if my parents knew! In their country they used to stone people for being gay. I can't believe how many good-looking guys there are here.'

Later that night Harry asked me the time. It was after one-thirty and he had missed his train. He asked if he could stay at my place. We split the bed. I put the mattress on the floor and gave him the base. Then he asked if anal sex hurt. I said only at first. There was a silence and then he asked me to screw him. 'I'm a virgin and I reckon you'd be gentle with me.'

'You're sweet, but I have a boyfriend.'

'He's not here. You don't think I'm attractive.' He said he was coming to join me on the floor. I tried to resist, but I was hard by the time he slid in beside me and held my cock against his arse.

I screwed Harry. He had no trouble doing what, for me, had been a painful thing. In fact he seemed to enjoy it immensely. *Has he done this before? Was this all a con-job?*

He left at five-thirty, to be home before his parents woke up. He kissed me goodbye and was gone. *Well, I've done it. I've crossed the line. I don't feel different. If anything I feel worse. Something was missing.*

I met Philip at a New Romantic night at Inflation where the punters were dressed in eighteenth-century dress with powdered wigs, or ballet costumes. He was cute, dressed in a white shirt with puffed sleeves and a white headband. He was with some guys from Young Gays. We kept catching each other's eyes. Hearing that he liked me, I got up the courage to go and dance with him. The rest of the night we carried on like boyfriends, holding hands, sitting together with an arm around each other's waist.

Philip was clearly an experienced lover. He manoeuvred himself around my cock with obvious expertise. But again I sensed that something was missing. I didn't know what.

The next day Philip rang me at the café where I was working to ask me out. I declined. 'It was really nice but I don't think we should. I couldn't bear it if my boyfriend found out.'

I could hear he was angry. 'You should've thought about that before you led me on.'

'I didn't lead you on. I was honest the whole way.'

His breath was fast and hard. He hung up. *All I ever do is upset people.*

My friend Karl was making a student film and asked me to come and work on it. Franco was production assistant on the film. Straight away he and I started flirting. It was a two-day drive from Melbourne to the location at Lake Eyre, two days of sitting next to a cute man in the back seat until I developed lover's nuts, a deep ache in my groin from not ejaculating.

The huge salt pan that was Lake Eyre looked like snow and reflected the burning sun. We set up camp among the fish and snake skeletons on its edge. It was a tough three days. There was no relief from the sun, and the nearest water was a hundred and fifty kilometres away. It forced us to be inventive, washing plates with a wet hand-towel and wearing tablecloths, Arab-style, as headdresses.

When the crew went out to shoot, Franco and I stole inside the tent and finally got down to what we'd been thinking of for days. Our bodies had the sweet smell of sweat as there'd been no bathing. Franco was a gentle, kissing lover. Our affair didn't finish with the film, but continued for a month in Sydney. He too had a long-term relationship but his lover was in New Zealand. Knowing it would be finite made the whole thing more intense.

Separation

Part of me wanted to share these experiences with John. He was my best friend with whom I shared everything, but I didn't think I should share this. I knew he'd be disappointed. I hoped I wouldn't get the guilts and confess it all. I seemed to be swimming in a pool of negative feelings about our relationship. I felt claustrophobic. His devotion to me was so strong that it made me nervous. When friends told me how much in love with me he was, I felt obligated to him. And John could be very straight sometimes. I wanted more craziness. Maybe I needed some time out.

We were sitting on the couch in my flat one day when I said, 'I'd like to have a trial separation. I need some space. We've been together five years and I'm starting to lose my identity. I'm no longer Tim but a part of Tim-and-John.'

'What's wrong with that?'

'There are things I want to do that wouldn't involve you.'

'You mean sex with other men?' John was angry. 'How long do you want the separation to be?'

'A couple of months.'

'When does this start? Now?'

That's too soon. Maybe I've made a mistake. 'Are you okay about it?'

'No, why would I be?'

I went to the barber and got a number-two-blade crewcut. A few days later Pepe's friend Prue invited the gang down to her mother's holiday house among the white sand dunes at Venus Bay. I was greeted with cries of 'Tim! Your hair!' They ran their hands over the stubble.

John was as cheery as could be. 'Hello, bald eagle.' *I find his cheer a little hard to comprehend. It's better than him being the martyr, but why is he so buoyant? Maybe he's glad to be out of the relationship? Or didn't he understand what I said?*

Later in the afternoon Prue said, 'John told me that you and he are separated.'

'I keep wondering if I've done the right thing.'

'He was crying this morning.'

As we made preparations for bed, cheery John said, 'Don't sleep over there. Bring your li-lo closer.'

'Did you understand what we talked about the other day?'

'It doesn't mean we can't cuddle.'

'I think it does.' John looked upset. He climbed into his bed with his back to me. I hoped to God that he wouldn't start crying. He looked so cute, his little ear sticking out from his head. *I can't bear hurting him like this.* I dragged my li-lo over to where he was and put my arm around him. He took my hand. I lay awake for ages.

John dropped in at my flat while I was rehearsing monologues for my audition for the National Institute of Dramatic Art. We had hardly spoken over the past month and spent the first moments gauging each other's emotional state. He looked calm. *He's doing okay.*

In the kitchen we waited for the kettle to boil and the popcorn to pop. John rinsed out the teapot and said bashfully, 'I'm seeing someone.'

Suddenly everything had changed. 'Anyone I know?'

'Peter.'

'Lucky you. He's sweet. And very cute. Have you slept together?'

'A couple of times.'

'What's he like?'

John looked hurt. 'You're not even jealous!'

'No. I'm not. Is that why you told me?'

'Maybe. I don't know. Yes,' he spat out.

'I think it's great, a chance to experience something different.' I remembered that when I had tried to crack onto him, Peter said he couldn't do it to John. And here he was doing it with John.

Just as the popcorn stopped doing its stuff, the kettle started to whistle. I took the lid off the popcorn and emptied in the kettle. John laughed almost hysterically. My heart was struck with something warm and fuzzy.

We sat on the couch and caught up on what had been happening since we separated. 'Peter and I were supposed to be driving up to Queensland but Dad came home with a ticket for New Zealand. I'm leaving in a week. I can't help wondering if he's just doing it to keep Peter and me apart.'

We smiled. There was an understanding between us brought about by a common foe. It felt like old times.

I had auditioned for NIDA the year before, so I knew the shape of the day. This year I was approaching the audition differently. I had decided to present myself as a confident, masculine actor. I wore a black T-shirt and jeans. In my mind I was James Dean, quiet, brooding, keeping to myself.

We did our second pieces for the head of acting and the head of NIDA, and a number of people were let go. I was relieved still to be in the running; this was farther than I had got last time.

After a lunch that I abandoned out of nausea, we spent the afternoon doing improvisations and working on our pieces. At the end of the day there were six of us, myself included, on a short-list.

Weeks later, I began rehearsing an expressionist play called *Ruins* for Anthill, still waiting to hear if I'd got in. Each day, while we were climbing through the alps or listening to *Das Rheingold*, the director would ask me if I'd heard. By the fourth day he said they needed to know and asked me to ring the school.

They told me I had been accepted. I was ecstatic. I hung up the phone and saw one of the cast nearby. 'Julie, I got in!'

'That's good, turtle, if that's what you want.'

'Of course it's what I want. It's the school Mel Gibson and

Judy Davis went to.' I wanted to tell everybody, the woman in the café, the old man in the street, but I also didn't want to appear to be bragging. *'A cappuccino thanks and by the way, I just got into NIDA.'*

When I told John, he tried to sound happy. Then he said, 'I'm not going to see you much, am I?'

'I'll be coming back for the term breaks. And I'll write.'

He wanted to see me before I left. I suggested dinner at Rob's Carousel on Albert Park Lake, a very kitsch restaurant where we used to go as kids. I was struck again by how loyal John was to me. *I don't deserve it. And he deserves better.*

The restaurant was a fantasy in pink. A large revolving bar had a carousel horse at its centre. I talked about my fears of going to NIDA. 'What if they've got the wrong person? I turn up on the day and they say they thought Tim Conigrave was the boy with the black curly hair. Maybe I just fluked my way in on the day.'

'You're such a worry-wart. Of course you didn't fluke it. You'll be fine.' The fountains outside the window came on, a water wonderland with jets that spun in groups and streams spraying from the roof, all bathed in pink light. John smiled like a little boy at the Myer Christmas windows.

I asked if he'd meet me in town next day. 'I want to buy you a ring as a kind of memento and to say thanks for the last five years. You need to be there so we can check the size.'

'I'd like to buy you one too.'

'Most couples give each other rings at the start of a relationship, and here we are doing it when we break up.'

'Are we breaking up? I thought we were just separating.'

'I think NIDA's changed that. It'll be hard to maintain anything over such a distance.' I could see he was feeling dejected. 'I'm sorry, John, but don't you think the relationship was winding down? It was getting a bit stale.'

John sighed. 'Oh well, I guess I knew it was coming.'

After dinner we went for a walk on the shores of the lake,

holding hands under the cover of darkness. I wanted to kiss him and tell him I loved him, because in that moment I did, but I knew that would make things harder for him.

'I don't feel like going home,' John mused. 'Do you wanna go for a dance?'

Wednesday night at Inflation was gay night. Depeche Mode's 'Just Can't Get Enough' was playing. John took my hand, dragging me onto the dancefloor, and we mouthed the words to each other. Anyone would have thought we were on our first date. I leant over to John. 'This could be our song.'

Next day, John and I scoured the jewellery stores for rings. Two men buying rings got some fairly cold responses, but eventually we found a pair of cheap eighteen-carat gold rings, sold to us by a pleasant sales assistant.

I put mine on my wedding finger.

I had packed all my acting books, some linen, records and kitchenware into two tea chests ready to catch the overnight train to Sydney. Dad helped me hand them over the baggage counter, hugged me, rubbed my hair and left. In the foyer of the station I was greeted by the gang: Prue, Pepe, Jackie, Juliet, Eric, and of course John. Pepe held my face and said, 'I'm really proud of you. I'm going to miss you.'

John seemed nervous, fidgety. He handed me a photo album. On the first page were the words 'This is Your Life (actually only the last five years).' I flicked through and saw photos of John and me and the gang with commentary beside each. 'How did you get all this together?'

'The others pitched in.' They said John did the most work. He smiled shyly.

'It's wonderful. I'll read it on the train.'

They walked me out to my carriage, and as the station master blew his whistle, they started to hug me goodbye.

Pepe wiped tears from her cheeks. John, like a frightened boy, hugged me tightly and said, 'I love you.' As I pulled away I could see that he too had tears in his eyes.

I boarded the train. I had done this trip a few times before. I was used to sharing my sleep with snorers, drunken yobbos, and the largest array of bad haircuts ever seen. The seat next to mine was vacant. If it stayed that way I could stretch out and sleep.

The train blew its horn and started rolling. I was having trouble seeing my friends past a fat man blocking the window. *He'll be the one who snores.* I left my seat to wave as they ran alongside.

I sat with the photo album on my lap but I didn't want to read it yet. It felt too important to be read in such an environment. I wanted to make a ritual of it. I went down to the dining-car and bought a pie and sauce, a coffee, and a Wagon Wheel in honour of John – it was one of his favourites. Placing the album on my lap I began my journey. There were photos of John, Eric and me skateboarding down a freeway ramp, Christmas Eve on the Yarra bank, some of me in plays, and even a photo of the gang flashing our bums at the camera. John's commentary was very funny.

I sat holding the album. *I don't feel sad. Maybe it's the excitement and fear of what's coming.* I was leaving behind a group of loyal friends and a man with whom I had shared five years of my life. But I would be working on my acting skills with new friends in a very exciting city.

The Next Three Years

The next three years were about acting school. Gruelling days followed by homework: writing diaries for voice and movement, practising dialects, creating movement pieces, working on scenes with other students. It was a very vibrant and creative experience but my psyche took a lashing as we were pulled apart, examined and reassembled. Lots of pop psychology was thrown around: we'd hear things like 'You have a block with anger.'

I would compare myself to my classmates and feel inadequate. I was not the only one. In second year, when they tried to stretch us by giving us roles that were out of our range, a lot of us toyed with the idea of leaving, partly because we couldn't see the horizon – graduation.

The friendships we formed were intense and dynamic. When you've rolled around on the floor together, undressed in front of each other, talked about your deepest feelings, mingled sweat, and farted in front of each other, there's little left to hide. You'd have a best friend who would change with each project. A third-year student told me, 'The friends you make here will be your friends for life.'

Those three years were also about Craig. He was a northern-beaches surfie with a barrel chest and icy-blue eyes that never quite looked straight at you. He was probably aware of their power. When he looked at me I felt he could read my soul. He was straight and had a girlfriend. He knew I was gay but it didn't worry him. I never made a pass at him but I manoeuvred things so we'd sit together or have lunch together. I had always had a fantasy of friendship with a straight man, where we shared our deepest secrets. But my attempts at intimate discussions with Craig invariably failed.

'When did you lose your virginity?'

'Why do you need to know that?'

The ache of unrequited love appeared again. I started to wonder if this was an addiction, if I was like the women who always fell for married men. Watching *Brideshead Revisited* I was haunted by the eccentric homosexual Sebastian and his crush on his heterosexual friend Charles. I thought their relationship was like mine and Craig's, but when I asked him if he thought so he didn't know what I meant. I didn't have the guts to explain.

It was never going to be anything but a friendship. I did the only thing I could do. I took him home in my head and made him a part of my nocturnal fantasies.

Those years were about being perceived as soft. On our first day we had sat in the steamy confines of the NIDA theatre listening to welcome speeches from the staff. The administrator told us about the industry week the school had run at the end of the previous year. There had been a panel of casting agents and the students had had a go at doing screen tests. 'Barry, your movement teacher, gave a demonstration showing the girls how to be feminine and boys to walk like men, and not like they were carrying a handbag.' *My God, what have I got myself into?*

Fortunately my year was brimming with gays and lesbians. We managed to find each other very quickly. Nicholas asked me outright if I had a boyfriend, then told me that he thought he was gay. Libby always talked about her 'friend' Dotty, and told me that Veronica, the spunk of the year, was also gay.

One night Craig and Paul – another guy in my year – and I were checking our pimples in the mirror when Paul said he had heard that Veronica was gay. Craig pulled a face of derision. 'You poofters think everyone is gay.' Paul and I smiled at each other. It turned out that there were eight of us who were gay or bisexual, a third of the year.

At the end of first term we did a student cabaret, where we could do anything we chose. My group did the seven deadly sins. I was Vanity and elected to play him in Berlin white-face, lying across the top of a piano admiring himself in a hand-mirror.

After this performance Barry asked me to his place for dinner and a little chat.

'I've given this talk a number of times over the years, and with good results. It's about gesture, carriage and tone of voice. I'm sure I don't need to tell you that effeminate actors don't get much work. The public want their leading men to be masculine. If they detect any softness they're not going to believe that this man really wants this woman. You're a handsome young man, reasonably well built, and yet that all falls away when your gestures are affected. Look at the way you're sitting now.' I was leaning on one elbow, my index finger against my cheek and the other fingers rolled into a fist. 'It's a very womanly way to sit. Understand?' I nodded. 'You are more than your sexuality and I'm sure that when you're at home by yourself you're not like this.'

I knew what he was talking about, I'd known it for some time. But Barry was a gay man, a member of the cardigan set, and here he was asking me to betray my sexuality. It went against all the politics I had learnt at uni.

I began to explore my sexuality. It started in the bars. I had never walked up to a stranger and started a conversation and was sure I'd look like a real dick if I did. So I would sit on my beer, watching the passing trade, wondering what it would be like to bonk with them, hoping that if someone tried to pick me up I'd like them. But nobody did, probably because I looked like a depressed desperate.

It continued at student parties. At one party Paul – who had strawberry-blond hair and pale blue eyes and always wore pastel colours, so that he looked like a watercolour – was stretched out on the couch looking edible. Feeling game after a few beers I lay down next to him. 'I really like you, Paul.' I kissed his ear gently.

'Thanks, but I'd rather not.' He sat up. 'I don't think you like me as much as I like you.'

A few weekends later, after I had convinced him that I liked him, we fell into bed. Paul and I started going out, but it wasn't long before he complained that I wasn't affectionate enough and that I never wanted sex. I was finding our sex difficult. I would always come before Paul – I would try to help him but it was hard when all I wanted to do was sleep.

The more Paul complained, the more I backed off, until he angrily confronted me under the fig trees at NIDA. 'It's obvious that you have no commitment to this relationship and yet you don't have the guts to break it off. So I am going to.' He took a deep breath. 'I feel used.' Then he walked away. I felt like shit.

At a barbecue later in the year, to the sensual sounds of Grace Jones, I made eye contact with a guy from the year above, a beautiful blond named Brett. I had heard that he and his lover had recently broken up. I offered him a lift home. Sitting in the front seat he said he needed to piss, so we stopped at my place. I went into the kitchen and put the kettle on so that he might stick around.

When I opened the fridge he spotted a bottle of amyl. 'May I?'

'Sure.' He took a snort and handed me the bottle. My heart started to race, thumping away in my chest. 'You should feel my heart,' I said.

'You should feel this.' He pointed to his crutch. I asked him to stay. 'We should stay at my place,' he said, 'because Sam is calling me from Chicago first thing in the morning.'

'I thought you two had broken up.'

Brett seemed surprised. 'Who told you that?' I couldn't remember. Perhaps it was just wishful thinking.

When we were in his bedroom undressing I was so desperate to impress him that I lost my erection. 'It's all right, we don't have to do anything. Let's just go to sleep.' We curled up in the bed. It was then that I cracked a fat. I placed it on his thigh and we started to play. There was something about the sex that felt young, the sort of sex that I'd had as a schoolboy.

The next morning I had to leave early for rehearsal. I said goodbye to the blond angel in the bed, but I wanted to continue the contact. I wrote him notes and left messages on his machine. Absolute silence. It was confusing and painful. *Is it something I've done?* Eventually I confronted him at the end-of-term drinks. 'Just because we had sex doesn't mean you can treat me like shit. The way you've ignored me is hurtful.'

Brett was obviously uncomfortable. 'I'm sorry you're upset but I was looking for a one-night stand. I've already got a relationship.' At least I knew it wasn't about me.

Then I met Greg, an artist who had survived a severe head

injury. The doctors had replaced part of his skull with a metal plate which you could push in. We met at a party at his house in Melbourne during the Christmas break. As the last of the guests were being bid farewell at the front door, I started to follow them out. He took my hand, led me to his bedroom and began to undress me. There was something horny about his speed. I was in the hands of an expert.

Greg and I continued to see each other. He would take me to expensive restaurants and the theatre and then back to his place to romp. One night over dinner I said to him, 'Darling, you've chipped your front tooth.'

'I dropped them in the sink last night.' He pushed them out with his tongue, both sets. A shiver raced up my spine.

'I can't believe I've been going out with you for two weeks and I never knew.'

'Just wait till we get home and I'll give you a gum job.' Another shiver went up my spine.

We never got round to the gum job. He sat on my cock and I fucked him until we both came. Greg jumped off me, grabbed a towel to wipe the come and started rubbing my genitals furiously. I didn't realise what he was doing until I got home and saw my undies stained with shit. I felt a wave of disgust. Such a thing had never happened to me before and it revived my fears of anal sex as something dirty, practised only by unnatural dirty homos.

One day during that vacation Brenton Lewis came to lunch at my parents' house. He had recently left the Jesuits because he'd been assigned to look after dying priests. He believed this was punishment for having worked with a non-Catholic organisation – the Salvation Army – to set up a youth refuge.

He asked me how I was getting on. 'NIDA's been lots of fun but I seem to be having problems with relationships. I've had some fairly awful experiences.'

He asked if I'd like to come and chat during the week. When I saw him I talked about feeling inadequate, inexperienced and immature. I mentioned my fascination with the idea of saunas, how I felt tempted to go but frightened of doing so.

'While you haven't experienced it, it will have power over you.'

I decided I had to confront my fear. I rang a friend of mine who went to saunas quite a lot and asked him to accompany me. We put our clothes into lockers and wrapped small towels around our waist. My friend gave me a tour, then left me. I sat in the steam-room. Through the cloud of steam appeared a very muscular man. He sat next to me and rubbed his thigh against mine. I had an instant erection which he could see sticking out from under my towel. He followed me out of the steam-room and into a cubicle, where he grabbed me, kissed me and pushed my head down onto his cock. He said he wanted me to screw him. We lay on a squeaky vinyl bed and I lost my erection. He tried to turn me on by sucking me but it wasn't going to happen. Then he tried to screw me. I didn't really want him inside me, so my arse was shut tight. I had to work at relaxing so he wouldn't hurt me. There I was being fucked by a body-builder, having no erection and feeling like a semen receptacle.

After coming, he held me and said, 'There's nothing like being held in a man's arms after a hard day at work.' All I felt was the desire to get out of there.

'It felt so impersonal,' I explained to Brenton. 'I felt used. Another disaster.'

'It's obviously not what you're looking for. So what *do* you think you are looking for?'

I thought about his question. 'Someone to hold, to love and care for, and who loves me.'

'Have you ever been in love?' I nodded. 'With John?' I nodded. 'Do you still love him?'

I knew my answer instantly but was nervous about saying it. 'Yeah, I still love him.'

'So what's your problem?'

He was right. All the things I really wanted were there in John. Okay, maybe not wild sex but I hadn't been having great success with that anyway.

I rang John, told him I was going to see my Grandma in Adelaide and asked if he would like to come. He said he would and the next day we loaded up his car and headed off.

The drive was like a dream, listening to *Shabooh Shabah* by INXS under a hot glary sun, driving through the Coorong with its pink sand and pelicans and virtually not a car to be seen. John and I were relaxed, cracking funnies all the way and laughing. When he complained about the car not having airconditioning, I used my coffee cup to scoop air inside. John laughed hard, a laugh I hadn't heard for some time.

I told John what Brenton had said. 'I love you, John, and I would like to us to get back together, if you'll have me back.'

His answer was understated. 'Good.' But I could tell he was happy. I think it was during this drive that I really fell in love with John.

In Adelaide we stayed with a friend of John's from college named Roger. Roger had been at the beat on the River Torrens when Professor Duncan was allegedly bashed by cops and thrown into the river, where he drowned. The cops were acquitted but Roger said angrily, 'I know what I saw.'

Visiting Grandma was a little tense. Many years before, Dad had asked me not to tell her I was gay. 'It would kill her.' Now it saddened me to introduce the man I loved as a schoolmate. I wanted her blessing. However, she was so welcoming to John that I thought she might have picked up on the truth. When she died a year later, I regretted that my grandmother never really knew me.

We returned to Melbourne. I was due back at NIDA. John and I agreed that when we had both graduated we would try living together, but while we were apart we could have sex outside the relationship.

I took it a little further than that. When I was in third year I had a relationship with Harvey, a big boy who looked a bit like Matt Dillon. He knew about John but probably hoped I would leave John for him. We spent a weekend in a holiday house on the south coast, and on the Sunday morning I found myself avoiding his sexual advances.

'There's something I want to talk about.' I took a deep breath. 'I'm not really happy at the moment. I'm wondering whether it would be better for us to –'

'Break up?' Harvey flew into a rage. 'Get your things. We're going home.' It was the worst car trip of my life. Harvey refused to talk to me, refused to answer my questions; he just drove. It confirmed one of the reasons for my unhappiness. He was intense and quick to anger.

A couple of days later Harvey told me that he felt used, that I was merely amusing myself while I waited to get back with John. Deep down I felt he was probably right.

Those three years were also about a strange new disease. Gay cancer became GRID: Gay Related Immune Dysfunction. There was lots of speculation about its cause. Was it immune overload from all the sexually transmitted diseases gay men got? The use of recreational drugs like amyl nitrate? Or perhaps the enormous amounts of semen taken into the rectum were immunosuppressive?

Reading these theories I breathed a sigh of relief. Neither John nor I had participated much in any of them. We were not fast-lane gays.

As the disease became known as AIDS, the jokes started. 'What disease do the Village People have? Bandaids.'

Over our group of friends lay a pall of fear. Discussions would revolve around the latest theory or rumour. 'We're going to know people who will die from this.'

We'd all nod, sadly. 'Who do you reckon?'

'So-and-so is such a slut. He uses the beat every day.'

'A friend of mine saw Rock Hudson in a sauna in LA and he was lying on a bed with a towel over his head taking anyone who wanted him.'

'If Rock had a towel over his head how did your friend know who it was?'

My reaction was a mixture of repulsion and titillation.

The world was changing. The words 'anal sex' were starting to appear on the front pages of newspapers, and gay men's lives were combed thoroughly. There was a lot of hysteria. 'Mosquitoes Spread AIDS,' screamed one headline. 'Die Poofter, Die!' read another, quoting a father whose newborn triplets died after a blood transfusion traced to a gay man. AIDS and the fear of it were chipping away at us.

Having lunch with a woman in my class, I asked for a sip of her orange juice. She handed me the glass. I took a sip and handed it back to her. She suddenly looked tense. 'You can have it. I don't want any more.'

'Are you afraid that I might have AIDS?' She was. 'I don't think I do, but even if I did you can't get it from sharing a drink.'

'That's what they tell you. What about all those people who don't know how they got it?'

'If it was that easily spread, a lot more people would have it.'

I didn't feel like a leper but I was concerned for her, living in such a frightened world.

PART THREE

Soft Targets

Chapter *SEVEN*

Tested

John was already working as a chiropractor when I graduated from NIDA. We wanted to be together, and since my agent and professional contacts were all in Sydney he agreed to move up from Melbourne, excited by the prospect of starting his own practice. His parents discouraged the move.

'Dad's worried I might get AIDS,' he told me.

'What, gay means AIDS?'

'For Dad I guess it does.'

I wondered whether the prospect of moving away from his parents had helped him make his decision.

We decided to share with Franco and found a cute little old shop with weird angles, wooden floors and salmon-pink walls. I had moved house many times over the past three years and had learnt persistence. John found it harder than me. His legs were aching by the end of the day. 'I don't understand it. They feel burnt out, like I've been for a very long run.' He said he had noticed this before, when he was climbing hills. I suggested he see a doctor. 'They'd only give me painkillers. I should get my spine looked at.'

I was watching Rock Hudson and Doris Day in *Pillow Talk* when Franco arrived home. 'Great film.' He went to make tea, then put his head around the kitchen door. 'There was a doco on the radio last night. I taped it. The first half is about the gay community's response to AIDS and the second is interviews with people with AIDS. It's very moving.'

I put it on. The first part described a demonstration in San Francisco and then eavesdropped on the Gay Men's Health Crisis phone-line. 'Safe sex doesn't have to be boring, you just gotta use your imagination. Honey, I'd rather be telling you this now than giving you the name of a doctor in two years. I know it's hard but you just gotta hang in there.'

The second part crept up on me and wrapped its hands around my throat. There was a woman talking about her home-care client. 'When I first met Patrick, I was a little shocked. He was so thin but his spirit was extraordinary. Here was a guy who could barely breathe, cracking jokes. Laughing makes it a lot easier. Our friendship has been wonderful, but now that he's really sick again . . .' She started to choke back the tears and took a deep breath. 'It's a disaster. If this had been five hundred schoolkids, things would have been very different. You wonder sometimes if anyone cares.'

There was a nun whose patient had sat up in bed and said, That's all, Sister, I think I'll go now, and died. 'It was the happiest death I have ever seen.'

And there was a man who had had to seal his lover's body in two plastic bags. 'Dignity in death? Ha fucking ha!'

I was stunned by what these people had been put through. These were real people with lovers, family and friends. Why wasn't the media dealing with these stories, rather than all that sex-death-horror shit? I started to wonder what I could do. Maybe I should get a group of actors together and devise a piece. I was listening to This Mortal Coil and when 'The Siren's Song' came on I saw a stage with a mother holding her dying son. 'Swim to me, swim to me. Let me enfold you.'

The next Monday night at the Griffin Theatre in Darlinghurst I approached the gay actors I knew and told them my idea. Monday nights were members' meetings, when the space was full of actors drinking beer, exchanging gossip and trying to talk to directors. I got an enthusiastic reception, particularly from one guy, whom I will call Paul One, who had already lost friends. We wanted to reclaim an issue that had been hijacked by the media.

The following week we presented the idea and called a meeting in the theatre. As you would expect, every try-hard actor saw an opportunity to get into a play. I told them that it was great to see so much interest, but that we couldn't use them all. The project was more important than any individual. Paul outlined the workshop we were planning. One of the guys had access to a hall and we decided to meet there in a couple of days.

The hall was in East Sydney High, a school for difficult students. Many of the kids were sex workers and junkies. It had parquet floors and large windows that overlooked William Street. We broke into groups and wrote on large pieces of butcher's paper all the things we'd heard about AIDS. There was silence as we worked, kneeling over the paper. It was like a ritual. I then got each group to improvise something around the ideas they came up with.

While they were working a beautiful man came into the room, a Renaissance angel, strongly built, with red curly hair. I found out that Paul Two worked as a doctor at the Albion Street AIDS clinic but was interested in being an actor. He had heard about the project from his lover and wanted to be involved.

He sat with me and watched the improvisations: AIDS as an octopus, a plague, a whirlpool. Paul Two was not comfortable. 'This doesn't feel real. I could get some people to talk to you. There are some amazing stories.'

I was taken aback. A total stranger had walked in and changed everything. I knew he was right but I felt territorial.

'I'd better put it to the group.' Over cappuccinos we decided we would use only real stories. The two Pauls would organise some interviews. We left the café on a high, feeling that we'd come up with a good idea and that we might be able to make a difference.

Around this time I saw a South African general talking on the news about the Namibian border war. He referred to civilians as soft targets. I was appalled at his inability to see that those targets were people. It struck me that we could use this as a title. I put it to the group. Someone said it sounded like an anus. I snapped back, 'Would you prefer *Fuck Me Dead*?'

'You are off, Conigrave,' someone said. That's me, the one who says the things you're not meant to say.

The group talked about the title for a while and agreed that it was a good reference to the siege mentality in the gay community, the way we were all banding together like people in a war. We decided to go with it as a working title.

Later that night my head was filled with AIDS, young people dying in pain. *My relationship with John is not forever. Either we break up or one of us dies.* There was no relief from this thought.

Paul One's flatmate Richard was sick. Paul thought it would be good to interview him but didn't want to do it himself. I said I would.

When I arrived at the house with my tape-recorder, Paul let me in. I suddenly felt wary. *Is it safe to breathe? Paul's been living with him, sharing cups and toilet seats, and he's all right.* My fear heightened when I was taken up to Richard's room. He was half asleep. There was nothing to indicate he was a person with AIDS other than the large jar of liquid morphine beside his bed.

Paul introduced us and left us alone. Richard held out his hand. I shook it but wanted to wipe my hand on my jeans. I sat down on the edge of the mattress. The sheets were clammy. *He must be having night sweats.* Often when I asked a question he would collapse into coughing fits that doubled him up. I held my breath.

As we talked I calmed down. 'What's the morphine for?'

'For headaches that nothing else touches. It also helps with the cough.'

'You must have good parties.'

'Oh p-*lease*. It's not a party drug, it's hideous. It tastes revolting and it cuts you out of the world.'

Richard described a recurring dream. 'My boat has broken down in the Amazon but everyone else gets a nice little boat ride. I have to walk through this jungle with snakes and spiders and quicksand. When I fall into it someone pulls me out but I always sink back in. People drop supplies from a helicopter but it can't land. I'm angry and lonely. But I learn a lot. I see a leopard having a baby. Everyone has seen a leopard in a book but the actual experience is something else.'

I posed the question we had decided to ask all the people we interviewed. 'Is there a message about living with AIDS that you want the world to know?'

'That it's hard, bloody hard.' He looked so vulnerable. I rubbed his knee gently.

I left wondering if I'd ever see him again. A couple of weeks later when I was having coffee with Paul, Richard walked through the room in a sari, carrying a lit candle. He didn't acknowledge us. 'He's been a bit weird of late. Probably dementia.'

Franco asked me how the interview had gone. I admitted I had been afraid of contagion.

'Afraid of getting AIDS?'

'Well, maybe a little but also the other things he has. He was coughing violently. I feel bad because I judged him.'

'Why don't you get tested before the next interview? You're making assumptions about your own status that may be incorrect.'

I sat thinking about what Franco had said. *Imagine what it would be like to be told I had it. Franco and I had anal sex only six months ago and he is negative. And Paul from my year at NIDA is also negative. But there was that guy in the sauna . . .*

When John arrived home, I told him about Richard and what Franco had said. He too had been thinking about getting tested, for his own peace of mind. 'There was that boy Darrin I was seeing a couple of years ago. He gave me warts and who knows what else.'

John and I sat in the foyer of the Albion Street clinic, fascinated by the passing traffic: a couple from the cardigan set, two young queens laughing hysterically at something in *Vogue,* a moustached man wearing a leather vest. *Reckon he'd be at risk.* Every time the front door opened, I'd hope to God I wouldn't see anyone I knew.

'John 2118,' called a short, bearded gnome of a doctor. John bounced up to follow him. Being left by myself was even more unnerving.

Someone came out with a grin on his face. 'I'm okay,' he announced. *That'll be me in two weeks.* Eventually John emerged. He'd been asked questions, drilled about safe sex, given a physical and a blood test. My number was called. I didn't bounce out of my seat like John.

The almond smell of disinfectant hung in the air of the consulting room. I asked for an AIDS test. The doctor, who introduced himself as Ralph, asked if I was in a high-risk group and I told him I was gay.

The questions began. How do you define your sexuality: homosexual, bisexual, transsexual? How many men have you slept with in the last six months? How many women? Have you paid for sex in the last six months? Are you in a relationship? Would you say it was monogamous? *I wonder what John said to that? Probably not the same as me.* Do you practise anal sex? Are you active or passive? If both, what ratio? Then he looked in my mouth, my eyes, felt the glands in my neck, in my armpits (which I hated) and in my groin.

'How do you think you'd feel if in two weeks I told you you're positive?'

'I'm involved in a theatre project about AIDS, so I know it's not a death sentence.'

'I think you may be positive. Your glands are up all over your body. I'll take some blood now.'

I would have thought I'd be shocked, but weirdly I felt whole. I broke the news to John. 'It's probably the flu,' he said. 'Mine weren't up.' After that I didn't pay much attention to the possibility that I might be positive. I knew I wouldn't be. As John and I headed to Oxford Street for lunch, I walked proudly through the flocks of gay men. *Look at me. I'm a fast-lane gay.*

I'd been cast in the Australian touring production of *Brighton Beach Memoirs*, a comedy by Neil Simon about his adolescence. I had the part of Stanley, the hero's sixteen-year-old brother, and I was rapt. I felt uncomfortable about asking for time off to get my results. I told the stage manager that I had a specialist's appointment that I'd waited months to get. She checked with the director and he released me.

Sitting again in the clinic foyer, I glanced at a beer-bellied guy in stubbies and T-shirt who looked like he'd just stepped off a construction site. *I wonder what he's doing here?*

John was called in by a tall blond man. I sat reading an issue of *Campaign* but found it impossible to concentrate. Paul Two appeared and we waved to each other. *He must often see people he knows here.* He called in another patient and off they went.

Eventually John came out with a little smile on his face. 'Negative,' he said softly, and then grinned like a madman. *I must be okay.* I breathed a sigh of relief, put my arm around him and hugged him. Then Ralph beckoned to me.

I sat beside his desk. 'I'm sorry to inform you that you are positive.'

I felt like I'd been stabbed. 'Shit, you're kidding!' Ralph held my file up to my face: 2117, positive.

'It's not that I don't believe you, but my boyfriend is negative.'

Ralph excused himself and left the room. A minute later he returned with John's file and the man who had given John his results. 'Could you wait in the corridor, please?' Ralph said to me.

John came and sat with me. I told him I was positive. His brow furrowed. We heard Ralph tearing strips off the other man. *This doesn't sound good.* They called us back in together.

Ralph took a deep breath. 'I'm sorry, John, you've been given the wrong result. You are in fact positive.' *No! Not my John.* John's breathing quickened.

'I should explain. If your result is negative you see a counsellor, and if you are positive you see a doctor. The clerk put your file in the wrong pigeon-hole and the counsellor gave you the result without checking it.'

He took some more blood from each of us to do a cell-count. 'I'm really sorry about what's happened. I'd like to see you both in a few days.'

John and I went home, told Franco, and then went upstairs to lie down. Some people use drugs to blot out the world. I use sleep.

A little while later, Franco appeared with a tray. 'I thought you might like a cup of tea and some chocolate slices.'

'You're so sweet.'

'It's nothing. I feel terrible for you guys. If there's anything I can do, just ask. I'll let you get some sleep.' He kissed us both and left the room, pulling the door to. Every now and then I'd wake up hoping it was a bad dream, but then the gut-wrenching feeling would come. It was true. It was as though I had ants all over me and I was brushing them off but they kept coming back.

The next day at rehearsal the stage manager asked how I'd gone with the specialist.

'I've only got six months to live.'

She chuckled and walked back to her desk. What I really wanted to say was, 'Hug me.'

John and I had separate appointments to get the next results. I went by cab during my lunch break.

'You have a very high T8 count, the suppressor cells, which we believe indicates that you've only recently been infected. All your other cells are good, basically normal. Your T4 cell-count is 650. The normal range is 500 to 1100. T4s are the cells that the virus destroys and they're the ones that we monitor. You've been exposed to toxoplasmosis, which is a parasite carried by cats, and you may end up developing the disease if and when your immune system drops.'

'What does it do to you?'

'Sometimes it forms cysts in the brain, putting pressure on the lobes.'

'Glamorous.'

'The good news is you haven't been exposed to CMV, which is a virus that can make you go blind. You're very lucky. Most gay men have been. I want you to maximise your potential. Eat well, don't do too many drugs, exercise and get enough sleep. You're lucky. You're starting at a good place.'

John and I had decided to be careful who we told. I knew actors were huge gossips and the industry was not known for its acceptance of gay actors, let alone infected poofters. Foolishly, however, we'd told many people that we were getting tested and so there was lots of curiosity.

Paul from NIDA was in our kitchen and saw an HIV pamphlet stuck to the fridge. 'How did your test go? Negative, I bet.' I shook my head.

'Positive? You and John?'

I nodded.

'Unbelievable. I thought you guys would be the last ones to get it. How are you both?'

'John doesn't tend to talk about these things, but I think he feels he's failed. And I don't think it's hit me yet.'

Paul wanted to cheer me up. 'Trust you to be first.'

'The price of being a fashion leader, darling.'

Later that day the phone went. 'It's Veronica. Why haven't you rung me? I've been beside myself with worry.' *I can't tell her over the phone.*

'I'm fine. We're both fine.' *It's not a lie, we are fine at the moment.*

Veronica started to cry. 'I don't know what I'd have done if you told me you were positive. I couldn't stand it. I'm sorry.' *How am I ever going to tell her to her face?*

'Don't be sorry. It's nice that you care.' I got off the phone, shell-shocked, wanting John to hurry home so I could offload what had just happened.

That night we sat on our bed. 'Do you think I infected you?' pondered John. I was stunned, wondering where that thought had come from. 'The way our cells are, me being more advanced, you with your high T8s . . .'

'It's not important.'

'I just wish I hadn't infected you.'

'We don't know if that is what happened. We can never know. Don't blame yourself. We didn't know that such a thing was lurking. It didn't even have a name. We're both infected. That's all we can know. Come on, worry-wart.' I pulled him down onto the bed and took his T-shirt off, kissed him, and pulled his trackies down so he was lying in his jocks. Then I leapt off the bed. I had a surprise. 'Condoms and lube!'

'I don't want to have anal sex. That's how we got into this mess.' John's jaw was clenched.

I was taken aback. For me anal sex had an emotional dimension that other forms of sex lacked. But I didn't feel like challenging John, and I no longer felt like sex.

'Find a place that's comfortable for you, either lying down or sitting.'

I was at a meditation class at the clinic. Running it was Petrea, a gentle woman with rosy cheeks and a calming voice. People said she had had leukaemia and had cured herself by meditating in a cave in France for eighteen hours a day.

I was a little nervous about meeting other HIV-positive people. One guy's face was covered in the purple lesions of Kaposi's sarcoma and another was so thin he looked like he might snap in half if you sneezed on him. I tried hard not to stare, but I was so curious.

'Devote this next little while to getting in touch with and nurturing yourself, creating an environment for healing within your body. Visualise an elevator with five levels. With each level you descend, you feel more and more relaxed.' *Is someone snoring?*

'Begin to descend. Five . . . letting go of all outside sounds except the sound of my voice.' *With that racket going on? You've got to be kidding.*

'Four . . . allowing all tension in your body to drain away into the floor. Three . . . leaving all thoughts of the past and the future. Two . . . breathing quietly to your own rhythm. One . . . letting go and becoming more and more relaxed until you are completely relaxed.

'Stepping out of the elevator you find yourself on a beautiful golden sandy beach, stretching in both directions, a soft curve where the sand meets the sea. The water is shimmering. As you glance to the right, you see a hot-air balloon tethered to the ground. Its canopy has the full colours of the rainbow. Place into the basket any feelings that make you uncomfortable or create tension in your life: fear, anger, guilt, resentment.' *My God! Another snorer. I'd like to put them both in the basket.*

'Loosen the rope that secures the basket to earth. See it leave the ground. *It's like a zoo in here.* 'As it moves away from you, feel the sense of lightness, the sense of release, knowing you no longer need those thoughts and emotions. Watch them drift away from you till the earth becomes a speck in the distance, finally disappearing from view.'

We went on to fill our bodies with sparkles of energy from the sun. 'When a sparkle bumps into a healthy cell it bursts open, filling the cell with new vitality. And when diseased cells come in contact . . .'

I started to drift off. I could hear her voice but could no longer make sense of it. When the teacher stopped guiding us, my leg jolted and I realised that I too had been asleep. I felt the need to pretend that I hadn't. It was like being caught smoking at school.

After meditation came a support session where each person got to talk. The skinny guy told how tiring his diarrhoea was. He felt like an invalid because he now wore nappies in case of accidents. Someone else was waiting for a biopsy result. 'The doctors think it might be lymphoma.' His voice quivered. The teacher allowed him to sit in his pain. It was hard because I wanted to hug him and comfort him. I felt sorry for the sicker guys in the group but another part of me was thinking, I'm never going to let this happen to me.

I walked to the station with a guy who told me he'd started an anti-candida diet. A naturopath on the North Shore was getting some results with people with AIDS. You got rid of all moulds and funguses in your diet. This guy had been on it for three weeks and said he felt heaps better.

Over the next couple of weeks, John and I decided to take it on. We cleared the cupboards and refilled them with almond butter, yeast-free bread and acidophilus yoghurt. We bought a book of recipes and our life became plainer. I would have killed for a Pollywaffle.

My doctor Ralph was unimpressed. 'I don't think it's going to do much. It might cut down the candida but it won't do anything for your immune system. And people usually lose weight on it, which is not good. If you can maintain your weight I'll be happy.' *Bloody doctors! They never acknowledge anything alternative.*

The workshops for *Soft Targets* were encouraging, the actors enthusiastic. Scenes had been rolling in thick and fast. There was a father talking to his young sons. There was the story of a woman arriving from Cootamundra because her son was sick. She'd had little contact with him since he moved to Sydney. She didn't know he was gay, nor that he had AIDS. She had to come to terms with the fact that he was dying, and that she had to share him with his lover.

We started to play with placement, trying to get the maximum impact from the juxtapositions. We then ran the scenes for ourselves, and in the discussion afterwards the cast was bubbling as I gave notes.

Our next step was to present it to the Griffin Theatre members. The cast assembled in the theatre, some jittery but all full of expectation. I gave them a special warm-up to focus their energy. 'A go-go class. Could everyone get into a circle? One at a time we'll do a step to the music and the rest of us copy that.'

I put on 'Blister In The Sun' by the Violent Femmes. The group was hesitant at first, but then began to enjoy it, laughing at each other, blushing. It bonded us. Then followed one of those wonderful performances where the audience was totally attentive. It was a ritual broken by laughter and sniffles.

At the end of the reading, Penny Cook, chairperson of the board, leapt to her feet and others followed. As we celebrated in the foyer afterwards, Penny kept saying, 'We've got to do it next year.'

The feeling that comes from acceptance of your work is the best drug I know. I was feeling exhilarated, loved, whole.

Peter Kingston, the artistic director of the company, had been away on the night of the performance. We met among the black leather jackets at the Tropicana Café. Peter was spinning the ashtray as we talked. 'I've read the play and I think it's really good, but it definitely needs work.'

I suggested we apply for development money. He said we had missed the deadlines of the major funding bodies, and he felt the piece was so important we should get it on as quickly as we could.

'We could try getting money from an AIDS organisation.'

'Worth a try.' Peter took a deep breath. 'Now, are you wanting to direct this?'

'I'd like to.'

'I'm not sure you have enough experience. Let's see how things work out.'

The Bobby Goldsmith Foundation, an AIDS charity, sponsored a workshop on the understanding that they would get any future royalties. Meantime, there was some discussion about when the piece should be done. The Mardi Gras festival was to happen early in the new year and the group seemed keen on being part of it. It suddenly dawned on me that I wouldn't be available to direct it as I would be on tour with *Brighton Beach Memoirs*. I think I wanted the group to postpone the project till my return.

The group voted unanimously to try to get it on during Mardi Gras. I felt like someone had ripped my baby from my arms. I was hurt by the lack of recognition of my part in getting the piece together.

The workshop was held at the Juanita Nielsen Community Centre in Woolloomooloo, a sun-drenched building full of local kids. Paul One and I came to loggerheads. His character spoke in monologue. I thought he should dramatise the story.

'Tim, it works,' said one of the women. 'You get to see the charm and sense of humour of the guy.' I pointed out that I had other ideas about the piece.

'We've moved on.' Paul was getting angry. 'You're not the only person who wants to do a piece about AIDS.'

My blood was boiling. The baby that had been ripped from my arms now had a boot against its head. I wanted to get out of there. At the break I asked to speak to Peter. We went for a walk through Woolloomooloo.

'I want to leave the project. I'm finding it hard doing the show at night and the workshop during the day, and I guess the other thing I should tell you . . .' I took a breath. 'John and I have just found out that we're positive.' I wanted Peter to know that I wasn't just wimping out. 'The stress I'm feeling won't help my health. But I'd rather that the others didn't know. If you need to talk to someone you can talk to James Bean. He knows.' I walked away feeling like a soldier walking out of a blown-up building.

Later that night James rang me and told me that Peter was upset. James had said to him, 'This is why we are doing the play.'

'Your performance is really good,' said Veronica. *Brighton Beach Memoirs* was about to leave for Perth and we were sitting over a farewell cappuccino. 'That scene where you tell your mother you've gambled away your wages is the best work you've done.'

'I always thought my best work was playing Icee Bear at shopping malls.'

'You didn't! In a bear suit?'

'The kids used to grab my balls to see if I was a boy bear or a girl bear. Ms Icee wore a tight red T-shirt and the kids would grab her tits.' Veronica laughed loudly. 'The advantage of wearing a large fibreglass head was that I could bring it down on their heads and give them a good whack.'

'Do you still want to have kids?' Veronica and I had talked about having kids together, living in two semi-detached houses – she and her girlfriend in one and John and I in the other. We talked about using a turkey baster to get her pregnant. 'You never mention it anymore.' *I guess now is as good a time as any.*

'I don't know how to say this. Guess I just spit it out.' She fixed me with her gaze. 'John and I are HIV-positive.'

'You told me you were all right!'

'I did and we are. I didn't want to tell you over the phone. I wanted to be there. Sorry.'

She asked all kinds of questions until she started to cry

quietly. She put her head in her hands and let go. I rubbed her back. 'It's so unfair. You guys are some of the most beautiful people I know.'

Away From Home

Perth is a young city full of suntanned, sun-bleached teenagers, and architecture no more than ten years old. On tour there I felt on top of the world. I was working, had some money in my pocket and lots of time to enjoy the sunny weather.

After the opening night's performance there were drinks in the upstairs bar at His Majesty's Theatre. Over a plate of sandwiches I caught the eye of a boy smiling impishly at me from under his fringe. He'd liked the play and complimented me on my performance. He introduced himself as Nordin. 'A shortened version of Nor-el-din. My mother lived in Morocco for a while.' He was fixing me with that smile and I started to feel he was flirting with me.

A few nights later I went dancing at a gay bar called Connections with another boy I'd met at the gym, but he disappeared with the love of his life. As I drained my beer someone blew in my ear. I turned to see Nordin. I told him what had just happened. His response: 'Better for me.'

I was surprised. I couldn't believe I was getting this sort of attention from beautiful boys. We caught a cab to my place. Nordin had his hand on my leg. I was finding his forwardness a little disconcerting. *Is there something he wants?*

I took him out on the balcony among the mozzie coils. I was nervous. *Am I any good in bed? Is my body attractive? Should I tell him my status?* We did the 'getting to know you' stuff. He was born in France, came to Australia at five, and was studying physics at uni. I excused myself to go to the toilet. I looked in the mirror and tried to work out how to tell him about my status. When I came back I couldn't see him on the balcony. He was inside on the bed, where he asked me to join him.

My heart was beating fast. 'There's something I feel I should tell you. I'm HIV-positive.'

'Doesn't mean we can't have sex. Come here.' I lay next to him and he kissed me gently. 'You are so cute.'

'So are you.' He moved his mouth to my earlobe, biting it gently and making me goose-bumpy. Our clothes came off and we lay naked against each other, playing swords with our hard-ons. His body was suntanned and hairless. We licked each other, rubbed against each other, he sat on my back and massaged my shoulders. We then pulled each other off and as I came he twisted my nipple, increasing the intensity of my orgasm. Nordin grabbed the tissues and wiped the come off very quickly. *Is he afraid? I went down on him but he didn't go down on me. Still, it was good.*

The next couple of weeks were like a shipboard romance. We went out to bars as a couple, holding hands, dancing together, and standing with our arms around each other. He kept telling me how cute I was, and what a good actor. It was nice to hear.

The night I left Perth, he came to the airport. We talked about how good it had been and how much we were going to miss each other. He even talked of coming over to Sydney later that year. Saying goodbye was difficult. I didn't want to let go of him and when I boarded the plane I felt sad, really sad.

Our next touring date was my home town, Melbourne. The red-eye arrived at six-thirty in the morning. Standing at the exit gate was John, bleary eyed and suppressing a yawn. His face lit up. 'Timber!' he called. *A new nickname?* 'Hi, darling.' He rubbed my arms. 'Neggsie asked us over for breakfast, but it's a bit early to go round there. We could have coffee here.' Neggsie was a friend from student theatre.

We sat at a table. 'Did you meet anyone nice?' I smirked and raised my eyebrows. John sat stunned. 'I didn't mean like that. What are you saying?'

I wanted to share my joy, to say, 'John, he was so pretty,

a French boy with an amazing smile, and we had great sex. He made me feel good.' But I didn't. 'I'm sorry, I thought our agreement was that when we're apart we could sleep with other people.'

He gasped. Tears rolled down his face. 'I thought with this AIDS stuff that would have stopped.' He stared out the window as if he couldn't bear to look at me. He didn't say much after that. It was like when Dad was angry with me as a boy – I never knew why he wouldn't answer my questions and it made me feel bad. That's how I felt now.

Back at Neggsie's John sat next to me on the couch with his hand on my leg. *He's obviously not too upset. I hope he's forgiven me.* Neggsie headed off to work, telling us to make ourselves at home. I felt pooped and wanted to go and lie down.

'I'll come too.'

We stripped down and got under the sheet. John rolled on top of me and started kissing me intensely, reclaiming what was his. The sex was disconnected and mechanical. I started twisting his nipple. 'Ow! What are you doing?'

'Don't you think it feels good?'

'Where did you learn that? From your friend in Perth?' He shook his head and rolled over, turning away from me. *I guess I deserve this.*

A couple of weeks later I was missing the attention that Nordin had given me. I had received a letter from him that started 'Hello, spunk' and said how much he missed me. John and I were having dinner in an Italian café in Carlton. I asked him if he loved me. 'You know I do.'

'Why don't you ever tell me?'

'Words are cheap. Can't you see I love you?'

'It would be nice to hear it now and then.' I hesitated. 'I don't know if I want to be with you if you can't tell me.'

'Oh, Tim, you're a dag. I love you.'

It wasn't quite what I wanted, but neither was creating more of a fuss. I dropped it.

This year John's family had returned early from the Christmas break at their Mornington Peninsula beach-house; the weather hadn't been very good. So John and I went down to the white weatherboard cottage stumped in sandy soil, surrounded by ti-tree and couch grass.

For some time I had been asking to see photos of John as a little boy, and now he brought out his family's projector and boxes of slides. He got out a large block of chocolate and a bottle of Fanta. He closed the curtains.

The first couple of boxes were of Christmas Island. We saw the Navy radar installation where John's father worked, and a barbecue for all the ex-pats, with John's mother Lois looking very stylish in her beehive hairdo, floral tank-top and shorts.

Then John as a little boy. Standing in a golf hat and a short-sleeved shirt buttoned to the neck, about to take a putt with his child-size golf club. With his brothers and their Christmas toys, proudly showing his boat. Playing footy in the backyard. And the cutest one, him in his red jumper and black shorts holding up his first communion medal.

I loved this man and I think I would have loved him as a boy. I felt cheated of the chance to see him growing up. The closest I could get was to take copies of the slides.

I stood in the wings at the Comedy Theatre on opening night, waiting to make my second-act entrance where I tell my mother that I've gambled away my wages. Mum and Dad were in the audience. I was slightly nervous as this was my first big role and I wanted them to be proud of me, to see that I was a good actor.

I started the breathing rhythm that suggested I was choking back tears. Then I heard my cue, braced myself and ran on. I told my brother that I'd lost my wages in a poker game and made him swear that he wouldn't let on. Then I went up to our bedroom. My mother knocked on the door and came in.

'Stanley, can I have five dollars for Aunt Blanche?'

'I haven't got it.'

'Didn't you get paid today?'

'Yes, but I don't have the money.' But suddenly the tears were real. The shame that Stanley felt was my own feeling. *How am I ever going to tell Mum and Dad that I am positive, that John and I are positive? I have failed them.*

On Our Own

Soft Targets was still playing when I got back to Sydney. I'd heard good things about the production from friends, and their comments were confirmed when I saw it. Peter Kingston had taken a simple idea and found resonances in it.

The play opened with two cleaners in space suits vacuuming the set. Instantly we knew we were seeing a piece about contagion and fear.

A home-help worker talked about seeing his first client. 'There was hardly anything to him. He was in and out of a coma. I saw this photo behind a vase and realised that I knew the person in the bed. I hadn't seen him for a year.' A picture of Rock Hudson came up on a screen.

The character from Cootamundra was given a sponge bath by his boyfriend. No words were exchanged but plenty was going on. When the mother entered, watched for a moment and then left without saying a word, I started to sob. There were others crying but the audience was disappointingly small. Perhaps people were afraid of what they were going to see.

The cast were glad to see me afterwards. They came over to hug me. All the smiling faces made me feel I had returned to the fold.

John and I finally made the big move into a flat of our own.

I had found an old thirties place in Rose Bay with an unusual design, a hallway like a dog's leg which was initially confusing but made the space seem bigger. I tried to explain it over the phone. 'I trust your judgement,' John said. I put in the application, leaning heavily on John's professional status as a chiropractor.

On Saturday morning I took him over to see it. He seemed to like it, particularly the balcony and the wooden toilet seat. We went off to the agent and signed the lease.

Living on our own was a fabulous thing. John and I knew each other's rhythms and so there were none of the old problems of timing. 'We're going to bed now, could you turn the music off please?' Or personal politics. Franco watching a news item on migrant health: 'That is so racist!' Me: 'Why's that racist?' Franco: 'I'm sick of you challenging me. I don't expect to be challenged in my own house.' There was an incredible freedom in being together by ourselves. We could walk around the house naked, or take a crap with the toilet door open. We could eat whatever we wanted without the pettiness of wondering, Who ate my yoghurt? We could run around like two-year-olds, talking baby talk.

In setting up our house, John was obsessive about making sure we had everything, hunting the best can opener or garlic crusher, traipsing through Bondi Junction armed with a sales catalogue as we looked for a juicer. And because he earned more than me (I was selling towels over the phone for the Guide Dog Association), he often paid for things, and never grudgingly.

At the Albion Street clinic I talked to my counsellor Mark, a big teddy bear, about the affair in Perth. Nordin had made me feel so good, telling me how much he liked me. 'I wish John would tell me he loved me.'

'Have you discussed it with him?' I said I had. 'And what does he say?'

' "Words are cheap. Can't you see I love you?" I told him it'd be nice to hear it now and then.'

Mark smiled. 'It's a classic case of different communication systems. You use lots of auditory words. "Tell me. Nice to hear it." John says, "Can't you see?" He processes things differently. No doubt he shows you he loves you. Maybe all you need to do is look around and see what kinds of things he does.'

On the way home I thought about what Mark had said, and slowly the things that John did came into my head. *The way his hand brushes mine as we are walking, his little finger hooks mine, our secretive version of holding hands. The smile that breaks out on his face when he sees me. His pet names for me: Conabear, honeybear, Timber, and the new one, Tim Salad, short for Tim Salad Bim. And my favourite, him playing with my hair while my head is in his lap as we watch television.* I was warmed by these memories and realised that I only had to look around to see that he indeed loved me.

His birthday was on the horizon and I thought I could show him that I loved him. I made a card. The front of a strangely shaped piece of cardboard read, 'Excuse me, are you the boy with the cutest ears on the block?' It opened to reveal a pop-up heart with wings flying amongst the clouds. 'Then this is for you. Happy twenty-sixth, I love you.'

When I gave it to John he seemed touched. 'It's beautiful, thank you. I'll put it on my desk.' He sat it up on one corner. That's how he showed me he loved me.

Nicholas, an actor in *Soft Targets*, had told me that he was a volunteer at the AIDS Hotline and that it was good fun. I wanted to do something about the disease, something active rather than just wallowing in self-pity. He told me how to apply.

I was trained by a gentle older man, a heavy smoker named Edward. 'We don't counsel people. If they need to speak to a counsellor we put them through to the appointments desk.' He then gave me a pile of stuff to read. He took some calls with me listening in and eventually I took my first call.

A man wanted to know the symptoms of AIDS. 'Do you have any reason to believe you've been exposed to the virus?' I asked. He'd had a girl who was 'a bit of a slag'. 'Do you mean she was a prostitute? Did you use a condom?' He didn't trust condoms. 'Did you penetrate her? If so, there is a possibility that you've exposed yourself.' He asked for a test. I transferred him to the appointments desk.

Edward debriefed me. 'That was very good. You left out one thing. They have to wait three months after exposure before they can test. I liked you saying he'd exposed himself. You made him sound like a flasher.'

I enjoyed working there. It was a safe place to be openly gay and openly HIV-positive and there were lots of laughs. In the phone-calls you'd hear about a side of life that very few got to. The Grim Reaper commercials, above all the image of the little girl bowled over at random, her doll flying into the air, brought a lot of sexual guilt out of the closet.

'Does it matter how much semen?'

'It's more important what happens to it, whether it gets into your bloodstream through cuts or through unprotected sex.'

A young woman with a Greek accent, quite distressed, rang. 'My doctor has just told me I'm antibody-positive to measles. Does this mean I have AIDS?'

'No, it means you have measles, or you have had it in the past, and your body has made antibodies to the virus that causes it.' I could hear friends in the background priming her with questions.

'What are the symptoms of AIDS?'

'We don't like to give them out. Most of them are similar to cold symptoms. We don't want you to panic when it could be just a flu. If you are worried, you could come in for a test.'

'Oh no! What if I saw someone I knew?'

An adolescent boy: 'Me and my mates got into a punch-up and I got some blood on me.'

'Do you have any reason to believe the blood was infected?'

'She was a hooker, one of those boy/girl ones.'

'Did you have any open wounds?'

'She scratched my face.'

'There may be some risk, then. Perhaps you should come in for a test, but you'll have to wait three months.'

'Three months? If I'm infected she's dead.'

I hung up and growled. 'Boy bashes a tranny and he's concerned about getting HIV. I should have told him he definitely had it.'

Nicholas was on the next phone and shushed me. Edward called me over to his desk. 'It's hard when you get a call like that, but you can't say that sort of thing. We don't judge people.'

I went home, full of rage, to bad news. A while back Karl, my film-maker friend, had fallen in love in a way I'd never seen before, with a guy called Marcus. They started a teddy bear collection that grew until their bedroom walls were lined with fuzzy bears. When they went out to the clubs Marcus would wear a leather harness and a dog collar with a leash, but it was actually Marcus who led Karl. Then Marcus had fallen ill with meningitis and I had wondered at the time whether he had AIDS. He was put in Melbourne's Fairfield Hospital, where the AIDS wards were. Karl rang me one night to say he was deteriorating. 'He's gone blind. The meningitis has chewed out that part of his brain. Poor Booboo is so scared.'

Now John greeted me with the news that Marcus had died. The thought hung in the air like an orb. *Marcus is dead. Not here anymore*. I struggled to get my head around it.

I tried to ring Karl but he was engaged for the next hour. Finally I got through. 'Have you had a chance to cry?'

'I think I'm still in shock.' He paused. 'I should tell you

Marcus had AIDS. But he didn't want anyone to know.' *How am I going to tell Karl about me and John? Not now. He has enough on his plate.*

A few weeks later he came up to visit us. I got home from work to find him there with John. He hugged me, the kind of hug you give when you say goodbye to someone you won't be seeing for a long time. 'John told me about you guys being positive. I wish it wasn't true. You guys helped me come out. I remember you dancing together at my twenty-first like you didn't care what anyone thought. It showed me I could be gay and not ashamed of it.'

We walked down to the harbour. 'It's funny that neither of us told the other what was happening,' I said.

'It's good that you guys have been working hard at staying well. Marcus didn't do any of that. I don't think we realised what we were dealing with. I believed that all we needed was a positive attitude, and everything would turn out right. What a way to find out we were wrong.'

We reached a seat that looked out over the harbour. Beyond the bay a yacht race looked like a flock of pelicans. 'These are strange times,' I pondered. 'Who would have thought when we were involved in Young Gays that this is where we'd end up.' The idea sat heavily on us. I asked about Marcus's estate.

'He didn't have anything except his clothes. I gave them to the Brotherhood.'

In my best old-woman voice I said, 'Joyce, how much should we charge for this leather brace and dog collar?'

We chuckled. 'Have you tested?' I ventured.

'I don't want to know. I'm assuming I'm positive.' We sat there a little longer. Karl put his arm around my shoulder. 'I love you,' he said.

Craig was a chiropractor from John's year at college. He and John had been toying with the idea of starting their own practice. Craig found one for sale in the association newsletter. The chiropractor was retiring and was less concerned about money than about his patients. John and Craig met him and liked him, and got his agreement to sell them the practice.

Craig came to dinner to discuss the details of the deal, and whether they would be a gay-identified practice, advertising in the gay press. They talked about what they would do if John got sick. Craig felt they could deal with that when it happened. 'It's more important that you have this goal. If things do deteriorate someone else might buy your share, or maybe I might.'

Craig went away on a locum, leaving John to find premises and fit them out. He asked our friend James Bean and me to help him move into the new building. I hate moving at the best of times. This was easier than moving house as there wasn't as much stuff, but some of it was back-breakingly heavy.

With the first load James and I were like kids in a new treehouse. I found a sign that read 'Chiropractor' and slipped it inside my shirt so that it read 'actor'. John had his camera and got a picture. James got into the act and we took a photo of me adjusting him as he grimaced in pain.

We started to load things for the tip. I spotted a moulded sixties chair that looked like an insect, an ant perhaps.

'Why are you throwing that out?'

'It won't look right in the practice.'

'But it's fantastic. It'd be worth a fortune.' I put it in the back seat of the car and added a beige shag-pile rug which had printed on it: 'Chiropractic adds years to life and life to years'.

'Why do you want that!'

'I think it's kitsch.'

John sighed. We struggled up the stairs with a heavy steel desk. Finally everything was in place. We collapsed on the floor and feasted on cappuccino and banana cake. 'I think I need a chiropractor,' I joked. 'I've pulled something in my lower back.'

A week later, the night before the official opening, John said, 'Craig saw the ant chair here and asked if he could have it.'

'I've done all this work for you guys and you're going to begrudge me a chair that nearly went to the tip.'

'So you expected a reward? Is that why you did it?'

'Fuck you!' Anger rose in my throat like lava. 'You can forget your flowers tomorrow.'

John snapped. He started yelling. 'Why are you being like this? You're making everything hard for me.' He stormed out of the room. There was a large bang. I heard John whimpering in pain. I ran in to him. 'I smashed my arm on the table.'

It was our first real screaming fight and it had gone as fast as it came.

'I'm sorry about what I said. Of course the flowers will be there.' *Blown that surprise.* We kept the ant chair.

Chapter *EIGHT*

Italy

November 1988 and John and I were off to Europe. I sat in the back of Craig's car on the way to the airport totally unnerved. 'We haven't left the iron on? And all the timers for the lights are on? What about the kettle?'

John had had a few health scares recently. While on a double-blind AZT trial he developed a barking dry cough. It was assumed to be PCP, an AIDS-related pneumonia, and John was started on Bactrim. When the cough cleared up the diagnosis seemed confirmed. The code of his AZT was broken and we learnt he had been on a placebo. If he'd been on the real stuff he might not have got sick. I felt angry that my boyfriend had been used like that.

Around this time John's T-cell count seemed to drop somewhat, probably because of the PCP. He was very upset. He lay face down on the bed. 'What am I doing wrong? I've been seeing a naturopath, meditating and doing the anti-candida diet.'

'Maybe it's stress. You seem fairly stressed at the moment. Maybe you need to express your feelings more.' Later that night it struck me that I was being unfair to John, blaming him when the problem was a virus.

And so we decided on Italy. We flew into Rome and got straight on a train to meet John's college friend Steve in Florence.

Steve was dressed like a Renaissance Florentine in black tights, a green suede tunic with puffed sleeves, and a beret sitting on top of his bobbed hair. He greeted us and led us out to a small Fiat with his girlfriend Marina behind the wheel. She was an elfin beauty with a bright, open manner – until she started driving, when she became a Roman taxi driver, tooting and abusing people. Every time we turned a corner my heart was in my mouth. I was convinced we were on the wrong side of the road.

We drove through an old archway flanked by icons of the Blessed Virgin. Suddenly we were in the Tuscan countryside – rolling hills with silhouettes of churches and conifers. The road was now a winding dirt track. 'That is where we live,' Marina said, proudly pointing to an old building with a tower. 'It was a monastery eight hundred years ago. We live on the top two floors.'

We climbed the stairs to a large room with wooden floors, adzed furniture and the smell of burning olive branches. *Steve's really into this Renaissance thing*. After a lunch of gnocchi in melted gorgonzola John and I went for a walk to a small lake beyond the monastery. 'Well, Doompson, here we are in Italy.'

'Wahoo!' John yelped.

Across the hills we could hear the crack of gunshots, which Steve later explained were boys shooting sparrows.

Florence is a dream, cobbled streets and endless beautiful vistas. And art treasures in every church, cathedral and museum, even on street corners. *How do people live in such beauty?* I was stunned by how large and majestic the David was, the way it made marble seem sensual. *His hands are disproportionately big; he could never be a convincing drag queen.*

John wanted to see the Pitti Palace with its Boboli gardens, a name he thought hilarious. As in the rest of Florence you could see how rich the Renaissance had been, but you had to wonder who painted the frescos, who clipped the hedges in the gardens, who wove the tapestries. Then on to Botticelli's *Birth of Venus* and *Primavera*, Caravaggio's *Medusa* at the Uffizi. I started to understand why Stendhal fainted, earning himself extra fame in having a syndrome named after him.

On the third morning John woke complaining of feeling sick.

'Darling, you're bright red.' I felt his forehead. 'You're burning up.'

We were in a bind. We didn't want to tell Steve and Marina about our HIV but something could be seriously wrong with John.

Steve drove us into town to a doctor who worked in the same building as him, and acted as translator. 'It looks like an allergic reaction. He wants to know if you're taking drugs.'

'No,' John lied. At least we now knew that Bactrim was probably the cause.

'He wants you to go home and rest up for a few days, drink lots of water.'

Bummer, not going to see much more of Florence but I hope my boy will get well. When John got back to the tower he went straight to bed and slept till the next morning. He was still hot but greatly improved. I made him some toast on the fire and he sat up, eating and smiling. 'My top lip is really itchy.' He was biting his lips to soothe them, which looked so cute. I couldn't see anything.

We headed off to Venice. In the train carriage I noticed that John's lip was blistering. 'I can feel it. I think it's cold sores.'

I looked closely and could count ten blisters in a triangle from his lip to his nose. When we went to buy cold-sore cream at the station, the pharmacist was intrigued and called his assistant out to look. He gave John a cream to dry out the blisters, and over the next couple of days they became large scabs. If John smiled they cracked and bled. He started to look like the rock monster from *Lost in Space*.

If Florence had been a dream, Venice was a mirage, foggy in the autumn mists. We found a sweet pension on a small piazza. The manager was a beefy guy who walked with his bum sticking out. Without even asking, he showed us to a room with a double bed. When he left I did an impression of him and John started to laugh. His scabs cracked. I grabbed some toilet paper and blotted them for him and he reached out and patted my tummy. John sucked his lips in, trying to cool them by breathing on them.

'You look like a parrot.'

'Don't make me laugh,' John said without moving his lips. That made me laugh.

'I won't make you laugh,' I said without moving my lips.

'Don't!'

It astounded me how groups of schoolkids would point at John. Shop assistants did double takes. Even more astoundingly, John was unfazed by this, as though he hadn't noticed. I wondered if it was because he had such a strong sense of himself.

Everything about Rome was big. It didn't have the village feel of Florence or Venice. Biggest of all was St Peter's, the holy-water fonts held up by eight-foot cherubim, the baldaquin as big as a skyscraper and carved out of porphyry. Markings on the floor showed the relative size of other cathedrals, asserting it the largest in the world. It is considered good luck to kiss the feet of a small statue of St Peter – after hundreds of years the feet have been kissed down to small stubs.

John had wanted to see Michelangelo's *Pietà* for some time. He stood reverently in front of the bulletproof box; I never knew why it was so important to him but I guess it was to do with a mother and her dead son.

From Rome, John and I went south to Sorrento, a resort on top of a cliff. It was deserted, being autumn, and virtually everything was closed. From Sorrento we caught a ferry to Capri, a volcanic rock covered in glamorous shops: Versace, Mugler and Moschino set around small piazzas. It didn't feel very welcoming.

Taking the chairlift to the top of the island we stepped into a surreal world. Past old stone walls and a gate flanked by terracotta urns we looked out over pinnacles emerging from the sea. The horizon was bleached out by the salty mist. This was how I imagined the land of the gods would look. John sitting on the fence in the clouds looked like an apparition.

Italy was a sensual experience: spectacular vistas, moreish food. The gelato was sensational. My favourite was a tartufo in the Piazza Navona in Rome, a ball of dark chocolate icecream with cherries in the centre, covered in thick, thick chocolate. The barman smashed it on a plate, squirted cream over it and topped it with a glacé cherry. John and I went and sat on the fountain of the four rivers and indulged.

And the men were beautiful. They had good dress sense and carried themselves like they knew they were being looked at. They had beautiful bums that filled my head whenever John and I were having sex.

I knew as we left Italy that I would come back some day.

Blood and Honour

On our return from Europe I again volunteered for the Hotline. I was asked if I would be interested in relieving the night co-ordinator for three months. The day I accepted the job I was offered a month's work at the Film School, which I turned down. It was a turning point.

Towards the end of my shift the workers from the Bus would roll in. This was a mobile facility for testing, needle exchange and counselling. It went up to the Wall, where the boy sex-workers waited for tricks, and also to St Peter's Lane, where the transsexual workers hung out. The staff were working on the edge and I was impressed.

One of them, Diana, was transsexual. She was large and fat

with frizzy red hair and freckles. She looked like Buffy from *Family Affair* and had a wicked sense of humour. 'Want to see my new cunt?' She pulled up her skirt and pulled her panties to one side, revealing stitches. She took no shit from anyone. She had worked as a nurse and was still driving a taxi on dayshift. I loved her subversiveness.

Geofredo, a funky young nightclubbing gay boy, had been a junkie and probably a sex-worker. Through Narcotics Anonymous he'd really pulled his life together. He used to sit with me each night and we'd talk about his work. And we'd flirt.

My curiosity about boy sex-workers was almost overwhelming. I found it unthinkable to have to get it up with someone unattractive. 'Why do they do it?' I asked. 'To get money for drugs?'

'Some of them. Some of them enjoy it.' Geofredo fielded my questions without making me feel I was ignorant or a bleeding heart. I found out he also worked for Fun and Esteem, a group set up for men under twenty-six who have sex with other men. Its objective was to build self-confidence and give people a place to talk honestly in a supportive environment. He ran workshops over three consecutive nights. Since many of the clients were homeless, the theory was 'get 'em while you've got 'em'. He was planning a trip to England, and encouraged me to apply for his job.

Over breakfast one morning he posed the sort of problem I might get in the interview. 'You're running a workshop when one of the boys discloses that he is HIV-positive and that he still has unsafe sex. The other boys start openly attacking him. What do you do?'

Getting ready for the interview was like preparing for an audition: making sure I got there on time, deciding what to wear to give the right impression. I dressed as young as I could, wearing a pair of Frankenstein boots with metal plates.

The Fun and Esteem office was a basement room at the AIDS Council. I was ushered in by the other worker in the project, Brent, a small boyish man who seemed more nervous than me. He introduced me to Finlay, who worked at Twenty-Ten (a gay and lesbian youth refuge), and Simon, one of the AIDS Council education team.

I was calm and totally unfazed by their questions. 'How would you describe your knowledge of HIV and AIDS? Where do you get your information from?'

'I'm HIV-positive, so I try to keep up.' *I can't believe how easy that was to say.* 'I read the gay press and work at the Hotline.'

'We're going to pose some dilemmas for you. We'd like you to tell us how you'd respond.'

Finlay chipped in. 'You are running a workshop. One of the boys discloses that he is HIV-positive and that he's still having unsafe sex.' *Geofredo! Naughty!* Other problems they posed he had also discussed with me. I answered easily and confidently; it was like being in a play when the audience is with you. I left the interview feeling good, but as the day wore on I started to pick over the things I'd said. *I wish I hadn't made the comment that lesbians are less at risk.*

When I got home, just after six, there was a message from Finlay to call the refuge before five. *Damn!* I'd have to wait out the weekend. I played the message a number of times trying to determine the result from her tone, but she gave nothing away.

On Monday morning I rang Brent. He offered me the position. When could I start? Straight away, I told him. I hung the phone up and jumped around the Hotline. 'I got the job, I got the job.'

On my first day, Brent showed me a video the guys had made with a community artist. A pretty boy with streaked red-and-blond hair introduced us to Oxford Street and interviewed other young guys. Then there were scenes of boys picking each other up in bars, or talking about safe sex. One of the boys played Dr Crucci, who talked dirty about putting a condom on. The guys were all effeminate bitchy queens, camping it up. *What have I got myself into?* They didn't strike me as boys with self-esteem, but people putting themselves down for being gay.

Brent disagreed. 'They're being subversive and they don't give a fuck what other people think. That takes incredible self-esteem.'

Jeremy, the boy at the start of the video, had worked the Wall with his hair in dreadlocks and a black hat. The other boys on the Wall called him Boy George. He had been living at Twenty-Ten, and when I met him he was starting the two-year assessment to prepare him to become a woman.

The work at Fun and Esteem proved to be challenging, but it was also very rewarding. We'd take young men terrified by their sexuality, with their heads full of lies, and help them become proud gay men connected to their community.

We saw an angelic boy who was obsessed with Kylie and Madonna, and even looked like Madonna. He spent every cent he had on every single they released. He would come into the office with a new Japanese picture-disc of 'Get Into The Groove'. You had to wonder where he was getting the money. We heard from the boys that he'd been seen up at the Wall and one day I thought I'd raise it with him. He seemed distressed by my question. 'A number of boys have mentioned it,' I said. 'We're not interested in intervening in your life. We just want to make sure you're okay.'

'I am. I just wish everyone would butt out.' He left the office. I wished I'd said, 'Only magical people get talked about.'

A few days later I found him sitting at the spare desk doing a jigsaw puzzle. I said hello. He grunted. 'You doing a jigsaw?' He looked at me with disdain. 'Can I join in?'

'Do what you want.' We sat putting together a photo of a New York street. We didn't exchange a word but I could tell from his body language that he was relaxing with me.

A guy came into the office one day looking for a fight. He was a gothic with a pink mohawk, crucifixes hanging from his ears, and a black T-shirt with the sleeves ripped off. 'You older gays aren't doing anything for us young people. You think you're so fabulous because you've got some gay bars and a parade.'

We failed with him, as we did occasionally. A couple of years later he was found dead in his flat, with a needle in his arm. He'd been dead three days and his body had turned black.

John came through the front door, his breath short and wheezy. He'd been coughing all day but didn't want to go to the doctor. I gave him some Panadol and tucked him into bed. He slept peacefully through the night, but as soon as he sat up in the morning the cough started again. He was almost choking on his phlegm. 'We're going to the doctor,' I said.

'I've got to work.'

'John, you're sick. You can't work like this. You'll be coughing all over your patients. I'm sure Craig will manage.'

The doctor pulled John's lower lids down. 'You're looking a bit pale. I'd like to take some blood and check your haemoglobin, and then do an induced sputum so we can find what's going on in your lungs, and I hope rule out PCP.'

Induced sputums are a step on the road to hell. You breathe in salt-water steam through a mouthpiece to irritate your lungs and loosen the phlegm from the walls. The objective is to produce the biggest possible greeny. And in achieving that you are racked by a dreadful cough.

'I know it's uncomfortable but we're nearly there.' John was convulsed with coughing, but finally hoiked a greeny into a small jar.

We had to wait a couple of hours for John to get a result. 'Your haemoglobin is low,' the doctor told him. 'We want to give you a transfusion but we don't have a bed at the moment. We'll get in touch with you when one becomes available. Go home and rest up.'

John decided to stay home for a few days. I got him videos and nibblies, I wheeled the TV into the bedroom and made him a cup of chamomile tea. The next day he rang me at work. The hospital had a bed for him and wanted him to go in straight away.

As I walked along the corridor I could hear John coughing. When he saw me his face lit up. 'Timba.'

There was a doctor beside him doing something to his arm. 'First the local. Small prick.' John winced and the doctor threw the spent syringe into a kidney dish. 'Now the cannula.' He pushed a huge needle into John's arm. 'The nurses will be here in a minute to put up the blood.'

John and I sat holding hands, conscious of the old men in the other beds. 'What's new, Bubbyloo?' I asked.

'They want me to reduce my AZT so I don't become anaemic again.'

'That's a scary thought. Why can't they transfuse you once a month if it means you can keep up your AZT?'

John shrugged. 'They've grown something in my sputum, a bacteria called haemophilus.' *That translates as blood lover.* 'They're waiting to find out which antibiotics it responds to.'

Two nurses brought in a bag of blood labelled with a large yellow tag, which they checked against the request form. As I was leaving, John smiled. 'There's a surprise at home for you. On one of the speakers. I saw it and knew you'd love it.' I got home to find a set of white plastic tulips with light-bulbs in them. I laughed. 'Fabulous.' *My boyfriend knows me well.* I felt hugged.

John decided to leave work. He was now so sick he was finding it hard to deal with his clients' concerned questions. Fortunately, he had disability insurance.

My sister Anna and her boyfriend Tony had decided to get married. John and I were flying down to Melbourne for the wedding, and he decided this might be a good time to tell his family he was HIV-positive. I wondered how they'd take it. John shrugged. 'No idea, but I've got to do it. They'll want to know why I'm leaving work.'

Of late my sister had become more Catholic, so the wedding was to be a big church number, with a nuptial mass and communion. My discomfort burst over a dinner of Mum's vegetable lasagne as Dad described the reception, to be held in the ballroom at Ripponlea. There were to be a hundred guests and a small chamber orchestra.

'Bit over the top, isn't it?'

'She's my only daughter. This will be the only wedding I'll pay for. I want to make sure it is unforgettable.'

'The best wedding I ever saw was my friend Morna's. It was a simple exchange of vows in a room full of their friends. It was very moving.'

I could see the veins in Dad's neck. 'But this is what your sister wants.'

'I think it sounds pretty tasteless.'

My brother Nicholas intervened. 'Tim! Cool it.'

'No. This feels like a charade.'

'I won't have you destroy this wedding,' my father said. 'If you don't want to be involved then don't be.'

I left the room and went into my old bedroom. Anna came in later. 'You're my big brother and I want you to be part of my celebration.'

'It doesn't feel right.'

'Can I show you the reading I want you to do?'

I read, 'My lover says to me, come my love . . .'

Anna smiled mischievously. 'I knew you'd like it.'

I smiled back. 'I'm being a bit of a jerk, aren't I?'

'You wouldn't be you if you weren't.'

During Mass the catechism echoed out of my past and I could barely say the responsorial psalm. When the priest spoke about a man and a woman coming together to create a family, to bear offspring and raise them in the Catholic faith, my discomfort hung in my throat like vomit.

The reception was a fantasy in white. Anna wore a cream silk crinoline with pearls sewn into the bodice. The ballroom, its midnight-blue ceiling dotted with gold stars, was full of large round tables covered in white linen.

My mother's cousin Gae snuck over to me. 'Which one's John?' I pointed him out. 'He's gorgeous. I've never seen eyelashes like that on a boy.'

I was with him when my Aunt Mary came over and kissed me hello. I could smell stale cigarette smoke. 'You must be John.' Later she took me aside. 'What a beautiful man. You make such a nice couple. Extraordinary eyelashes.'

'They're false,' I winked.

My cousin Anthony, whom we all called Ant, a tall, beautifully built red-haired shearer, sidled up to me. 'Is he your boyfriend?'

'I didn't know you knew I was gay.'

'Your mother told me some time ago.'

I was flabbergasted. 'Really? When I came out Mum said she couldn't tell anyone. But everyone knows.'

'He seems sweet. Why don't you guys come up to Mudgee and stay for a while?'

At the end of the night I said to John, 'When I next see you you'll have done the dirty deed. How do you feel?'

'Fine.' That's my boyfriend. Here he was about to dump a large crisis on his family and he says he's fine.

'I've told them I want the whole family to be at lunch tomorrow because I have something I want to discuss with them.'

'I guess they'll be relieved that you're not pregnant.' I hugged him goodbye. 'I'll send positive vibes.'

Next day I sat at Karl's drinking coffee. I started to feel that telling Mum and Dad wouldn't be too hard. 'John has made this seem so easy,' I told Karl. 'I'm that close to telling my parents.'

'The weekend of your sister's wedding? I don't think so.' With one sentence he deflated my bravura. There was a knock at the door and Karl opened it to reveal John.

'Went pretty good. Dad had already suspected something. He found it strange that we went to Europe five months after I opened the practice. He asked about my disability insurance. Mum was concerned about my weight and just kept blowing her nose. I think she wanted to cry, but she wasn't going to in front of anyone else.'

Back in Sydney I felt pressure to do the same. It nagged like a paper cut, till I decided to fly down for a weekend and do it. When I had come out, my parents' reaction was totally different from the one I'd hoped for. This time I was expecting the worst. They'd blame me, or worse, blame John.

In the car on the way from the airport Dad asked about work.

'We're seeing a lot more boys from other agencies, like STD clinics or the AIDS bus that works up at the Wall. That's where boy sex-workers find their customers.' *I want them to know the heroic work we're doing.*

'Oh God,' Mum exclaimed. I fell silent.

Later that night we were setting the table when I asked if we could have lunch tomorrow. 'There's something I want to discuss.'

'What now?' Mum abandoned the knives and forks.

'I'd rather wait till tomorrow.'

'You're making me fret.'

'Come on son, you may as well get it over and done with now.'

I had prepared a speech that I was now struggling to retrieve from my memory: there's something I've wanted to tell you for some time but didn't think I could; I love you and I'm afraid it's going to hurt you. *Here goes* . . . 'John and I have HIV, the virus that causes AIDS.'

Dad stared at me from under his furrowed brow. Mum crossed her arms, put her head in her hand and started to shake. She was crying. 'What a waste. All that talent.'

'I'm not dead yet.'

'How long have you boys known?' Dad was going to get down to business.

'Four years.'

'And how is your health?'

'Mine's pretty good but John's is failing. He's already had pneumonia.'

'That beautiful boy. I knew something was up. He didn't look well at the wedding.'

I had already lined them up a counsellor at the AIDS Council. My father declined the offer. My mother was nervous of being seen there. I gave her the number and she promised to ring on Monday. Then I rang John in Sydney and told him it had gone okay.

'I'm on a roll. I think I'll tell Anna and Nicholas.'

I rang my brother. We agreed to meet at Dogs Bar in St Kilda. Things between Nicholas and me had been strained for some time. I think I was jealous of him and the way everything was handed to him on a plate because he was heterosexual. If he brought a girl home a big fuss was made, but when I brought John there was an air of embarrassment.

All through our coffee I was distracted, waiting for an opening to launch into my speech. *Now? No. What about now?* 'Let's go for a walk. Along the pier?' We crossed the highway on the flyover. About halfway across I found myself saying the words, 'John and I have HIV.'

Nicholas gasped as though he'd been punched in the stomach. He started to cry. 'I'm sorry, I'm sorry.' I rubbed his back as we looked down on the traffic. 'I can't believe it.' He started to cry again. 'You poor bastards, having to face the fact that you're dying.' *Not quite how I see it, but I'll leave it.*

We walked along the pier and stood at the rail, watching little waves bobbing up and down. Every now and then Nicholas would say,

'I can't believe it,' and start crying again. But each time he cried a little less.

Anna's reaction was quite unexpected. It didn't seem to upset her at all. It was like I'd told her I'd got a new job. She didn't grill me about my health, or ask who had infected whom. *Maybe she's trying not to upset me.*

I flew home, and a few days later I rang to see how Mum had got on with the counsellor.

'I saw her this afternoon. She's a riot. That Irish accent! We had a lot in common. We laughed and laughed.'

'Did you talk about me?'

'A little.'

'When are you seeing her again?'

'I don't think I need to.'

'Gert, wouldn't it be better to set up a relationship with her now, so that if things get worse you have something established?'

'It's not me. I've survived bigger crises. I was an orphan at eleven.'

John and I saw Alex Harding's play *Blood and Honour*. Michael, a Chinese boy, watches his lover Colin, a newsreader, being crushed by AIDS but slowly growing to acceptance. Colin's mother, a seventies feminist, moves in with them and tries to politicise both boys. The play's structure and style were refreshing: lean, precise, accurate, angry. Glaringly lit moments of the human condition went whizzing past at an extraordinary speed.

I was shocked to hear my thoughts coming out of Michael's mouth. And then I was shocked because he'd say something I hadn't thought of and I'd think, What's wrong with me? The play ended with Colin coming out on his news program, a fantasy about taking control.

John was crying by the end, and I was choking back tears.

We drove down to Bondi Beach and walked along the damp sand. We took off our shoes and paddled in the shallows. In the darkness, in the warm air, we were safe, trying to comprehend what we had seen. John said he was shocked. 'I hadn't seen my health from your side of the story. Alex should be proud of what he has done.'

We sat on the sand watching the waves rippling in to shore. Talking to him about my fears, my anger, was not easy. There was stuff I felt I could never bring up, for fear John would say I was undermining his positive thinking. But the play had given me courage. 'Do you think you are going to die from AIDS?'

'Probably.'

'How does it feel?'

'Scary.'

We spoke of our fears for ourselves and for each other. How long did we think we had? Was he going to die before me? He wanted to know it all.

We drove home to Rose Bay. In bed I was awake for many hours, thinking. *I wonder what the moment of death will be like? Will I be so bombed on morphine that I won't even notice? Or will my soul crack me open making its escape? And when John dies, what will it be like, life without him? I want it all to go away. Leave me alone.*

I had written a play called *Thieving Boy* which had been workshopped but not yet produced. When I applied for a development grant from the Australia Council I went the big guns and asked for everything I wanted: a director (Peter Kingston), five actors for two weeks, publicity costs, and hire of the Belvoir Street Theatre for the reading.

At school I always left things till the last minute and so it was now. I was due to fly out to Bali next morning to meet John and our friend Peter Craig from Melbourne. I spent the day and night making a clean copy of the script, and typing a covering letter with a budget and the actors' and my CVs. By the time I finished it was sunrise and the cockatoos were screeching. I showered, bundled myself into a cab for the airport, and asked the driver to pull over when he saw a letter-box so I could post my application.

I was tired in the way you get when you've been out all night, that nauseous kind of tired. As I waited to board the plane, my guts were grumbling. I went to the Men's and as soon as I sat down, I squirted out diarrhoea. *Great. I've got Bali belly and I haven't landed yet.* Fortunately I had an aisle seat on the flight.

The line at Customs moved slowly. I could see John through the doors, waiting at the baggage carousel, looking very tanned with a sharp, short haircut.

We hailed a bemo and drove to Legian. The air was pungent with the smell of burning wood, copha, and stagnant water. The smell of Asia. 'It reminds me of Christmas Island,' John said as we hurtled down narrow bitumen roads overhung by palm trees and lined with open-fronted, bamboo-framed shops.

The hotel had a large garden, and a swimming-pool with a carved bridge and a Balinese carving on its back wall. The Hindu influence was everywhere: elephant imagery all over an island that had never seen an elephant.

Next day we headed off to Ubud, past houses with little bamboo platforms on which daily offerings were put to distract evil spirits. At the Attini Homestay we chose a pair of first-floor rooms. The walls were of woven palm fronds, through which you could feel a breeze. We looked over a rich garden of frangipani and bananas. A young Balinese boy was picking off dead flowers and leaves. Beyond that were rice paddies where a man herded ducks. Life was bursting out of the soil.

The next morning I was woken by an urgent need to shit. I sat on the toilet and after a few squirts the pain became excruciating. I was panting to get my breath. I felt I was going to faint and I leant forward. The next moment was blackness and me underwater in honey. I could hear growling like a wolf. Then John was there, almost crying with panic, yelling, 'It's all right, it's me, John.'

'What's happening?' I struggled to consciousness, swimming to the surface. I was lying on the bathroom floor surrounded by little piles of shit. John was naked, yelling, 'Peter, get in here!' Peter ran in, followed by the hotel manager. 'Not drugs, is it?'

'No, he's just sick.'

I had hit my head in the fall and had a large bump on my forehead. I felt extremely hot. John told me later that he'd heard the toilet lid slam shut and called out to ask if I was all right. There was no answer, only a strange growling. I was sitting in the corner with my legs out, looking over my shoulder and twitching. It was very scary, he said. Peter reckoned it was probably a mild seizure. *Great. I'm losing my brain.* John poured me a bath and put gardenia oil in it. I slipped into the pungent water.

Bali is magical. Everyone is an artist: a carver, a painter, a dancer or a singer. Walking into town we would pass a number of gamelan orchestras rehearsing while young boys learned to dance, the music mixing with the sound of frogs, crickets and geckos. At night we'd sit on the balcony watching fireflies playing over the rice paddies. In the monkey forest the monkeys were tame enough to sit on our arms and the babies had mohawk hairdos. They'd steal your bag if you weren't careful. The Temple of the Dead was being prepared for a ceremony. The men decorated the temple in cloth and the women made offerings of fruit and squid.

But all these memories are coloured by my stinky diarrhoea and the cramp and nausea I felt every time I smelt oily food. When I got back to Sydney the doctor asked for a poo sample. The results showed I had campylobacter.

My doctor flipped through my file. 'Your haemoglobin is good. Your T-cell count is 370.' He saw my shock. 'What was it last time?' He flipped another page, '540.'

'Why has it dropped so much?'

'We sometimes get maverick readings. And the time of day can affect them. But we should assume it's accurate.'

'That means I'm now out of the normal range, doesn't it?'

He felt the glands all over my body, listened to my chest, took my blood pressure and pulse, and looked at my tongue. 'You have some leukoplakia on the side of your tongue. He held up a hand-mirror and I could see the striations. 'We think it's Epstein-Barr virus, which is the virus that causes glandular fever. When it presents as oral hairy leukoplakia it's considered an AIDS-defining illness.'

I thought about what he had just said. 'So I now have AIDS?' *That's a big thought.* 'What about AZT?'

'You have to have less than 200 T-cells to be eligible.'

'What am I supposed to do, sit back and watch the virus chew up my immune system?'

The registrar at the hospital had a totally different story. 'The leukoplakia makes you eligible. Your doctor should know that.' *Fuck.* 'I'd like to ask you some questions, do an examination, take some blood, and then I'll write you a script for the hospital pharmacy.'

AZT causes a number of side effects. Initially I had a strange taste in my throat, like parmesan cheese. Then I started to become anaemic, but not badly enough to be transfused, so I had to put up with breathlessness. Then my T-cells dropped even further, first to 270 and then to 180. I began to feel blue. It wasn't anger, it wasn't depression, it was just blue.

At a meeting at work one day I found it hard to concentrate. I felt achy in my joints and my heart was racing. Within half an hour I felt shithouse. As the meeting ended I said, 'I don't feel very well. I think I've got a fever.'

'You look very red, like you're sunburnt.' *Sounds like what John had in Florence. God, I feel like shit.*

Later, my doctor asked, 'How long have you been on Bactrim?'

'About two weeks.'

'You'd better stop it and we'll see if the reaction calms down.'

'What about my prophylaxis for PCP?'

'We'll put you on Dapsone, which has been used in treating leprosy. Unfortunately it's not a hundred percent effective. We do see breakthroughs. Would you like some Panadol to bring down your fever?'

'You can have your sister's old room.' Mum ushered me into the room with psychedelic fleur-de-lys wallpaper. 'The letter is on the shelf above the bed. See you after your shower.' I sank into the quilted coverlet. It felt secure.

Oh, the letter! I bounced up and retrieved a business envelope with the Red Cross symbol on it. *It's probably a request for a blood donation.*

> Dear Mr Conigrave,
>   With regard to your donation
> of blood in June 1981, your donation was pooled
> with nineteen others and given to a patient. That
> person has now gone on to full-blown AIDS. As
> part of our Lookback scheme we would like you
> to test for HIV and let us know the result. All
> information will be kept confidential. Please call
> Nurse Fowles if you have any queries. We thank
> you for your co-operation.

This changed a few things. It could mean that I had been infected for nine years instead of five. Shortened things a bit. I had had that strange viral illness back in 1981 – could have been my sero-conversion. It would probably mean that I had infected John.

I went outside. Mum and Dad sat drinking wine and nibbling peanuts. Dad read the letter and with a concerned look handed it to Mum. She sighed.

'It's awful to think that I may have infected someone.'

'In 1981 we didn't know there was an AIDS virus,' Mum comforted. 'You didn't know you were infected.'

'What if the family try to sue me?'

I called the AIDS Council legal officer, who told me I had nothing to worry about. Cases that were succeeding only went back as far as 1984 and it was only the Blood Bank that was being sued, not the donors. Armed with this knowledge I rang Nurse Fowles at the Red Cross. I told her I had tested positive in 1985.

She seemed a little flustered. 'Thank you. Thank you for your co-operation and your honesty. Could you give that result to us in writing?'

'Can I ask if any of the other donors has come up positive?'

She hesitated. 'No. Not so far. We've made contact with sixteen others, you're number seventeen and you're the only one. I'm sorry if this has upset you.'

I sat there, my mind swimming with thoughts of the man I had infected and the boyfriend I had infected. I was comfortable with the thought that John had infected me, but it was awful to think I may have infected him. *As though I have killed the man I love.*

I never wrote the letter.

Chapter *NINE*

Thieving Boy

I came home from work to find a letter from the Australia Council. I took a deep breath and ripped the envelope open.

'We are glad to inform you that your application for funding was successful . . .'

'I got it! I don't believe it. So fantastic.'

'Good boy.' John gave me a congratulatory hug. 'I'm proud of you.'

'I'm proud of me.'

A few days later Peter Kingston and I sat in the Café Tropicana planning the workshop. We decided to have some fun, hire the people we wanted to work with. We wanted Ben Franklin, Gia Carides, David Field, Valerie Bader and Yves Stening. It was my job to approach their agents, book a rehearsal space for two weeks and hire Belvoir Street Theatre for the performance.

On the first day of the workshop we decided to work outside, in a church garden beneath leafy poplars and a large elm. We read the script and the actors laughed a lot, which was very encouraging. We talked about what we liked and what we didn't like, exploring the elements that didn't work. Most of the comments were positive, and criticism was offered considerately. I remembered a director's advice at a young playwrights' conference a few years before: 'It's arrogant to think that your work is unchangeable. Don't resist, don't be defensive, try what is suggested.' I went home each night with the cast's thoughts, and returned next day with rewritten scenes I had photocopied on the way in.

John Stone the dramaturg said, 'It's impressive how fast you write. But these aren't just quick changes, they're good writing.'

I started to become very tired. I was working too hard and caught a cold. Cold-and-flu tablets made me feel okay for a couple of days. But then I developed a dry barking cough.

On the Thursday, four nights before the performance, I felt like shit and threw myself into bed thinking, I'll get up in an hour and finish those scenes. I woke up much later feeling very hot. My temperature was 39.4°. I thought I'd better go to the hospital. John dropped me at Casualty while he went to park.

The woman behind the counter asked me to take a seat. The waiting area had hard orange plastic benches and was sealed off from Casualty by bulletproof windows and an electronic door. *I guess it's to keep out the drunks and addicts.* I sat trying not to faint. I lay down but immediately thought I was going to throw up, so I went back to the counter. 'Excuse me. I'm sorry, but I'm feeling really sick. How much longer do I have to wait?'

'We'll be with you in a moment.'

Eventually a young nurse came to get me. I followed him into a cave full of people groaning. I caught a glimpse of someone bleeding through the curtains, and then someone swore at a nurse and a kidney dish crashed to the floor. The nurse took me into a cubicle and hooked me up to a machine that monitored blood pressure and pulse. He asked lots of questions. What operations had I had? When was I diagnosed positive? Had I moved my bowels today? I fell asleep and woke when John returned.

The registrar from the ward told us, 'The sputum you've been bringing up doesn't seem to contain anything, so we'd like to do an induced sputum. Get the stuff at the bottom.'

John rubbed my arm. 'Poor Tim.'

The nebuliser was wheeled in and they asked me to breathe through the cardboard tube. I coughed uncontrollably but nothing came up. After a number of attempts I finally brought up a gob and spat it into a jar.

'We've got a bed for you up in the ward.'

They wheeled the bed up to the seventeenth floor where I was placed in a room with five other guys. The ward was eerily silent, the others asleep or watching television with earplugs in. Down the corridor I could hear trolleys crashing. A strange chemical smell mixed with smelly feet and farty bedclothes. The silence was broken by a man groaning in pain and then by another very thin man using a urine bottle.

'Pretty scary,' John said quietly.

'Very scary. I never want to be like that.'

'Me neither.'

I told the doctor, 'I'm in the middle of a workshop of a play of mine and tomorrow is the last day's rehearsal. I want to be there.'

'Tim, you are very sick. It's important you look after yourself.'

'What about Monday? It's the performance.'

'If you feel all right by then, I'll be happy for you to go.'

John kissed me goodbye and I pulled the blankets up to my face like a child scared of monsters. The man in the bed across from me had the purple shadows of Kaposi's sarcoma on his face and body, like footprints of the devil. How did he get around in the world?

I slept the sleep of the dead, waking occasionally to use the bottle.

In the morning, after a hospital breakfast, I rang Peter Kingston with the news.

'Don't worry,' he told me. 'What do you want me to tell the others?'

'I guess you can tell them I have AIDS, but ask them not to tell anyone else.'

Later that day, after a lunch that resembled cat vomit, the registrar came in. 'We've grown nothing on your sputum but I'm not convinced it's not PCP, so we'd like to do a bronchoscopy this afternoon.'

A nurse came and gave me a pre-med of morphine to suppress my cough, and atropine to dry out secretions. I sat in the bed, slowly becoming drowsy. 'I'm off my face,' I said to no one in particular.

A trolley rolled up beside the bed and two nurses slid me onto it. They wheeled me through hallways and lifts. I drifted on a cloud of morphia down white corridors and into the theatre, where I finally fell asleep.

When I woke I was back in the ward. A nurse stood over me. 'You shouldn't have any food or drink for half an hour, your throat is numb and you might choke. You've got some visitors.'

Peter Kingston, John Stone and John were there waving. John had a big bunch of bird-of-paradise. He leant down to kiss me, almost sticking me in the eye with one of the flowers. 'How'd it go?'

'Didn't feel a thing. I still don't. I'm off my face.'

'Rehearsals went well today,' said Peter. 'Everything's ready to go.'

The registrar walked in and asked to be left alone with me, but I asked John to stay.

'The doctor who did your bronchoscopy said he saw the cysts that are consistent with PCP. I'd like to start you on Pentamidine. It's fairly toxic so we'll need to monitor your creatine level daily. You may notice a strange metallic taste in your mouth. It will also cause your blood pressure and blood sugar to drop.'

'Sounds like a party drug.'

The doctor left the room. I looked at John, who attempted a smile. John Stone and Peter came back in. 'Well guys, it's PCP.'

I spent most of the weekend vomiting. I felt it with every cell of my body, a cold clammy nausea. My body became so cold my teeth chattered. But through all this the cough seemed to be subsiding. My hopes of seeing the performance were raised.

On Monday night I was standing in the bathroom trying to shave, my legs wobbly. What was normally a simple task was now very difficult. I was feeling dizzy. The need to vomit hit me out of the blue and I threw up in the sink.

'Fuck it.' I sat on the toilet seat and buzzed the nurse. 'I don't think I can go.'

'We could organise a wheelchair.'

'Knowing my luck I'd vomit all over myself in the foyer.'

It was a hard decision to make, to miss my own party with three hundred friends and industry people, but I was feeling so bad I knew people would see something was wrong. And they would talk. I rang Peter at the theatre. 'I can't do it. I can't stop chucking. What should we tell people?'

'That you have really bad gastro.'

'I hate this. Can't believe I'm not going to see it.'

'Pretty tough, but it's important you get well.'

I have AIDS. I'm not afraid of dying but I don't want to be in pain. I want as much time as I can get. What's that? Six months? Three years? Will I ever see my play produced? Everything needs to be reassessed now.

I have AIDS. What will the boys in the project think? What will my friends think? I don't want them to be scared of me or of the fact that I'm dying. Am I dying? I don't know. I don't think so.

It was six o'clock. I was aware that the reading was about to commence. I sent the cast some positive vibes.

They all turned up to see me about two hours later. They were abuzz. 'It was fantastic. They pissed themselves.'

'Wait till you hear the laughter.' John Stone held up a cassette.

'You've taped it?'

'It's probably a bit rough. But it should all be there.'

'You guys are wonderful.'

John arrived, sat down shyly next to me and leant over and kissed me.

The cast were on such a high that I found it draining. Ben handed me a card as they lined up to kiss me goodbye. When they'd all gone, I opened the card and read, 'It was so nice to work with you after only knowing you at a distance. I think your play is fab and I want to thank you for asking me to be involved. I hope you get well soon, Tim. Ben.'

John read the card and smiled. 'It really was fab. So good. I'm proud of you. I love the end where the two boys are in the prison courtyard and they rub knees. I had real tears. It's what we used to do.' John sat quietly patting my hand.

'Want to get on the bed and have a cuddle?'

John struggled to get on the bed. Arms and legs got tangled but eventually we were lying side by side, kissing gently. We were startled by a nurse, who drew the curtains round us, mouthing an apology.

'How ridiculous. It's not like we were bonking.'

'My arm's gone to sleep,' said John, rubbing it. 'I might go home and have some dinner. Besides, you've got your play to listen to.' He kissed me goodbye.

I picked up the Walkman, nervous about playing the tape in case I didn't like it. It was hard to hear, but I knew all the lines. What I didn't expect was the raucous laughter. *I knew it was funny but not that funny.* Or the rousing applause. The cast had done a really good job. I should have been happy but I felt sad.

In the middle of the night I was woken by someone talking in his sleep. It sounded like a one-sided conversation. I strained to hear. 'You're dead. You died weeks ago. So young, so young.'

In the morning I couldn't determine if I'd heard these things or dreamt them.

The community nurse sat on the end of my bed talking about getting some help around the flat. 'I could ring the Community Support Network.'

'I'm all right. I feel fine. I'll be at work in a couple of days.'

'You'll be much weaker than you expect. You've lost quite a bit of weight, you need to conserve your energy.' She could see I wasn't convinced. 'You've been through a major illness. Think about it and call me if there's anything you need.'

Veronica dropped in to see how I was. 'I'm being discharged in a minute.'

'I'll drive you home if you like.'

On the way home in her rusty Mazda, Veronica suddenly said, 'I feel so bad. I've been a bad friend. I've barely spoken to you since you told me. I should have done more.' She started to melt into tears. I handed her a scrunched up tissue.

She carried my bags upstairs. My throat burned with the rasping attempt to get my breath. I found the stairs difficult. By the time I'd conquered them the muscles in my legs were burning too. *The nurse was right. I'm a lot weaker than I thought.*

I knocked on the door and John opened it. 'Timba!' He kissed me and hugged me. 'Welcome home, boy.'

Veronica took her leave. 'If there's anything you want, call me.'

There was a pile of messages on the machine for me.

'Tim, it's Libby. You beaut. *Thieving Boy* was great, I nearly wet myself. Hope you get a production and that your gastro gets better.'

'It's Craig. Hope your gastro is getting better. I loved your play. It deserves a production. Call me.'

'Hi Tim, it's Morna. James Bean told me you were in hospital. I hope everything's all right.'

'It's James. I told Morna you were in hospital. I assumed she already knew. Sorry. Call me.'

'Christina Totos here. I think your play is fabulous and hope it gets picked up. How's the gastro?'

I rang Morna. 'Darling, how are you?' she asked.

'Not bad.'

'You were in hospital? Why didn't you tell us? Is everything okay?'

'Sort of.'

'Sorry to ask, but everyone is wondering if you have AIDS.'

'Yes, I do.'

'And John? You poor boys, how long have you known?'

'Six years.'

'You never told us.'

'I didn't think it was worth worrying people.'

Morna started to cry. 'I'm sorry.'

'It's okay.'

We sat there for a while as Morna let it flow. 'Do you want me to tell people?'

'That'd be great.'

The phone rang. 'Hi Tim, It's Annie.' She went silent for a moment. 'I've just heard that you were in hospital and that you have AIDS. Is that true?'

'I'm afraid it is.'

'That's terrible. I don't want you to die.'

'It's not going to happen for some time.'

'I'm scared.'

Later: 'It's Denise. I've just heard you guys are not well, that you have AIDS. I'm really sorry to hear it. You guys were the ones I would have least expected to get it. How sick are you?'

'I've just had pneumonia and I've lost quite a bit of weight. John had pneumonia a couple of years ago.'

I heard her blow her nose. I thought she was crying. 'This is terrible. I love you guys.' She blew her nose again. 'I'm sorry.'

'Don't apologise. We're going to be all right.'

I rang Morna. 'When you tell people, could you ask them to fall apart elsewhere? I'm finding it too draining. I end up counselling them and I don't have the energy at the moment.'

When a friend from NIDA called he said, 'Mate, I've just heard and I want you to know how sorry I am. And that I love you.'

The new plan was working.

An Ulcer, a Headache

I sat on our balcony enjoying a cigarette. John appeared in the doorway and stopped in his tracks. 'What are you doing! You've just had pneumonia. Don't you want to get well?'

'Of course I do.'

'Then why are you eating McDonald's and Tim Tams, and smoking!' He stormed inside and I followed. 'It's really stressing me out. I think I'm getting an ulcer.'

At dinner that night John had difficulty eating. He'd take a mouthful and grimace as the food passed into his stomach. Antacid didn't seem to give relief. John decided to see his doctor. *Have I caused this?* She thought it probably was an ulcer and she wanted to scope it to make sure that it was nothing too sinister. Like what? 'Cytomegalovirus or lymphoma. But it's probably just a gastric reflex ulcer.' She gave John a referral. 'Call his assistant and make a time.'

The waiting room at the surgery was the side alley of a terrace house roofed over with clear corrugated plastic. We sat against the wall. John leant his head back and lamented, 'I'm starving.' He'd been fasting since midnight the night before. 'My stomach is hurting.'

At that moment the doctor came out and called us both into

his office. 'We're going to have a look, and if there's anything suspicious we'll take a biopsy. Then we'll put you in the recovery room for about half an hour.'

An hour later John emerged with a look of contentment. He was obviously enjoying the anaesthetic. The receptionist came out with a plastic cup of water. 'I want you to sip this to make sure you are swallowing properly.'

John did it and said, 'No wuckers.'

The doctor came out. 'Would you boys like to come in?'

It'll be all right. It'll just be a normal ulcer. I was scared that if I let go of the thought, this thing would be lymphoma.

'It's definitely an ulcer and my guess is that it is lymphoma.' He paused, letting this sink in. 'Let's not get too worried yet. I want Sam Milliken, the haematologist at St V's, to look at the biopsies.'

'Hope it all goes well,' he said gently, shaking our hands. I was struck by warmth of his hand.

Days later John and I sat in Sam's room in the new St Vincent's Medical Centre. 'I'm sorry to say there's no good news. It's non-Hodgkins lymphoma.' He waited for our reaction. 'It's an aggressive cancer and most likely it is already disseminated. I should also tell you that survival beyond six months is unlikely, maybe a 10 percent chance. And with chemo the odds don't get much better.'

Sam examined John on the bed, looking in his mouth, checking reflexes and feeling his glands. 'The gland on this side of your neck is up. It's possibly a secondary. Have you been having sweats or fevers?'

Most nights lately John had been getting up two or three times to change his T-shirt. It would be clinging to him as though he'd been hit with a bucket of water. 'We should enter you in a wet T-shirt competition,' I said to him one night. He'd even started to put a pile of clean T-shirts and a towel on the bedside table.

'Radiation is only useful for one-off tumours. It won't catch any migrating cells. But we have the option of chemotherapy once a month for three months. We have a new regimen which seems to be working quite well, and it should provide some relief.' *I can't believe what I'm hearing. John. Cancer. Six months. Why am I not feeling anything?*

'The other option is not to treat it at all but to make sure that you are comfortable. Take some time to think it over and give me a call in a couple of days.'

I drove us home, neither of us saying much, and then John spoke. 'Six months is nothing. That's November.'

I felt like I'd been side-swiped. My tears were wrenched out of me and all the pain of the last few months came spewing forth. I could barely see the road. A car tooted as I veered into the next lane. 'Pull over,' John demanded. I tried to turn off into a side street but was going too fast. I mounted the curb, almost hitting a gum tree. We stopped on the nature strip.

'I'm really scared. I don't want you to die.'

'I don't want to either.'

'It's a fucken disaster.' I wiped my nose and eyes on my sleeve and turned to John. 'I'm so snotty, I must look ridiculous.'

'You look beautiful. C'mon, let's get home.'

When we got home we lay down on the bed and cuddled, just holding each other. *John is here in my arms.* But the sorrow rose up again.

'Why don't we treat ourselves and check into a five-star hotel, where we won't have to worry about a thing?' John didn't seem too keen. 'C'mon, we need some glamour.'

I booked a weekend package at the Ramada Renaissance in Circular Quay. Then I called our friends to let them know what had happened.

John and I were in our Sunday best as we drove into the hotel driveway. A valet in crimson uniform opened our doors. 'Good afternoon, sir. Could I have your name please?'

'Conigrave.' Our bags were loaded onto a trolley and we walked into reception. The foyer was grand, a large sweeping red granite staircase with brass railings surrounded by turn-of-the-century furniture and etched glass screens. I noticed I was speaking with a refined accent and holding myself upright.

The valet showed us into our room. 'Enjoy your stay.'

'Look at the bed. Huge!'

John cheered. 'Sticky Long goes for the mark!' He dived onto the bed pretending to mark the ball.

'Nice bed?'

He bounced on it. 'Pretty firm.' I jumped on. We were kids let run riot in the Giggle Palace.

'John, look at this. They've marked our baggage Mr and Mrs Conigrave.'

We had an afternoon nap, spruced up for dinner and walked down to the Quay. The lights of the city played on the water. It was a lovely cool night and people were out enjoying their harbour.

Dinner was just a couple of bowls of pasta and apple juice. Then we fell into bed. 'Have you come to any decision about treatment?'

'I'm going for the chemo,' he said indignantly.

'You say it like I should know.'

'It seems the obvious choice to me. I'm not going to give up without a fight.'

We talked about the regrets we each had. 'I'm sad that my acting career didn't take off.'

'You did all right. I'm sorry I never got to have sex with a woman. There's no way I could now.'

'Do you really desire to?'

He shrugged. 'I'm curious.'

'What if you decided you liked it better than with me?'

'Not a possibility. You're too cute.'

I was struck by a memory of my most recent affair. While John was in San Francisco for his brother Paul's wedding, I took the opportunity to play with a man who worked at the AIDS Council. He had almond eyes like a cat's. We had started flirting with each other some weeks before. We went bike riding together one afternoon and I asked him for dinner at Rose Bay the next night. I had set a table on the balcony with candles and flowers. Not very long into the meal we were caressing. Before dessert we were in the bedroom having touchy-feely, sensual, fantastic sex.

A few nights later I told Veronica. She didn't seem impressed. 'How would John feel if he knew you were telling people this?' I felt a bullet of guilt pass into my chest.

And now I could feel it again. A wave of panic came over me. *I've got to tell him. I couldn't bear the thought of him dying and me not being totally honest.*

'John, there's something I want to tell you.' I paused. 'I had a couple of affairs when you were in San Francisco last year.'

He sighed. 'Why do you do this to me? Was it anyone I know?'

'No, they were a couple of guys at the sauna,' I lied.

He sighed again. 'It hurts.'

'I'm really sorry.'

'I don't want to talk about it.' He turned away. He froze me out that night. I still hadn't told the whole truth but I didn't want to hurt him more.

In the morning at breakfast he mucked around with a pastry snail, holding it in front of his nose. 'Bwight wight, bwight wight.' He was himself again, as he had been after every other time I'd hurt him.

That afternoon Nicholas, from *Soft Targets*, opened the door to the apartment he was minding at the Quay. Our friends were there: Veronica and her girlfriend Tracy, Franco and his lover Paul, Ben,

James and his flatmate Denise, Morna and her husband Ian. I spied a zebra skin on the floor. 'Is that real? To think it died to be a rug.'

Nicholas took us on a tour of the apartment, the quilted Japanese silk walls, the antique bedside table, the stack of de rigueur reading (*Patrick White: A Life*) with a pair of reading glasses on top.

There was a mink blanket. 'Very decadent. It says: "Fuck off, we're rich, we can do what we like."'

It was wonderful to be with our friends, drinking tea and eating almond shortbread, standing on the balcony looking at the harbour. I felt we were supported, that no matter what happened from here on, we were going to be okay.

That night, John and I treated ourselves to a room-service dinner. Two attendants wheeled in a trolley that folded out into a table. They laid the silverware on a white linen tablecloth.

I popped the cork of our complimentary champagne. With a mouthful of salmon ravioli I raised my glass. 'My darling John, I want to thank you for the years of love, comfort and support.'

He was touched. 'I want to thank you for being my boyfriend.'

'I'd like to thank you for all the times you let me fall asleep in front of the TV with my head in your lap.'

'I'd like to say thanks for all the fun we've had.'

'Yeah, the baby talk and the laughs.'

'Thanks for all the holidays, Bali, Europe . . .'

'The Barrier Reef and Uluru . . .'

John said meekly, 'I really want to thank you for being here now.'

'I love you.' I leant across the table to kiss him. My elbow ended up in his gravy.

The haemotologist called John into the short-stay ward for his chemo. He was to be in overnight for observation, to make sure there was no adverse reaction.

He was at the naturopath for some herbs to get him through it when Craig rang. He was disapproving. 'I don't think he should be having chemo. He's only going to poison himself. Can't you talk him out of it?'

'Even if I could, I wouldn't.'

'It's gonna fuck up his bone marrow, destroy the lining of his bowel and make him nauseous. And his hair will fall out.'

'John knows all that but he still wants to do it. I support him in whatever he chooses.'

John returned, braced himself and rang Craig. He sat for some time grunting affirmatively, then took a deep breath. 'I know all that but I don't want to sit back and do nothing. At least this way there's a chance. If I don't have chemo there's no chance.' He listened, then raised his voice. 'Craig, it's my decision and I would like you to respect it, okay?' He hung up and took a deep breath and blew it through his cheeks.

We sat in an old Victorian ward with large windows and lino floor. John put on a pair of hospital pyjamas and climbed into bed. I sat at his feet rubbing his legs through the blanket. A nurse came in with a tablet and a glass of water. 'This should stop you getting nauseous. Julie will be with you in a moment.'

Julie arrived with a kidney dish and four large syringes. I knew her from the treatment room and my monthly dose of 'make me vomit' Pentamadine. She was a cute, sexy woman with a blond bob and blood-red lipstick. She reminded me of someone from the Mickey Mouse Club.

She put a butterfly needle into John's forearm while I gave him my hand to squeeze. 'I always thought chemo would be bigger than this, you know, drips all day.'

'They're fairly powerful drugs.'

'And they stay in your body for a month?'

'They're big guns. If you have any reaction like tingling on your lips and tongue or difficulty breathing, you must tell me.'

She loaded up each syringe and pushed it through slowly.

'Why so slow?' I asked.

'It can irritate the vein or damage it.'

'Is he going to lose his hair?'

'Tim, do you have to know everything!' John protested.

Julie answered my question. 'Not everyone does, but two of these can cause hair loss, so it's pretty likely.' *I'm not going to enjoy that, my beautiful boy without his thick black hair.* I was suddenly confronted by how much I valued his looks. It amazed me that after all these years I still found him attractive.

Julie was finished. 'I'll come back in half an hour to make sure you're okay.'

I sat holding his hand. 'How are you feeling?'

'Fine. No wuckers.'

His dinner arrived at five o'clock. He took the lid off a plate of dried chook and boiled vegetables. 'Kindy dinner. How do they expect anyone to get well eating this shit?'

I kissed him goodbye. 'See you in the morning about nine.'

Next morning I walked into the ward. John's bag was there but the bed was empty. I found out he was in Casualty. 'Is he all right?'

'Can I ask who you are?'

'I'm his lover.'

'He's having an X-ray. They think he may have popped a lung.' *Jesus, just what you want.*

I stood at the prison window. 'My lover John Caleo is in there having an X-ray.' *Hurry, my boyfriend needs me.* Eventually they let me in. I found him sitting in a wheelchair with an oxygen mask on. 'You look like a parrot,' I told him.

'Carpe Beakum,' John joked, quoting a *Fast Forward* sketch about the Dead Parrots Society. We laughed and then John grimaced. 'I woke up this morning with a really bad pain down one side.' He coughed and took some time to recover.

Tony, the registrar from the ward, appeared. 'We've seen the X-ray and you have a pneumothorax, a popped lung. We're going to put a pleural drain into your chest.'

They wheeled him into a cubicle and Tony scrubbed up. He asked John to open his pyjama shirt, sterilised his chest, referred to the X-ray, counted ribs and decided where to go in. 'A little local first,' he said, then punctured John with a needle. He then held up a metal tube cut at one end at an angle, so that it looked like a spearhead. The other end was attached to a piece of hose connected to a bottle with water in it.

'I hope this won't hurt too much.' He placed the spear against John's chest and with some exertion pushed it in.

There was a hiss as air escaped into the bottle. 'That's bubbling well. We'll do another chest X-ray.' Tony explained that pneumothoraces normally heal well, but less so in people with HIV. I asked if he thought the chemo might have caused this.

'No. It's more likely to be a burst PCP cyst. We may have to do a chemical pleurodesis, where we pour irritants in between the lung and the chest wall, hoping that they will scar together. When the bubbling stops we know it's healed.' He clamped off the tube and John was wheeled up to the ward, where the tube was attached to a suction port on the wall.

At the end of a week Tony came in. 'I'd like to get you back on your feet as soon as possible. It hasn't healed. We are going to have to do a pleurodesis, probably this afternoon.'

'Okay, honey.' In came a large nurse built like a ship. 'Got you some fun drugs. This is Midazolam. It's a sedative, but it also blocks the memory so you won't remember what happened. Do you want it in your bum?'

John rolled over onto the side without the tube. *He must be craving a chance to roll over on the other side.* I sat watching him becoming sedate. He took a deep breath, blew through his cheeks. 'Petty strong stuff,' he slurred.

Tony returned. 'This is going to hurt. If you find it too hard, tell us and we'll try to alleviate the pain. We're going to start now.'

John sucked air through his teeth. He was trying so hard to be brave but he started to groan loudly. They wheeled a gas tank over to him and placed the mask over his face.

'Breathe deeply.' John's breathing became relaxed and Tony continued pouring in the Tetracycline. 'It's good, the bubbling is reducing. Keep breathing the gas.'

'It's stopped,' said a nurse.

'We'll let you stay like this for a while, to give it a good chance of sticking. We'll come back in a couple of hours and unplug the suction.'

When they did the bottle remained still. There was jubilance among the staff.

Later that night, John and I were watching *Home and Away*. Out of the corner of my eye I saw something move in the bottle but when I looked closely I couldn't see anything. A couple of minutes later, there was more movement. *Don't alarm John. It'll heal.* But then it started bubbling in earnest.

John would have to go through it again. That too failed. By the third attempt I was finding things distressing, standing by while they hurt my lover, worrying whether this one would take. This time I held his hand. With us was Carole, John's Ankali (a volunteer carer in the program set up by the Albion Street clinic). She was a mother with a cuddly body and a gentle, spiritual manner.

John was breathing through gritted teeth and groaning now and then. I started to feel very sad. 'I'm hating this. It's like we're standing by watching him die.'

'Tim!' John chastised me through the mask. 'You're talking about me dying.' I was embarrassed, and I resented being ticked off.

Later that night the bottle started bubbling again. 'This is fucked. It's so unfair. Would you mind if I don't come to the next one? I find it distressing to see you in so much pain.'

'I want you to be there, to hold my hand.'

'It's giving me headaches.'

On the fourth attempt the lung stuck. They took the tube out of his chest wall and John was able to go home, very much weakened after not using his muscles for so long – he had spent nearly a month attached to the wall. He struggled up the stairs, stopping on the landing to get his breath. He braced himself and took on the challenge of the next flight. Once inside he started to cough, his body racked with rasping and wheezing.

'It's nice to have you home, my brave Boony.'

John enjoyed his freedom. He had a major shopping attack, buying a swanky can-opener, a toaster, a CD of Vince Jones and a new jumper. He'd spend his days reading the paper, watching videos and snoozing. Sometimes we'd go for a walk down by the harbour, where the winter sun sparkled on the water. John tried to keep a good pace in order to build his strength but every now and then he'd start coughing. He looked so cuddly rugged up in his woollen overcoat and his Bombers scarf.

He was re-establishing himself in normal life. And I could go to work without having to visit him two to three times a day in hospital. However his cough was a real bark. He would be at it through the night. I'd drift off to sleep only to be woken by him coughing. In the mornings I'd feel like I'd been through a mangle and my head would be thumping.

'I might sleep in the living-room tonight,' I said one morning.

'Please don't.'

'I'm going to break down if I don't get some sleep. I'll come to bed with you and we can cuddle, but when you fall asleep I'll go out to the living-room. Okay?' He agreed, resentfully.

I was at work when the phone went. It was John. 'You won't believe this. My lung's popped again.' He was crying and coughing. Carole had taken him to Casualty. 'They're going to put another drain in. Can you come?'

I hung up the phone and strode up the hill to the hospital so fast my legs were burning. *This is fucked. Why is he being punished like this? It's going to be another month of visiting him in my breaks, washing his pyjamas and running his errands.* I arrived at Casualty feeling tired, weighed down by what was happening.

Carole was there holding his hand. I kissed him and rubbed my hands through his hair and it came away in clumps. I secretly showed Carole, who raised her eyebrows. I chose not to say anything to John.

Next morning they had put him in a room of his own with a view over the eastern suburbs. He was sitting up in bed and smiled when he saw me. There was hair from arsehole to breakfast – hair on the pillow, on his shoulders, even caught in his eyelashes – and yet his head still looked normal.

By the next day he started to look mangy. 'Maybe we should pull it out?' I suggested.

'No, I don't want to.'

My headaches were still there. I was now getting a visual aura like the ones I used to have when I had migraines. At John's suggestion I booked in to see the Outpatients registrar.

'Your gait looks normal to me. And you seem fairly lucid. Are there any changes in your handwriting?'

'Don't think so. Should I have a brain scan?'

'You can if you want, but I don't think we're going to find anything. You don't look like someone with toxoplasmosis or a brain tumour. The headaches are probably due to the stress of having John in hospital. If they're still there in a week, come back and we'll talk about a scan.'

I went to Craig for an adjustment, which gave only partial relief. Then I tried massage from a warm cuddly bear of a man who ran a volunteer service for people with AIDS. He worked my neck and shoulders strongly and brought some relief.

I told him about John. 'No wonder you're getting headaches. Maybe you should think about relaxation or meditation.'

'I'm too tense to relax.'

One afternoon during an evaluation workshop, finding it impossible to concentrate, all I could think about was that John was in pain, he was very sick and going to die. I had an ache behind my eyes that meant there was a dam of tears waiting to burst. At the break I approached the staff counsellor, whom I had been seeing for some time. She was booked up all that day.

'I'm feeling suicidal.'

'Come and see me at five.' I felt so much better.

'Do you talk about this with your friends?'

'I don't want people avoiding me because all I talk about is John, AIDS and death.'

'Do you talk about it with John?'

I shook my head. 'If this was any other crisis he'd be the first person I'd turn to. But he is the problem and I can't make him feel like that.'

'What do you think life will be like without John?' I was taken aback. I'd never thought about it.

'I would feel like I'd lost one side of my body.' My voice started to rise. 'I don't want this to happen. I love him.' I was crying freely, venting all the anguish and fear.

When I got back to the hospital John was in the middle of yet another pleurodesis. I had a plastic bag with his pyjamas in it, nicely washed but flecked with tissue. 'I'm sorry, but they went through the wash with a Kleenex.'

'Didn't you check? Can't you get anything right?'

'Please don't talk to me like that. I'm really stressed. You're not the only one having a hard time here.'

'I'm sorry. You're right.'

I rubbed his arm. 'We're both pretty stressed at the moment. I've got you some apricot delight. Hows about we clip your hair? It really looks ratty.' I got some clippers from the nurses' station, got someone to take his tube off the suction, and wheeled him into the bathroom. I was feeling solemn. This was a symbol, a circumcision rite. I started the clippers and put them to the base of his neck. The hair fell away and his skull was transformed into a large peach with soft fuzz on it.

'Beautiful. It makes your eyes stand out even more. You look like Sinead O'Connor.'

As each pleurodesis failed, my back seized up even more. John was sent down to Casualty to have another X-ray and they decided to try again while we were down there. They were about to start when a woman commanded, 'Move.' I turned to see nurses and doctors wheeling in a trolley with a girl who was blue all over. 'Get out of here please. Crash trolley!'

We were moved into another cubicle. 'Probably an OD,' Carole said.

'I hate the fact that John is fighting so hard to stay alive and people like her are trying to leave the planet.'

Chapter *TEN*

Drifting

I had at last been booked in for a scan. I sat on a blue plastic chair and pulled out my knitting. I had almost finished a beanie for John, to cover his head in the cold weather. It was to be a surprise for him.

The nurse called me in and asked me to take off my earring and lie on the table. At one end was a large tunnel. She strapped my head down with a large band and urged me to stay still. The table started to move through the tunnel, where something whizzed around me.

Then a doctor came in and introduced himself. 'We're going to give you some contrast fluid, to enhance the tomography of the brain. Some people have an allergic reaction to it, so if you notice tingling in your lips or tongue, let us know. You may also get a rush.' He put a needle into my vein, an extremely uncomfortable procedure, attached a large syringe full of orange fluid, and pushed.

Suddenly I was falling. A wave of panic washed over me, but as I breathed deeply the feeling went.

The doctor went behind a screen with an operator, who

stuck her head around the corner and ordered me to stay still as my body moved slowly back into the tunnel. The staff were quiet after the scan, pointing at their screens. I was hoping someone would come and tell me that everything looked good, but no one did. They kept talking and pointing at the screens.

I was back sitting in John's room when the Outpatients registrar called me out. I followed her to the doctors' station and was shown some scans on the lightbox. I didn't know how to read them till the registrar took me through them. I had five lesions of toxoplasmosis in my brain. She pointed to some dark shapes in my head. 'They're colonies of a parasite that is transmitted by cat poo.'

'What are you saying? I ate some cat poo?'

'Probably playing in a sandpit as a kid. Because you're allergic to sulphur drugs we have to give you an alternative, Clindamycin. I'd like you to start straight away. Two tablets four times a day.' She gave me a prescription.

'Am I going to have brain damage from this?'

'Not likely. The lesions don't eat the brain, but they put pressure on it, which is why you get the manifestations.'

I went to the chemist and then struggled home, feeling nauseous. I wheeled the television into the bedroom. Topolino, the Mickey Mouse doll John had bought for me in San Francisco, sat smiling with startled eyes. *Who does he remind me of? John.* I crawled into bed and played with Topolino, making him do the things that John does, like John's famous impersonation of a charging rhino.

I got worse, as though I'd been given permission to collapse under the weight of the headaches. My head thumped, expanding and contracting like a balloon with every heartbeat.

Within the world of sleep I was able to find relief from the burden of pain. I woke some hours later, straining to read the clock: 20.40. *I don't know what that means. Twenty to nine? In the morning? Don't know. Got to take tablets.*

This drifting continued for a couple of days. I rang John to say I felt too bad to come in. By the third day I was quite disoriented. I rang the hospital and spoke to the consultant microbiologist. I told her I was having trouble knowing which drugs to take, even what day it was. She asked me to come in.

I rang my Ankali, Geoff, at work. While I was waiting for him I packed some things, no easy feat. I kept going over and over what I was taking. Socks, Topolino, an apple, and the Clindamycin.

I sat in Casualty, my headache blurring my vision. Geoff sat beside me and I was able to let go, knowing that I was in good hands.

Then someone came to say they had a bed upstairs. It was the single room next to John's and there was a door between them.

'Hi John,' I waved.

The next few days I drifted in suspended animation, waking in distress calling, 'The curtains are on fire.' Sitting up and saying to a visiting friend, 'I really like you but I wish you'd stop having affairs.' Waking up and seeing my mother standing next to a friend from my NIDA class. 'You two look like you could be sisters.'

A few days later, I slowly swam out of the fog to see a tall blond nurse doing my temperature and blood pressure. 'We thought you were dying. You and John being in here together has given us all a big fright.'

I sat reading the *Star Observer* when Dominic, one of the Fun and Esteem boys, put his head round the door.

He had come to the project as a straight boy who was a sex-worker, and had thrown himself into a workshop with gusto, revealing his childhood sexual abuse, his drug use and the fact that he was HIV-positive. The group had been discussing whether people should disclose their status.

'Why? If you're having safe sex, it's irrelevant.'

'Do you believe safe sex works?'

'I wouldn't sleep with someone if they were positive. And I reckon I should have the right to know.'

'You may miss out on a major spunk.'

Suddenly Dominic spoke. 'You guys don't know what it's like.' He was crying. 'It's so hard. I've probably infected people and I don't feel good about it. I've come close to topping myself.' At the end of the workshop when thanked for his honesty he looked ready to cry again.

At the hospital he smiled, holding up a large bag of Darrell Lea chocolates. 'You helped me so much. I'm very sad that you're sick.'

'I'm okay, this one's not going to get me.'

John had had some painkillers and was drifting on an opiate cloud. I sat watching him, thinking about all that was happening to us. *I don't want him to die. I'm scared that it'll be the last time I see him. I don't know if I believe in an afterlife. What if John's soul is just reabsorbed into the greater power of the universe? I don't want him to become blended energy. I want him to be there waiting for me. I want us to be distinct entities. He looks so peaceful, like an angel asleep. Innocent. Serene. Calm. No pain. No fear.*

Some years later I would hear a song called 'Venus As A Boy' and would cry as I was reminded of this moment, of the divine being incarnated as a boy.

I looked up to see John's father in the doorway. He approached John without acknowledging my presence. 'Hi, Bob,' I said.

'Hello.' *I have a name!* He leant over John and called his name.

'Bob, he's asleep,' I whispered.

John opened his eyes. 'Dad.'

'Hi, son.'

I watched Bob. *I wonder what John would look like at that age? I reckon he'd still be good-looking. I reckon I could still love him even if he looked like Bob. I would adore seeing John grow old.*

'What have the doctors been saying?'

John struggled to talk. 'They just want to keep trying to fix my lungs by –' He coughed. 'By putting antibiotics in between –'

'I'm sorry, I can't hear you.'

'Haven't you got your hearing aid?' John strained to shout and ended up coughing.

'I don't like wearing it.'

'Bob,' I interrupted, 'John can't talk loudly, it makes him cough. I'll translate for you, John.' And so I did. It was hard work. I was hurt by Bob's disregard for me but I figured it was because he thought I'd corrupted John, and probably infected him.

I woke up scratching at little red dots all over my forearms.

'Would you guys like to have breakfast together?' asked a nurse, Malcolm. 'I can put your trolleys together.'

I pulled up my pyjama sleeves and showed Malcolm my forearms. 'Make sure you show the doctors when they do their morning round,' he told me.

Malcolm set up tables with breakfast trays, left the room and came back with a carnation in a glass. 'You divine man,' I said. 'Where'd you get it?'

'You don't want to know. Enjoy.' He went out again.

'Probably from some dead guy's flowers.'

'Tim!' scolded John.

When the doctors appeared, Tony asked me to take off my top and poked away at my skin. 'It looks like an allergic reaction. This is tricky. You're on a number of new drugs. I don't want to take you off an essential one. I think we should stop the least important ones first. And we'll give you some antihistamines.'

They didn't touch the rash. By late afternoon I was maddeningly itchy. 'Tim, stop scratching,' a nurse said. 'It'll only make it worse.'

When I next spoke to Tony he was distressed at the lack of improvement. The microbiologist suggested a drug that blocks the itch receptor site. One of the nurses suggested soda baths. 'As cold as you can stand it; it takes the heat out of the rash.'

Before bed, I poured a cold bath and braced myself as I lowered my torso under the water. Being cold was an unpleasant experience but so was the itch. Within minutes there was relief, but when my teeth started chattering I wimped out. I patted myself dry with a towel, walked back to the suite and kissed John goodnight. 'Your lips are cold,' John gasped.

'I'm the Snow Queen.' I climbed into bed and took a sleeper and the last Clindamycin for the day. Within minutes I felt a rush, prickling all over. I buzzed the nurse. 'I've just had a rush from the Clindamycin.'

'I was surprised the doctors didn't take you off it, I would have thought it was the obvious one.'

'So can I stop it?'

'I don't have the authority to tell you to, but if I were you I would.'

Next morning I told Tony that I'd taken myself off the drug. 'I'm not happy about that, but it's done now. We still need something to combat the toxo, so we have to desensitise you to Bactrim.'

This meant exposure to the drug in very small steps. 'It's every three hours, exactly three hours, not three hours and one minute, or the whole thing collapses.' I was woken up through the night, to have the nurse squirting Bactrim into my mouth.

A couple of days later, I arose feeling very bright. My headaches were under control and the itching was a little improved. I'd stepped out of the forest of madness.

I spent the morning explaining my situation to John. 'The

drug may have left my body by now but the allergic reaction can continue for weeks. Isn't that boring? Oh, yeah, one of the nurses told me this morning about this allergic reaction called Stevens-Johnston syndrome where all your skin falls off. Isn't that gross? I'm so allergic these days that I'll probably get it.'

John's and my friends were running our errands, bringing in surprises and mail. I loved having them coming in, and got excited telling them all my news: the soda baths, the toxo, the allergy to Clindamycin. I was talking faster and faster. There was so much I wanted to report. 'It's fantastic being in here, being able to be with John but not having to worry about him or look after him. Penny Cook brought me a bag of coffee from Café Hernandez. It's fabulous, best coffee I've ever had. Would you like one?'

I held court around John's bed, entertaining friends. Their laughter only encouraged me more. Each new pair of ears would get the whole trip: coffee, toxo, allergy. Eventually Carole said, 'Tim, stop talking, you're giving me a headache.'

I was crushed and anxious. I wanted to talk.

Later that afternoon, I noticed that when I looked to one side of the television, it disappeared. I sat testing this phenomenon until I concluded my peripheral vision had shrunk. I buzzed and asked for Tony, who fetched an ophthalmoscope. 'Pick a spot on the wall and keep focussed on it.' This was not easy, as Tony's head was in the way.

'It's amazing, the television is suddenly not there.'

'Can you stop talking for a minute?' Tony kept looking into my eyes. I could smell his aftershave. 'There seems to be a large white spot on your retina but it doesn't look like CMV. Shut your left eye and tell me when you can see my finger.' He tested the size of the blind spot. It was fairly large and in both eyes.

'I suspect it's the lesion on your occipital lobe.'

'Is this brain damage? Is it permanent?'

'Maybe, maybe not. As your toxo improves we'll know. And I'd like you to speak to a psychiatrist.' I was appalled. 'You're a bit hypermanic. You seem very up, very chatty, talking at a hundred miles an hour.'

'I'm not up. I just feel good. It's the first time I can be with John and not have to look after him . . .'

'Tim!' Tony interrupted. 'It's important that we bring you down before you become grandiose, thinking you're Jesus or spending all your money.'

I saw the psychiatrist. 'I'd like to ask you some questions,' she said. 'How do you feel today?'

'I feel really good.'

She scribbled away in her notebook. 'Happy? Excited? How is being in hospital for you?'

'Great, I'm really enjoying it. I'm having the best time.'

'What sort of things have you been doing to occupy your time?'

'I'm working on a play called *Jimmy, an Angel, Stars and That* about a gay relationship where one partner is dying.'

'How's it going?'

'Good, I'm feeling very creative.'

'Anything else?'

'Just sitting around here with our friends, chewing the fat. Which has been great. So much to tell them.'

'How do they think you are?'

'Very bright, happy. John's Ankali asked me to be quiet once because I was talking too much.'

'Okay,' she said making some final notes. 'I'm going to put you on Haliperidol. You're manic because the cells in your brain have become hypersensitive to certain neuro-transmitters. Haliperidol reduces that sensitivity. I'll come and see you in a week.'

The first tablet arrived with lunch. I took it resentfully while the nurse watched. I slept the sleep of the dead, all afternoon and overnight.

Somewhere Warm

John had just been scoped again and was snoozing. I sat beside him playing with Topolino. When John woke and stretched I dragged my chair to the side of the bed and leant on it with my elbows. 'I'm feeling a lot less speedy.' I was seeking approval. 'Hey, what's this?' I bounced Topolino towards him. 'A charging rhino.'

'Big dag.'

'What's this?' Topolino clapped his hands. 'Joy. And this?' He clapped one hand. 'Wanking.' John grinned.

Sam stuck his head in the doorway. 'Good news. Your scope was clear. There's no ulcer and no inflammation. It's probably fair to say that your cancer is in remission.' Sam was looking pretty pleased with himself. 'This new regimen seems to be getting good results. So now we've got to concentrate on fixing your lung.' He left.

'Wahoo!' I yelped. John looked shocked, his eyes moist. I realised how scared he'd been.

Early that afternoon I'd fallen asleep in the chair next to John. I was woken when Bob arrived and bent over to kiss him.

'Good news, Dad.' Bob pulled his hearing-aid out of his pocket and screwed it into his ear. 'Got some good news. The cancer has resolved.'

Bob smiled. 'You worked hard for it, son.'

'Here, Bob, have the seat.' I sat on the bed.

Bob pulled out a white envelope. 'I was reading your will this morning –'

'Where'd you get it from?' John demanded.

'It was in the drawer of your desk.' Bob had been staying in our flat while we were in hospital. John rolled his eyes at me. 'I have some concerns,' Bob went on. 'Why is everything going to Tim?'

John was stunned. 'I want to make sure he's all right if I die.'

'And Tim, is your will set out similarly?' I said it was. 'And if John doesn't survive you?'

'It goes to my family.'

'So if John dies, you inherit his belongings. And then say a month later you die? Everything goes to your family? I don't think that's fair. I would like half. I put John through school and college and I think I deserve it.' He pulled out a list. 'Now, who owns the television and video?' John sighed. It was his. Bob ticked his list. 'And the stereo?' His list was thorough, almost down to the Vegemite. I wondered if he was going to go back to the flat and stick little yellow dots on everything.

'What about the car? You don't want it, Tim, do you? With all the stuff going on in your brain and the eye stuff?'

'They're resolving, Bob.' I sighed. 'But I'm not going to fight you for it. You can have it.'

Bob trundled downstairs to get some lunch. 'I wonder if he found our boy videos,' I said and John hooted in embarrassment. 'Who owns *Hung Like a Horse*? The whole thing's a bit offensive.'

'It's just Dad.'

Tony came in. 'Had some good news? Happy? Now, about your lung. We have a number of options. We can keep up the pleurodesis until it sticks.'

'How many times can you do it?'

'Pretty well forever, if you can stand the pain. Or we can do nothing, just wait for the inevitable and make you as comfortable as possible. Or we can operate, open you up and sew up the holes. You'll end up with reduced lung capacity and there is a chance you won't survive.' John looked worried. 'I'll get the anaesthetist to assess you. They don't like operating on people with underlying chronic illnesses.'

The anaesthetist was a scrawny man with glasses and hair full of Brylcreem. Tony stood by as he listened to John's chest, tapping around, checking liver and spleen.

'You sound okay, a few crackles in the bottom left lobe, but when you have an underlying chronic illness there is a risk of failure. I'd rate yours at about 25 percent.'

'Failure?'

'Death.' *Oh, is that all?* 'Take some time to think about it.' He and Tony left the room.

'I don't want to do nothing.' John coughed. 'That's giving up, and I don't know how many more pleurodeses I can stand. What do you think?' I told him I would support whatever he chose. 'I think I'm going to have the operation.'

'Okay. You are such a brave boy.'

John had a visit from a good-looking man with curly black hair. I noticed the eyes, those eyelashes: cousin Tim. 'I'm boyfriend Tim,' I told him. John and he had come out to each other at a family dinner a year ago. When John got home from the dinner he was thrilled. At last he wasn't the only poofter in his family.

Tim didn't know till now that we had AIDS. His mother had swallowed Lois's story that John had cancer.

A nurse came in and handed John the portable phone. 'John, it's your mother.'

John looked at us, as though bracing himself, and then said as sweetly as possible, 'Hi Mum . . . Not too bad. They're going to operate tomorrow . . . To sew up the holes in my lungs . . . A little scared . . . Tim Cookson's here. Mum, he says you told his family that I have cancer . . . But it's AIDS-related cancer . . . I'm not ashamed of what I have. I want you to tell people the truth. Please try for me.'

Whatever Lois said next took John aback.

'That's a shame.' He nodded, his breathing getting shallower. 'It's a shame. Yes, it is.' He chewed his lips. 'Okay, goodbye.' He slumped forward. 'She reckons that if I insist on her telling people, she doesn't know if she can be my mother.'

'She doesn't mean it.'

'I know, but it hurts.'

The next morning Tony came back in. 'The theatre list is full today, but if there's a cancellation or if they finish early they'll try to squeeze you in.'

Mark, a college friend of John's, arrived with two paintings from his daughters, the kind of abstract paintings that four-year-olds do with a message in texta pen: 'Get well, John. Love, Sophie.' He stuck them up on the wall in front of John's bed.

Later that day a nurse arrived with a pre-med. John turned over and pulled back his hospital gown, revealing what was left of his bottom. *His bum looks like two skin flaps.* A rush of revulsion went up my spine. I was shocked.

Before I knew it, the transport guys appeared at the door. They brought in a trolley, undid the suction and helped John on board. He was very weak. As they wheeled him out he gave a small wave. Then he was whisked away from me. A moment later James Bean arrived. 'I just saw John. He's going to have an operation.'

'They're going to sew up his lungs.'

'He held my hand and said he was scared.'

James and Mark sat sharing memories of John. 'I can't believe how hard he's fighting. When I came in the other day he was lying in bed with strap-on weights doing leg-lifts.'

John's brother Michael appeared. We told him what was happening. The four of us knew that at any moment John could die. I couldn't think of anything to say to Michael. We'd never been close. I tried to read a copy of *Outrage* but it all floated past me. All I could think about was Tony coming in to tell us they had lost John.

After an hour of nervous silence, the door swung open and an inanimate John was wheeled in and loaded back into bed. As he slowly came around I said, 'Welcome home, my John.' But in my sick fantasies I had been saying, 'Walk towards the light.'

The scar was huge and angry-red, from his solar plexus to the back of his ribs. I wish I could have seen the operation. I would love to know what my boyfriend looked like inside, a privilege that most couples don't get. Slugs and snails and puppy-dogs' tails.

Malcolm was inserting a naso-gastric tube through John's nose and throat down into his stomach. Every now and then John would gag. 'Take a deep breath.' John started to dry-retch. 'Are you okay to go on?' John nodded. 'Nearly there.' John had lost so much weight he was put on a 24-hour drip-feed, about 3000 calories a day.

Once John was ambulatory we talked about the future. 'I want to go somewhere warm, Noosa maybe.'

'It may be a bit early for that,' said Tony. 'Why don't you think about going to the hospice?'

'I thought that was for people who are dying?'

'Not solely. People recuperate there. They even offer respite care for family members who need a break. It's a nice place, the food's quite a bit better than here, and the staff are pretty friendly.' *I wonder what it'll be like being around a lot of dying people?*

'Can we be together?' I asked.

'If there's room available.'

A couple of days later John, unplugged from the drip machine, the tube hanging over his ear like a piece of punk jewellery, wandered into the six-bed ward where I had been moved. He was grinning broadly. 'Good news. We've got into the hospice and the best bit is we have a double room to ourselves.'

'Fantastic! Anything would be better than staying here. There're some really creepy guys in here.' I lowered my voice. 'See that guy over there? His body is bizarre, huge pendulous breasts, and he doesn't have teeth so he sounds like someone with cerebral palsy. The only thing he says is, Fuck off, poofter – to every nurse, male or female.'

A nurse gave me blue and white plastic bags with the words 'Patient's personal belongings' blazoned across them. As I packed I was shocked at how much stuff I'd accumulated over four weeks, but when I saw John's pile I was flabbergasted. I wondered if there was anything left in the flat.

At the hospice John was pushed up the hill in a wheelchair by the nursing unit manager, with the bags stacked on top of him. He looked like a bad Mardi Gras float. We entered the foyer of the hospice and it struck me how much like a hotel it was – spacious, with a large flower arrangement on the desk.

We were shown into a largish room painted a relaxing blue, with vinyl floors and our own bathroom. Everything had the sweet smell of disinfectant. There were two beds. 'We can push them together.'

'Sorry,' a nurse said. 'We need to be able to get around the bed.' She smiled apologetically. 'I guess I need to tell you that we don't do any medical interventions. You have to go across the road to have those. And we don't resuscitate. Enjoy your stay.'

I wandered to the window and realised that we could see the Wall, where boy sex-workers worked under the monster figs. It struck me as symbolic: if those boys were not practising safe sex they could end up in here. The TV room looked down onto Oxford Street. 'It's like living in a city apartment. I'd love to live somewhere like this, to step out into café land and gay-boy city.'

The first meal we had was delicious: Beef Burgundy and rice, a green salad and coconut apricot pie. 'Should be able to put some weight on in here, Johnny.'

I had been put on steroids so that I could take a sulphur drug to which I was allergic. My appetite had increased enormously. I couldn't get food down my throat fast enough, and if there wasn't food around I would get anxious. I got a thick neck and a moon face, and began to look like a renal patient.

The phone in our room rang. I jumped up and answered it. It was Peter Craig, in Melbourne. He was now working in the AIDS ward at

Fairfield Hospital and was about to take annual leave. 'I thought I'd come up and see you guys.'

'There's an eager puppy here who wants to talk to you. I'll put him on.'

'Pete! You can stay in our flat, while we're in here. It'll be great. I can't wait to see you.'

When Peter arrived he asked when we thought we'd be going home. 'Will you need someone to help you? If you like, I could stay. I've got three weeks of leave left.'

'I want to go somewhere warm,' John said. 'Noosa.'

Peter sucked air through his teeth. 'The airlines won't take you if you've had a pneumothorax in the last six months. The change in air pressure can cause it to happen again. Maybe you should think about somewhere closer? Coffs Harbour?'

'I want warmth.'

When it was time to go home, we put John in the front seat of Peter's car and loaded the plastic bags in the back with me. On my lap I nursed a drip-stand that the hospice had lent us for John's naso-gastric feeds. The car was struggling with the extra weight. We took off, stalled and started again. We must have looked like the Beverly Hillbillies.

As if to welcome us home, the sun came out as we pulled up outside our block. Our neighbour, old John, was sitting on the fence where he spent most of his afternoons. He and his wife Merna had been collecting our mail, even remembering us in their prayers. 'Hello, boys. Home again? Nothing better.'

Peter put my John's arm around his shoulder to support him as they climbed the stairs. I struggled behind carrying some of the bags and the drip-stand. *He used to be so physical, playing footy, tennis and jogging. Now he's just an old man.*

Arriving home was like crawling under a crisp cotton doona. The old familiar smells, the plants on the balcony, and a bunch of flowers with a note: 'Welcome home boys, Love Morna.'

Peter had washed our bedding and done our laundry and

filled our fridge. He unpacked while John and I sat on the bed. 'I'll make you some dinner and then I'll go.' He had arranged to stay with a friend in Bondi.

When he'd left, we lay down on the bed beside each other, the first time we'd been alone for months. 'Hello,' John said shyly.

'This crew-cut is pretty sexy.' I ran my fingers over his fuzzy head. I moved closer to him and kissed him gently on the lips. He kissed me back, his mouth lightly opened. I could smell the vanilla of the drip-feed as our tongues mingled. I put my hand under his T-shirt and was struck by how thin he was. I could feel the outline of his ribs, and my spine tingled.

John rolled over on top of me. I placed my hand on his hard-on through his tracksuit pants and then ventured inside. He was groaning in my ear, his warm breath against my neck. 'I want you to screw me,' he whispered. I was shocked. We hadn't had anal sex since we had found out we were positive. I could still hear John's angry cry: 'That's how we got into this mess in the first place.'

John flicked his eyebrows up and down, smiling seductively. He started undressing me and kissing my hard-on. I undressed him, revealing his skeletal body, his skin hanging loose. I tried hard not to let him see that I was shocked. I hugged him and we rolled around the bed naked, his tube swinging and getting caught up in our bodies.

I reached over to the bedside table and pulled out a condom and lube. I undid the packet, squeezed the teat and rolled it on; John ripped open the packet of lube and smeared it on. He then climbed over me, reached behind him and grabbed my cock and attempted to push it past his sphincter. He wasn't having much luck, but he kept trying. My cock was starting to bend. 'We don't have to do this if you don't want to,' I said.

'I want to.' We persisted and eventually he opened and took me inside him. He leant back and pulled his cock and slid up and down on me. When he came there was very little fluid, another reminder of how unwell he was.

I withdrew, pulled the condom off and brought myself to orgasm, my come splashing onto my belly. John smeared it and then licked his fingers clean. 'Mmm.' We lay there. I felt sad. *That was such a gift, giving of himself. I love him for it.* We drifted off to sleep, content.

The next day John wanted to go for a drive. When we got downstairs I went to open the passenger door for him. 'No, I want to drive.'

'Are you up to it?'

'Think so.'

He started the car but found the clutch difficult and stalled it. I didn't say anything. He tried again and this time he was able to back us out, but when he attempted to take off we kangaroo-hopped until John disengaged and put on the handbrake. 'Bloody hell.' We were sitting in the middle of the road, the engine still running. I offered to drive. 'No!'

We started up and drove out to the Gap, a place famous for its suicides, a high cliff with rocks below to crush the life out of you. We walked over the rocky outcrop with its little windblown ti-trees to the fence on the edge of the cliff. The exertion started John coughing. He recovered his breath and we stood watching huge waves crash against the rocky wall.

The dome of the blue sky above and the dark green horizon made me aware that we were standing on a large rock hurtling through space. I walked to the edge. Being up this high was making me charged. I had a strong desire to run off the cliff and freefall through space. *Perhaps vertigo is not fear of falling but the desire to jump?*

John drove back along the clifftop and I could see a police breathalysing station ahead. A cop flagged us onto the side of the road. 'Good evening, driver. Have you been drinking this afternoon? I require you to undergo a breath test for the purpose of indicating the concentration of alcohol in your blood, and I instruct you to exhale deeply in one single breath from your lungs into this approved device.'

This should be fun. John took a deep breath and exhaled as best he could, but he only wheezed until a cough broke through.

'I'm sorry, driver, I'm going to have to ask you to do it again.' John took another breath and blew very hard, venting his anger. Then he started coughing again. The policeman looked at the meter. 'Thank you, you may proceed.' John pulled over to let the cough run its course.

'What a bastard. Couldn't he see that you were unwell? Let me drive, got to get you home.' When we arrived John went to his codeine linctus like an alcoholic to vodka.

In the morning we were sitting on the lounge watching mindless morning television. I started playing with the wrist weights he had used in hospital to keep up his strength: dayglo green with a black velcro stripe. They were sensual, squishy, sand-filled. I rolled one of them up tightly and secured it with the velcro, making an hourglass shape. Looks like a little hat. 'Put it on.'

He looked amazing, his bald head topped by the little green hat – like a clown from a thirties film.

'You look so cute,' I laughed. 'Have we got some film in the camera?' I found the camera but there was no film.

I walked down to the shops, sticking my head in at the laundry and saying hello to Rosa. 'You been away?'

'You could say that.' Living here had a wonderful community feel about it. Bruce the chemist always greeted me by name. And old John was like a grandfather to John and me. I went to the camera shop and bought film. In the shopping centre I found other things that I could stick to John's head.

John sat at the dining-table. 'Put the little hat on.' John did so with a grudging smile. Click. I dug into the shopping bag and pulled out a stick-on bow, the kind that you put on presents, and put it to one side of his forehead. 'You look like a drag queen.'

'Great.'

'Next trick.' I pulled an icecream cone out of the bag. I stuck it to his forehead with Blutack. It looked like a unicorn's horn. He was so beautiful; his big brown eyes and their heavy-duty eyelashes made him look like a baby seal.

'And now for the grand finale.' I pulled out a packet of plastic farm animals and proceeded to fasten them to his head. Two cows, a sheep, a pig and a piece of fencing. It looked hilarious and I couldn't stop laughing while I tried to take the photo. John was irritated.

'You're making fun of me.'

'I'm not. It's because I love you.'

The next day when I returned with the prints, John slowly went through them, cracking a smile and even chuckling. 'You are such a dag.'

Peter and I had managed to argue John down from Noosa to Byron Bay, only eight hours away. We decided to break the journey at Coffs Harbour. Peter was driving, John in the passenger seat, and I was in the back seat behind him as we hurtled along the freeway. John's little ears looked so cute, I couldn't resist gently flicking them with my fingers. He would reach up and play with my hand, *rub rub rub, pat pat pat*, and then kiss it.

We reached Coffs Harbour mid-afternoon and drove through industrial estates looking for the motel John had chosen from the NRMA accommodation guide. When we found it we realised why it was called the Aqua-jet. In front of it loomed a blue plastic mountain of waterslides.

'Oh, wow, can we go please Dad, please please?' I said.

'Yeah, yeah, after lunch.'

In the changing-shed I caught sight of a chubby white body. *Nice fat white bum?* I was looking in the mirror. *Oh God, it's me.* I stood there appalled by the spare tyre I was carrying. *Can't wait to get off the cortisone.* It was so ridiculous. John's body was starved for fat and here I was piling it on.

John had decided not to try the slides. Peter and I grabbed rubber mats and ran up the stairs like twelve-year-olds. Halfway up I ran out of breath. I hadn't realised how unfit I was. At the top, the gaping mouths of the slides greeted us. We raced each other, turning nearly 360 degrees, speeding downwards and slamming into the pool. Peter crashed into the water beside me.

As we made our way back to the stairs John called, 'Smile!' He had the camera up to his face.

'No, I'm too fat.' Click. 'Thanks.'

Peter said, 'It's good to have some fat. At John's stage the body is cannibalising its muscle to get the energy it needs. Look how hard it is for him to put weight on.'

Next day at Byron Bay there were lots of alternative types walking along the main street among the rural folk, and a community centre painted with a large rainbow and dolphins. We found the Lord Byron Motel, an attractive building, mid-eighties with vari-coloured brickwork. Our room was very large, with exposed brickwork, a double bed and a single. Peter and I unpacked the boxes of drip-feed, the drip-stand and our bags. Then he headed off to Belongil Beach House where he was staying, promising to return to take us for dinner.

We had a pleasant meal and after dinner John was asleep within minutes. Having asked us down to the Beach House for lunch the next day, Peter left. I turned on the television and sat on the bed next to John. He started mumbling, his eyes half open, then began to twitch. *This doesn't feel good. It's like the spirit of a troubled soul has possessed him. Maybe the lymphoma has gone to his brain. Jesus!* Steve Vizard was doing his Top Ten on the screen. I lay beside John. *I love you.*

Belongil Beach House was built around a large courtyard, with an open café on one side. The place looked pleasant enough, but Peter's accommodation was a fibro lean-to with holes punched in the wall and a mattress covered in stains. John pressed it. 'Bit soft. You might need a chiropractor after sleeping on this.' The common-room held the sweet smell of dope and a bunch of young hippies. We waved at them and made our way to the café. Halfway through the meal John stood up abruptly. 'I've got to go to the toilet.' He was moving from leg to leg, holding his penis through his jeans.

In the toilet John anxiously fumbled with his fly and pulled out his squirting penis. He was ashamed of wetting himself.

I took him back to the table. After lunch I asked him to let me walk back alone along the beach.

At the end of the bush track a beautiful white sandy beach opened up before me. Bright azure water pulsed at the shore. It was low tide. I took my shoes and socks off and walked at the water's edge. Warm breezes played over me as the waves rippled to shore and the water flowed around my ankles. *Water is so accommodating, it moves around me and continues on its way.*

I sat below the dunes and rubbed the sand off my feet, watching the cloud shadows move along the beach. *If John's going mad, where does his soul go? Trapped inside his madness, or maybe floating free?* My eyes filled with tears. One ran down my cheek and into my mouth. Before I knew it my face was tightly screwed up, as if I were trying to squeeze out the tears and the pain. *I don't want him to go. I don't want him to die. He's slipping through my fingers like wet spaghetti.*

I walked back to the motel, feeling a little unburdened after having a good cry. Peter sat on the single bed reading the paper. John was asleep again, hooked up to his drip-feed. He was twitching, his eyes half open.

A couple of days later a friend, Beth, whom I had met when I was at TNT Couriers doing shit work to pay the rent, drove down from Brisbane. She was a striking woman, large with short hair bleached white. We had become good friends, sitting in cafés, laughing and ripping up the latest films and plays. She had also been a great support when things with John got heavy. A believer in the New Age, she was able to see things from an 'own your own life' perspective.

As we wandered through the scrub to the beach I told Beth about my fears. 'I think he's getting demented. He's very vague and he sleeps all night with his eyes half open. I'm not coping very well.'

'You're going through a very difficult time, you're about to lose your boyfriend of fifteen years. It's okay not to cope.' She put her arms around me and I was pressed against her breast in warmth, comfort, safety.

'Sorry, I've cried all over your shirt.'

'It'll dry.'

'I love this place. I get a lot of comfort from walking along these beaches. I've been coming down here and crying. There's something healing about it.' A movement out beyond the waves caught my eye. I saw a group of three dolphins, their fins breaking the water, revolving. 'So beautiful.'

'It augurs well, they're a powerful healing symbol.'

'I'd love to be out there swimming with them. They look such sensual animals.' I stood on the rocks and thanked the beach for its solace.

All along the Pacific Highway back to Sydney, John kept needing to go to the toilet. We would pull over to a petrol station, John would run and get the key from the manager and then rush to the toilet. We'd head off again only to be stopped half an hour later. Once we pulled up on the gravel shoulder as semitrailers hurtled down the hill, rocking the car. John stumbled across the rocky ground to a tree and marked its trunk.

We decided to break our journey at Port Macquarie and checked into Sails Resort on the Hastings River. I went for a drive around the cliffs. I spotted a beach, parked the car and climbed down a dirt track. It was like walking into a tourism ad, families picnicking, playing French cricket, boys floating on surf mats in the mouth of the river, riding the small waves. A large fishing trawler passed and the boys rode the wake.

I sat on a rock, looking across the mouth of the river, listening to the sound of the waves. I wanted to cry but didn't feel safe enough;

there were too many people. *I feel the earth is shifting beneath my feet. Nothing feels stable.* A year ago John had been strong, playing tennis. Now he was dying and I was thinking of resigning from Fun and Esteem. It was too hard to work with AIDS during the day and come home to it. I started thinking about the moment of John's death. *What will that be like? A flash? A clang? Will I feel angels descending and whisking his spirit away? I don't want him to die. Who will look after me when I get sick?*

Back at the hotel John was sitting up on the bed reading a pamphlet for the Port Macquarie Koala Hospital. 'Sick koalis,' he said in a baby voice. 'Koalis in wheelchairs with oxygen masks.'

The reality was far more devastating. The hospital's display area showed photos of koalas with severed arms and smashed-in faces. Underneath each was a small piece of text: 'Polly was hit by a truck on the Pacific Highway. She was brought in with one arm and one leg broken and internal injuries. She was carrying a baby who survived, but Polly didn't.'

John and I stood looking at the photos, me leaning on his shoulder, reading the gruesome stories. In the yards we saw the same devastation in the flesh: koalas with amputated limbs, missing eyes, legs in plaster. I found myself talking to one, apologising on behalf of the human race. Driving back to the hotel, we were silent.

That night we had dinner at the hotel restaurant. It was quite swanky, its patrons dressed up. We were wearing T-shirts and track pants. John had his naso-gastric tube in and was carrying his Big John bag. I noticed that people were mumbling to each other and secretly looking at us. I caught the eye of a woman with a very tight perm, smiled at her and waved. She waved back, embarrassed. I wanted to say, 'This is what someone looks like when he's dying.' But instead I called, 'Hi, love your hair.'

'Tim!' said Peter under his breath.

'I'm sick to death of people staring at him.'

Chapter *ELEVEN*

Reality Check

Back home in Sydney I was in the lounge-room reading about Neneh Cherry in *The Face*. John called to me from the bedroom. I rushed in to him.

'We have to get the cricket whites! The other team will be here in a minute.'

'John, what team are you talking about?'

'The Australian cricket team. They're coming on the supply ship.'

'Where are we?'

'Christmas Island.' *Do I humour him, or try to give him a reality check?*

'John, we're in Rose Bay in Sydney.'

'What about the team?' His face was scrunched with worry.

'There is no team.' He tried to comprehend what was happening to him. He started to whimper.

'It's all right, Johnny. I think we should go to see the doctor.'

'I'm not sick.'

'I have to go to see the doctor and I'd like you to come with me.'

I rang Carole. I didn't want John to hear so I lowered my voice. 'I'm taking John into hospital. He's absolutely mental, hallucinating. I'm worried the lymphoma may have gone to his brain.'

'I'll be there as soon as I can.'

I drove John into Emergency. 'You can't park there, mate.'

'I'm just dropping my friend off. He's very sick.'

'It's parking for ambulances, mate. Just pray they don't clamp your wheels.'

Carole was waiting in the foyer. John had to be admitted: name, address, what drugs? Then the nurse took us down to a cubicle.

Tony the registrar appeared. 'Hi John, what's going on for you?' John looked confused.

'He's been behaving oddly, sleeping with his eyes half open, sleep-talking, and this morning he was hallucinating.' Tony said they would run some tests and hurried away. I told Carole I should move the car and realised I would have to go home anyway to get John's things.

The flat felt odd, like no one had been living there for a while. I grabbed a couple of pairs of sleep shorts, some T-shirts and John's slippers. He always put on his brown corduroy slippers when he got home from work, much to the amusement of his flatmates down the years. I put everything into a sports bag and I was about to head off when the phone rang. It was Carole.

'You're not going to believe this. He's diabetic. They did a blood sugar reading and found that it was 42. Apparently he should have been in a coma.'

I laughed. 'I can't believe it. Sorry to laugh.'

At the hospital John was sitting up in the bed, smiling.

'Johnny, you're back.' He didn't understand. 'You've been away, to Christmas Island.'

'I sort of remember.'

Tony turned up again. I asked how this could have happened.

'It was probably the Pentamadine that they used for his PCP. We're concerned at how much weight he has lost. We think he should be on naso-gastric feeds, but he'll have to be in here so we can monitor his blood sugar. We've got a bed up on the ward.'

John complained of pain when he ate, as he had when he had lymphoma. Sam suggested another endoscope, which showed the ulcer in the same place as before. Chemo was no longer feasible, but they might be able to use radiotherapy. The radiologist saw us after he had the biopsy results and told us he could start treatment early in January. 'In the meantime we need to run some more tests to determine how disseminated it is.'

'We're going to Melbourne for Christmas.'

'We'll start when you get back.'

That night I dreamt that John had been bitten in the stomach by the devil himself.

Home for Christmas

I was sick of sitting in the back seat of the car. But we would soon be home for Christmas, which meant sleeping in, Mum's smoked salmon platter, and the smell of pine needles.

When we reached Melbourne we dropped Peter off at the nurses' home at Fairfield Hospital, thanking him for everything he'd done for us in the last months. I drove John to his family home in East Ivanhoe. Lois was watering the garden in her turquoise shell suit. She opened John's door and smiled, offering him a hand to get out of the car.

John sat on the lounge. Lois brought him a cup of tea and asked about Byron Bay. 'I believe it's magnificent. I've never been anywhere other than Sorrento or Sydney.' She thanked me for driving John home and asked what I was doing for Christmas day.

'Lunch with the family, I guess.'

At home Mum was sitting at the dining-table with the usual book. She asked after John.

'He's now having difficulty breathing, I think because he's anaemic. I want to say to God, Just give him a break, will you?'

'It'll be over soon.'

'I don't want to hear that.'

Next morning I was woken by Peter ringing from Fairfield. 'John can scarcely breathe this morning. He asked me to bring him into hospital.'

'I'll be there as soon as I can.' I drove off with the tape of Prince's *Diamonds and Pearls* blaring away.

Fairfield, the infectious diseases hospital, is surrounded by magnificent lawns, and at this time of year the gardens were filled with peacocks and agapanthus in full bloom.

In the ward I asked a nurse for directions.

'You're John's lover? He's very sweet. Beautiful eyelashes.'

In John's room a tall woman with sensual lips painted fire-engine red was standing next to Peter. I went to kiss John but he was wearing an oxygen mask. I kept pretending I was trying to kiss him through the mask. 'I can't do it, there's this thing on your face.' He smiled, lifted the mask and pouted his lips. The doctor introduced herself.

'We think it's pneumonia but we don't know which kind, and I don't want to do an induced sputum or bronchoscopy in case it causes another pneumothorax. I suggest that we treat for both PCP and bacterial pneumonia. Are you happy with that, John?'

'You're the doctor.'

'I'm afraid it means that you'll be in here for Christmas.' John sighed. 'I'm sorry. I'll see you in the morning.' She left.

'Fuck. In here for Christmas.'

'Don't worry, we'll make it the best Christmas ever.'

Peter left and I crawled onto the bed beside John, holding

him close to me. *Stay with me, don't go just yet.* Like a puppy crawling up to its mother I drew comfort from his heartbeat.

A chubby man with thinning hair came in carrying two bags of drugs and a kidney dish. He introduced himself as Michael. I held John's hand while Michael swabbed John's forearm. 'Good veins. Most of the patients in here would kill for veins like these. Right, anaesthetic, small prick.' John grimaced. 'Now the cannula.' He flashed its steel tip. 'Should be numb enough now.' He speared John's forearm. John groaned. 'It's in.' He secured the cannula with tape. 'I'll see you guys later. Don't hesitate to buzz me. Oh Tim, do you want to stay tonight? There's a camp stretcher we can set up for you. And we may be able to get you some dinner, even though we're not meant to feed visitors.'

I lay on the stretcher waiting for John to wake. When he stirred I sat beside him and leant on the bed. I sang softly, 'We wish you a merry Christmas.' John opened his bleary eyes, smiled and stretched. I kissed him gently and he ran his fingers through my hair.

'My Timba.'

'My John. Time for presents?' I handed him a box wrapped in silver paper. He opened it. 'It's a Stable Table. It's like a tray with a pillow under it so you can eat in front of the teev.'

'Thanks. There's something for you under the bed. I got Peter to get it for me.'

I ripped off the paper. I didn't know what it was. 'It's a document holder. It's got a little motorised clamp that moves up and down when you use the foot pedal.' John grabbed the pedal from the box and set the clamp running.

'It's bizarre.'

'You don't like it?'

'It's good, but I don't know if the clamp is all that useful.' *You always have to tell the truth, don't you Timothy?*

The nurse came in with John's breakfast tray decked in tinsel. She was dressed as an angel with cardboard wings.

'You look fabulous!'

'Thank you. Christmas breakfast: fruit muffins, fruit salad, scrambled eggs and a chocky. Tim, would you like some eggs?'

'Please.'

Later that morning John's youngest brother Anthony and Lois arrived with shopping bags. Anthony stood shyly on the outer, smiling bashfully. 'We've got some treats for you. Some Christmas cake,' Lois said. Anthony hung a gold-foil Season's Greetings banner. John smiled contentedly. Lois handed him his present, a pair of pyjamas. 'It's not much but I thought they'd be useful.'

Anthony handed him his present, a book about Australian cricket.

A man stuck his head round the door. 'Can we come in?' He brought three children into the room. One handed John a small cactus in a terracotta pot with a ribbon around it. Another handed him a bag of mixed lollies, and the third handed him a handmade card that read, 'Hope you get well soon, Merry Christmas, the Baileys.' They shuffled out again.

The kids must have known which ward they were walking into. Very touching. 'Isn't that fantastic?'

'A piece of human kindness,' Lois pondered.

When lunch arrived, Lois took the lid off the meal. 'Roast turkey. Lucky boy. Would you like me to cut it up for you?'

She started feeding him like a baby. I felt she was infantilising him, but when I saw the comfort he was getting I knew she was right. I left to have lunch with my own family.

I was getting into the car at the supermarket after getting nibblies for John and noticed a big scratch in the driver's door. When I got home I started to tell Mum someone had dinged her car.

'That happened weeks ago. The doctor from the hospital rang and wants you to call as soon as you can.' My heart was in my throat. *Please be all right. Please.*

'John's had a respiratory arrest but we were able to resuscitate him. I think you should come in as soon as you can.'

Mum made me ask Anna to drive me. 'We don't want you to have an accident.'

We drove to Fairfield talking about her pregnancy. 'Is it like having an alien inside you?'

'Yes, it's this thing that takes over your body, making all the decisions.' I started to wonder if John might come back as Anna's baby. We drifted into silence. I felt numb. What could I do to change what was happening? My friend Ken at work would suggest sacrificing a chicken or burning ginseng.

We went into the ward and Lois was there. 'How's the baby coming along? Are you hoping for a boy or a girl?'

'Don't mind.'

Lois and Anna left us alone. I sat next to John's head. He turned to me with tears in his eyes. 'It didn't hurt a bit. I was just not here and now my ribs are all bruised from the bloody cardiac massage.'

He looked at me with those big brown eyes. 'I wish I'd gone. It was so easy.' I could feel tears in my eyes. 'Are you okay hearing that?'

'No, I'm not ready for you to go.'

'We've said goodbye, haven't we?' I hugged him and we both cried.

'What did you see on the other side?'

'Nothing.'

I was relieved that he hadn't died. I'd always had this fantasy of being there holding his hand as he slipped away. And we had made a pact that if one of us was dying he would wait until the other was there.

Lois, John, the registrar and I discussed John's decision that he didn't want to be resuscitated again.

Our friend David had been sitting with John and asked me if I wanted to go to a movie. He suggested *Truly Madly Deeply*. Had I heard about it?

I had. Another friend raved about the performance of Juliet Stevenson. Her boyfriend had died suddenly under anaesthetic and she was sitting with a counsellor. 'It's an amazing performance, so undignified. She's got tears running down her cheeks and she's really snotty.'

There was a crowd queuing for tickets. I wanted to tell them all about John. I wanted them to know how brave I was being.

I braced myself in my velvet seat, terrified I might howl. The film started. Juliet Stevenson talks to her counsellor. She is sitting with her head in her hands. She says bitterly, 'I miss him, I miss him, I miss him! I know I shouldn't do this.' The counsellor says nothing. 'There's no point going to bed because he's not there. I'm so angry with him. I can't forgive him for not being here.' She was snotty and hysterical. *I don't know if I can sit it out. Don't cry yet. Not yet.*

As we were leaving the cinema, I remembered that first moment and started to cry. Over coffee David told me about his conversation with John that morning. 'He's getting really tired. He wishes he'd died but feels that's giving in. I said, "Buddy we all know how hard this has been for you and we wouldn't think any less of you. And it's not giving in, it's taking control."'

I told him I wished I could be brave enough to say that.

'You will be.'

John was being wheeled into the shower. I watched the nurse undress him, revealing his skeletal body. 'We should change that dressing on your pressure sore after the shower.' *Oh God, a pressure sore, he's falling apart.* 'Are we washing your hair today?'

I want to wash him; a chance to be together in a way that we haven't for some time. 'Can I wash him?' John agreed unenthusiastically.

I turned on the hose, felt its temperature and swung it onto John. He reeled. 'Ow! Too cold.'

I fumbled nervously. Now it was too hot. 'You're not doing it right. Can you get the nurse to do it please?' I sat on the window-sill feeling rejected and sooky, chewing my nails. The nurse caught my eye and winked.

As we wheeled him back to bed she confided to me, 'He loves you, and that's why he feels he can trust that you won't leave.'

Later that day the physio came into the room. 'Are you ready for some chest work?'

'No. I hate it,' John whinged.

'We have to get the mucus out of your lungs or you'll drown.' He tilted the bed, put John on his side and started gently percussing his ribs. 'Playing the bongos, eh Johnny?' John coughed furiously, bringing up sputum into a tissue. *It's weird that the way to treat your cough is to make you cough more.*

The physio did it a couple more times and started on the other side, until John said, 'No more.' He lay back on the bed, exhausted. His cough didn't stop there. Every time he tried to catch his breath he would splutter. I buzzed and Michael came in, then fetched some morphine. John winced as he drank it. 'It's so bitter.'

Michael asked me to step outside. 'Sorry to tell you, but we think he'll be dead by the end of the week.' He let the thought sit for a moment. I was in shock, my hands shaking. 'Why don't you take him home, or down to Sorrento?' When I suggested it to John he said no. He wanted to stay here.

I walked through the hospital grounds. Agapanthus gave way to scrappy Australian bush and the Yarra River opened up before me. I sat on a bench that overlooked a Victorian boatshed. There were kids paddling in small dinghies and canoes, splashing each other with their oars. Their laughter echoed through the gorge. *Life goes on. I'm jealous. I used to love these kind of afternoons.* I noticed a coin-operated barbecue.

I found some enclosures with scrawny sheep and goats. The goats had pustules, growths around their mouths. *They must be experimental animals, infected to see what happens.* They stared through the fence with big weeping eyes, as if asking for help. I couldn't handle it and turned away. The ground in front of me moved dramatically. Rabbits, millions of rabbits. Probably escapees from the lab. *Hope none of them is carrying disease.*

Back in the ward I told John what I'd seen. 'There's a coin-operated barbecue down there. I reckon we should get all our friends to come and have a barbecue.' John liked the idea.

My friend Tom had gone to Cleveland to further his English studies. He and his wife Laura, a stunning Italo-American, were back in Melbourne to spend Christmas with Tom's family. They turned up to see John. Tom looked staggered and his sadness leaked out from behind his attempt to appear cheerful.

I asked Laura about her research.

'I'm still digging for pig bones in Kenya, and going through drawers and drawers of bones in the archaeological museum.'

John asked why, and then started coughing. Tom held his hand.

'There has always been a relationship between the migrations of pigs and man.'

'Because man feeds on the pig?'

'No, I believe they have similar needs for water, warmth and food. That's what my thesis is trying to prove.'

We sat chatting. John was coughing. None of us said anything, pretending it wasn't happening. He kept apologising.

Tom and Laura were going to Sydney for a few days. We lent them our flat. They asked if there was anything we would like brought back. I asked for mail and our photo albums. John had always been a camera bug and we had photos from every holiday we'd been on. I wanted John to see them again, hoping to give him a little something to cling to.

Tom said goodbye with tears in his eyes. Laura bent down and kissed John. I saw them out. Tom put his arm through mine. 'He is such a beautiful man, kind and warm. I feel very sorry for you both.' We hugged and they were gone.

I went back into the room. 'It's a really nice day outside, John, quite warm. Do you want to go for a walk? I'll get us a wheelchair.'

I came back with a tall nurse with a beautiful Danish accent. We lifted him into the chair and put a rug over his knees. I wheeled him out to the garden and then across the paddock towards the river. The ground jumped. 'Oh, bunnies,' John gasped. 'Millions of bunnies.' He was ecstatic.

We sat on the bench and held hands like an old couple on a verandah, listening to the birds and enjoying the cool breeze and the sun.

I wheeled him back to the ward. The Danish nurse was waiting for us. 'How vos det, John?' We lifted him into bed. 'You see the peacocks?'

'No. Lots of bunnies.' John started coughing again. She left to get some medication. I put my head in John's lap.

Jackie and Juliet came tumbling into John's room, laughing hysterically, and then pulled up. 'Sorry,' said Juliet. 'We were asking the nurse about you, and Miss Fluffy here farted loudly.'

'Don't I get a hug or anything?' John asked like a little boy. They rushed him, making a big fuss.

At that moment a group of people piled in: two of John's mates from the school footy team, another old school friend Eric and his wife Andy with a big bunch of flowers. John loved seeing his old friends. He was grinning from ear to ear. I hadn't seen him so happy for weeks. We lifted him into the chair and our little entourage wheeled him across the bumpy lawn, nearly bouncing him out once or twice.

Down by the barbecue other friends stood silently. I was expecting them to break into applause. They walked towards us, trying not to crowd John in, taking turns to say hello and kiss him. Prue held her daughter on one hip. 'Sinead, do you want to kiss John?' She buried her head in Prue's chest.

'Hello, John.' Pepe's son Tashi held a daisy that he'd picked out of the garden.

'Tashi, haven't you grown!' Tashi smiled contentedly.

Peter was there with his New Zealand boyfriend Daryl; so was Prue's boyfriend Kevin; Andrew, who had lived with John and Peter in the fabulous Patty Duke house; Mark, who had brought his daughters' paintings into St Vincent's.

Some friends sat on others' knees, arms around each other. Kids played chasey around the trees. The barbecue was under way, the air filled with the smoke of charred meat.

I overheard John telling Kevin about his respiratory arrest. 'It was so easy, I didn't feel a thing. I wish I hadn't been resuscitated.'

Franco and James walked over to John and hugged him. 'What are you guys doing here!'

'I'm down here for the film I'm working on.'

'And I've come down to see you, my friend.'

People chewed on sausages, water crackers with paté, or Tim Tams, talking about John. I was aware that John kept saying he wished he hadn't been resuscitated. I heard him complaining to Jackie and Juliet about his bruised ribs. At that moment he broke into paroxysms of coughing, but continued when he had recovered his breath. 'I want to go down to Sorrento and then back to Sydney, but it doesn't look like I'll get there,' he said sadly and started coughing again.

It was starting to chip away at me. *Why is he saying this? He's saying he wants to die.* I sat down by Pepe. 'I can't stand hearing John wishing he was dead.'

'It's going to happen, Tim.'

'I don't want it to.' I cried on her shoulder.

John was coughing furiously now. I announced that we were going indoors. Some people started clearing up, others came over and hugged him or kissed him. Many of them realised they might not see him again. James and Pepe walked back with us. *The next time the group will see each other is probably going to be at John's funeral.*

Back in a warm bed, John was still coughing. 'I'm so tired, it exhausts me.'

'Why don't you have a sleep?'

'If I could stop coughing I might.' I rubbed his back. When I brought the resident in, John barked at him. 'Fucken oath! Can you stop it? I want you to stop me coughing.'

'What would you like us to do?'

'Double my morphine.'

'I can't authorise that, you'll have to ask the registrar in the morning.' John sighed a world-weary sigh. 'I'm sorry.' The resident left and John started crying. 'It's so unfair.'

After a hard night of coughing John got to sleep at dawn. I lay in bed with that sick feeling you get when you're over-tired, but with John asleep I was able to catch some zeds.

I woke a few hours later as Tom and Laura crept in and sat on the verandah. They had some photo albums with them. I hopped out of bed and joined them outside.

'Sorry we didn't bring more, we couldn't fit them in our luggage. It was fun trying to work out which ones to bring.'

We looked through them: our trips to Italy, Kakadu and the Daintree, and the daiquiri party for John's thirtieth.

John coughed. 'Hi guys.' He stretched and coughed again. 'Ow, my lungs hurt.'

The registrar appeared. 'I believe you're having trouble with the coughing. With the antibiotics you're on that shouldn't be happening. What would you like us to do?'

'Double my morphine.'

'I have no problem with that as long as you understand you may have another respiratory arrest.'

John squeezed out the words, 'Fine by me.' The registrar said he would organise it. 'What would happen if I ceased treatment altogether?' John wanted to know.

'You'd probably be overwhelmed by bacterial infections and drown in your own mucus.' *These thoughts are like arrows in my side.*

A nurse came and gave John more morphine. His coughing stopped, which cheered him as much as the albums. He chuckled, pointing at a photo of me in speedos at the beach. 'Thick thighs.' Tom loved seeing me being put down. John turned another page and smiled again at me standing in front of a pylon under the graffiti 'Free Tim'.

The morphine took hold and John drifted off to sleep. Tom and Laura said they would stay a while, so I wrote John a note: 'Gone home to get some sleep, hope you get some too. See you tomorrow, I love you. Timba.' I left Tom and Laura sitting with their arms around each other.

Next afternoon I dropped into the Clifton Hill pool on my way to the hospital. The water was warm, sensual, pleasurable; it caressed my body. I swam hard, as if trying to rid myself of something.

My muscles got tired so I lay on the grass. I turned onto my stomach, enjoying the sun and the view of a young man in electric-blue speedos, imagining what it would be like to bury my face in his armpits. I started to get aroused and turned away, but I lay there a while longer, drifting on the edge of sleep. Suddenly I was side-swiped by fear. *Something's changed. It doesn't feel right. God, I hope he hasn't died.*

I drove to the hospital as calmly as I could. John was alive but quite out of it. His breathing had changed.

The registrar appeared. 'We've given him Largactil to help suppress the cough and Atavan to remove any anxiety.' He was watching me closely. 'Are you happy with that?' It wasn't till some time later I realised that the doctor was suggesting the drugs would kill him.

Lois arrived with bags of shopping. 'Bob and I found a nice grave this morning. It's under a tree, and we're having a boulder as a headstone with a brass plaque on it. Do you like the sound of that?' I did. 'And Bob and I are going to be buried with him.'

I was stunned. *What about me? He is my husband of fifteen years.* I chose to say nothing. *That hurts. I feel invisible.*

She admired my T-shirt, which showed a Keith Haring cartoon for ACTUP. 'John bought it for me when he was in San Francisco.'

'Ignorance equals fear, silence equals death. Lovely.'

Bob arrived, and after kissing John he asked if we could have a word outside. We went into the corridor. I sat on a table with my arms crossed, feeling defensive. 'The funeral is going to be here in Melbourne at a Catholic church. And we don't want anyone making a statement.'

'You mean about AIDS?'

'That and the gay thing. Everyone already knows, so there's no need.' *So what's the problem?*

'You know that's against John's wishes. Be it on your conscience,' I said acidly. We stood uncomfortably together in the corridor.

Eventually he spoke again. 'It's such a tragedy. How did this happen?'

I wanted to say, 'Your son takes it up the arse,' but chose to say instead, 'I'm sorry Bob, I don't know.'

I didn't want to ring people in front of John and have him

hear me saying that he could go that night. I scavenged coins from the nursing staff and used the public phone. I rang our friends in Sydney. Beth asked if I'd like her to come down. I said I'd love that.

During the night John's breathing was so relaxed its hypnotic rhythm sent me off to sleep. I was woken later by him sighing. He moaned with every breath, like a wind through a piece of bamboo.

I asked a nurse if he was all right. She called his name loudly. It didn't rouse him. ' John, are you in pain?' He grunted no. I stayed sitting with him, watching him breathe slowly, enjoying the rhythm.

Then it was morning. I asked the nurse to keep an eye on him while I had a shower and some breakfast. When I returned to the ward, my hair dripping from the shower, Lois was spoon-feeding her son. 'Hello, my little mate. You've been asleep for days.' He nodded with a big smile on his face. I asked Lois how he had been.

'Bit mad, we've been doing all sorts of things, like playing basketball, haven't we John?' She finished feeding him and pushed the trolley away.

'Do you feel good?' I asked.

'I'm not coughing.'

It was nice to spend some time with John while he was almost intelligible. But as the day wore on he drifted back to his dreams and the constant rhythm of the moaning.

Our friend Kate from Darwin rang. 'Pepe's just told me about John. She said he was close to dying. Is that him groaning? Can you give him my love?'

'I'll hold the phone to his ear and you can tell him.' I could hear her telling him she loved him, how sad she was for him. John groaned loudly. I took the phone away. Kate was crying.

'It seems so unfair. He's the nicest person I know. I want to come down but I can't afford it, I'm sorry.'

'He knows you're thinking of him.' I hung up and sat there with him. 'Johnny, I hope you know how loved you are.'

As the afternoon wore on, John drifted into unconsciousness. Lois fell asleep in the chair and I was feeling drowsy. It was as if we were in space, floating towards an unknown planet.

I was roused by the rustle of Beth's skirt as she struggled to get her luggage through the door. She'd come straight from the airport.

'You look like you're moving house.'

'Girl's got to have her accessories.' She sat beside John. Lois opened her eyes and Beth introduced herself. I noticed the sun had gone down. It was nine-thirty. Beth offered to go and get us something to eat but Lois insisted on going herself. 'I need a break, anyway.'

When she'd gone, Beth entwined herself around me. 'This groaning thing is interesting. My great-aunt did this too.'

'What do you think it's about?'

She looked intently at John. 'Perhaps asserting that he is still alive. Or comforting himself.' John suddenly groaned louder.

I was startled. 'It's like he can hear us.'

'No doubt he can.'

Beth and I sat gossiping on the verandah in the warm night air. 'I saw *Truly Madly Deeply* the other night. I hope John will visit me like that.'

'When you're ready he will.'

I asked for some time on my own with John. Beth headed off to the waiting-room with *Harper's Bazaar*. John and I were alone again, alone with his groaning. I placed my head on his chest and put my arm across him as though I was holding him to this world. The moaning vibrating through his chest sounded like our sex, emotional, the end of climax as we drift off to sleep. It comforted me.

The groaning started to sound like wailing, but he wasn't crying. I gently rubbed his hand. *Rub rub rub, pat pat pat.* It seemed to calm him.

Beth came back in. She sat next to me and put her hand on

my knee. I rested my head on her shoulder. Lois returned wearing her turquoise shell suit. She dug into her bag and produced three salad rolls in Gladwrap. It was one a.m. We were in for the long haul. We settled ourselves. Beth and I top-and-tailed on the camp mattress.

Peter joined us. He sat on the floor with his back against the wall. We sat through the night with John groaning. It was wonderful. We shared memories and laughed.

'Lois, do you remember the time I was staying at your house and I forgot to bring my school pants?'

'The only pair we had were old ones of Chris's. I'll never forget seeing you walking to the bus in very tight pants with the legs at half-mast.'

We talked about John. 'He was such a good-looking boy,' Beth said.

It amazes me how beautiful he still is, even when he's ravaged by this virus. 'He is such a gentle soul.'

'He was my favourite. I shouldn't say it, all my boys are wonderful. But he was my favourite. Never a problem.' The night was like a celebration of John, our lover, our son, our friend.

Later, as we drifted off to sleep, the kind of shallow sleep where your head is filled with your worries, John groaned loudly. 'John, will you shut up, we're trying to sleep,' Lois joked. We all laughed.

This night was special for me because it re-established my friendship with his mother, a relationship that had been destroyed by the carry-on thirteen years before.

Chapter TWELVE

Wish You Were Here

It was morning now, Australia Day 1992. Lois had gone home and Beth and I sat with our heads on each other's shoulders. Beth suddenly laughed. 'She's fabulous, a very funny woman. And much stronger than she appears.'

Pepe appeared in the doorway, carrying a wicker basket with a baguette sticking out of it. 'Breakfast. Bread and cheese and real coffee.' John moaned. She caught sight of him and sadness washed across her face. She stroked his head gently.

Beth and I left her with him. In the corridor we opened the basket, revealing pâté, two chunks of cheese and a coffee plunger.

Jackie and Juliet arrived, followed by Tom and Laura, James, Prue, and our old friend David Bonney. There were kisses and hugs all round. Daryl came in with a box of croissants from the restaurant where he was working.

'Can we go in now?' asked James. 'I've got to leave in half an hour to get my plane.' He seemed close to tears. 'I wish I could stay.'

'I'll call you tonight.' He went in and a few minutes later Pepe emerged, eyes swollen with tears. Prue put her arms around her. Laura served coffee.

I put my head round the door to see if James wanted coffee. He was sitting with his elbows on his knees, holding his head.

A lot of tears were shed for John that day. *I hope he knows how much we all love him.* The photo albums created a good opportunity for us to share. Jackie pointed to a photo of me with dreadlocks. 'When did you have that done?'

'Or more importantly, why?' laughed Tom.

As the morning progressed, John's breathing became more laboured. The nurses were coming in every hour to turn him, hoping to stop pressure sores. *Why are they bothering? Wouldn't it be better to leave him asleep?*

Every now and then he would stop breathing. 'Why's he doing that?' I asked a nurse.

'It's Cheyne-Stokesing. It means he's probably about to die.'

'Is he in pain?' She shook her head.

The resident came in and stood looking at John's rhythmic groaning and occasional hiatus.

Lois arrived, followed by Bob – like a queen and her manservant. 'Peace at last,' she sighed. She sat by John stroking his head. 'My boy.' She pulled out a little floral hankie and wiped away her tears delicately. Bob sat on the other side.

A good-looking man in his forties with salt-and-pepper hair came in. He greeted Lois and Bob. 'You must be Tim,' he said to me. 'I'm Peter Wood, the pastoral-care worker here.' We shook hands. 'Bob and Lois have requested the last rites for John.'

He pulled out a scapular, a book of Catholic ritual and a small bottle of oil. He made the sign of the cross on John's forehead with the oil.

'In the name of God the almighty Father who created you, in the name of Jesus Christ, Son of the living God who suffered for you, in the name of the Holy Spirit who was poured out upon you, go forth faithful Christian. May you live in peace this day. May your home be with God in Zion, with Mary the Virgin Mother of God, with Joseph and all the angels and saints. My brother in faith, I entrust you to God who created you.' *This is really happening. But it all seems so unreal, like watching a movie.*

I vagued out. I didn't hear the rest of it. *This time tomorrow he'll be dead. No more cuddle bunnies. No more 'Timba'. But I'm not feeling anything. I just feel numb.*

Father Wood asked if we could have a word in the garden. 'I believe things between you and the family are pretty tense at the moment, particularly with Bob.'

'He treats me like I'm not there. It's like he's trying to reclaim John, save him from the dirty poofter who corrupted him. All this stuff about not mentioning 'gay' or AIDS at the funeral.'

'I want you to know that I will try my best to include you in the funeral. I'll talk about you as his friend. Are you happy about that?'

'He's my husband, we've been together fifteen years.'

'I understand, but you must understand there'll be nothing gained by alienating his parents.'

A nurse called me in. Father Wood patted my back and quietly wished me good luck. I went in, feeling the blind fear of a schoolboy about to get the strap.

Bob and Lois were holding John's hands. Beth and Peter were at his feet. *Where am I supposed to sit?*

I slid in between Bob and the wall and sat at John's head, lightly stroking his hair. Bob pushed in front of me and kissed John's forehead without so much as an 'excuse me'.

John's groans had become almost whispers. Every time he stopped breathing we all sat upright holding our breath. 'John, you're tricking us,' Lois said.

This went on for some time, his breathing becoming shallower, quieter. He began blowing saliva bubbles. His mouth filled with saliva which started to run down his chin. Bob grabbed a tissue and started to wipe it. There was the sweet smell of faeces in the air. *Not a lot of dignity in death, eh?*

John stopped breathing.

He was dead.

I walked out along the colonnade. The sun was shining. *Such a beautiful day.*

Then I was hit by grief. The tears came and kept coming. Snot ran out of my nose as though it was being wrung out of me. *I wish you were here to help me get through this. I'm not going to see you again, am I?*

A pigeon was startled by me and took flight. *Was that John? I wish you were here.* I shut my eyes and felt him put his arms around me from behind. I wanted to lean back and put my head on his chest but he wasn't there. The feeling had been so strong that I wasn't sure it hadn't happened. I put my arms around myself and started crying again.

A family walked past me. A little girl asked her mother, 'Has someone died?'

'I think so.'

I went back into the room. The resident was listening with his stethoscope. He felt for John's pulse and held a mirror to his mouth to check for breath. There was nothing, no sign of life. He filled out the death certificate.

'Do you want an autopsy? It could take a few days.' A shiver of horror went through Lois. She shook her head.

A nurse came in with a bowl of water and some towels to wash the body.

'Could Peter and I do it?' I asked.

We pulled the blanket back, revealing his ravaged body. There was a small turd sitting between his legs. Peter picked it up in a tissue and threw it into a contaminated-waste bin. We started to bathe him, caressing his body with sponges. It was a chance to say goodbye. I had a strong desire to kiss his penis but was well aware that Bob was crashing around the room putting everything into plastic bags. Peter rolled John towards me and washed his back and then lay him back down.

The nurse placed weights on his eyelids and put a towel around his neck. 'I'll call you when I'm finished.'

'What is she going to do? Sew his eyelids down?'

'She'll make him look peaceful,' said Peter.

I rang Mum and Dad. 'You poor boy.' I could hear that Mum's nose was chocka with snot. 'You shouldn't have to go through this.'

'I think it was a huge privilege. Not many people get to be there when their lover dies.'

We were called into the room. There he was, covered in a morgue gown with a red carnation on his chest. His eyes and jaw were shut. He looked at peace.

I sat on the verandah with Beth and Peter. 'It's weird how it doesn't look like him,' said Beth. 'Just a body and no spirit.'

I drove David to his house and went inside for a cup of tea. We listened to the new Frankie Knuckles album. David sat beside me and put his hand on my knee, asking how I was.

'Okay, I guess. I don't think I believe it yet.'

'One thing I want to say. Just because John is dead, doesn't mean it's your turn. You've been looking after him for the last two years and you're going to have to deal with him not being there. I don't want you to give up.'

'Thanks. You've become so wise, David.'

'All the drugs, darling.'

I left and drove home to Mum and Dad's. When I walked in the back gate they were sitting at the outside table, glasses of wine in hand. Dad walked over to me and hugged me. 'I love you, son,' he said with tears in his eyes.

'I've got to make some calls.'

'Leave it till the morning. Sit down and have a drink.'

But I wanted to get them over with. I went into the psychedelic bedroom, sat on the window-sill and started ringing people. James was still distressed about not having been able to stay. 'He knows you were there.'

I rang old John at our block of flats. He said Merna and he would remember us in their prayers.

Most friends were expecting the call and wanted to know how it was. Some started crying, which I couldn't handle. I'd wimp out, saying I had other calls to make. In the end I lay down and cried myself to sleep. *I wonder where you are? I just want to know you're all right.* Every time I woke I'd be hit with the thought, John's dead!

Early next morning old John called. 'I know this is the last thing you need right now, but your flat was broken into last night. It doesn't look like anything was taken but I think you should get one of your friends to come round and have the door put back on.' *God, why are you doing this to me? What is the lesson here?*

I rang Veronica and asked her to do it. 'Maybe it's John's ghost trying to get stuff before his father does,' I said.

Anna called. 'I had an amazing dream last night. It was a poem, and so clear I had to get up and write it down.' She asked if I wanted to hear it. And of course I did.

There's a new star in the sky tonight
And that star is my lover John.
He died after a fight for life,
A fight he could not have won.
In these early days of mourning,
When the glare of the sun is too bright,
And the sound of children pains me,
I love by the cool of the night.

I was speechless, moved by its sentiments and the love I felt from Anna.

I sat at the dining-table eating cornflakes with Mum's stewed rhubarb. She appeared in her burgundy velvet dressing-gown holding the newspaper open at the death notices.

> Caleo, John Robert, passed away Jan 26.
> Sleep peacefully my son, now there's no more pain.
> You will always be remembered until we meet again.
> All our love, Mum, Dad, Michael, Paul, Christopher, Anthony.

And: 'Caleo, John. A kind and loving young man, nephew of Joan and cousin to Lisa. Now in God's care.'

None of them mentioned me. I started to feel invisible again. I didn't want the end of my relationship marked by denial of its existence. I rang James in Sydney and asked him to place an obituary in the *Star Observer.* '"Thanks for the laughter, I love you. Tim." I'll pay you when I get back to Sydney.'

'Don't worry about it.'

'I want to. It won't be mine if I don't.'

The next day there were more notices, some of which were a bit on the edge, gay urban terrorism.

'Part of oppression is having other people tell your story. Luv ya, Karl Steinberg.'

'Beloved partner of Tim. Sadly missed by his friends. At rest, in our memories he lives.' *No name. I wonder who that was?* I felt relieved. The truth was out.

I went to our local newsagency to place one myself. 'You have to be family, or have the death certificate.'

'If you look in today's paper you will see there are already notices to him.' He conceded and I filled the form out: 'In loving memory of John Caleo who was taken from us Jan 26. I miss you terribly and pray that one day we'll be together again.'

'What about music? Did John have a favourite song?'

'The Essendon club song,' I joked. We were in Father Wood's office planning the funeral. 'I can't think.' *Don't Panic. How embarrassing, not knowing his favourite song.* 'Vince Jones, but which song? Perhaps Enya?'

'What about "On Your Shore"?' Peter offered. 'They played it at Stephen's funeral. It's really nice.' Then he handed me a photocopy of a poem called 'Life Unbroken'.

'It's great, Pete, thanks.'

As we were leaving, Bob asked what was happening about the car. I had thought I'd buy it from the leasing company.

'You said you didn't want it,' he said.

'I'm sorry Bob, but I do now.'

'So do I.'

'Everyone in your family already has a car.'

'Have you seen the bomb that Anthony is driving?' Lois walked up to us. 'Excuse me Lois, I'm talking to Tim.'

'Yes, and I'm listening.' And listen she did. It made him nervous. I said I'd let him have it if he agreed to give me first option to buy it.

Lois took me aside. 'You don't have to deal with Bob. You come to me or Christopher.'

The funeral was on Friday, five days after John had died. Mum woke me that morning. I kicked the sheet back, turned my weary body towards the floor, and sat on the edge of the bed waiting for my hard-on to recede. I crawled into the shower and stood under the water. Coming through the window was the kind of glary light that said it was going to be a hot day.

As I was about to leave, Anna handed me a small parcel. It

was an enamelled Mickey Mouse badge. I was moved almost to tears. She understood what I was feeling. 'I love it. A little bit of John.' I put it on John's wool jacket over my heart.

When I arrived at the Caleos' the front lawn was covered in cars, including two large white limousines. Among the family friends in their Sunday best there was only one face I recognised, his Aunt Grace. We waved at each other politely across the lawn.

Lois came up. 'Tim, you and Peter are in the family car with Anthony and me.' Peter was already sitting in the back seat. I slid in beside him. Lois and Anthony got in. I felt unsettled, my guts were churning. *I don't want to do this. This makes it real.*

Arriving at the church was like going to the Academy Awards. I stepped out among our friends, some of whom I had not seen for years. People were queuing to sign the register. Inside, the organ was playing. The coffin was covered in wreaths of flowers. *That's my John in that box. Probably rotting by now.* I had fantasies of running up to it and throwing the lid off and hugging him. Wailing.

The organist started a hymn, 'As Gentle As Silence'. Not many people knew it. Father Wood in ceremonial vestments entered, followed by Father Wallbridge – our headmaster from school – and then another four priests. The surprises kept coming. There were six boys in school blazers. *Oh my God, they're prefects.*

'We are here today to mourn the loss of our dear son. Our hearts go out to Bob and Lois and his brothers Michael, Paul, Chris and Anthony. And then his friends, Tim and Peter, who were a wonderful support to him in the last few months.'

Chris did the first reading from the Book of Lamentations. 'It is good to wait in silence for the Lord to save.' Anthony read the responsorial psalm. 'I hope in the Lord, I trust in his word.' *This is so Catholic. I wonder what the hell John is thinking about it. It's like they're trying to claim a lost soul.*

It was my turn. I got out of my seat, trying not to tread on people's feet. I was nervous. I wanted it to be fabulous. I read 'Life Unbroken'.

> Death is nothing at all . . .
> I have only slipped away into the next room.
> I am I and you are you . . .
> Whatever we were to each other, that we are still.
> Call me by my old familiar name.
> Speak to me in the easy way which you always used to.
> Put no difference into your tone:
> Wear no forced air of solemnity or sorrow.
> Laugh as we always laughed at the little jokes we
>   enjoyed together.

I had a flash of John and me rolling on our bed, laughing. I started to get choked up.

> Play, smile, think of me.
> I am waiting for you for an interval,
> Somewhere very near, just around the corner.
> All is well.

John's brother Michael gave the eulogy, talking about him and John as boys, the rough and tumble of footy in the backyard, how he would call him Bubby John, teasing him.

Chris, Anthony, Peter and I were the pallbearers. I carried the coffin with my dead lover in it, my head pressed against it where his head would have been. We placed him in the back of the hearse.

Outside the church Prue said, 'It didn't feel like John, did it?' I agreed.

Karl interrupted. 'It's interesting that Michael couldn't talk about John after the age of fifteen. Is it because that was when John became gay?'

Father Wallbridge came over to me, looking at me as though trying to work out what to say. 'Lost your little mate?'

I nodded.

'Very sad. You've got some hard times ahead.' He touched my arm and left. *Wow, how bizarre. I would never have believed it.*

We drove off to the cemetery, its lawns dotted with rose bushes. John was to be buried in the lawn. The boulder was there, but no plaque yet. We placed him in the ground where he was to be food for worms.

At the Caleos' the tables were laden with sandwiches, chocolate crackles and fruit salad. Lois made pots of tea while Bob did a circuit with a bottle of beer.

A woman in her fifties introduced herself as Shirley Cookson, Tim's mother. 'Tim has been taking John's death very badly.' She watched my reaction. 'When I confronted him about it, he told me he was gay. He'd been scared that we might reject him. Such a silly boy. I'd suspected for some time. I was waiting for him to tell me.'

'He's a lovely man.'

'Yes he is.' Over Shirley's shoulder I could see a couple deaf-signing. 'Who are they?'

'Cousins of John's, I think.'

'How bizarre. I've been learning to sign for a couple of years and John never told me.'

'Why don't you go and talk to them? I bet you they'd love it.'

I went over to them and signed, 'Excuse me . . .'

The woman's face lit up. 'You're deaf?'

'I work with deaf people. At the AIDS Council.'

'Good for you.' She asked how I knew John.

'We were at school together.' *Should I risk it?* 'And then we became boyfriends.'

She signed, 'Beautiful couple.'

Later I found myself with Trevor Cookson, Tim's father. 'I was surprised when I heard that John had AIDS. Lois had told us it was cancer. I was hurt. She couldn't trust me. I confronted her about it and she burst into tears.' *I don't really want to be counselling Tim Cookson's family.*

Father Wood and I got talking about his sexuality. 'I was gay until I became celibate.' I had never met a gay priest. 'We're not that freakish. Lots of clerics are gay, although celibate. It's just another way of expressing the love of Jesus.'

I drove to Fitzroy, to Prue and Kevin's house, where there was a large metallic aerial on the roof that looked like a spaceship. *Obviously one of Kevin's creations.* In the living-room people were sitting on the arms of couches and cushions. Mum and Dad and Anna were there.

'It was a nice funeral,' said Dad. 'It wasn't easy seeing Bob. He walked over to shake my hand and I was tempted to refuse.'

'Are you still angry with him?'

'Course I bloody am. That was the most humiliating day in my life.'

'Can we drop it? It's John's day.'

I plonked on the couch next to Pepe. Her mother Marie held out her arms. I got up and gave her a kiss. She held my face. 'Beautiful boy.'

At the piano Tim Cookson played Satie. I put my arm around him. He said hi. He seemed tipsy. 'I'm very upset about John. Here I am coming out and he is dead. He was really important to me in my coming out. It was good to know that you could be a good guy and be gay.' He took a swig of beer from his can. 'Mum asked me why I was taking it so hard and I told her I was gay. She was fantastic.'

Tom asked if I wanted to make a toast to John. He called for silence.

'To our dear friend who can't be with us today. *God I'm going to cry.* You are my lover, my friend and my soulmate. I miss you terribly, we all miss you terribly.' I stood there crying, until Prue gave me a tissue.

People started leaving. I didn't want to go, though the beer was making me sleepy. I stretched out on the couch and drifted off to la-la land. There I met an angel sitting on a rock.

'What did you learn from John?'

'That you don't need to be concerned about what people think of you.'

'Anything else?'

'The value of unconditional love.'

The angel held open his hand, revealing a small glowing orb. 'It's a kiss from John. Shut your eyes.' He placed it against my lips and I could feel John's warm lips. My body was alive with emotion. I was falling through free space.

I opened my eyes. John wasn't there, the angel wasn't there. *Was it a dream? It doesn't matter. It felt real.*

Epilogue

Italy

Dear John,

  I am sitting in the garden at the back of my hotel, surrounded by orange trees and bougainvillaeas. After the madness of the northern cities, the island of Lipari is paradise.

  I associate so many things here with our time in Italy, even the café where we bought our first real gelato, but they are not the same without you. I'm not aware of your absence as much as I would have thought, although I wonder what all the tourists thought of me as I sat in the Duomo in Florence, openly weeping.

  Here on Lipari is where I most miss you. I think you would have loved this place. It's warm and very strong, and the Liparoti are very amiable. You would almost think you were on a Greek island, but the whirr of Vespas ridden by the ragazzi places you smack bang in Italy.

  Margaret and I visited the island of Salina yesterday, the island where your grandparents were born, and Margaret's husband's grandparents. It was a bit like a private pilgrimage. It is almost barren, lots of rock and caper bushes. The café is only open for an hour and you can understand why they emigrated.

The most unnerving thing: here on Lipari there is a beautiful boy who works in the bar in our hotel. He is so like you he could easily be one of your brothers. Margaret asked, 'Tim, have you seen the boy behind the bar? Don't you think he is like John?'

'I do but I thought I was seeing things.'

He was born here but his family is not Caleo. He is so gentle and so shy. We try to talk but he speaks Liparota, a dialect I can't understand. He occupies my dreams: I fall in love so easily these days.

Life is pretty good at the moment: I have my health and − seem to be doing many of the things I want to do before I die, including hiring a Vespa and circumnavigating the island twice. I kept thinking, John would love this, and then I remembered you would never have let me do it.

I guess the hardest thing is having so much love for you and it somehow not being returned. I develop crushes all the time but that is just misdirected need for you. You are a hole in my life, a black hole. Anything I place there cannot be returned. I miss you terribly.

Ci vedremo lassù, angelo.

ACKNOWLEDGEMENTS

The publishers acknowledge the editorial contribution of
Nick Enright. On behalf of the author the publishers would also
like to thank Timothy's friends and colleagues, with particular
thanks to Tony Ayres, Nellie Flannery and Morna Seres.

The song lyric on page 46 is from 'Dreamer' (Hodgson/Davies),
© Delicate Music (Almo Music USA). Reprinted by permission of
Universal Music Publishing Pty Ltd.